"A master of the craft [...] and [...]"
—*New York Times* bestselling author Maggie Shayne

Praise for The Otherworld series

# BONE MAGIC

"*Bone Magic* turns up the heat on the D'Artigo sisters. Galenorn writes another winner in The Otherworld series."
—*New York Times* bestselling author Jeaniene Frost

# DEMON MISTRESS

"This book pulls no punches; it's a boot to the head one moment and a full-mouthed kiss on the lips the next that leaves you begging for more."
—*Bitten by Books*

"Ms. Galenorn weaves a tale where the strong flow of magic and danger entice the reader deeper into the story...fast-moving, engrossing, and filled with chemistry and passion."
—*Darque Reviews*

# NIGHT HUNTRESS

"Galenorn hits the stars with *Night Huntress*. Urban fantasy at its best."
—*New York Times* bestselling author Stella Cameron

"Ms. Galenorn did an outstanding job...I can hardly wait until the sixth book is released to find out what happens next!"
—*The Romance Studio*

"A thrilling ride from start to finish."
—*The Romance Readers Connection*

"Fascinating and eminently enjoyable from the first page to the last, this skillfully written book is populated with unique characters who never bore. *Night Huntress* rocks! Don't miss it!"
—*Romance Reviews Today*

*continued . . .*

# DRAGON WYTCH

"Action and sexy sensuality make this book hot to the touch."
—*Romantic Times* (four stars)

"Ms. Galenorn has a great gift for spinning a compelling story. The supernatural action is a great blend of both fresh and familiar, the characters are each charming in their own way, the heroine's love life is scorching, and the worlds they all live in are well-defined."
—*Darque Reviews*

"This is the kind of series that even those who do not care for the supernatural will find a very good read."
—*Affaire de Coeur*

"If you're looking for an out-of-this-world, enchanting tale of magic and passion, *Dragon Wytch* is the story for you. I will be recommending this wickedly bewitching tale to everyone I know!"
—*Dark Angel Reviews*

# DARKLING

"The most fulfilling journey of self-discovery to date in The Otherworld series . . . An eclectic blend that works well."
—*Booklist*

"Galenorn does a remarkable job of delving into the psyches and fears of her characters. As this series matures, so do her heroines. The sex sizzles and the danger fascinates."
—*Romantic Times*

"The story is nonstop action and has deep, dark plots that kept me up reading long past my bedtime. Here be Dark Fantasy with a unique twist. YES!"
—*Huntress Book Reviews*

"Pure fantasy enjoyment from start to finish. I adored the world that Yasmine Galenorn has crafted within the pages of this adventurous urban fantasy story. The characters come alive off the pages of the story with so many unique personalities . . . Yasmine Galenorn is a new author on my list of favorite authors."
—*Night Owl Romance*

# CHANGELING

# WITCHLING

# NIGHT MYST

## An Indigo Court Novel

## YASMINE GALENORN

JOVE BOOKS, NEW YORK

**THE BERKLEY PUBLISHING GROUP**
**Published by the Penguin Group**
**Penguin Group (USA) Inc.**
**375 Hudson Street, New York, New York 10014, USA**
Penguin Group (Canada), 90 Eglinton Avenue East, Suite 700, Toronto, Ontario M4P 2Y3, Canada
(a division of Pearson Penguin Canada Inc.)
Penguin Books Ltd., 80 Strand, London WC2R 0RL, England
Penguin Group Ireland, 25 St. Stephen's Green, Dublin 2, Ireland (a division of Penguin Books Ltd.)
Penguin Group (Australia), 250 Camberwell Road, Camberwell, Victoria 3124, Australia
(a division of Pearson Australia Group Pty. Ltd.)
Penguin Books India Pvt. Ltd., 11 Community Centre, Panchsheel Park, New Delhi—110 017, India
Penguin Books (NZ), 67 Apollo Drive, Rosedale, North Shore 0632, New Zealand
(a division of Pearson New Zealand Ltd.)
Penguin Books (South Africa) (Pty.) Ltd., 24 Sturdee Avenue, Rosebank, Johannesburg 2196,
South Africa

Penguin Books Ltd., Registered Offices: 80 Strand, London WC2R 0RL, England

This is a work of fiction. Names, characters, places, and incidents either are the product of the author's imagination or are used fictitiously, and any resemblance to actual persons, living or dead, business establishments, events, or locales is entirely coincidental. The publisher does not have any control over and does not assume any responsibility for author or third-party websites or their content.

NIGHT MYST

A Jove Book / published by arrangement with the author

PRINTING HISTORY
Jove mass-market edition / July 2010

Copyright © 2010 by Yasmine Galenorn.
Excerpt from *Harvest Hunting* copyright © by Yasmine Galenorn.
Cover art by Tony Mauro.
Cover design by Rita Frangie.
Text design by Laura K. Corless.

ISBN: 978-0-515-14814-5

JOVE®
Jove Books are published by The Berkley Publishing Group,
a division of Penguin Group (USA) Inc.,
375 Hudson Street, New York, New York 10014.
JOVE® is a registered trademark of Penguin Group (USA) Inc.
The "J" design is a trademark of Penguin Group (USA) Inc.

PRINTED IN THE UNITED STATES OF AMERICA

10   9   8   7   6   5   4   3   2   1

*Dedicated to:*

*Andrew Marshall,*
*one of my dearest friends,*
*who also understands the Hunt,*
*and whispers on the wind,*
*and the desire to fly away.*

# ACKNOWLEDGMENTS

Thank you to my beloved Samwise. You make life a joy, always and forever. And to my agent, Meredith Bernstein, and to my editor, Kate Seaver: Thank you both for helping me stretch my wings and soar. To my cover artist, Tony Mauro, who I am thrilled to work with again. To my supportive Witchy Chicks. To my "Galenorn Gurlz," those still with me, those who have come into my life the past year, and those who crossed over the Bridge in 2008–2009—I will always love you, even through the veil.

Most reverent devotion to Ukko—who rules over the wind and sky, Rauni—queen of the harvest, Tapio—lord of the woodlands, and Mielikki, goddess of the Woodlands and Fae Queen in her own right. All, my spiritual guardians. And to the Fae—both dark and light—who walk this world beside us.

And the biggest thank you of all: *To my readers*. Your support helps me continue to write the books you love to read! You can find me on the net at Galenorn En/Visions: www.galenorn.com. I'm on Twitter, Facebook, and MySpace—all links can be found on my main website. If you write to me via snail mail (see website for address or write via publisher), please enclose a self-addressed stamped envelope if you would like a reply. Promo goodies are available.

The Painted Panther
Yasmine Galenorn, December 2009

There's a whisper on the night-wind, there's a star
    agleam to guide us,
And the Wild is calling, calling . . . let us go.

ROBERT SERVICE, "THE CALL OF THE WILD"


O wild West Wind, thou breath of Autumn's being,
Thou, from whose unseen presence the leaves dead
Are driven, like ghosts from an enchanter fleeing . . .

PERCY BYSSHE SHELLEY

# The Beginning

*And she arose from her deathbed in a gossamer gown, with eyes the color of starlight and hair as black as the night. And those who were her captors trembled, for the scent of death and madness emanated from her soul, and yet—she was not dead. She moved like the spiders that creep in the treetops, and none could look away. Taking her first captor in hand, she fed deep and ravenous. And so it was that Myst, Queen of the Indigo Court, was born from the blood of the dead.*

# Chapter 1

The women in my family have always been witches, which is why when Ulean, my wind Elemental, tossed my hair early on a balmy, breezy December morning and whispered in my ear to listen to the wind, there was a message for me riding the currents—I did. Pausing to close my eyes and lower myself into the slipstream, I heard a faint, feminine voice calling my name. When it told me that my aunt Heather and cousin Rhiannon were in trouble, I didn't wait for a second warning. I called them to tell them I was on my way and got my second surprise of the day.

"Marta's dead." Heather's voice was strained.

I stared at the phone. *Marta, dead?* The woman had been ancient the last time I was home, but we all expected her to outlive the entire town. That she was dead seemed incomprehensible. "She's dead? What happened?"

"I don't know, Cicely. We found her in her garden. She was drained of blood and her throat had been . . . ripped apart. And I do mean *ripped*."

The obvious answer was a rogue vampire, except for one thing: the ripped part. Most vampires were fairly tidy with their work. The Northwest Regent for the Vampire Nation lived in New Forest and kept order in the area. Geoffrey was a good sort—if you can call a vampire a good sort—and it was hard for me to believe that any one of the vamps under his control would be so stupid as to kill Marta. She had charms aplenty for warding them off and the repercussions would be harsh, even for the vamps.

"You think one of Geoffrey's people killed her? What do the police say?"

My aunt paused. "I'm not sure of anything, to be honest. There are some strange things going on and the town is . . . changing. The cops didn't seem too interested in investigating Marta's death."

A chill ran up my spine.

*Strange is not the word for it,* Ulean whispered. *There are so many traps in New Forest now. The entire town is in danger.*

"Are you sure you're okay? A voice on the wind told me that you and Rhiannon are in danger. I was about to pack."

A pause. Then, "Please come home. I'd love to have you come home for good. It's time, Cicely. Krystal's gone, and we need you. Right now, I'm not sure what that danger is, but yes, it's lurking on the edges and in truth, it has me afraid."

My aunt never admitted fear. That she would do so now sealed my decision to return to New Forest.

Heather paused, then added, "I think at this point, everyone's fair game, but the magic-born seem to be getting hit the hardest. I'll explain when you get here. And there's another reason you should return."

"What?" Family duty, I had no problem with, unlike my mother. But Heather's voice sounded odd and a tingling at the back of my neck told me that something else was in play.

"Marta passed the torch to you. She left you her practice. The town can't do without her, and apparently she's chosen you to take her place. You'll have to move the business over here to Veil House. It will take a little while for you to get everything set up again, but she left you all her supplies."

Stunned, I blinked. Marta was the town witch. People went to her for help. She was also the elder of the secret Thirteen Moons Society—the coterie my aunt belonged to. No one but family members knew about the Society and it was kept that way on purpose. Hell, even I didn't know what they *did*—only when you were inducted into the Society were you told what went on.

"Marta left *me* her business? Are you sure of that?" I had been home once a year from the time I was thirteen until I turned seventeen, and that had been the last time I'd set foot in New Forest. And my mother had been persona non grata with the elder witch. "Why would Marta do that?"

Heather laughed. "Oh, Cicely, you may be twenty-six now and on your own, but you're still one of us. You've always been one of us, even though your mother tried to distance the both of you. It's time to come home to New Forest." Her voice turned serious. "Krystal's dead. You don't have to run anymore. Come back. We need you. *I* need you. And you . . . you need us."

She was right. In my heart, I knew it was time to go home. I'd been running for years, but now there was no more reason. There hadn't been a reason for me to stay on the road for two years, since Krystal had died. Except that sometimes running felt like all I knew how to do. But now . . . Marta left me her business. I had something to go home to—something to focus my life on other than keeping my mother and me alive.

"Be there in three days tops," I told Heather. "Can I have my mother's room?" Memories of the violet-and-ivory trimmed room loomed in my mind.

"Of course you can, and you can use the back parlor for your business and one of the spare rooms on the third floor for your supplies and workroom." Heather laughed again. "Oh Cicely, I've missed you so much. I'm so glad you're coming home again for more than a visit. We've missed you."

And with that, I tossed the few boxes containing my possessions and my backpack in Favonis—my 1966 navy blue Pontiac GTO that I'd won in a game of street craps—and headed out of California without a single look over my shoulder.

LA was like every other city I'd lived in since I was six: a pit stop in the rambling journey that had been my life. But now, after twenty years, my past was about to become my future. As I pressed my foot against the accelerator, Favonis sped along the I-5 corridor.

I was wearing a pair of black jeans, a black tank top, and my best boots—a kickass pair of Icon's Bombshell motorcycle boots. I had no job to give notice to—I'd picked up odd jobs here and there since I was twelve but never anything permanent. All through the years, I knew there was something I was supposed to do—supposed to accomplish—but I'd never known what. Maybe this was it. Maybe taking Marta's place would fill the void.

"Come on, baby," I coaxed. "Don't let me down."

And Favonis didn't. She purred like a kitten, all the way up the coast.

Speeding along the freeway, fueled by numerous stops at Starbucks and espresso stands along the way, I kept my eyes peeled for the exit that would take me to I-90. New Forest was snuggled against the northwestern foothills of the Washington Cascades and the promise of going home for real this time dangled in front of me like a vial of crack in front of a junkie.

Twenty years ago, I'd kicked and screamed my way down the front steps of Veil House, begging Krystal to leave me with Heather, but my mother had just dragged me to the taxi, bitching at me to shut up. Now, after a thousand miles on the road, and a thousand years in my heart, I was heading back to live in the only house I'd ever thought of as home. And this time I planned on staying.

*Only now, I'm twenty-six and my mother's dead. Something is terribly wrong in New Forest. And my wolf has woken up again.*

❧

Twenty miles out from town, I began to see spots of snow, and by the time I passed the WELCOME TO NEW FOREST sign, snow blanketed the ground. Not wanting to bother my aunt till morning, I eased into the parking lot of the Starlight 5 Motel. I stared at the flickering light that illuminated the VACANCY sign. I was in New Forest. *I was really back.*

Grabbing my backpack, I hauled ass out of the car and stood there shivering as I listened to the air currents washing around me. Something *was* off—I could feel it. New Forest didn't feel like I remembered it. A glance across the street showed me an all-night diner. The windows of Anadey's—a twenty-four-hour joint— glimmered with Christmas lights. I vaguely remembered Anadey from my visits. She was Marta's daughter, if I remembered correctly. I wondered what she was doing running a diner, but decided to check in first and then snag a bite to eat.

The motel clerk stared at me, unblinking. "You want a room?"

I nodded. "Single. One night." As I pulled out my

wallet, he shoved the register across to me and I scribbled my name down and tossed fifty bucks on the counter in tens. He counted the bills, then nodded and held out a key.

"Room 105-A. Checkout by noon."

"I'll be gone earlier than that. You have anything on the second floor?" I'd long ago learned it was safer to be higher up.

He looked me over again and then handed me a different key. "Room 210-B. Nonsmoking and no hot plates."

"No problem on either front."

I took the key and headed outside again. The motel was a U shape and wrapped around the parking lot. I squinted at the upper story until I found my room and jogged up the stairs. As I unlocked the door, force of habit made me check the surrounding area, looking for anybody or anything suspicious. Krystal had raised me to be on guard, even though she had lost her own savvy over the years, thanks to the crack and the heroin.

No one in sight. I opened the door.

Cautiously, I scoped out the room. Queen-sized bed, a little lumpy. Headboard bolted to the wall. Utilitarian dresser and mirror with the TV atop it. Usable, clean bathroom with thin white towels. Typical cheapie motel. I dropped on the bed but was too pent up from the drive to sleep. My stomach rumbled and I realized I was hungry, so I gathered up my pack—no way would I leave anything in this joint while I was gone—and headed out to the sidewalk in front of the motel. I waited for the light to change and crossed the street to Anadey's Diner.

The café had that truck-stop vibe, though there weren't any places for semis to park. As I pushed through the doors, the dim light from the overheads filtered through the long, narrow restaurant. Utilitarian blinds gave a slatted view to the parking lot, and Formica ruled supreme. Booths lined one wall, while on the other, a long counter flanked the kitchen, with bar stools attached to the floor.

A tall, narrow Christmas tree nestled against one corner, sparkling with lights and gleaming ornaments. The tree was pretty and it made me smile.

Several late-nighters were scattered through the café. Two of the men sitting at the counter looked odd—they weren't magic-born, that was obvious, but they weren't human. I could read the difference just by looking at them. Both swarthy, with shaggy black hair and topaz eyes ringed with black circles, they watched as I passed by them, giving them a wide berth.

I chose an open stool at the opposite end of the counter and slid onto it. Picking up the menu, I pulled one of the saucers to me and flipped over the mug.

The waitress saw me and headed my way, coffeepot in hand. I recognized her.

"Hi, honey. I'm Anadey. What will you have? My daughter's the best short-order cook in town." She nodded toward the kitchen, where a tall, solid young woman flipped burgers behind the grill. A sparkle of magic flickered in the girl's aura, and also surrounded Anadey, only stronger. I gave her a slow smile. She didn't seem to recognize me, so I decided to wait until I was settled in before coming back and introducing myself. For all I knew, she could be angry that her mother had chosen to give me the family business.

"Your daughter's lovely."

"That she is, my dear. You want coffee?" Anadey hovered over the mug.

"Yes, and cream, please."

The coffee steamed hot and black as she poured it into my cup. Anadey hesitated for a moment, then said, "Her name is Peyton. Come back in sometime when you're not so tired. I think you'd hit it off. I'll get your cream now. You want another minute with that menu?"

"Yeah. Thanks."

She bustled off, returning with the cream as I added

three packets of sugar to my coffee. I gave her a soft smile—she looked somewhere in her early fifties and exhausted—and flipped open the menu. The words all seemed to run together and I closed it again, turning to gaze at the posters on the wall. Fatigue from the trip was setting in big-time.

I motioned to Anadey. "Make my order to go, would you? A large chocolate shake. Cheeseburger and fries. Butter only on the bun. Hold the pickles and condiments. And a piece of apple pie if you have some. Oh—and make sure nothing has any sort of fish added into it, please. I'm allergic to fish and shellfish." I reached into my pocket and produced my EpiPen for emphasis. Some diners didn't take food issues seriously unless you hit them hard with the *I can die* speech.

"I have several friends with various allergies, so I keep a strict watch on my kitchen. We have a dedicated fryer for French fries to avoid cross contamination. And one section of the grill is reserved for unbreaded patties only and cleaned every time." She gave me a wink. "You look like you're about ready to crash, honey."

I nodded. "Long trip to get here. Been driving for two days with very little rest along the way."

"I'll get your order going so you can get some shut-eye. You look about done in." She hurried off and I sipped at my coffee. As I sat there, I became aware that the guy at the other end of the counter had gotten up and was strolling my way, his eyes glued to me. He didn't look impressed.

I gave him the once-over as he passed by, on his way toward the restrooms. As he crossed behind me, I heard him whisper, "Magic bitch, watch yourself. New Forest doesn't like your kind anymore."

Taken aback, I swiveled full around, but he just went on walking. Normally I'd get in his face—I'd been in enough street fights to hold my own—but I was too tired to deal with a confrontation. Instead, I just memorized his looks and turned back to Anadey, who was polishing the counter in front of me, a concerned expression on her face.

"Regular?" I asked, nodding at his back.

She gave me a short nod, her lips pressed together and I could see the flash of fear in her eyes. "Don't cross him, child. He's a mean one and a drunk. Just let it go. Your food should be ready in a few minutes." She glanced at the other end of the counter where his buddy was sitting. She didn't say a word, but the look in her eyes told me all I wanted to know.

*Bad news . . . don't trust them . . . they are not mortal.* Ulean's voice tickled my ears and I let out a low *Umm-hmm.*

As Anadey packaged my food and handed it to me, Snarly Dude came back from the bathroom, his full lips curling in a derisive, leering manner. I returned his gaze, keeping my expression neutral. Tossing a ten and a couple bucks for a tip on the counter, I headed toward the door, my senses on high alert.

*Watch my back.*

*As always, Cicely . . . as always,* came Ulean's calming thoughts.

Once I was in the parking lot, a shift in the current alerted me. I paused, listening.

*They're following you . . .*

*I know,* I whispered gently. *I can feel them.*

*Not just them. Another. Older, more dangerous. I don't recognize the energy though.*

I slowly exhaled, relaxing into my body. Tension could ruin a good punch, could turn a good fight into a bad one. I gave the parking lot a look-see. Five cars to my left. Another three to my right. Gauging how long it would take me to dash across the street, across the snow and ice, I headed for the sidewalk. The street was mostly empty; there were few cars on the road at this time of night, although two long, dark limos with tinted windows passed by, gliding silently, the sound of their engines muffled by the falling snow.

*Vampires hunting.* Ulean's thoughts were filled with distaste.

I gave an imperceptible nod and set a foot into the road. Immediately I sensed the men behind me speed up. I was two yards across the street before I broke into a run. The sound of footsteps told me they had done the same.

*Crap.* I still didn't know who they were or what they wanted, but it was obvious they didn't like me and I wasn't going to stick around to find out why.

I made a break for it, Ulean whipping along behind me, pushing me forward. With a shout, my followers picked up the pace as their boots drummed a tattoo of running steps. On the other side of the road, I assessed my best option.

No way in hell could I go up to my room—they could easily break through the flimsy lock. Favonis was my best bet. I'd rigged her with an automatic key and kept my keychain hooked on my belt loop just for situations like this. I'd spent my life ditching danger of one sort or another with my mother and had learned a thing or two along the way.

I tossed the bag of food to the side and fumbled for my key, but even as I hit the shadows surrounding my car, a noise cut through the night behind me—a sharp scream, choked off before it barely began. I whirled, only to see Snarly Dude turning tail to race back across the street into the light. He slipped once on a spot of black ice, righted himself, then disappeared into a truck and squealed out of the parking lot.

As I squinted, trying to figure out what the hell had happened, another sound echoed in the parking lot—a sickly gurgle—and the scent of blood washed over me.

As I backed toward my car, another shift in energy cut through the night and whatever the hidden force was vanished.

*Gone . . . and so is the man who cried out.*

*Crap. Gone?* Where the fuck could he have *gone?* He'd been right behind me. I slowly edged my way toward the shadow that had engulfed him. The scent of blood hung thick but when I shone my pen flashlight on the ground, I could see only a few drops scattered red against the snow. I looked right and left—there was no place he could have disappeared to, but the man had definitely pulled a disappearing act. Not voluntarily, though.

I scanned the other side of the street. Nothing.

*What the fuck is going on, Ulean?*

*I don't know, Cicely, but that's what we're here to find out.*

*What was the thing that took him? Vampire?*

A pause, then, *No . . . not vampire. Do not be so quick to blame the Vein Lords. This . . . is much darker than vampire signature. Dangerous, feral . . . hungry in a way the vampires cannot even begin to match.*

Cripes. Vamps were at the top of the food chain—predators, often without mercy. If this was worse than they were . . . I didn't want to know what it was.

Without another word, I sucked in a deep breath, retrieved my dinner, and headed up the stairs toward my room. New Forest had changed all right, and I had the feeling I was just skirting the tip of the iceberg.

# Chapter 2

The next morning I stared up at the rambling three-story house that had been my only home for the first six years of my life, and sucked in a deep breath, shivering in the twenty-two-degree morning.

I couldn't wait to see Aunt Heather and my cousin Rhiannon again. They were the only family I had, and they were good people. I knocked on the door and Rhiannon answered.

It had been nine years since I'd seen her, but my cousin looked the same—just a little older. Tall, willowy, with flaming red hair just like Aunt Heather's. But one look at her face told me something was wrong. Her eyes were red and puffy, and she looked like her head hadn't touched a pillow for a while.

"What's going on?"

She shook her head. "Heather disappeared."

*Fuck.* I was too late. "But I just talked to her a few days ago."

I leaned against one of the columns of the front porch

as Rhiannon came out to join me. She was wrapped in an oversized fuzzy robe, and she stood, staring across the lawn at the wood, her eyes flickering like two amber cabochons.

"I came home from work yesterday and she was gone. Vanished. Like she'd never been here."

I winced. Heather had been more *mother* to me than my own mother.

"Did you call the cops?"

"For all the good it did. They won't file missing person reports for forty-eight hours, and they tried to convince me that she went on a trip and forgot to tell me." Rhiannon pressed her lips together so hard they turned white. "Heather left her purse and her keys in the house. Her car's in the driveway. She's out there, Cicely." She nodded toward the forest. "*I know it.*"

I crossed my arms, shivering as I surveyed the ravine buttressing the edge of the vast lawn. Veil House—my aunt's home—was situated on a triple-sized lot at the end of Vyne Street, a half-empty cul-de-sac. The lawn bordered a thicket of trees, which rode the ravine down one side and up the other. A copse blended into a wooded glade. The wood was thick with firs and cedars, but a pall hung over the area like invisible smog and the air felt dusty, like in an abandoned house that had been closed off for too long.

A gust of wind slashed through me and I thought I heard a snarl.

*Someone isn't happy you're back.* Ulean whisked the air around me, stirring it up into a cloak that wrapped around my shoulders. *You are in danger.*

*From what?*

*I don't know. The energy is hard to read, but this is the same sort of creature we sensed last night in the parking lot. It's deadly and it's powerful, and it's watching you.*

*Fuck,* I thought as I pulled my leather jacket tighter.

Danger, I could handle, if I knew what the danger was. Another gust came whipping by, sending a swirling haze of snowflakes up on the porch. *Too cold*—it was too cold even for December here. New Forest got snow, but not a lot and it never stayed long.

"I know it's cold out here, but is there any chance you can pick up on where she might be?" Rhiannon leaned against the opposite beam. "You were always a powerful witch, even when we were small. Can you read the wind for me?"

"Not really so powerful," I said, thinking about how much had slid by the wayside while I was on the road with Krystal. "But I'll try." I closed my eyes, focusing on the sharp-edged breeze that whistled past. Sometimes it was Ulean who spoke to me. Other times it was the wind itself.

Flutterings rode the breeze, scattered whispers and thoughts, the usual stuff. But behind the gusts and sudden drafts crept a shadow that made me uneasy. Some shadows are comforting and protective. Others steal the light. And this one sucked the warmth and life right out of the day.

I reached further, seeking Heather's energy—latching on to what I best remembered about her: the lavender and cinnamon scents that clung to her skin and clothing. As my energy stretched thin, seeking any clue, a whisper raced past. *"They have her. They have her."* And then it was gone again.

Rhiannon was right—something had snatched my aunt. And whatever it was, it was big and it was bad and it was out there, in the forest.

I opened my eyes and yawned, shaking off the sudden surge of energy.

"Let's get inside."

When we entered the house, the warmth hit me like a blast from a furnace and I peeled off my jacket and walked into the living room I remembered so well, drawing back the curtain to gaze out the window by my aunt's desk. The forest was a wonderland, covered in white, looking pristine and beautiful, but there was something dark there now, a shadow that hid under the sparkling cloak of snow.

"I only know that she's been abducted. Somebody has her, but I don't know who." I didn't want to ask the next question, but I had to. "Have you seen Grieve? He might know what's going on."

Just speaking his name made my heart ache. I missed him. But the last time I came home—nine years ago—he'd asked me to stay. I couldn't, and he turned distant and aloof. I'd left without saying good-bye.

Rhiannon wrapped her arm around my shoulder, pressing her cheek to mine. "No, he hasn't shown himself since you last went away."

That figured. I had the feeling he wouldn't, either, until I apologized. And even then, I might have blown my chance forever. Another fear I'd been running away from since my mother died. But now . . . my wolf whimpered and I gently rubbed my hand across my stomach, feeling the tattoo stir with worry. Grieve was out there, and he knew I was home.

"I have to go look for him. He might be able to help us."

"Are you sure? Maybe he doesn't want to be found, considering you turned him down."

"Maybe," I said. "But I have to try."

Rhiannon yawned, looking more exhausted than I felt. "I'm so tired. I haven't slept a wink since night before last. When I realized Heather was gone and not just out on an errand somewhere . . ." Her voice softened and she looked near tears. Rhiannon called her mother by her first name, as did I. It seemed to run in the family.

"I didn't sleep so well myself. I had a little adventure

out near the diner. Not one I care to repeat." As we headed into the kitchen and she poured me a cup of tea, I told her about my experience at the motel.

We settled in at the big oak table and Rhiannon let out a long sigh. "I think the men who followed you might have been from the Lupa Clan. Remember, lycanthropes have a strong dislike and distrust of the magic-born and they've been on edge lately. The whole town has. And whatever that thing in the shadows was . . . I don't know. All I know is that nobody hangs out after dark anymore except the vamps."

"What the hell is happening, Rhia?"

"It's all over town. The kids at the school feel it. I can tell—I watch them. They hurry to their classes, as if they don't want to be outside too long."

Rhiannon worked at the New Forest Conservatory, one of several academies across the country for the gifted. And by *gifted*, I mean advanced students with supernatural talents, who aren't entirely human. Mostly the magic-born. Some vampires, a few Fae. The Weres usually kept to themselves.

I stared at my cup. "This is a nice friendly street, with nice friendly neighbors. Everything looked so normal as I drove across town today."

Rhiannon bit her lip as if she was trying to decide how much to say. "Be cautious, Cicely. You actually *use* your powers, unlike me. I think whatever this thing is, it eats magic, like food. People have gone missing, people have died. I don't know if Heather told you on the phone, but a number of members of the Thirteen Moons Society have vanished or turned up dead."

I closed my eyes and inhaled deeply. *The faint taste of leather and sweat and passion.* And something behind it. *Magic rode the currents. Shadow magic, spider magic, blood magic. The taste of sweet poison and wine.* The energy swept over me like a web, muting my ability to sense my touchstone. Whatever this force was, it was strong. *Powerful. Old.*

Dizzy, I glanced at her. "Did Marta say anything about what's going on? And by the way, I'll need to talk to her lawyer, if Heather was right and I inherited her business."

"Oh, you are her beneficiary, all right. I'll give you his name and you can talk to him tomorrow." Rhiannon shrugged. "The past six months, Marta closed down. She kept to herself a lot, and now she's dead. In the past three months, five members of the Society vanished without a trace, and three others are dead."

"*Fucking A*. That leaves . . ."

"*Four*. There are only four left of the local group. Rupert and Tyne. LeAnn, and Heather. And now Heather's gone. And it's not just the magic-born, but townsfolk. Marta mentioned a few weeks ago that she was getting a lot of business for protection charms and amulets. People are afraid."

She was whispering, but that wouldn't stop prying ears. There were always creatures listening. The wind carried secrets. I could hear them.

"Whatever attacked me, whatever's behind the shift in this town, it's hiding in the ravine out there. And the woods beyond." I frowned, thinking. "When was the last time you went into the forest? Or Heather, that you know of?"

She thought for a moment, then said, "At least a couple of years for me. As far as my mother . . . I don't know. She does a lot of wildcrafting in the forest. I doubt if it's been more than a few months. The energy was slow to show itself at first, like a storm gathering offshore. Nobody thought it would stick around. I guess we didn't take it seriously. And then, one day a few months ago, we woke up and the town was engulfed in a shadow. Shortly after that, the Society started to fall apart. People began to vanish."

"Heather said Marta's throat had been ripped apart, she'd been drained of blood. But your mother also said she didn't think it was the vamps that did it. What about you? What do you think? I know the bloodsuckers aren't to blame for everything, but when trouble comes home to roost in a supernatural way, nine times out of ten vampires are involved."

Rhiannon blushed. "Honestly? No, I don't believe they did it. My boyfriend, Leo, is a day runner for Geoffrey. And while Geoffrey admits that the energy feels similar to his people's, he insists that they aren't to blame for what's been going on."

That was news. First that Rhiannon had a boyfriend—she'd always been rather shy—and second, that she was dating someone who worked for the vamps.

The Vein Lords—also known as the Crimson Court—kept to themselves for the most part, but on occasion, they mingled with people. As in socially, not a feeding frenzy. They tended to hang out with the magic-born more than anybody else. The vamps had their bloodwhores, but most of them were willing humans, only too happy to play *host* for their masters.

My aunt and cousin had kept me abreast of the latest exploits of the *bite-me* set over the course of our phone calls and my brief visits home.

"But can we believe Geoffrey? I'm not up to snuff on vampire lore, but they are predators. There's nothing to say they can't lie."

"I think we can take his word for it. The Vampire Nation has a lot to lose if they're lying. They're stronger than we are, but they *are* stuck in stasis half the time, and the retaliation would be horrible if they turned on their word. No, our problem is hiding out there.

"No." She shook her head and glanced out the kitchen window. "Whatever caused those deaths, and the deaths of our Society members, whatever is taking the people of New Forest, isn't human. And I don't think it ever was."

"Then I guess our next step is to search the forest, and for me to contact Grieve. Do you have anybody that can help us? Maybe your boyfriend?"

She let out a long sigh and nodded. "I haven't talked to him about Heather yet, because his sister was one of the Society members and she vanished, too. And he was studying wortcunning—herbal lore—with Heather. She really liked him and ever since Elise vanished, Heather acted as kind of a buffer for him—almost like his aunt. I didn't want to put him through the pain of losing someone all over again until I knew for sure. But I guess . . . do you think she's really gone? Could I be wrong?"

I hated breaking the fragile hope in her voice, but right now, we needed to face reality. "Yeah, and if we don't find her soon, who knows if we'll ever have the chance? You call Leo while I get my things from the car and take a shower. Then we'll bundle up, and head out to the woods to see what we can find."

And just like that, without ceremony or even time to sit and chat, I was home.

# Chapter 3

While Rhiannon called Leo, I headed upstairs to my mother's old room, to unpack and take a shower. The incident at the hotel had made me so uneasy that I'd slept in my clothes, not wanting to be caught unprepared. After two days on the road, I was overripe and ready to hose myself off.

The thought of looking for Grieve weighed heavily on my heart, but I had to face him sometime. The memory of his skin against mine, of his lips against my lips, flashed through my mind and I bit back my heartache.

I loved him. I'd always loved him, but when he wanted me to stay, I'd still been too young to commit myself . . . too afraid of what it meant to bind myself to someone so strong and so different. Now, at twenty-six, nine years distance had put a lot of mileage on my soul. I'd seen the worst of the worst. I was ready to come in out of the cold, to build a hearth fire. The only question was: Did I still have a chance with him? Was he even still around?

The room was just like I remembered it, in shades of violet and ivory, which seemed out of place for my junkie mother, but then again, she'd just been starting down that road the last time she was here.

Deciding to leave the unpacking for later, I pulled my tank top over my head. The room was cool and I shivered as I exposed my skin to the air.

Banding my upper left arm, a pair of blackwork owls flew over a silver moon with a dagger stuck through its center. A matching tat banded my upper right arm. The owl was my familiar, though I didn't have one, and never had. Owls responded to me, though, and I was drawn to them. I gazed at them, and once again, it felt like they were there for a reason, but I didn't know why.

Every tattoo inked on me had a meaning. My fingers trailed down my left breast, lingering over the gently raised skin against which blossomed a deadly nightshade plant. A feral, wild girl peeked out from behind the glossy leaves and drooping violet blooms, with her shadow creeping along behind her. I didn't know what she stood for, either, but she was there for a reason.

Slipping out of my jeans, I traced the vine, dappled with silver roses, that trailed up my left thigh, across my lower stomach, ending near my ribs under my right arm. Entwined among the roses glimmered a trail of violet skulls, and right above my navel, a wolf stared out at the world through emerald eyes.

*Grieve* . . . the wolf was for Grieve, though I couldn't remember why I associated him with the animal. I'd had it inked on me when I was fourteen. As I gazed at the tattoo, a shiver raced through my stomach, and the wolf let out a low growl, his breath light against my skin. My body was hungry, and the feel of his soft breathing made me ache.

I closed my eyes and sucked in a deep breath. Time

to get moving. We had no time to waste—Heather could be out there, hurt. Or worse. Practical possibilities raced through my mind—she might have fallen and hit her head, or broken a leg and found it impossible to manage the walk home. Any number of things could have happened. And yet . . . and yet . . . I knew that wasn't the case.

After jumping in the shower to rinse off, I towel dried and dressed in a clean pair of black jeans and a black knit turtleneck. Shrugging into my leather jacket, I took another look in the mirror.

"Right on." I might be Value-Mart chic, but I had the goth rocker chick look going on, and I wore it well. Turning sideways, I patted my abs. Tight, but not concave. While most women angsted over their weight, I didn't mind packing an extra twenty pounds. At five four, and one hundred-forty pounds, I was solid and muscled from my workouts and life on the road.

My hair was straight, draping just past my shoulders, jet-black and in need of a trim. I pushed the long bangs back behind my ears and stared at my face. The smooth, straight-as-silk strands contrasted against my green eyes and pale skin.

A gust blew against the window, startling me out of my thoughts. *Welcome back, Cicely. Aren't you going to come say hello?*

Cautiously, I opened the sash. The inner radiance I'd always associated with the copse had faded. The welcome mat had been pulled. As I stared at the forest, a shadow covered the wood. I leaned on the sill and stared out at the thicket, fat flakes of snow drifting down to blanket it in a lacework of white.

"Are you really still out there?" I whispered. "Are you waiting for me? Do you still want me? What happened, Grieve? The light's gone from the trees."

*Grieve . . .* You never forget your first love. I'd been six years old when we first met, but it was on a visit when I was seventeen that he took me in hand, laid me down, made love to me, and stole my heart. And I'd broken his.

*Grieve* . . . Was he still out there? My wolf told me he was. Was he waiting for me to find him again? Time would only tell. And did he know what happened to Heather? That . . . I could only hope.

There was only one way to find out the answers to my questions. I headed downstairs.

✢

Leo Bryne was in the living room. I wasn't sure what I'd expected a day runner to look like, but whatever my expectations were, Leo didn't meet them. He was in his late twenties, tall with tawny hair and a crooked but sweet smile. Lean and a little gangly, the Windbreaker he wore made him look younger. Rhiannon introduced us.

"What's your specialty? Were? Magic-born?"

He grinned. "Witch. Herbs and healing." Then, sobering, he added, "Your aunt is training me in advanced studies. I can't believe she just upped and walked away without telling anybody."

"That's because she didn't. You know it. Rhiannon knows it. I know it. The only people deluding themselves are the cops. So, tell me, what does a day runner do?"

He blushed. "I run errands for Geoffrey and his wife that they can't do during the day. Pick up dry cleaning, personal shopping, mail off stuff at the post office, things like that."

"They pay well?" I knew I was being nosy but it didn't hurt to find out my options. Marta might have left me her business, but I doubted it brought much in the way of money.

"Eh—not bad. I get benefits, which helps." He caught Rhiannon around the waist with one arm and she rested her head on his shoulder. It was obvious they'd been going out for a while—they seemed so comfortable together. "And benefits will be important over the next few years."

Blushing, she swatted him off. "I haven't set the date yet, and until we find my mother, I can't even think about it. So shoo, pest."

Staring at the pair, I noticed then that Rhiannon was wearing a thin silver band on the right fourth finger of her hand. It had a diamond in it—minuscule, but a diamond nonetheless.

"You two are getting married?"

She smiled softly. "We're engaged to be engaged. But yeah, Leo is the one. We've been dating for three years now. Cicely, can we go look for Heather? It's getting colder out there and if she's caught somewhere . . ."

"Yeah. She could die of hypothermia. Bring a blanket, just in case we find her." Blankets were bulky but better safe than sorry.

I slipped out onto the back porch. Down the steps, a narrow stone path led into the backyard where the kitchen garden and herb gardens sprawled. There was no lack for privacy, that was for sure.

I was about to call out Heather's name, but then realized that it was ridiculous to hope she'd answer. I started walking the perimeter of the land toward the forest, leaving a trail of footprints in the fresh snow. I motioned for Leo and Rhiannon to head the other way.

Maybe my aunt had fallen and hurt herself. Maybe she'd hit her head on a rock and had knocked herself out. *Maybe* . . . a flash of snow lightning—a phenomenon that happened around the Pacific Northwest now and then— illuminated the sky, directly over the wood. I stared at the flickering light as the thunder hit, slamming through the air like a sledgehammer.

*If Heather's around, please, blow me in her direction*, I thought.

A gust sprang up, chilling me through, pushing me toward the northeast. Right toward the forest. *Shit. Four members of the Society were dead. Five members were missing.*

I headed toward the wood, first reluctantly, then my fear broke through and I set off, jogging across the lawn. As I neared the tree line I heard shouts behind me and looked over my shoulder to see Rhiannon and Leo following. I skidded to a halt and turned, waiting for them.

"You think she's in there?" Rhiannon said.

"The wind led me here." I glanced over my shoulder at the dark path that beckoned. At that moment, a figure came racing out, dark and spindly on two legs, with a bloated belly and long, jointed arms.

"What the fuck?"

The creature went straight for my throat and I stumbled back, clawing at it as it wrapped unnaturally strong arms around my neck. I smashed the palm of my hand into its nose, but it tightened its grip and everything began to go fuzzy. The next thing I knew, an owl swept out of the trees, savaging my attacker with its talons. As the bird spiraled up to get a better vantage, Leo jumped in, beating the creature off of me while Rhiannon tugged me away by one arm.

I scrambled to my feet, rubbing my throat as the thing let out a screech and backed off, hissing before it turned to disappear in the foliage.

"Crap and double crap. What the hell was that?" As I stared at the departing silhouette, I thought, *Shadow, it reminds me of a thin, nasty shadow.* And the owl—where had the owl come from? Owls were nocturnal, but this one had been on full alert. The owls banding my arms stirred. Startled, I stared down at my sleeves, but the sensation stopped.

*Ulean, what's going on?*

*I don't know. But that creature was out for your*

*blood. Be cautious, Cicely—this woodland is not what it once was.*

"I don't know," Leo said. "I've never seen anything like it."

"Fae?" Rhiannon asked.

"I have no idea," I murmured. "Whatever it is, it's horribly strong. I don't think it expected you guys to help me. And the owl startled it."

Rhiannon turned to the forest, staring mutely at the trees. After a moment, she let out a long breath. "Do you think my mother came this way?"

Leo swallowed hard. "Maybe Heather went searching for my sister." He turned to me. "Elise, my sister, is one of the members of the Thirteen Moons Society. She vanished a few months ago."

"Somehow, I don't think Heather went in the forest to look for her," I said softly. "What about the Society? Can they help us?"

"Only Rupert, Tyne, and LeAnn are left, now that Heather's vanished," Rhiannon said. "With Marta dead, and Heather missing, I guess we could go to LeAnn."

"LeAnn has a new baby," Leo said. "We can't ask *her* to risk—"

But he was cut off when Rhiannon's head dropped back.

"She's here . . ." Her voice sounded far away, as if she were speaking through a tunnel, and her eyes glazed over with a white sheen.

"What is it? What do you see?" I let go of her hand and stepped back, motioning for Leo to give her some space. "Rhiannon, can you hear me?"

"That's what my sister looked like whenever she went into trance. She was a seer." Leo circled around behind her. "If she falls, I'll catch her."

"I hope she's okay. Rhiannon, can you hear me? Where

are you?" If she didn't answer in another moment, I was going to shake her out of it. A trance as deep as the one she was in could suck a person under so far they'd never resurface. But then, her throat rattled and she opened her mouth. The voice that came out was ancient and keening, to where it might shatter like glass.

"The Indigo Court has risen. The Hunt has begun. All of my enemies, tremble with desire, and let your hearts fear."

Rhiannon crumpled into Leo's arms and he braced her up as she began to regain consciousness.

I stared at the forest. What the hell was the Indigo Court? As the breeze stirred the fern fronds near my feet, scattering snow from their leaves, something sparkling from beneath one of the maidenhair ferns caught my attention. Quietly, I knelt down to pick it up. A crescent moon necklace in white gold, and on the back, one engraved word: *Heather.*

Another look at the snow-shrouded ground showed droplets of blood near where the necklace had rested. I knew, without a shadow of a doubt, that whatever was hiding in these woods had kidnapped my aunt. The question wasn't *Where was she*, but *Was she alive*?

❋

I squatted on my heels beside the blood, fingering the leaves around it. The snow was compact, new snow hadn't managed to cover it yet, and I found several footprints. They were the right size and shape for my aunt's boots.

"What is it?" Leo knelt beside me.

I glanced over my shoulder. "Trouble. That's what." I stood up, wiping my hands on my jeans. Rhiannon was standing on her own, looking pale but composed. "You okay?"

She nodded. "What just happened?"

"You fell into a trance," Leo said. "I recognized the signs. What the hell is the Indigo Court? And what's the Hunt?"

"I don't know." I looked at my cousin. "Do you remember anything you said? Any images that might have been running through your mind when you were channeling whoever that was?"

Rhiannon rubbed the back of her hand across her forehead, squinting in concentration. "I think . . . I remember seeing something. But I'm not sure what to make of it. I was standing in a forest that was bathed in dark blue. The silhouettes of the trees were silver and barren . . . surreal. Real, but yet, not quite. And there were nets . . . webs? . . . stretching through the branches."

Just where had she been?

"Anything else?"

"Yes," she said softly. "A woman was standing there. A tall, thin woman. Her arms reminded me of a spider's legs, all jointy and spindly. She was dressed in a diaphanous gown. The woman stretched out her arms and a cloud of sparkling mist rose from her body."

Rhiannon hugged herself. "She looked at me, and when she smiled, her teeth were sharp, like tiny needles. She had black eyes—like a vampire's—except there was a swirl of stars in them. Her hair was long and black, and she wore a silver circlet on her head. When she saw me, she crooked her finger and said, '*Join us.*' And the horrible thing is . . . I wanted to. I wanted to go to her."

I stared at her. "I don't like the direction this is taking."

"What's that?" Rhiannon pointed to my hand.

I glanced down. For a moment, I'd forgotten that I was holding Aunt Heather's necklace. I silently handed it over to her.

"This is my mother's necklace," she said softly. "Where did you find it?"

"By the fern." I shook my head, warning her back. "There's blood there. Not much but . . . I think . . ."

"They've got her." Leo winced. "Just like Elise. Whoever's doing this, they're systematically getting rid of the Society. Which means all the magic-born around here may be in danger. But why?"

"They aren't just taking the magic-born. People from all walks of life are disappearing." Rhiannon frowned. "Heather was keeping tabs on the disappearances. The strange thing is, the cops haven't been doing anything— they keep hemming and hawing, stalling. I'd think they were in on it but . . . that sounds outrageous. Maybe they're being influenced, though."

"Which means at best, they may ignore us. At worst, they may hinder us. What do you guys think? Should we head into the forest? Look for Heather?" I stared at the trees, knowing in my gut that we wouldn't find any sign of my aunt. Whatever—whoever—had her, wouldn't leave us a trail of breadcrumbs. And we might encounter more of the creatures like the one that had attacked me.

Rhiannon stared up at the treetops, a single tear running down her cheek. "There's nothing we can do for her right now. If we go looking for trouble, we're bound to find it, and we aren't prepared. We'd better talk this through before charging off on a rescue mission. Find out what my vision meant, if we can. See if LeAnn will help us. You need to meet with the lawyer. Maybe Marta had something among her supplies that will help us."

Leo nodded and put his arm around her shoulder, kissing her gently on the cheek as they turned back to the house. I paused.

"I'll catch up. I'm going to send out the word for Grieve first." When they gave me a worried look, I reassured them. "I'll be careful. I promise."

Leo shrugged, leading Rhiannon toward the house.

I turned back to the wood and took one step onto the path, feeling the hush descend the moment I crossed the border.

I closed my eyes, praying that the creep-show Fae who had attacked me was long gone. After a moment, I caught the scent of a passing breeze and focused on tapping into the slipstream. For a moment, everything seemed normal and then, the next thing I knew, something yanked me onto the breeze and I went hurtling through the woods at a breakneck speed, like an otter caught in the roaring current of a powerful river.

The trees, the undergrowth, the path were all a blur as I sped along, buffeted like a leaf in the wind. I tried to disentangle myself from the current, but found myself wrestling with something holding me tight. And then I caught sight of a face, carved in ice, captured in a haze of mist. A snow Elemental, with concave eyes and a crazed laugh on its lips.

*Let me go. Please let me go . . .*

The lace-winged creature tightened its grip, squeezing me so hard I thought a rib might break. Then, with another laugh, it let go and I tumbled toward the ground, flailing as I went. We'd been high in the canopy—I was going to break my neck. But as I careened toward the forest floor, my fall slowed and, like a feather, I drifted back down and . . .

*. . . back into my body.*

Blinking, I looked around. I was right where I'd been standing when the Elemental caught me up.

*You mustn't stay here. That one is old, and I can't fight his strength. This is his territory. If he took you body as well as soul, I couldn't stop him.* Ulean's whisper cloaked me like velvet fog.

Shivering, not understanding what had just happened, I cautiously forced a thought into the next wisp of breeze floating past. *Grieve, Chatter. We need you. My aunt has disappeared. Something in the woods took her. Please, help us.*

When there was no answer, I turned and hurried back to the house. I didn't have to look back to know that the owl was watching me from high in one of the cedars as I raced across the lawn.

# Chapter 4

A quick call to LeAnn proved our fears.

"I can't help you," she said over the speakerphone. "I wish I could but I have my baby to think of. I'm sorry, but I've resigned from what there is left of the local Society. It's over, Rhiannon. Your mother, along with Elise and the others, they're probably dead. I suggest you get the hell out of Dodge while you can. By tomorrow, my family will be two hundred miles away, and safe." She hung up without even saying good-bye.

"That's it." Rhiannon dropped onto the sofa. "Tyne is Marta's grandson—he might help us but I don't have any clue of where he is. And Rupert wasn't at home when I called him. Oh man, I'm tired."

"Let me make some tea for us." I found my way around the kitchen, glad Leo was here to help. Rhiannon's slip into trance freaked me out and whoever the hell the Indigo Court was, I didn't want them mucking inside my cousin's head.

When the tea finished steeping, I carried the tray to

the living room and sat near the window, steaming cup in hand as I stared out at the woodland.

"What are you thinking?" Rhiannon sipped her tea, and some of the tension fell away from her face.

"I'm thinking I need to get my ass back out there to find Grieve."

"I'm sorry, Cicely. This isn't fair. You just got home this morning, you haven't even had a chance to unpack."

"Not a problem. I'm used to living out of my car. And when Krystal was alive, we were always on the run. This is nothing compared to nights when we were trying to get out of this city or that before the goons she hooked up with found us to collect on her drug debts."

Memories of dark nights spent running through back alleys, trying to get to the freeway so we could hitch another ride to another city, flooded my mind. I'd learned early how to cage rides, and more than once Ulean had protected me from the rapists and serial killers who prowled the highways.

"I can't begin to understand the life she put you through," Rhiannon said. "Heather wanted to bring you back more than once, but every time she talked to Krystal, she'd get off the phone crying because your mother was such a basket case and wouldn't let you come home. And by the time you did . . ."

"I felt obligated to go back to help my mother. She trained me well with guilt. I wanted to stay every time I came home for a visit. Hell, I know Heather did everything she could short of kidnapping me. But I'm here, now. That's what counts."

I set down my teacup and shrugged back into my jacket. "Call the lawyer and make an appointment for me later today, if possible. Tomorrow, if not. I'm going in search of Grieve. If I'm not back in an hour, come to the edge of the wood and call my name, but whatever you do, don't step inside."

Leo nodded. "Got it. And Cicely—be careful. Your cousin needs you."

"You're really going out there?" Rhiannon pushed herself to her feet.

"Yeah. I'll be careful," I said, zipping up my jacket. "Do you have a pair of gloves I could wear? I didn't count on snow."

Rhiannon handed me a leather pair of gloves and a scarf. "Bundle up, it's cold out there. And please, be careful. I don't want to lose you, too."

Before I headed outside, I ran upstairs and grabbed my switchblade. Highly illegal to carry but I didn't give a damn. I'd learned early that protecting myself was worth getting ragged on by the police if they caught me. As I stepped out onto the porch, Rhiannon was on the phone, talking to the lawyer.

The snow had let up, the clouds parting just enough to show the moon rising, full and round in the afternoon sky. The air was ripe with the tang of ozone that presaged a hard winter storm.

I crossed the yard. When I was little, Rhiannon and I weren't supposed to go into the ravine alone, but we always found a way to sneak off without being caught. I suspected my aunt always knew, but she never said anything.

The glade didn't have an official name. Huge, it sprawled for a good twenty miles, winding its way through the foothills of the western Cascades that bordered the back end of New Forest, Washington.

Grieve had called the thicket the *Golden Wood* but I thought of it as spider heaven. In spring, summer, and fall, golden and white orb weavers hung thick in the copse, spinning their webs from tree branch to bush to giant fern, a thick lacy net for catching flies and mosquitoes and the occasional dragonfly.

I jammed my hands in the pockets of my jeans as I

came to the edge of the lawn and glanced back at the house. Rhiannon was sitting in the living room at Heather's desk as she spoke on the phone, illuminated by the light spilling out from the bay window. I stared at her through narrowed eyes. For some reason, the realization that I could see her so clearly from here made me nervous, as if I were a hunter, watching a doe through a rifle scope.

Taking a deep breath, I shook off the feeling and approached the edge of the ravine, my boots squeaking on the powdery snow. The undergrowth thickened, rich with bracken and brambles, and maidenhair ferns stood half as tall as I. Every sound grew muffled as I stepped into the shelter of the towering firs. I let out a long breath, glancing around. Nothing jumped out at me, or caught me up, and I took another step, then another.

Dim light splashed through the trees, making for an eerie play of shadow puppets against the falling leaves and trunks. My boots scrunched along the trail as I scrambled my way down the overgrown path leading into the heart of the ravine. Pausing, I closed my eyes and *listened*.

At first all I could hear was the scuffle of small animals rustling through the brush and the call of birdsong that echoed in the frozen air. After a moment, I caught the cadence of wind and let my mind roam.

*There—voices from off to my right.*

*"Grieve?"* I whispered his name, sending it along the slipstream. It had been a while since I'd tried to harness the breeze this way. There wasn't much call for it in the city, but here . . . here, everything came streaming back.

After a moment, I whispered his name again. *"Grieve, are you here? Are you really still here?"*

*Never hurry.* Grieve's voice echoed in my memory. *Give it time. Don't try so hard—I know it's hard to be patient when you're still so young, but you'll need these skills, Cicely. You'll need them as you grow up.*

He'd known, I thought. He'd known that I was leaving soon, and he'd tried to prepare me.

Another pause. Then, slowly, the wind picked up, carrying the sounds of arguing headed my way. Before I could blink, two men stood beside me.

My heart thudded in my chest and I wanted to cry. It had been so long, so many years, and yet—here he was. *Grieve . . . it was Grieve.* And Chatter stood beside him. Both gorgeous and mesmerizing.

Olive-skinned, Grieve and Chatter had slanted eyes and their chins were sharp and narrow, as if the flesh had been stretched taut across their faces. Grieve had a thick head of platinum hair that curled down his back, while Chatter—slightly stockier—wore his hair in a raven-black ponytail. They were dressed in camo jeans. *Tight, form-fitting jeans and long dusters that looked oh so hot.*

But something was different . . . While Chatter's eyes still glistened pale blue, the blue of cornflowers, Grieve's had changed. They'd grown dark—no white showed, and no pupils, just glistening ebony orbs. But unlike a vamp's, scattered amid the inky blackness sparkled a field of glowing white stars. *Like the woman in Rhiannon's vision.*

"Grieve . . . what happened to you?" My whisper sliced through the silence, my heart thudding in my chest. As I took a step forward, Ulean hissed in my ear, stopping me.

*Be cautious, be careful.*

I paused, tuning in to the energy and went reeling. Grieve had an edge to him that I didn't remember, a palpable arrogance. Chatter—not so much. But Grieve felt wary, almost hostile.

I caught my breath, wanting to throw myself in his arms, but I restrained myself and gave them a gentle nod. *Play it light, keep it superficial at first.*

"I'm back, boys. I'm home. To stay. Did you miss me?"

Chatter broke the silence first. He held out his arms, pulling me close.

"Dear Cicely. Of course we missed you. We heard word on the wind that you were home." He smelled like sweet grass and raspberries and his hug ran through me like sheets fresh from the dryer on a cold night.

"But you shouldn't be here. Not now. You need to leave the wood," he whispered so low I had a feeling that even Grieve couldn't hear him. "Before the dark comes, get out of here for your own safety."

I stepped back, staring into his eyes. He looked frightened.

"Chatter—I missed you." I turned to Grieve, hesitating before I said, "I missed you, too." *Please, oh please, don't reject me.*

Grieve held back. He didn't reach out like Chatter had. "You returned." There was a hint of distrust in his voice and he looked angry. "I thought you were done with me. With New Forest. You said as much, last time."

"I guess I deserve that," I said, stung even though I knew he had every right to be angry. I scuffed the ground. "Are you so unhappy to see me?"

He took a step back and shook his head. "You must leave. You have to get out of this wood. *Now.* And stay away, *especially* during the night." But as he watched my face, his eyes lit up and the tip of his tongue crept out to lick the corner of his lips.

Confused, I wasn't sure what to think but my body answered for me, hunger welling up as I watched his thick, full lips curl into the hint of a smile. Just the look of him made me want to reach out and . . . *Touch me, take me, taste me, feel me, hold me.* My wolf let loose a low growl, hungry.

Grieve had implanted himself on my heart years ago, the roots taking strong hold. His rejection hurt, even though I knew I'd brought it on myself.

"If I'm so unwelcome, why are you worried about me?" I crossed my arms. "I can take care of myself, you know."

"You're the one who should be worried, Cicely," Grieve said, his eyes narrowing. A hint of threat rode the wind and I eyed him cautiously. Oh yes, Grieve had changed drastically.

*Never show fear if you're not sure whether they're friend or foe.* Lesson number twenty-nine from Uncle Brody, an old black man who lived in the first rooming house we'd stayed in after leaving the Veil House. I still thanked that old geezer. He gave me a running start— his cautions a guidebook to living the life into which my mother had dragged me.

"I'm not six years old anymore. Too old to be captured for a changeling."

"Not the subject to joke about. Not now, not here." Grieve slowly reached out for my hand. "You've fully grown up. You're more beautiful than you were the last time you came to visit." His gaze raked over me like hot coals.

"I'm home to stay, Grieve. Marta's dead and I'm taking over her business."

I froze, forcing myself to breathe normally as he took hold of my hand and brought it to his lips where, one by one, he brushed a kiss against each fingertip, soft silk against my skin. Slowly, he turned my arm so my palm was facing up, and lowered his lips to my wrist. I closed my eyes, sinking into his touch. I remembered that touch, those lips.

His feral smile was punctuated by dimples that were neither cute nor comforting. Sharp, brilliant white teeth shone against the dim light of the forest, and, as I watched, he grazed my skin with them, leaving a trail of thin, red marks from two tiny fangs I'd never noticed before.

*What the fuck . . . What was he doing? Biting me?*

My skin welted up and a flush raced from the wounds through my bloodstream. I was spinning, like when I had the flu or the one time I'd eaten tuna fish and ended up passing out from an allergic reaction.

As the spiraling heat flared through me, all I could think about was what it would feel like if he took hold with those teeth and never let go. Common sense warred with my body. I shook my head to clear my mind, and managed to throw off the glamour.

Chatter shook his head, looking browbeat. "Grieve . . . please . . . not her." He stepped forward, stopping as Grieve motioned with his other hand. "Grieve, *she's our Cicely.*"

"Hush. You talk too much, Chatter." Grieve never took his gaze from my face. Afraid to make any sudden move, I kept silent as Grieve brought his hand to my mouth.

As he traced my lips, I slowly parted them, unable to resist as he slid a finger just barely inside. I slowly wrapped my tongue around it, tasting him gently. *Cloyingly sweet, like sugared dates.* He tasted different than I remembered. I tried to back away, but he grabbed my wrist and held fast, staring into my eyes.

Ulean brushed by me on the wind. *Don't lose yourself to him. It's not safe here. Snap out of it. Wake and beware.*

The abrupt sting of her touch against my skin cleared my thoughts again. I forced myself to focus. "Grieve, let go of me. *Now.*"

His brow narrowed and a nasty look crossed his face, but he acquiesced. I slowly backed away, then hopped onto a deadfall where I brushed away the snow and squatted, my chin on my hands, elbows resting on my knees. I knew two things: Grieve had changed, and change or not, I still wanted him. I was ready to curl up inside his embrace for good.

When I felt steady enough, I said, "What the fuck's going on, guys? What's happening out here?"

The dark look fading, Grieve shook his head. "Go. Don't stick around this town, Cicely."

Chatter spoke up. "It's bad, Cicely. We've lost so much over the past few years—"

"Shut up," Grieve said, not even glancing at him. Chatter closed his mouth and bowed his head, looking contrite. I caught sight of a series of bruises on the back of his neck that looked like thumbprints. *Please tell me Grieve didn't do that* . . . but I didn't say anything. I couldn't bear to think the marks were Grieve's doing.

I tried to sort out the interaction between them. Grieve was a prince in the Court of Rivers and Rushes, nephew to Lainule, the Queen. Chatter was his cousin, but not one of the nobility. Grieve had always been a control freak, but he'd been fair. Now, his heightened sense of authority set me on edge. Chatter had always been jovial. Now he darted glances over his shoulder. He reminded me of a whipped puppy.

"People have died. You know that, don't you? Members of the Thirteen Moons Society are dying and disappearing. Marta is dead, her throat ripped out. *Heather*, my *aunt*, is missing." I stared at Grieve, forcing myself to not break eye contact.

Chatter glanced at Grieve, who gave him one shake of the head.

After a moment, Grieve said, "I'm going to tell you this once, and only once. And I only tell you because I once loved you. Convince your cousin that it's in her best interest to leave. Take her and get out of town. This wood . . . *all of New Forest* . . . is now ruled by Myst, the Mistress of Mayhem, Queen of the Indigo Court. Any more than this would be unhealthy for you to know."

*Once loved you* . . . I reeled, but tried to keep my composure. I'd known he probably wouldn't wait for me, but the proof hit me like a sledgehammer in the gut. And then I realized he'd mentioned the Indigo Court, and a cold sweat washed over me. What did Grieve have to do with Rhiannon's vision?

"Grieve, I'm staying. I missed you. And I need your help."

"Stick around and you'll get more than my help," he said, taunting me.

Tears sprang to my eyes, but I dashed them away. I wouldn't let him make me cry. "That sounds like a threat."

"Take it any way you want."

Sliding off the tree, I wiped my hands on the legs of my jeans. "Our roots are here. My aunt's home is here. She's a member of the Society." Impulsively, I added, "So, what will it take to get you to help me? You want me to beg? To cry? I will—for her life, I'll get down on my knees and beg your forgiveness."

Grieve's eyes flashed and he grabbed my arm again, twisting the leather of my sleeve. "Don't challenge me, Cicely. It's not safe."

The weight of his hand on my body was like fire.

Angry and embarrassed, I tried to pull away. *"And don't you push me.* I'm harder than you think, and I won't put up with anybody treating me like crap."

Grieve was dangerously close. The truth: I *was* afraid, but I knew better than to show it. This new Grieve scared the hell out of me, and yet—for all of his fierceness, the headiness I remembered was still there, compounded by whatever this new energy was. I wanted to push his buttons, to throw down the gauntlet. The wolf on my stomach growled, but whether in warning or challenge, I wasn't sure and right now, I didn't care.

"Listen to me and listen good. If you insist on being

stupid and staying, then *I can't help you. And I very well may . . .*" He paused.

"You might *what*?"

"You are so beautiful and strong," he said, his voice husky. "Your energy still sings to me . . ." His lips were near my ear and his tongue flicked out to tickle my neck. I couldn't help myself. I pressed against him.

He fisted my hair, holding me fast as he whispered, "You know what the men of the Indigo Court do with beautiful women, don't you? You want to find out just how I've changed, don't you, Cicely? I could teach you what it means to be paramour to a dark prince."

"I refuse to play your game," I whispered back. "You can't frighten me."

One more inch and he'd be kissing me. As Grieve pressed his lips to my neck, I caught an odd smell. Dust and chill evenings under the autumn stars. Fields burnt to ashes and musk. The metallic tang of blood. A primal scent that set me on edge and reminded me of graveyards.

"Grieve!" Chatter's voice shattered the silence.

It also seemed to shatter Grieve's focus. He furrowed his brow and roughly shoved me away, ignoring me when I tripped over a root and fell into a soft pile of snow and leaves. "Don't come into the ravine again. Stick to the land around the house. Stay out of the town at night, and you *might* be safe. At least for now."

"But *why* is it dangerous for me to be here? What's out here? Why are you pushing me away? What's the Indigo Court? Tell me!"

Chatter backed away as Grieve motioned to him.

"Stubborn woman," Grieve said. "I don't *want* you here." But the tone of his voice said otherwise. "You don't belong here anymore, Cicely Waters, and if you insist on staying, there's nothing we can do to help you or your aunt. Take my advice and keep your nose out of the world of Fae. It's never been a safe place to play and it's far more dangerous now. Mortals are play toys . . . expendable. The magic-born are in danger."

He paused, then added, "*Especially* witches. *Especially you.*"

A sudden gust rose up, blowing leaves and snow around my head. As I turned away, shading my eyes from the swirl, there was a quick noise and I heard a faint, "*Goodbye, Cicely. It was good to see you again. I'm glad you're back but I sure wish things were different,*" whirling in the wind.

*Chatter's voice.* As quickly as it had come, the breeze died and I turned back to find both of them gone. I looked behind a few bushes, but could find no sign that they'd ever been there.

A moment later, a noise from a nearby tree startled me. The owl—a great horned owl—ears tufted up, eyes round and brilliant topaz in the dim afternoon, let out a deep, resonant series of five hoots, sending a chill up my spine as it stared at me with its round, glittering eyes. The bird was huge and I could swear it was studying me. Nervous, I backed away, heading toward the edge of the forest, stopping once to glance behind me. The owl still stared, like it was waiting for me to say something. Hurrying, I turned the bend and broke into the open.

As I raced back across the lawn to the house, Rhiannon and Leo were standing on the porch. When she caught sight of me, she hustled me inside.

"You look frozen through, and scared to death," she said, bustling me into the living room. "What happened? Did you find anything?"

I shook my head, barely able to find my voice. I didn't want to talk about Grieve, about how he'd changed and pushed me away.

"It's . . . Don't go in the woods. Please promise me that you won't go in the woods without me."

She gave me a long look, then nodded and let me go. "The lawyer's booked but he'll meet us in a couple of hours, after he gets off work. He'll meet us at Anadey's Diner."

"Fine. I need a bath." Even though I'd showered before we went out to search for Heather, I felt oddly dirty.

I jogged up to my room and began filling the bathtub with water as hot as I could stand. I poured in several caps of Heather's lavender bubble bath and the steam rose, working its magic as it began to calm me down. The encounter with Grieve had left me feeling like spiders were crawling over my body and I nervously scratched my arm as I waited for the water to warm up.

As the afternoon began to settle, an odd light flickered from somewhere deep in the Golden Wood. I closed my eyes to listen for anything the wind might have to say, but the only image I could see was that of a great horned owl, screeching in the trees. And its piercing shriek sounded for all the world like someone saying, "Leave this place, Cicely—leave while you still can."

Suddenly terrified, I made sure the window was locked and closed the curtains. Even so, I still felt vulnerable and exposed.

# Chapter 5

When I was finished and dressed again—I'd have to do laundry soon considering how many times I was changing clothes today and how few clothes I actually owned—I sat on the bed, taking stock of the situation.

Grieve had changed. His eyes haunted me and I couldn't figure out what the hell had happened. And he'd mentioned the Indigo Court. But mostly, I felt the sting of his rejection. Would he ever forgive me? And more important—could I love this new Grieve, who was far harsher and crueler? Would I even want to?

We headed out to meet the lawyer at the diner, taking Favonis since Rhiannon was too upset to drive and Leo wanted a ride in my Pontiac GTO. His enthusiasm would have made me smile any other time, but after everything that had happened today, I really wasn't up for an automobile lovefest.

As we pulled into the parking lot, I glanced around, nervous, but there didn't seem to be any mysterious creatures hiding out. Last night I'd been running for my life here. Today it was quiet, almost serene.

As we filed through the door, Rhiannon nodded to a gentleman who was probably in his mid-forties, waiting in one of the booths.

He was very suit-and-tie, but I had the feeling that beneath that professional exterior, he couldn't wait to get home to blue jeans and a T-shirt. He just had that look in his eye. Plus, instead of coffee, he was sipping on a milkshake, and a piece of apple pie smothered in whipped cream waited in front of him. Somehow, pie and a strawberry shake made him seem less imposing.

We slipped into the booth.

"How you doing? Jim Fischer." The lawyer held out his hand and I shook it. Nothing spectacular, just warm, firm, and strong. The kind of handshake that offered confidence and security.

"Cicely Waters. And I'm fine, thank you."

Anadey was at the table immediately with menus and coffee. I was the only one who turned over my mug and I noticed she'd brought cream with her.

"You just take your time looking over the menu," she said, "unless you already know what you want. Cicely, it's good to see you again. I was worried last night when those two ruffians left right after you, but I watched and made sure you got to your motel room safely enough."

"You know who I am, then?" Surprised, I wondered why she hadn't introduced herself the night before if she'd recognized me.

"Of course, but you were so tired last night, I didn't want to push you into a long talk. Now then, what can I get you all?" She held up her order pad.

I handed the menu back to her. "Chicken soup, and grilled cheese. Plain—make sure nothing with fish comes near either, please."

Leo and Rhiannon asked for hamburgers and fries,

and Anadey ran the order over to Peyton, who glanced out from the kitchen and waved.

"She's had a hard life, that girl," Rhiannon said.

"Why? Her mother seems nice enough."

"Marta's daughter *is* nice, Cicely," Jim said. "But Peyton's father was a werepuma. And some of the Weres—lycanthropes especially—don't see magical Weres as true to their nature. Peyton was teased unmercifully as a child by the werewolves, especially the Lupa Clan."

"So you're Marta's lawyer? You seem kind of young." I'd expected some elderly family retainer.

"Marta transferred her business to me ten years ago, when I first took up practice. She never would say why, and I learned not to question. Anadey is Marta's oldest child. She also had a younger son, who died a few years ago. The mother left town, but Marta's grandson—Tyne—is a member of the Thirteen Moons Society."

"That much, I know."

"Jim's right," Anadey said, overhearing our conversation as she returned to pour more coffee, and bring Leo and Rhiannon their Cokes. "Unfortunately, Tyne and Mother never saw eye to eye, and she left him out of the family inheritance. He's stubborn, and he butted heads with every woman in the coterie."

"But he's still part of the Society?"

"Yes, and he always ended up deferring to Mother, as is proper, but only after an argument. Mother used to say they wasted more time bickering than they did actually getting the work done."

It occurred to me that if he didn't like women in the Society, then maybe he saw his chance to ascend to power after his grandmother died, and might somehow be tied to the disappearance of my aunt, but I discreetly kept that thought to myself. I'd talk to Rhiannon about it later.

"I asked Jim to meet you here because I wanted to reassure you ahead of time that I'm fine with you taking over Mother's business." Anadey held up her hand. "Just a second." She called back to the other waitress, "Jenny, fill in for me, and have Rob man the grill. Peyton and I will be taking a couple hours off this afternoon."

I stared at Anadey. Nothing but sincerity seemed to flow from her. "Are you *sure*? I don't want to horn in on something you wanted from your mother. Hell, I never even really knew her, more than just a passing hello on one of my few visits back to New Forest."

Anadey laughed. "Don't worry. I get the house, and gods only know, Peyton and I need it, but honestly, I have *no* interest in running Mother's business. You may come get her supplies any time you like. Besides, she was adamant about you being the one to carry on for her. I trust her. I always did, even if we didn't see eye to eye. And so now, on her word, I'll trust you to do right by her. You know, of course, that means you are automatically a member of the Society, though not much remains of the local membership. I suggest you begin building it back up from scratch. You'll need every scrap of what she left to you, I'm afraid. What with the way things are going in this town." Her expression told me she knew more about it than I did.

"How much do you know?"

"I know your aunt has vanished. I know the Society is being systematically eradicated." Anadey frowned. "The energy of the town has changed, people are disappearing, and I have a really bad feeling about what the wind's blowing our way. Now if you'll excuse me, I'll just run some last-minute instructions by my staff and then Peyton and I will be right back."

She excused herself. As soon as she was out of earshot, I said, "I'm confused. Why didn't Marta leave her daughter the business? Or her grandson? They're both magic-born. It doesn't make sense."

Jim spoke up. "Oh, yes it does, Cicely. Marta knew

something. We're not sure what, but she changed her will about two months ago. Anadey was with her and agreed to all the changes. Tyne was pissy about it, but since he's not her closest of kin, he can't very well challenge what Marta's daughter won't."

He pulled out a sheath of documents. "Here are all the legalities. Marta left enough money for me to change the ownership and file new papers for you. All you have to do is take possession of the assets and supplies. I'll put in for a business license for you as soon as you give me your information."

Pulling out a checkbook from the briefcase, he handed it to me. "Here's the business checkbook—I've made all the necessary changes to move it to your name. I just need you to sign this form for the name change and proof of signature, and I'll turn it in to the bank today. Then you can take over the business account." He placed a sheath of papers in front of me and handed me a pen.

As Anadey returned with our meals, I glanced over the documents and was shocked to see a balance of four thousand dollars in the checkbook. Hell, Marta did pretty good for being the town witch. I still felt odd accepting the gift, but everything seemed in order. At least as far as I could tell.

"What next?"

"You sign those papers, give them to me, then get your things from Marta's house. I'll file all the pertinent documents."

Anadey paused. "Jim, I'm going to run over to the house with them and start sorting out things." She looked at me. "There's a lot of stuff, it may take you a little while to go through it, but you can get an idea of how much there is today, and take a load home with you."

She wiped a strand of hair out of her eyes and at that moment, I saw the exhaustion and sorrow hiding behind her smile. It occurred to me that since her mother had recently died, I should say something comforting, but I honestly had no idea what would be right. I didn't have much practice at cushioning the blows of life for others. Or for myself, either, for that matter.

Anadey seemed to sense my hesitation. "It's okay, truly. Mother wanted you to have these things. I'm a powerful witch in my own right, but I never had any desire to work with the Society, or to hire myself out. I've always been the solitary type when it comes to magic. But if you ever need me, I'm here to help."

"I don't know what to say." I bit my lip. "I'm just sorry . . ."

Placing a hand on my shoulder, she smiled down at me. "Cicely, my mother had faith in you. I'm not sure what she expected you to do, but she was waiting for you to return. Don't let her down."

We finished up quietly, then Anadey removed her apron and called to Peyton while Jim paid the bill. Over my protest, he paid for all of us.

Once out on the street, Leo excused himself. "My employers are going to wake up soon for the night. I have work to do before then."

Rhiannon frowned. "It doesn't do to keep Geoffrey waiting, does it?"

Leo shook his head. "No. No, it doesn't. I have to change before I make my daily report. They require more formal clothes than Windbreakers and torn jeans." He gave Rhiannon a kiss and jogged down the street.

"Call me if you need anything. I'll get the paperwork started and let you know when things are ready for you to officially open the business. It will probably take about a week or so for everything to go through." Jim headed toward a silver Beemer.

As Peyton and her mother got in the backseat, and Rhiannon and I climbed in the front of Favonis, I couldn't help but wonder just how much Marta had known about what we were facing. And if there was any way of contacting her spirit to find out.

✤

Marta's house had to be a hundred if it was a day. One of those wonderful places with a wide veranda, it included the requisite swing, and if we had warmer summers here in western Washington, I could imagine the parties that porch would have seen. As it was, Marta appeared to have used most of the space to store various bags and boxes—rock salt, sulfur, and potting soil; what looked like a huge box of short, white taper candles; crystals and other odd-looking rocks; pieces of wood that I guessed were for wands and short staves.

A sign was tacked on one of the newel posts. It read: BEWITCHERY GARDENS: FOR ALL YOUR MAGICAL NEEDS. Well, I knew I'd be changing *that* name. Just not my style.

"All of this stuff is yours. Well, maybe not the potting soil, but I won't begrudge you that if you want it."

Anadey unlocked the door and we followed her through the foyer into the living room, which totally upset my expectations. The furniture was sleek, not heavy and upholstered. A lot of chrome and glass, a gray leather sofa, bookshelves stained with ebony rather than a dark mahogany. Modern, with a minimalist bent. Not at all what I'd been expecting. A few scattered pictures of Anadey and Peyton ornamented the walls, and there were even fewer doilies and tchotchkes.

"Please, make yourselves comfortable while I find my list here . . ."

She hunted through a desk in the corner as I wandered around the living room. Marta had been tidy, that was obvious. Meticulous, in fact. Everything pointed the same direction, everything was lined up perfectly. As I moved over to the DVD shelf, I noticed all the movies were in alphabetical order by title.

Peyton wandered up beside me. "My grandmother was one of those everything-in-its-place people. I used to drive her nuts when I was little by dragging things off the shelves or out of drawers and putting them back wrong."

I glanced at her. Peyton was tall, taller than either Rhiannon or me, and she looked part Native American, with long, brown hair and a slightly flat nose, and eyes that were the color of dark chocolate. She wasn't classically beautiful, but something shone through that gave her a smoldering, sexy feel.

"Do you like working with your mother?"

She shrugged. "She started the diner a few years back and needed me to cook. We're getting to the point where she'll be able to hire someone new, soon, and I can do what I really want to do."

"What's that?"

"I want to open a shop called *Magical Investigations*. I'd like to work as a psychic investigator. I'm half-Were, but also half-magic-born, and I have a real knack with the cards. I've also got martial arts training. I moonlight now, taking a few private clients, but I'd love to do it full-time."

That gave me an idea. "Hmm. That sounds interesting. And it might be even more fun if you had another witch attached to the business. What do you think about working out of my shop once I get it going? We could team up if needed, especially since I know nothing about running a business. Our first case can be finding out where the hell my aunt is."

Peyton grinned. "My grandma was right—you're a go-getter. I'll think about it. Seriously, it might be a perfect match."

A moment later, Anadey had spread out several sheets of paper on the old oak dining table. "Come on over. She motioned to Peyton, Rhiannon, and me. "Sit down, please. There's a room upstairs with my mother's magical tools, but I'd like to wait on those. There may be something I want—for sentimental value."

"Of course," I said, once again not wanting to overstep my bounds.

"Then there are the supplies on the front porch, another room filled with supplies, and the books. On that shelf over there"—she pointed to one of the wide wall-to-wall built-in bookshelves—"the entire middle section is yours. Why don't you start with them? We've got some boxes and can easily pack them up this afternoon."

Rhiannon and I wandered over to the bookshelves while Peyton ran to get boxes for us. Tome after tome of magical work lined up, all for the taking. I was practically drooling by the time I had scanned two shelves.

Anadey let out a long sigh as she wearily rubbed her feet and leaned back in the rocking chair.

Peyton returned with a half dozen boxes for us, and then dropped by her mother's side. "Let me rub your feet, you've been on them too long today."

Sighing with relief, Anadey sat back. "So, tell me," she said after a moment. "Tell me about Heather."

Rhiannon put down the book she'd been looking at. "Not much to tell. I came home from work and she was gone." She crossed over to Anadey and held out the necklace. "This was all we found. Well, this and some blood."

"We think whatever's . . . in the woods . . . got her," I said.

Anadey looked at us, holding each of our gazes in turn. When she came to me, she smiled softly. "I don't think Marta expected everything to snowball so soon. Tell me, Cicely, whatever happened to your mother? I knew her when we were teenagers, before she got pregnant. We drifted apart after that."

I swallowed. "She couldn't handle her powers and ran, taking me with her. She died a couple years ago, killed by a vampire."

Rhiannon jerked her head up, and she turned to me. "You didn't tell me *that*. All you said was that your mother was dead."

"Not much to be proud of in her death, is there? Krystal was strung out. A crack addict. That's how she got the money for her drugs—she was a bloodwhore. Her last trick went apeshit on her and drained her. I found her bathed in her own blood and urine." I shrugged. "I don't have a whole lot of love for vampires. Or pushers."

Rhiannon glanced at me. "Does it bother you that Leo's a day runner?"

I shrugged. "I haven't really had time to even think about it. I don't know how I feel about his job. But I do like *him*."

Anadey interrupted. "I'm sorry to hear that. Krystal had so much promise. Let's focus on Heather. Tell me everything. Maybe I can help."

Rhiannon looked at me and I nodded. We couldn't keep our secret any longer. We were no longer children, but women, long past our childhood.

I took a deep breath. "Everything started when Rhiannon and I were barely six . . . and first stumbled into the spiders' wood . . ."

⚜

Rhiannon followed me into the wood, glancing over her shoulder to make sure we weren't followed. The path was shady. It was *always* shady regardless of how much sunlight beamed through the branches. Aunt Heather had warned us time and again to stay out of the copse, but my own mother didn't care—she was always off at a party or away on some trip. And so I had persuaded Rhiannon to join me in my explorations. And now, we had a precious secret.

At six years old, the trees towered so high they were growing into the heavens. Maybe if we climbed them, we'd find Valhalla. Heather called it the home of the gods. My mother said it didn't exist. But either way, I wasn't afraid, and after a few times of sneaking into the wood, neither was Rhiannon. We were magic-born, the daughters of witches, and nothing could hurt us.

*Even though my mother isn't happy about being a witch,* I thought. I'd heard the arguments late at night, when I was supposed to be asleep.

"Krystal, you keep denying your birthright and the power's going to destroy you. You can't repress it forever. Not to mention, you have an obligation to the family. To the Thirteen Moons Society. And most of all, you have a responsibility to your daughter to see she gets the training she needs." Heather's accusations echoed up the stairs.

"Fuck you and fuck the Society," my mother would counter. "I don't give a *crap* about family tradition or magical powers. I never asked to be born with this fucking ability, and I wish somebody would just rip it out of my head. Do you know what it's like, being able to hear voices all the time? The voices of people who laugh at you? Who think you're a slut just because you want to have a little fun? *Do you?*"

A murmured whisper from Heather.

Then, Krystal's voice again. "Well, that's what I hear *every day* when I go out. The only things that help drown them out are booze and pills, and let me tell you, I'll bow down in front of a jug of Gallo faster than I'll ever kneel at the feet of that sorry-assed Society or that priggish, self-righteous old biddy."

"Marta's just worried about you—"

"Tell her not to bother!"

And Krystal would stomp out of the house—the door slamming behind her—and my aunt would cry. Sometimes Heather didn't cry, though. Sometimes she just remained silent but I could hear her grumbling, all the way up in my room. Her words filtered in on the breeze.

"Hurry up," I urged Rhiannon as she lagged behind. "Grieve and Chatter are waiting for us."

"How do you know?" she asked, but she quickened her pace. I could run faster and play rougher than she could, but Rhiannon was the graceful one. She could be a dancer, I thought. When she grew up, she could be a ballerina, she was so tall and lithe.

"They're waiting. I can hear them. Now come on."

I started to run and she followed me. We came to a skidding halt in front of one of the huge old cedars and I bit my lip. Every time we came out here, a little voice whispered that this was a dangerous thing to do, that we could get hurt. But overriding my aunt's orders and common sense was the absolute *need* to visit with our odd friends.

I reached out and knocked on the tree trunk three times. The third time, there was a noise to the left of the path and we turned to see Grieve and Chatter slipping out from behind a bush. They were older—grown-up, but they'd always been polite and nice and never did anything to make us uncomfortable.

I never thought of them as *boys*. Boys were loud and obnoxious and only wanted to follow their girlfriends around. Grieve and Chatter never said anything about girls, and they were . . . well . . . *different*. They weren't human, we knew that, or magic-born. They were Fae and seemed so very exotic and dangerously strange. We knew all about other Supes in the area, but mostly met others like us.

Grieve motioned for us to follow them and held the bushes aside as we slipped off the path and into the woods, avoiding the ravine as he led us into a clearing to the left.

Another moment and we were sitting by a small pond where the trees opened up and the sun actually shone down, scattering light through the branches. I clambered up onto a tree trunk and took a deep breath, inhaling the scents of mushrooms and moss. Rhiannon shyly hopped up beside me. She liked Chatter better than Grieve. He made her laugh.

"Our time together is coming to an end," Grieve said, kneeling beside the tree trunk. He had a sad smile on his face and looked like he was going to cry.

"How come?" I didn't want our visits to stop. Grieve and Chatter had taught us how to make friends with the Elementals and coax them out to play. At least, sometimes. It didn't always work, but he said that the more we practiced, the better we'd get at it.

"Cicely, your mother—" Chatter started to say, but Grieve held up his hand and shook his head.

"Stop. We're not allowed to tell her," he said. "Cicely, everything will be all right. It's just that we won't be able to talk to you much longer. Not for a very long time. Years, maybe. And Lainule—you remember the beautiful woman who came with us to talk to you last time?"

I nodded, proud of my memory. "She's the Queen of Rivers and Rushes."

"That's right, you've done well. Anyway, Lainule wants to make sure you have a friend who can help you send messages along the wind. She says this is *very important*. Do you understand? And you must remember: You can always contact our people through the wind and someone will be there to help you, even if you don't see them."

I stared at him, my lower lip trembling. Somehow, even at my young age, I knew he was saying good-bye and it made me want to cry. But I forced my tears back because when Grieve said something was important, he meant it. He was a prince—he'd told me so. And I'd seen him get angry before—not so much at us, but at Chatter. An angry Grieve was fierce and unpredictable.

After a moment, I nodded. "You need to teach me to talk to the wind, right?"

"Right. You can already hear it speak, but you need to learn to talk back, to send information on what we call the *slipstream*. And at your age, to do that, you need to befriend a wind Elemental. I know some of this won't make any sense for a while, but I'll try to teach you the easy way to communicate with the creature. She'll always be there to help you. You have to promise me something, though."

"What?" I would have promised him anything.

"Promise me that you won't forget *this*. The magic we've taught you. Promise me that you'll keep practicing, even if you're a thousand miles away." He squatted in front of me and took my hands in his, smiling softly. "And when you're older, come back. Come back to me . . . to us. I'd like very much to know how you turned out." There was something in his voice, almost a promise of a future to come, and it made me both incredibly sad and yet—happy.

I gazed into his eyes as the smooth silk of his voice slid over me. The funny-looking man with eyes so clear, so blue, that they looked like twin oceans against the olive skin of his face . . . Grieve was kind to me, and I knew he'd never hurt me.

Solemnly, I nodded. "Promise," I said, "cross my heart and hope to—"

"No," he interrupted me, his eyes glowing. "Don't finish the rhyme, Cicely. Too many nasty creatures listen to the wind. They listen to secrets whispered in dark halls, to promises made in secret, to oaths and alliances forged. Don't ever promise your life—not for anyone."

"Okay," I said, a little afraid. I'd never seen him look quite so imposing. It was as if he'd shed a cloak and he looked even less human than usual. His chin was sharp, his cheekbones ridged, and his lips were full.

"Now come with me, and I will introduce you to your Elemental, and teach you to *speak*." And he set about the ritual that bonded me to Ulean, and taught me to harness the wind and call it to my command.

※

Anadey remained silent as we spilled out our secrets about Grieve and Chatter, and how Chatter had taught Rhiannon to conjure fire, and how Grieve had taught me the ways of the wind.

"Then, Krystal took me away," I said. "And nothing was ever the same. But I remembered, and I kept my promise. Ulean helped me, and eventually, things began to happen. She warned me when we were in danger. The wind would grab a paper out of my hand and I'd go chasing it and bingo, there'd be a twenty-dollar bill in the street just when we were running out of food. And sometimes, the breeze tripped people who threatened to hurt me, like this one guy . . . He was about to beat the crap out of me and a sudden gust caught up a nearby garbage can and hit him from the back with it, giving me time to run."

"You came back before, several times, then left again. Why?"

I'd thought about her question a thousand times. "My mother needed me. I couldn't leave her out there alone—she was so . . . helpless, so fragile. And I wasn't ready, I guess. Wasn't ready to turn my back on wandering. To commit to the life that I knew would be waiting for me here." *And the last time, at seventeen, I wasn't ready to commit to Grieve, as much as I loved him.* But I didn't want to say it aloud.

"And now, the wind has brought you home. You, and Ulean." Anadey looked like she wanted to say a whole lot more but she kept her silence.

"We went looking for Heather today, just to the edge of the wood. And we were attacked. Twice—well, *I* was attacked twice. But Rhiannon and Leo fought off the first creature that threatened to choke me. When I returned,

I found Grieve. But he was much changed." I gave her a condensed version of what had happened, including the difference I'd noticed in Grieve.

"The creature you describe is a tillynok, but they're usually peaceful. Something must have set it off. And the snow Elemental—they're not known to play tricks on humans. Unless they're bonded, like your Ulean, they usually just ignore us. A strange magic has taken over the forest."

"What about Grieve? What about the Indigo Court that he mentioned? That Rhiannon envisioned?"

"I don't know," Anadey said.

"Cicely? Look." Rhiannon turned around, holding one of the books she'd picked up off the shelf.

A strange tingling started through my hand as I reached out to take the volume from Rhiannon. The energy surrounding the book was frightening, wild, ancient. I didn't know if I *really* wanted to touch it, but I had no choice. I had to look. The tome was large, with a navy cover. I flipped open the cover—which was blank—and read the title, which appeared only on the inside.

*The Rise of the Indigo Court.*

"It would seem we've found an answer."

"Somehow, I think your answer is just going to lead to more questions," Anadey said, glancing at it. "Why do I feel like we're opening Pandora's box?"

"Because we are." And I opened it to the first page.

# Chapter 6

I slowly made my way to the dining room table, and the others followed me. Setting the book on the table, I opened it to the first yellowed page. The words were handwritten, in a tight, clear text. Old ink. Old pages. The smell of library dust and time gone by.

> *Steeped in a secrecy far deeper than even that of the Unseelie Court is the Indigo Court. While the Unseelie are nefarious and dangerous, the Indigo Court are considered the Fallen Fae, corrupt for they not only bear their own bloodline, but the blood of the Vampire Nation. The merging of the two races evolved into a breed stronger than either, and yet with their own unique vulnerabilities.*

I stopped, looking up. "Vampiric Fae?" The thought made me cringe. Somehow that just seemed . . . *so wrong.* "I've never heard of them before. Has Leo ever mentioned them? He works for the vampires."

Rhiannon shook her head.

"I've never heard of them either, but obviously Mother knew about them or she wouldn't have the book." Anadey leaned in to look over my shoulder.

"How did they start? How on earth could the vampires mix with the Fae? Did they turn them like they do humans?" Peyton looked as confused as I felt.

I skimmed through until I came to a passage that seemed to answer her question.

*Some thousand years ago, a scouting group from the Vampire Nation led by Geoffrey the Great attempted a raid on the Unseelie Court. They took prisoners—a group of the bewitching dark Fae. Intent upon siring the women as vampires in order to infiltrate the Unseelie, they used the techniques that they'd always used successfully on humans.*

*What they did not expect was for the women—nearing death and forced to drink of the vampires' blood—to live and regain their strength at an alarming rate. But the vampire blood had changed their makeup.*

*First, the vampires quickly discovered their new daughters weren't bound to them the way humans would be. Second, the Unseelie women could still use most of their magic, as well as having the vampires' strength. But they'd shifted even further into the shadow realm.*

*The Vampiric Fae quickly took control of their captors, forcing them to bring in males of their race and turn them. Since the Vampiric Fae are alive, rather than undead, they can still mate. Their offspring keep all characteristics from their parents.*

*A war broke out within the Unseelie Court, who considered the tainted Fae to be abominations, and the Fallen Fae were cast out, pariah. These nests of*

*living vampires—the Vampiric Fae—were driven off,*
*but only due to their lack of numbers.*

*Ruthless, far more terrifying than either of their*
*sires, they crossed an ocean and retreated into the*
*dark forests to create their own social structure. The*
*Indigo Court is ruled over by Queen Myst, the Mis-*
*tress of Mayhem, the original Faerie who was turned*
*by the vampires. She is awesome in her beauty, seduc-*
*ing before she strikes.*

*Over the years, the Indigo Court faded from view*
*while growing in numbers and strength. The Vampire*
*Nation has sworn they will gain revenge for their*
*defeat and humiliation. A prophecy of theirs, first*
*put forth by Crawl, the Blood Oracle, discusses the*
*breakout of an eventual war between the two races.*

"Holy fucking hell." I pushed the book back. "We're
facing a group of living, breathing Vampiric Fae. And
their mortal enemies are the . . . I guess you'd call them
the true vampires."

The thought washed over me like a river of glacial
water, as chilling as the huge mountains of ice they came
down from. Queen Myst . . . Grieve had mentioned she
now ruled the forest. We were living next to a nest of
vipers, of hunters. Predators, first created by . . .

"I wonder, is that the Geoffrey that we know? Regent
for this area?"

Anadey shook her head. "I don't know, but he's old
enough to be the one."

"And Myst lives in the forest next to our home," Rhiannon whispered, voicing my thoughts.

I shivered, feeling an alarm ring in the pit of my stomach. "And now they're ready to climb out of obscurity,
back into the light. That could well mean the destruction
of everyone and everything they touch. And . . . I think
they've turned Grieve."

I crossed to the window and stared out. The snow was back, lightly drifting down. If we were right, the world had just turned upside down and we were a step away from chaos. I turned back to the others.

"So what do we do to stop them?"

Anadey let out a long sigh. "I suppose we find out what their weaknesses are. We have to scour that book for information. Rhiannon, Leo works as a day runner. Do you think he can ask his employers about the Indigo Court? Apparently they hate each other so much the true vampires believe there's a war coming. We might find out some useful information from them."

Rhiannon wrinkled her nose. "I can ask, but that seems dangerous to me. But . . . I'll see what I can find out."

"I need to read this book from cover to cover," I said. "For some reason Marta entrusted me with her business. Could it have something to do with what New Forest is facing? I mean, I'm a competent witch, but totally self-taught, and Ulean's really the reason I'm alive."

*No, that's not true. You do much without my help. I just offer what I can.* Ulean swept around me, her soft currents embracing me. *I'll be here to help you as much as I can in this. You know that.*

"I don't know," Anadey said. "But now, more than ever, I think she foresaw something that called out to have you take over her business and her place in the Society. I'll see if I can find her information on how to get in touch with the leaders of the greater organization. I have no idea who they are. Meanwhile, I'll do what I can to help. Trust me, there's a reason she invested you with her magical practice. We just don't know what it is. Yet."

I didn't voice my thoughts, but couldn't help but wish that my aunt were around to help guide me. Heather could handle this—I had no idea what to do. I'd managed to keep myself alive on the streets over the years, but that was different. People were easier to deal with than Supes, and from what we'd just read, the Indigo Court basically made me think of vampires on steroids.

And now, Grieve was one of them—or at least it appeared so. I should back away, hold on to my heart until I knew more about what had happened to him. The thought made me want to cry, but I'd learned the hard way: Trust people when they warn you *not* to trust them. Grieve had given me plenty of warning.

"Okay, what do we know about the Vampiric Fae? How do they differ from the vampires? We're going to have to figure out if what works on vamps will work on the members of the Indigo Court." I looked around. "Got a notepad?"

"Better than that," Peyton said. She pulled out her netbook and booted it up. "What's your e-mail address? I'll e-mail you a copy of my notes."

"E-mail?" I snorted. "I don't even have a computer."

"We can take care of that at home," Rhiannon said. "Heather has a laptop that she used for a backup in case the desktop went down. And I've got my own laptop. Send it to my addy, Peyton. When we get Cicely set up with her own address, I'll forward it to her."

Peyton grinned. "A woman after my own heart— multiple computers. I like that. Okay, what's *your* e-mail?"

"Fire_Maiden at bestwebmail dot com."

I glanced at her. "At least you're owning your power through the magic of the Internet."

Rhiannon stared at me for a moment, then broke out laughing. "Oh man, I needed that smile. I didn't even think about it when I chose that user name."

"Yeah," I said softly. "I think we all need a laugh, however small. Okay, getting to the matter at hand. Let's see—silver hurts vampires, right?"

"Yes, but the Fae tend to like it," Anadey said. When I glanced at her, she added, "I may own a restaurant but my degree is in mythology and folklore."

"So would Vampiric Fae love or hate it?" I mulled over both and decided we didn't have enough to go on for that. "Okay, just put a question mark after it. What else? Garlic? Holy water?"

"Garlic—another maybe," Anadey said, pushing back her chair. "But we know that religious artifacts only have power over mortals. And even then, they only have power over the living who believe in the religion, and over ghosts who followed that particular religious system. A cross won't harm a ghost who was an atheist in life, a Star of David won't touch a Christian spirit. And astral creatures who were never human aren't bothered by any of them." Pausing, she shook her head. "I'm going to make some tea. I'll be back in a moment."

While she was in the kitchen, I turned to Rhiannon. "If Myst now rules the wood, I wonder what happened to Lainule. If there's any way to get in touch with her? The Queen of Rivers and Rushes always seemed to be friendly to humans. I hope she's not dead." A thought crossed my mind. "If she's still alive, will she help us? Another task."

Peyton blinked. "I can do a tarot reading and see what I can find out."

"I thought of another question," Rhiannon said. "Do the Vampiric Fae make meals off humans? Do they drink blood like other vampires?" Her voice was low and I knew she was thinking of Heather. "Maybe they're keeping people as cattle—as blood donors."

I'd been thinking along the same lines myself and began to flip through the book. It was dense, and much of it talked about things that I didn't understand—people long dead, places I'd never heard of. I skimmed, letting Peyton and Rhiannon talk.

After a moment, I came to a couple of passages that seemed to address our question. "I think we found our answer, guys. Listen to this."

*And so they fed, and drank deep of their enemy's blood, and rent the flesh of their victims until they were unrecognizable. But their thirst was unquench-able until Myst discovered one of their newfound powers born from their vampire bloodline: Members of the Indigo Court could drink from the souls of their victims . . . and a whole new round of terror began as the Shadow Hunters began to feed on humans and Fae alike . . .*

"So they drink blood, and tear people apart . . ." I glanced over at Peyton.

"Grandma's throat." Her voice was clear, but I could hear the tremor in it.

"Yeah, I was thinking that myself." I went back to skimming pages until I found another passage that seemed important.

*Those turned by the Indigo Court must be Fae them-selves for the turning to take. Unlike true vampires, the Vampiric Fae cannot turn humans or most Supernaturals. They can only turn other Fae and the magic-born. Their bite will enthrall, and that thrall can last a lifetime, but if they drain a mortal—a true mortal—that mortal will die.*

*The magic-born, however, respond to the turning in much the way the Vampiric Fae do. They will die rather than regenerate, but when they return to walk among the living, they retain their magical powers along with diluted Fae abilities. But they will never—as far as this research committee knows—match their sires in strength and power.*

Both Peyton and Rhiannon fell silent. Anadey, who had been standing in the archway leading into the kitchen, shook her head.

"Then, we can safely assume that Myst and her people are the ones snatching the other magic-born, as well as the townspeople. They feed on both blood and energy, and they can turn the magic-born and use them for their own ends. A terrifying combination."

She turned to Rhiannon. "We have to talk to Geoffrey. The two factions are mortal—or rather, immortal—enemies. While the Indigo Court can't turn humans the same way a vampire can, they certainly can make a meal of them. We may have to ask the Vampire Nation for help."

I closed the book, staring out into the street. Everything looked so normal, but beneath the current of everyday life ran a dark river of energy. It's what I'd felt when I first looked out into the ravine next to Veil House, and it had followed us here. The thought of asking the vampires for help turned my stomach, after what had happened to my mother, but Anadey might be right. We needed help—we couldn't fight the entire Indigo Court by ourselves.

Without looking over my shoulder, I said, "So . . . I guess our next step is to talk to Geoffrey?"

Anadey's voice was soft but firm. "I'm sorry—but yes. I think we have to. The Society's fallen apart. We're on our own here. And regardless of our magic, we're no match for Myst and her people."

As I turned away from the window, I could feel someone from outside trying to peer in. Marta's wards were strong and whatever it was couldn't get past them. *Yet.* But I was certain that Myst's spies knew we were here.

⚜

After we loaded three boxes of books and four boxes of magical supplies into Favonis's trunk, we dropped Peyton and Anadey off at the diner again.

On the way home, I told Rhiannon, "I like them—especially Peyton. She's quiet and soft-spoken, but there's a strength behind her."

"She was always picked on when we were students in the conservatory," Rhiannon said. "So was I, but because I did so poorly. She was picked on because of her half-breed nature."

I nodded. "That had to be hard, growing up. At least she's half-werepuma and not werewolf—that would be far worse. We were chatting and discovered we both like sparring. We're meeting at the conservatory gym tomorrow morning to work out together. If we get along, I gather the fee's only twenty dollars a month. I can swing that."

"Sounds good. What about tonight?"

"I still need to unpack, and I think we should ward the house. We have to do something to protect ourselves."

Rhiannon nodded, slowly. "What would you say if I asked Leo to come stay for a while? I'd feel better with someone else in the house. Especially now, after what we've found out. And since he works for Geoffrey, and the vampires hate the Indigo Court . . ."

I picked up on her line of thought—if they knew one of their employees was living near danger, maybe they'd be apt to protect us. Trying to push my conflicted feelings over Grieve out of the way, I bit my lip and nodded. "Yeah. Why don't you call him now. See if he's home."

She put in the call and we lucked out. Leo had been given light duty for the evening and was hanging out at his apartment. We headed over there before going home, all too aware that dusk was falling.

Leo lived in an apartment smack in the middle of downtown New Forest, on the fourth floor. It was modern, but modest, and felt like just one of a dozen other buildings dotting the town.

The minute we got inside, without further to-do, Rhiannon asked him if he'd stay out at the house with us for a while. She stumbled over her words, and I wondered if she was worrying about how this would affect their relationship, but Leo took it in stride.

"Crap," he said as we explained what we'd found out. "Okay, I'm in. I'll feel better knowing the two of you aren't out there alone, so this will ease all our minds."

"But what about your rent here?" I asked.

He shrugged. "Don't sweat it. If it looks like I'm going to be over at the Veil House longer than a month or two, I'll give notice. Now that Elise is gone—we shared the apartment—there's just a lot of baggage here." He put his arm around Rhiannon. "We were talking about moving in together, anyway. This seems like as good a time as any. Can you grab my cat, Bart?"

He threw together a bag while I coaxed Bart off the top of the refrigerator. The Maine Coon was frisky, but when I opened the cat carrier, he let out a *purp* and looked at Leo, who was stuffing his backpack. He'd already filled two suitcases, one with clothing and one with spell components and herbs.

Leo gave a three-toned whistle and Bart delicately leapt down to the counter, then to the floor. He strolled over to the carrier and made himself at home, curling up on the thick cushion inside. I shut the door and fastened the latch.

"I've never seen a cat so responsive. How did you train him?"

Leo laughed. "*You* don't train *cats*. *They* train *you*. Marta gave him to me when he was nine weeks old, and performed a binding ritual for us. Apparently, Bart needed to be with a healer, and so Marta presented him to me and Bart approved. We've been together five years now, and he's been a great help. And a real friend," he added softly.

I peered into the carrier. I loved cats, but there had been no chance to have any sort of pet when Krystal and I were on the road. After she died I'd been too restless to settle down. I'd befriended the strays wherever I went, until it hurt too much to leave them behind.

"Hey there, Bart," I whispered.

*Hello.* It didn't come as a word, but an impression in the current of air streaming from the air cleaner on the floor near the desk. I stared at the cat. The greeting had definitely come from the Maine Coon, but he just stared at me and blinked, long and slow. I blinked back.

"I'm ready," Leo said, interrupting my thoughts. "It's almost five thirty. We should head out."

"Yeah, the light's starting to fade." I peeked out the front window. "We'd better get going."

Rhiannon started to pick up Bart's carrier. "Come on. Let's go home, little dude. I . . . I . . ." A catch in her voice made me turn. She set down the cat and slid into a nearby chair, rubbing her head. "Heather's the only family I have. I can't lose my mother—*I can't.*"

"Hush," I whispered, stroking her back. "We'll find her. We'll bring her home and everything will be okay." I wished to hell I meant what I was saying, but my stomach twisted in knots. We had a long way to go before we ever found Heather. *If* we found her. "I'm here, I'm your family."

"I'm not family yet, but I'm here, and I love you," Leo said, stricken. "We'll all look out for each other."

She looked up at him. "And I love you, Leo . . ."

He smiled softly. "I know."

She stood and he enfolded her in his arms, kissing away her tears. I looked away, wanting to give them some privacy.

"Come on." Rhiannon wiped her eyes and picked up the cat carrier as I grabbed one of the suitcases. "We'd better go before it gets dark."

Leo hoisted his pack over one shoulder and picked up the other suitcase. Taking one last look around the silent apartment, he flipped the lights and locked the door. But even though he said nothing, as we clattered down the front steps, I could tell he was thinking about his sister.

The ride back to Veil House was quiet except for the occasional yowl from Bart. "He doesn't like cars?" I asked.

"Not many cats do," Leo said, shaking his head. "But Bart's not really complaining, he's just asking how much longer he has to stay in the carrier."

"He an indoor-only?"

"Yeah, he's afraid of the outdoors. I don't trust the forest near your house. Do you let the cats out?"

"Not the indoor babies," Rhiannon said. "Four of them are feral and won't put up with being caged. But the other three stay inside the house." As we pulled into the driveway, she looked at me. "Be sure to lock Favonis. We don't want any nasty surprises waiting in case we have to take off during the middle of the night."

The Fae could probably unlock the car, I thought, but then again, with the steel and iron, maybe not. I hoped that side of legend and lore stood to the test.

Dusk had hit by the time we got back to Veil House. As we headed for the front porch, I kept a close eye on the forest. Nothing stirred, nothing showed itself, but I could feel them there, watching us.

"Check every room," I said, setting down Bart's cat carrier. "Before anything else, let's secure the house."

We spread out. Rhiannon and I checked the upstairs while Leo combed the main floor. Rhiannon did a head count of the indoor cats. All but two were sprawled in the living room, and the third—Beastbaby—was waiting by the food dish, yowling for his dinner. As we gathered in the living room, I shut the drapes.

"So, what now?" Leo said.

We looked at each other. Heather was missing. We were facing a group of Vampiric Fae who were far more deadly than their dark kin on either side. I was about to embark on starting a business I knew nothing about, didn't know how to run, and wasn't sure I could pull off.

Oh yes, and we were sitting ducks, just waiting for the other shoe to drop.

"We eat dinner and then we ward the house. You call Geoffrey and get us an appointment if you can. We read up on the Indigo Court and find out every scrap of information that we can on them."

Rhiannon nodded. "And you and Peyton start planning your business. The more magic you work with, the better for us in the long run."

"I still think we're going to need more help." Leo pulled Bart's carrier over to the table and opened it. Bart slowly slunk out, glancing around. Leo sprawled on the sofa, crossing his legs in the lotus position. He whistled and Bart leisurely leapt up on his lap. Stroking the Maine Coon around the ears and chin, he said, "Who else can we trust?"

"Don't look at me," I said. "I just hit town. I don't know anybody. Except Peyton."

"I think she's going to be very useful. Tomorrow during your workout with her, steer the conversation around to asking just what she's strongest at." Rhiannon sat down at Heather's desk and snapped her fingers. "I know! What about Kaylin?"

"Who's he?" I pulled off my jacket and sat on the corner of the sofa arm.

"Kaylin Chen. He's a goth-type computer geek. He's also a martial arts sensei. He could probably snap your neck with one blow. Quiet. Intense. Independently wealthy. And he can sing and play kodo drums like there's no tomorrow. He teaches martial arts at the conservatory." She glanced over at Leo. "I bet he'd get along with Cicely."

Leo snorted. "You might be right."

Feeling simultaneously left out and picked on, I folded my arms across my chest and tapped my toe. "Don't count your chickens before they turn into KFC. Just why do you think he might be able to help us?"

"Because he's a rebel, and his best friend was a member of the Society. He was killed in a car wreck, though I suspect now it was the Indigo Court." Leo's face went dark. "Kaylin . . . is a special sort. He's far more than he lets on to be. He went into hiding. Right now, *nobody* knows where he's at, but I bet I can get him over here. I'll give him a call."

I stared at Leo as he fished out his cell phone. It began to dawn on me just how far things had gone. People were missing, people were *dead*, the cops couldn't be trusted . . .

"Why haven't the Feds sent in an investigation team?"

Rhiannon shook her head, a grim look on her face as she stood up. "My guess is that the news never hit the major papers. Heather thought . . . *I* think information's being squelched."

"Conspiracy?"

"Think about it. The cops don't give a damn that people are dying and vanishing. Grieve himself told you that Myst controls the town. She must have some way of controlling the authorities. It's probably easy for her to keep stories like this from ever making it out of this burg." She began searching through the desk.

"But surely people talk . . . What are you looking for?"

"Anything that might help us. Anything my mother might have written down or hidden that we can use." Pausing, she glanced over her shoulder. "We should go through the entire house. Can you check out the buffet over there?" She nodded to an antique buffet standing against the wall.

I slowly opened the drawer and began rifling through the papers inside, feeling uncomfortably like a voyeur. This was my aunt's home and I was pawing through her stuff like a common thief. Not that I wasn't familiar with copping a wallet here or there, but this was different.

But then I happened to look up and found myself staring through a slight part in the curtains. The trees were dark and shaded in the growing dusk, and something about the path leading to the forest gave me the creeps. Like a frost-covered open mouth, waiting to gobble up anybody who got too near.

I went back to my search.

"What's this?" Rhiannon said, pulling out a small notebook. She held it up. "This looks like . . . hmm, see what you make of this, would you?" As she returned to the table, I shoved the drawer shut and joined her.

The notebook was a field study book—filled with page after page of diagrams, figures, and notations on the graph paper. I frowned. As I flipped back to the beginning, I glanced at the inscription on the inside cover: Heather's name, and the words *A Magical Study of New Forest*. And then something clicked as I studied the pages.

"It appears to be a diagram of the town." I pointed to a schematic that looked very much like what I imagined Vyne Street to look like from above. "Isn't this our street? And there's the house."

"You're right." Rhiannon tapped her nails on the table. "But what's that mark—and that?" She gestured to a dark circle over where the wood and ravine were indicated. In the center of a diagram of Veil House, a pentacle had been inscribed.

"Dark circle. Dark moon, maybe? The new moon?" I shrugged.

"At least the pentacle over the house makes sense, since it's a magical symbol."

Leo interrupted, flipping his phone shut. "Kaylin will be over tomorrow morning. He doesn't like to travel alone at night."

We showed him the book and he recognized it.

"Your mother was using this when I was practicing my wildcrafting. Heather told me that New Forest is built over a very powerful energy field and that's why the plants here are so potent. She said the Society sources a lot of energy from the land around here and she keeps track of the ley lines."

"You've got to be kidding." Rhiannon looked up.

"No, I'm not." He shook his head. "New Forest is built over a powerful series of ley lines."

Ley lines were energy grids that traveled through the earth. I could feel them when I was near a mountaintop or at high elevation, and sometimes around ponds or streams or lakes. But since my powers were sourced from the wind, I couldn't always pinpoint where they were.

*You haven't tried to feel them in the air,* Ulean whispered.

*They can be felt through the slipstream?*

*Of course.*

"*You* can feel them, can't you?" I turned to Rhiannon. "You work with fire—you must be able to really tune in to the area because of the Cascade volcanoes."

She pressed her lips together. "I haven't tapped into the fire since . . ." Slumping into a chair, she pressed her hand to her forehead.

"Since what?" Leo looked at her, then turned to me. "What am I missing?"

I started to shake my head, but Rhiannon held up her hand. "I haven't told him. But I was going to, when I thought the time was right. I guess that would be now. And it's time I told *you* the full story, too, Cicely." She stared at her hands. "Both of you might be in danger living here, and not just because of the Indigo Court."

"Why? What are you talking about?" Leo knelt beside her.

Rhiannon shrugged. "You may not be so quick to reach for my hand when I tell you the truth."

"You were about thirteen, weren't you?" I knew a little of the story, but very little.

"Yes, I'd just turned thirteen. Just started my period and the hormones were flying. Heather and I were shopping one day. We were in the parking lot of the Dalewood Mall. I wanted a new pair of sneakers and she said no." Her voice caught and she trembled, her neck taut, her expression bleak. "I was angry and I automatically reached for the flame. Without thinking, I conjured fire. It sparked off the fuel in the gas tank of a nearby car and there was an explosion."

"Shit." Leo slowly dropped to the sofa. "Were you hurt?"

When Rhiannon spoke again, her voice was so low we could barely hear her. "No, I wish I was. But it gets worse. The flames . . . I will never forget the smell. There was a ten-year-old girl in the car and she couldn't get out. Nobody could get to her because the fire was raging so hot and then, the car exploded. She died. *I killed her.* She died because of *me.*"

Leo put his arm around her and she leaned against his shoulder.

I sat beside them and took her hand. I'd never known exactly what had happened but it didn't surprise me. "You never meant to do it. It was an accident."

She shook her head, her eyes furious. "I didn't mean to do it, but Cicely, I killed that little girl and over a decade later, I can still remember her screaming, pounding on the window, trying to get out. And the flames were so hot . . . so hot. And then the explosion . . . I watched her die, and I still see her every day. She haunts my dreams. I haven't touched my flame since that day."

"You can't run from the fire. If you keep running from it, the flames will build up inside you. They'll devour you! Look at what happened to Krystal. She ran from her powers and ended up a strung-out bloodwhore, and she died in a nameless alley because she was *afraid*. Rhiannon, you need to be strong."

She let out a snort. "The Society said I was tainted— that I'll never be able to control my powers. Marta threatened to kick Heather out if she ever taught me to use my abilities. I found *that* out by accident, so one day I told her they'd vanished, to keep her from worrying. She never believed me."

"What?" I gave her a long look. "The Society said *what* to you?"

"Marta refused to sanction any further training for me because my hands were sullied with blood, and since Heather is a member of the Society, she had to obey."

I snorted. "*Fuck them, then*. Where were they when you needed help? Fuck them and their rules. Marta's dead and Heather needs you. She's out there, the Indigo Court has her, and we don't know what the hell they're doing to her. And since the Society wouldn't do its job, then *we'll* help you."

Leo kissed the top of Rhiannon's head and gently guided her to her feet. She was shaky, but he braced her elbow.

I shook my head. "The Thirteen Moons Society is almost defunct. We can't rely on anybody but ourselves. We're in this by our lonesome. Ask Kaylin if he's interested in joining us. If you trust him, go for it. And Leo— can you please give Geoffrey a call now that the sun's down?"

"I still don't think it's a good idea, but I'll set up a meeting." The look on his face told me he thought I was crazy.

"You do that." Weary—the day had seemed long beyond words—I sighed and pushed to my feet. "Meanwhile, I need to unpack."

"We'll make dinner while you're doing that. Then we'll figure out how to ward the house."

As I headed upstairs, I whispered to Ulean, *Back me up, friend. I think we're all in trouble.*

*Always and forever* came the reply.

# Chapter 7

Once in my room, I pulled out my wallet and counted how much cash I had left. Checking accounts had never been a part of my life. Five hundred and twenty-three dollars. Add to that the four thousand in Marta's business checking and I still needed a job before long.

The wallet had been Krystal's. I'd always suspected she'd lifted it off some john. Why I kept it, I didn't know, but it was one of the few links I had to my mother. It had contained a single photo when I found it on her bruised and bloodied body. I slid the photo out of the wallet and flipped it over.

A crinkled picture of my mother and Heather, arms around each other. Krystal and Heather had been twenty years old, according to the date written on the back. They looked so young, and Heather was smiling, the wind blowing her hair in her face. Krystal was also smiling, but there was something in her gaze—a fear that had never left her.

"You just couldn't get it right, could you? You always fucked up." I hadn't cried when I found her dead, and two years later, I still couldn't cry. There was just a void—a hole filled with dark smoke.

I glanced at the picture again, then sighed. The past was gone. There was nothing I could do to change it now, and in truth, despite the problems of my childhood, I liked myself. And if I'd had it easier, who knows who I would have turned out to be?

After a moment, I propped the photo against the lamp on the desk and carefully laid out a soft black cloth, rolled and tied with a ribbon. Thanks to my nomadic childhood, I'd kept my magical tools to a minimum, too, making each item multitask.

I untied the ribbon and spread out the cloth to reveal a stiletto athame—my ritual dagger. Double-bladed, the silver hilt was engraved with an owl motif, the blade highly polished. Next to it, wrapped in tissue paper to keep it safe, was an owl feather. The very possession of the feather could land me a hefty fine and/or time in jail since it was protected by wildlife laws, so I kept it out of sight. As I touched it, it hummed.

*Whoa.* The feather had never done that before.

I waited, but it didn't do anything else and, after a moment I shrugged and laid it down, then set out the few other assorted tools I had: a smudge stick, a quartz crystal that I'd attuned to myself, a ritual fan . . . that was the extent of my magical goody bag.

But with what I inherited from Marta, my stash of magical tools and components would drastically increase. The thought of being able to practice on a regular basis, with enough supplies to really delve into my wind magic, made me all shivery in a good way. Even though it came all bundled up with Heather's disappearance and Grieve and the Indigo Court, I couldn't help but smile.

First, though, we had to do something about Rhiannon. Stifling up all that magical energy couldn't be good for her.

My cousin and I had been born on the same day—
the summer solstice—twelve hours apart. Rhiannon was
born at daybreak, a daughter of the sun, when the year
was still waxing, I was born at dusk, a daughter of the
moon, when the year had shifted over to waning. We
grew up calling ourselves twins, even though we didn't
look anything alike. She took after her mother; I took
after Krystal.

*Amber and jet*, Aunt Heather called us when we were
little. *Fire and ice.*

Rhiannon had always been the quieter one, more intent
on thinking things through before acting. She wasn't
exactly timid, but she seemed delicate to me—almost
like a hollow reed.

*Reeds are strong, you know,* Ulean whispered to me.
*They bend during storms, rather than break.*

I blinked. *Yes, but reeds won't hold up a house.*

*They make a good raft, so don't write them off so
fast.*

Shaking away the thought of Rhiannon being a life
raft, I headed downstairs to find her finishing up on the
kitchen. It looked spotless.

I yawned as I slid into one of the kitchen chairs.

"So what next? We . . ." I stopped, realizing that we
had no idea of what to do after we warded the house.
At least as far as finding Heather. "What the hell *are* we
going to do next?"

"Yeah, I know," Rhiannon said, softly. "I've been
thinking the same thing. My mother's gone, and I may
never see her again. I love Heather. I know we had our
differences, but she stood up for me and I love her. I'm
not sure what I'm going to do if she's gone for good."

"Don't say that! We'll find her, we'll bring her back."
Even as I said the words, I didn't know if I believed
them.

"I can't think about this right now. Everything's too much to take in. So tell me what happened with Grieve."

I shook my head. "What can I say? He's dangerous and I love him. The two are mutually exclusive, aren't they? I guess I never stopped loving him. No man in the past nine years has ever meant anything to me beyond being a one-night stand. Or a friend. Now I know why."

Rhiannon wrapped her arms around my neck and hugged me tight. "I know it hurts to hear, but Cicely, if he warned you away, there must be a reason." One look at my face and she slipped into the chair next to me. "You've got it bad."

"I wasn't ready to stay when I was here before. I wasn't ready to commit myself to him, and Krystal needed me. But now I am. And now it's too late. He belongs to the enemy."

She rubbed my shoulders. "Let it be. What will happen, will happen. And maybe . . . maybe he's still who he was. Maybe he can shake the turning somehow—it's not like he's dead, if what the book says is correct."

There was a sound, like knocking. I glanced at my cousin, who shook her head. "Don't," she said.

*I'm here,* Ulean whispered.

Slowly, I made my way to the front door and opened it. There was no one there. I stepped out onto the porch, looking right and left, and almost immediately felt someone's gaze focused on me from the ravine. A look over at the trailhead showed that a wolf stood half-on, half-off the path.

*Grieve.*

He padded toward me through the snow, and the next thing I knew, I was on the lawn, then halfway across toward the thicket with the wolf approaching me, eyes brilliant emerald, fur a silvery gray.

I reached out and he touched his nose to my hand.

A spark ricocheted up and down my spine, then spread through my stomach where my wolf's head tattoo was located. A resonance tingled across my lower abs, singing through the ink. I gasped as the wolf jumped up, its forepaws on my shoulders, and gazed into my eyes. In another flash, the animal was gone as Grieve pulled me into his arms and pressed his lips against mine.

"Let go of me." Grieve held me so tight I could barely breathe. I elbowed him, trying to break away.

"Stop squirming," he whispered. "It drives me crazy when you struggle, and I could hurt you." And there it was, in his voice. The hypnotic pull. And a deadly threat hiding behind the desire.

"Grieve, please stop." I'd been in enough situations with crack-crazed junkies looking for drug money or a quick fuck that I'd learned how to relax and avoid setting off panic buttons. Grieve might not be a druggie, but I recognized the razor's edge in his voice. He was walking a thin line and I didn't want to push him over the brink.

I forced myself to hold still. Struggle, and I was prey. Submit, and he might come to his senses. Closing my eyes, I willed the wind to give me strength, to shore me up and calm my fears. As a cool breeze raced over me, my pulse slowed and my heart stopped racing.

Grieve loosened his embrace, but my wolf tattoo kept up a warm keening throughout my body. ·

I stumbled away, keeping my eyes on him. Never turn your back on a predator. Too dangerous. A deviant little smile crinkled the corner of his lips and he darted his tongue out as he brought his fingers up to his mouth, licking them.

"I can taste your sweat," he said, never taking his gaze off of me. "I can smell you. You still want me. Don't even try to lie about it."

I stared at him. *He knew* . . . Part of me didn't want him knowing how I felt because that knowledge would give him an advantage, and part of me wanted to rush right back into his embrace.

"Back off. Don't do anything you'd regret later."

He let out a sharp bark. "Regret? I have no regrets. Not anymore," he added softly, but something in his voice told me he was lying. At least to himself.

"I almost forgot you could change into a wolf." Which I hadn't, but it was something to say, something to ease us back to safety.

"I am born of the Cambyra Fae, the Shifting Ones. There's a great deal you seem to have forgotten about me, Cicely Waters. About *us*." He glanced at the house. Rhiannon and Leo were watching from the porch and I prayed they wouldn't make any sudden movements. "I'm sorry about your aunt. But she should have been more careful." He circled me slowly.

I turned, mirroring his movements. "Did you take her? Did you kidnap Heather?"

"Kidnap is such a pale word, don't you think?" He stopped, his face deadpan. Then he shook his head. "No, I didn't take her; I swear on my life that I did not. But I know who did. I told you, Myst rules the town. And she always gets whatever she wants."

"Is Heather still alive?"

"That's information I'm not privy to, Cicely."

I sucked in a deep breath. "So, I guess my next question is, does Myst rule *your* actions? Are *you* truly now a part of the Indigo Court, Grieve? What happened to your devotion to the Queen of Rivers and Rushes? Is Lainule still alive?"

He leaned toward me and I thought he might kiss me again but instead he lingered a few inches away from my lips. "Devotion is an honorable attribute but unfortunately not one apt to prolong my life under certain circumstances."

I narrowed my eyes. He hadn't hurt me yet, but that

was no guarantee my luck would hold. I tensed to run should he decide to come at me.

"I'll ask you again: Do you answer to the Indigo Court? Are you . . . are you one of the Vampiric Fae? What happened to Lainule?"

Grieve's eyes flashed. He laughed, low and throaty.

"I was born of the Cambyra . . . but ask you this: How do you think those of us belonging to the nobility saved our necks? The Queen of Rivers and Rushes managed to escape. We don't know where she is, and for that I am grateful. I would not want to see her at the mercy of Myst. But hundreds in the court were slaughtered. Massacred. I watched them die, torn to bits, their souls drained even as their veins were bled dry."

He shuddered, a look of revulsion filling his face. "The Indigo Court feed in a frenzy, Cicely. Like sharks or piranha. They can devour their victims alive. They're bloody and terrifying, and entirely without remorse. I decided to forego the pleasure of that particular demise. Chatter was spared for two reasons only: he's not one of the nobility, and I begged them to let me keep him as my pet. I went down on my knees for him, and that is why he lives."

He reached out and stroked my cheek. "Chatter was worried I'd kill you. But trust me on this: I will never deliberately destroy you. I will never deliberately hurt you. Long ago I caught a glimpse of the future, a glimpse of what potential you had, and of who you would become. And of who you are. We're meant to be together, Cicely. I always knew you'd come back to me when you were ready. I told you to go away but . . . I can't bear the thought of seeing you leave again."

I started to back away, but he began to follow. Stopping, I whispered, "You've changed so much."

"More than you can ever know." With another laugh, he ran his hand down my arm, then hooked me around the waist. The cold seeped into my body but I barely noticed it. A swirl of snowflakes fell, twirling around our faces as his breath came in soft puffs, warming my face.

"I can save you and your friends from Myst, as long as you obey me. There's nothing I can do to help your aunt. But you . . . and your cousin . . . I can keep you alive if you cooperate. *If you look the other way.*"

Barely able to breathe, I slowly shook my head. "We can't do that. We can't leave Heather—or the town—to the mercy of the Indigo Court. This is no game, and Heather's life isn't up for grabs, even in order to keep us alive."

He let out a low breath. "Then the only way I can help is to keep silent about what you've told me," he whispered, his breath trailing down my neck in a thin line of mist. He moaned softly and pressed his teeth against my skin.

I stood perfectly still as the razor-sharp points nicked my flesh, poised for the bite. A drop of saliva hit my skin, then another, and—reacting to the warmth of his body—I leaned against him.

"Grieve." I murmured his name. "Oh, Grieve . . ."

As if he sensed I'd lost control, Grieve shuddered and pushed me away. "Go. Go before I take you right here. I can no longer help my nature."

I stared at him, my breath ragged. "You're lying. You wouldn't be here, warning me, if you couldn't control your instincts."

"Don't doubt me! I know who I am. I know *what* I am. Now, go, damn you!" He whirled, his eyes blazing, then the air shimmered as he shifted back into a wolf and bared his teeth.

Ever so slowly, I backed away toward the house, praying that neither Rhiannon nor Leo would utter a word till we made it inside. One wrong move, one wrong sound, and Grieve would be on me and he'd either tear me to shreds or carry me off. As I reached the porch and climbed the steps, he turned and loped back toward the ravine.

"Get indoors," I said hoarsely. *"Now!"*

Leo slammed the door behind us, then locked it. A thin plank of wood was all that stood between us and the dangerously seductive Indigo Court.

※

"How are those protection charms coming?" I hurried from room to room, making certain all the windows and doors were locked. "We've got to have some sort of protection for the doors tonight."

Rhiannon motioned for us to follow her into the utility room. "I found the batch of protection oil that Heather made up. While you were upstairs unpacking, I covered enough wooden pentacles with it to hold the windows fast."

"And I charged up several witches' bottles." Leo lifted the bottles, clear glass filled with threads and sparkling salts and herbs. "Set one by each door leading to the outside. Then a drop or two of blood on them should trigger the spell and they'll keep out intruders. But they won't last against a sustained assault and I have no doubt that any magicians the Indigo Court has within its ranks will be able to break through. I wouldn't trust these for more than two days, tops."

"Let's get to it then. I'll hang the protection charms over the windows upstairs. Rhiannon, take the downstairs windows. Leo—you made the bottles, so you should put them by the doors. Make sure all the cats are inside for the night."

Rhiannon and Leo grabbed their supplies and took off. I headed for the stairs, but stopped in the living room, drawing back the curtain to peer out of the window. Twilight had fallen and lights flickered from the ravine.

Faerie lights, they looked like Christmas lights, twinkling against the snowscape, but I know they were will-o'-the-wisps. Masks of illusion, the corpse candles were harbingers of death and I knew without a doubt that Myst controlled their movements. The Mistress of Mayhem was in charge, and one of her servants had a direct feed into my body and heart.

# Chapter 8

The next morning, on my way to the gym at New Forest Conservatory, I kept my eyes open, but nothing seemed out of place. I'd promised Rhiannon I'd meet her for coffee after my workout before she headed into work.

Early morning, the skies were brighter than they'd been the day before, but a silvery luminescence to the clouds promised more snow later. The chill seeped right through my leather jacket and I decided to take it in to an alterations shop and have it lined.

On my way across campus, it struck me how silent the conservatory seemed. New Forest Conservatory was a small school on a large campus. Along with a focus on basic learning, the school taught magical and physical skills to the magic-born in the area, as well as community service classes for older Supes—vamps and Fae primarily—in order to help them adjust to life out in the open. But the majority attending were under eighteen, and of the magic-born.

Set on a thousand acres of wooded land on the outskirts of the town, the school accepted a total of one thousand students each year, with preference granted to returning students who met the strict requirements for progress.

The conservatory had an Old World feel to it, which wasn't a surprise, considering Geoffrey's people were in charge. The vamps ran just about every school like this. They were the ones with the money. Most of the magic-born did okay, but nothing like what the vamps could pull in.

I glanced at the large bay windows dotting the sides of the buildings. Lights shone from within, except for two buildings, which seemed to have no windows at all. At first I couldn't figure it out, but then it clicked—*vampires*. Must be the buildings where most of the night classes were held.

"Man, this place has a lot of trees," I said, staring up at thick stands of oak, cedar, and fir that towered around the buildings. That's one thing I'd missed down in LA— the trees.

As I came to Terrance Hall, the center where the gymnasium was located, I looked around for Peyton, but she wasn't anywhere in sight. We were supposed to meet at the front desk, but I thought we might run into each other entering the building. Pushing through the double doors, I jogged over to the gym and stopped at the check-in counter. A young woman was sitting behind the desk, her eyes brilliant topaz, ringed with black. Fae? No . . . were-wolf. I could smell her right off. Odd that she'd work here, but at least New Forest Conservatory didn't discriminate in employment.

"I'm looking for Peyton Moon Runner. Has she checked in yet?"

The girl's nose twitched and she gave me a disdainful look, but checked the register without a word. She shook her head. "I'm sorry, I don't see her listed here. Everyone who enters is required to leave their membership card at the desk, so I'd know if she came through."

"Are you sure?" I glanced up at the clock. Seven thirty. Right on time.

"I'm positive," she said, less friendly. "You want to check yourself?"

Shaking my head, I moved over to one of the benches by the large window looking out to the main square. By seven forty, I was growing concerned. I pulled out my cell phone and punched in Peyton's number.

After five rings her voice messaging came on and I left a brief message. By seven fifty I was getting worried, and by eight, I grabbed my duffel bag and headed out. I debated whether to call Anadey or the police, but decided to wait to see what Rhiannon had to say.

I crossed the campus to the Grove, the main eatery at the school, and called Rhiannon on the way. "Listen, can you meet me early? . . . Yeah, the Grove, it is . . . I don't know if anything's wrong but I don't have a good feeling about this."

As I hung up, I entered Brekhart Hall and took the stairs down to the bottom story. The halls were wide and welcoming, if old, and made me wish I'd been able to attend here when I was younger. But those days were long past.

*Maybe you can attend a night class or two, a community-sponsored class,* Ulean said.

*Maybe . . . but with what's going on, I'm not too sure that's a good idea.*

The Grove was a pleasant, airy room. In place of long dining tables stood dozens of square tables, each sitting four to six people. The atmosphere definitely felt more *restaurant* than cafeteria. The average age of students seemed in line with what I'd read—early teens to mid-twenties. And all of them felt tingly with energy.

Rhiannon came rushing in just as I picked up my order—a triple-shot mocha and a sausage and cheese breakfast sandwich—and slid into the seat opposite. She was shivering.

"Let me get hot coffee—it's snowing hard." While she hurried up to the counter, I tried Peyton again. And again, no answer. Now I was getting seriously freaked. Peyton didn't strike me as the type to blow off an appointment without calling.

When she returned, Rhia was carrying a white chocolate mocha, a bowl of oatmeal, and two hard-boiled eggs. She slipped out of her coat and took a sip of the steaming mocha, her eyes closing in gratitude.

"Cripes, it's cold out. But this makes me feel almost human." She let out a long sigh. "What's up?"

"What's up is that Peyton didn't show and I can't get her on the phone. I tried calling her several times. Nothing."

Rhiannon's expression dropped. "Crap. Have you called Anadey?"

"I was waiting for your advice. I don't want to scare her in case it's just car trouble. But Peyton had my phone number and I'm sure she would have called me if it had been that."

"Unless she forgot her phone at home. But then, Anadey would have answered when you called, wouldn't she? Give her a call. She won't be at the diner yet—she usually works afternoons and evenings."

While Rhia warmed herself with her coffee, I phoned Anadey, who answered on the second ring.

"Cicely? Why hello—I thought you were with Peyton."

"She was supposed to meet me this morning for a workout, yes, but . . ." I paused, not knowing exactly how to phrase it.

*Just say it outright, child. That's the only way you*

*can.* Ulean's calming presence helped and I cleared my throat.

"Peyton never showed and she hasn't called. I thought maybe she forgot her cell phone at home and has had car trouble?"

Silence. Then, a soft but audible gasping for air, as if someone had knocked the wind out of her. "No, she had it with her when she left. She was fully intending on meeting you, Cicely. I think I'd better call the police."

"Do you want me to come over? Rhiannon has to work, but I can be there in ten minutes." I pushed back my chair.

"Would you, please? Though I don't know what good the cops will do. They aren't helping anybody much lately." She gave me her address and hung up.

I turned to my cousin. "Peyton left home with her cell phone, all right. But she hasn't checked in. I'm headed over there now. Anadey's calling the cops. I'll give you a ring and let you know what's going on after we talk to them. And, Rhia . . ."

"Yes?" Her brow pinched as if she were trying not to cry.

"Be careful, okay? Don't leave campus without calling me. Too many people are disappearing lately."

I grabbed my coffee and sandwich and headed for Favonis on the run, trying to dart between the tiny, stinging flakes that were whipping down from angry skies. By the time I go to the car, I looked like I had a horrible case of dandruff. Sliding behind the wheel, I let out a long sigh. Today was starting off on a very bad note.

❀

Anadey was waiting for me when I got to her apartment. I could see why she was planning to move into Marta's house—the place was tiny and she and Peyton had to feel cramped.

She led me into the living room, which was smaller than my bedroom at the Veil House, and motioned for me to sit down. The cops were already there, and they looked bored. One of them gave me a nod and continued with what he'd apparently been saying when I'd interrupted. "Like I said, she probably forgot the appointment and stopped off at a store. Maybe she saw a pair of shoes that caught her eye or something."

I bristled. "Listen, Peyton was coming to the gym to spar with me, not talk nail polish or the latest fashions. I've tried calling her several times and there's no answer. Can you at least have your cruisers out on the street look around for any sign of an accident? What if she's hurt? In case you haven't noticed, it's damned cold and snowing hard. She might have had an accident."

I didn't for the moment believe it, but just in case—and to get them off their butts—I decided to push that possibility.

"We've put out a call to all our men. We've checked the gas station and everywhere else Peyton might have stopped at. Ms. Moon Runner gave us her daughter's license plate number and car description. But ladies, that's all I can do for now. I'm sorry."

He stood and, together with his partner, sauntered out of the apartment. Anadey watched them go, then slammed the door, furious. "That is the attitude all the cops have had since . . . since all this started happening. I'm surprised Geoffrey's putting up with it. The vamps run the town, you know—they always have. Now it seems there's a new queen calling the shots and that can't be going over well." She leaned against the counter, her lips pressed tightly together.

I joined her, awkwardly patting her back. "Maybe we're wrong. Maybe she did stop somewhere."

*You know that's not true,* Ulean whispered.

*I know, but what else can I say? The woman has to*

*hold on to some hope and that's the only thing I can think of. It won't last long, granted, but it will get her through the next hour or so.*

"Was she supposed to stop for anything before she drove to the gym? If so, we can follow her progress."

Anadey's head snapped up. "Yes, actually, she was. She mentioned she needed to stop for gas before she met you, which is why she left early. She drives a Kia—a small red compact. We always go to the station on Twelfth Avenue— they have the lowest prices and we have an account there."

"I'm on it," I said. "You have a picture of Peyton I can take with me? I think you should stay here in case she calls and needs help."

"Here, take this one." Anadey pulled open a small ornate silver frame and withdrew the picture, handing it to me. "Thank you, Cicely. Thank you for looking for my baby. I know she's a grown woman but . . ."

"But she's your child." I paused. "And Heather's my aunt. We can't just act as if nothing happened and go on as usual. Listen, while I'm out looking for her, can you do me a favor and write up a good, strong protection spell? We have to ward the house. I'll tell you why later."

Anadey nodded. "Of course. Go now, please. Find my daughter for me."

I leapt into Favonis and gunned the motor. Time to make tracks.

※

I stopped at the gas station on Twelfth and filled up Favonis. As I headed inside to pay for my purchases, I pulled out Peyton's picture. Nobody else besides the clerk was in the store and so I tossed a ten on the counter for my gas, then held out the photo.

"Can you tell me if Peyton Moon Runner was in this morning to fill up her car? I need to get in touch with her and she said she'd be coming here. Wanted to see if she showed yet."

The guy pushed the picture back to me. "I know Peyton. And yeah, she dropped by to fill up her tank. She in trouble?"

"I hope not," I muttered. Then louder, said, "Not from me. I'm just trying to track her down. Listen, did the cops come by to check whether she'd been in?"

He blinked. "Cops? No. I've been here all morning and you're the second customer I've had since she was in. Why do you ask?"

"No reason . . . apparently," I said, adding a candy bar to my purchase, then headed back to the car. So the cops hadn't even bothered to see if she'd been at the station. Which she had. Which meant that she'd vanished after she'd gassed up.

I stood beside Favonis, closing my eyes as I tried to listen to the wind for any whispers that might give me a clue. *Any clue.*

First layer down . . . human contact . . . emotionally charged discussions . . .

*She said that she was at her girlfriend's house, but I found out later she was fucking my best friend . . .*

*Mother has cancer. Are you going to come visit or not?*

*What the hell are you talking about? I didn't scrape your car—you've got the wrong guy, you idiot.*

And then, I lowered myself a little further, tuning into the astral, the world of the unseen, the world of the elements themselves.

*Winter comes hard this year.*

*There's been a migration of Fae away from the area since the Shadow Hunters have come out to play. They hunt by day and night. Dangerous.*

And then . . . into the level of magic itself.

The energy buzzed, and I caught hold of the tail. I

opened my eyes, now able to visibly see the strands surrounding the area. It was like watching electrical impulses
running through a body, only what I was seeing was residue from those who walked along the streets, who flew
through the air, from magic-born and those not born to
the human world alike.

At the pump next to mine, I saw a trail of purple sparkles, and they led out of the lot and down the street. Something called to me and I sensed . . . Peyton. I'd picked up
her energy signature.

I jumped back into Favonis, and cautiously eased out
onto the street. It was hard to see through the strands of
energy lining the sidewalks and road, but I did my best to
keep my focus carefully divided so I didn't get in an accident or lose track of the tracers I knew had come from
Peyton. And then, they turned into a driveway ahead. I
eased Favonis down to speed and followed.

As the car jostled over a speed bump, I glanced at the
signs posted on either side of the drive. SUNSET PARK.
Great. A four-hundred-acre park complete with jogging
trails through the woods and a bicycle path. Wild wood.
Perfect place for Fae to hang out. *Or the Indigo Court.*

I parked in the lot and slowly stepped out of my car,
scanning for anything that might tell me . . . *Hello?* A red
Kia, compact, sitting on the far side of the lot. Dreading
what I'd find, I broke into a run and sprinted across the
lot, skidding to a halt just behind the car. A glance around
and a listen on the wind told me nobody was near here—
but the energy trails led right to the car and then abruptly
cut off, as if they'd been dampened.

The driver's door was unlocked and so I opened it, peek-
ing inside. Peyton's purse was on the passenger seat, but
the keys were nowhere to be seen. I glanced around, but
found nothing unusual. Her gym bag was in the back so
she'd definitely been on her way to meet me. A receipt for
the gas poked out of the cup holder.

Stepping back away from the car, I glanced around. A trail led off to the left, into the woods. A faint wisp of energy tapped me on the shoulder.

*Did she go that way, Ulean?*

*I believe so—a faint residue of her aura remains. But she is nowhere near here, that I can tell you.*

I shaded my eyes from the silvery overcast glare and looked around. There was no way I was going in those woods alone. Too dangerous. I could feel it creeping around me like tendrils from a vine. Just then, a glint of shine caught my eye and I squinted. Something was in the snow near the trailhead.

Cautiously, I jogged over to it.

*Watch my back.*

*You've got it, but there's nothing near here now. Not even prying eyes. Just the energy residue.*

I leaned over, still carefully keeping my eye on the woods—Ulean was right most of the time but I wasn't going to let down my guard—and snatched up a set of keys. With a sinking heart, I saw the symbol for *Kia* printed on the car key. Heading back to the lot, I tried it in the lock. Sure enough, these were Peyton's keys. The thought that I should call the police crossed my mind but I dismissed it. Not a good idea, considering how nonchalant they'd been with us.

Instead, I punched in Anadey's number. She answered immediately.

"Yes? Peyton?"

"Sorry, no. It's Cicely. Listen, I found Peyton's car, and I found her purse and keys. Her energy heads directly into the woods and then vanishes. Does she often visit Sunset Park?"

Anadey let out a strangled cough. "Yes, she goes there to run sometimes, though she used to go a lot more, before the shadow came over the town. Cicely, do you think . . . *they* have her?"

I didn't want to say yes but the words spilled out before I could stop them. "I think we can assume so." I glanced around, wondering what had drawn her here. "You want me to lock up her car and bring her purse and keys back so you can come get it?"

"Would you?" Her voice had fallen, and with it her hope. I could hear the fear hiding behind her words; it had hold of me, too. I scooped up Peyton's purse and locked the Kia, then slid back into Favonis. With one last look at the trailhead, I pulled out of the parking lot and headed back to Anadey's.

# Chapter 9

I spent an hour at Anadey's, trying to reassure her and collecting another load of supplies from Marta's stash. I hadn't a clue how to go about setting up the business, but I'd figure it out. It was noon by the time I drove back to the Veil House and unloaded everything.

The house seemed terribly quiet. Rhiannon was at work, and Leo was still asleep. He slept through the mornings, waking up in the early afternoon to run errands for Geoffrey and the vamps and then prepare for whatever they wanted him to do at night.

I stood out on the front porch for a while, staring at the forest, wondering if Grieve was near, but my wolf was silent. It occurred to me that the Indigo Court seemed able to exist in the light, so there was another difference between them and their vampire ancestors.

Finally, not knowing what to do next, I headed back inside. I'd no sooner locked the door behind me when Bart came rushing over to me and rubbed against my leg. I leaned down and gathered the powder puff of a cat—he was huge and heavy—into my arms and snuggled my face in his fur.

"You be careful, okay? You tell my cousin's cats to be careful, too. There are beasties out there that eat little ones like you." As I set the now-squirming Maine Coon down, the doorbell rang. Cautiously, I pulled back the curtains.

The FedEx truck was out front and I opened the door, feeling myself relax just a hair. The driver handed me a flat envelope and held out the register for me to sign. Afterward, he tipped his hat and headed back to the truck without a word. Wondering if he was always that silent, I glanced at the packet.

It was addressed to me. I ripped it open while speed-dialing Rhia at work. "Package came for me. I'm opening it right now."

The shuffle of papers told me Rhiannon was at her desk. "Did you ever find Peyton?"

"No. No, and they have her. The fucking Indigo Court has taken her."

The sound of silence, and then, "Hell. Does Anadey know?"

"I told her right before I came home. Hmm, I think there's an invitation in the package. Ivory paper, red rose wax seal on the back. Should I open it?"

"How else are you going to find out what it is?"

I slit the envelope with my switchblade and drew out a heavy parchment-style folded card. The front read *You're Invited* . . . and on the inside:

*From the Crimson Court to Ms. Cicely Waters.*

———

*Please consider this a summons to a party this evening at 7:30 P.M. We also have a business proposition we would like to discuss. Your presence is required, and your friends may attend. Address: 12495 Ranchivo Drive. Dress: Formal.*

———

*Best, Regina Altos*
*Emissary to the Crimson Court.*

Sweet heaven. Or *hell*. An invitation to a Crimson Court party was like receiving a summons from the Queen of England. In a way, it *was* a summons from a queen. The Vein Lords ruled over the Crimson Court.

"I think Geoffrey got our message." I read the invitation to her.

"I think you'd better wake Leo up. I'll get off early and come home. This sounds important. Cicely . . ." She paused.

"What is it?"

"Regina Altos has a brother who teaches here at the school. His name is Lannan. He's . . . don't cross him. Don't get involved with him. Rumors about his habits and preferences are frightening." Her words were constrained but I sensed a serious bout of worry behind them.

"Why do you think I would?"

"Because Lannan takes what he wants. And from what I've seen around campus, you're—" Again, a pause, then, "I have to go. We'll talk more tonight."

I slowly put down the receiver and looked at the invitation again. Regina was Emissary to the Crimson Court. Her brother was a professor. A thought occurred to me and I dug through the boxes of books I'd brought back from Marta's house. Sure enough, a book that had caught my notice was sitting near *The Rise of the Indigo Court*.

Another history . . . this one *A History of the Vampire Nation* . . . The leather-bound volume smelled like garlic, and it had a silver belt holding it shut. Which meant that Marta hadn't wanted the vampires getting their hands on it.

Picking it up, I began to flip through the pages. It was typeset, not written by hand, but my bet was that there were no e-books or audio versions of this book.

> *The Crimson Court is the ruling body of the Vampire Nation. Ruled for millennia by a vampire known only as the Crimson Queen, the actual location of the court is held secret, and no living person knows where it is. Several investigative journalists who have made an attempt to track down the location of the court died odd and sudden deaths.*
>
> *The Queen of the Crimson Court is said to be half-mad from her age—it's rumored she's well over seven thousand years old. Still other rumors place her as having never truly been human, but rather a creature from the astral plane coming into physical form. The vampire race was said to have started with her, but this is regarded as speculation.*
>
> *The Queen has a harem of thirteen emissaries scattered around the world and they carry out her bidding. They are accorded authority above the jurisdiction of local vampire nests and lairs, and even the Vein Lords cannot touch the emissaries, who are—for all intents and purposes—the Queen's eyes, tongue, and hands.*

And Regina Altos was an emissary, therefore not even Geoffrey could thwart her. Which meant . . . well, I wasn't sure what it meant except that Regina had to be treated with kid gloves. I glanced back at the book, rifling through the pages until I caught mention of the words *deal* and *business*.

*A deal made with vampires can be a make-or-break affair. Throughout history, we've seen how the Vampire Nation has become rich through the skilled use of prognostication and by playing on the greed of mortals. Much like King Midas, many of those who could have had prosperous dealings with the vampires ruined their chances by asking for too much—or by promising too much in return.*

*From religious institution to world leader to rock star, a number of humans have sold themselves to the vampires with dreams of becoming rich, not realizing that the arrogance of the Vampire Nation is one that enjoys seeing others make fools of themselves, and play puppet for the Crimson Court.*

Slowly closing the book, I thought about our plan to ask Geoffrey for help. Obviously, Leo had talked to him—wait a minute . . . had Leo talked to him? And if not, why had we been issued the invitation?

I set the book back down on the pile and took the stairs two at a time to Rhiannon's room, where I tapped softly on the door. No answer. I opened it a crack and saw Leo, dead to the world, sprawled in her bed.

"Leo? Leo! *Hey you*." Not wanting to take a chance on embarrassing both him and me—the blanket was barely covering his nether regions and I didn't want to startle it off of him—I raised my voice.

Blinking, he began to come around, then shook his head and propped himself up on his elbows, squinting at me. "What's up?"

"Need to talk to you about something. Meet me downstairs? I'll make you some breakfast."

"Sure. Be down in ten." His tousled hair was sticking every which way as he rubbed his eyes and yawned.

I slipped back outside the room and returned to the

kitchen, where I pulled out a skillet and the eggs, then found the bread and butter. I popped four slices of bread in the toaster, then scrambled half a dozen eggs. Might as well make some for my lunch, as well.

Leo came into the room, freshly shaven and dressed. "What's up that you would disturb my beauty sleep?"

"Lots going on today and most of it bad," I told him.

"I guess you'd better give me the bad first." He poured orange juice for both of us and added a jar of jam to the table as I set his plate in front of him and sat opposite with my own food.

"Where to start?" I told him about Peyton and everything I'd found out.

"Shit." He hit the table with his fist. "Not Peyton, too? She doesn't deserve this—she's had a hard life and now . . . now we don't even know if she's alive. So what else . . . and I hope it gets better."

"That remains to be seen. Did you talk to Geoffrey about us wanting to see him yet?" I leaned back in my chair and savored the hot food. I was hungrier than I'd thought.

"Yeah, he said he'd decide in a few days."

"Well, it would seem he's already made up his mind." I handed him the invitation. "What can you tell me about Regina . . . and Lannan? Rhia told me to be careful around Lannan."

Leo's gaze flickered up to meet mine. "Yeah, I can see why she would. Lannan's . . . Lannan is a pervert, pure and simple. He thrives on the decadent vamp scene—the bloodwhores and the raves. In fact, I have a feeling that's what this little party is all about. And for some reason they want you there."

"Give me the lowdown on decorum. I need to know what *not* to do."

"Good idea. Formality among the vamps is never to be taken lightly. If they were responding to my question, the invitation would have been addressed to me. No, they want to see *you* for some reason. Don't trust any of them, but you can't refuse to show up. Nobody can refuse the Emissary."

I fingered the invitation, my stomach lurching. *Decadent vamp scene* didn't sit well with me. And bloodwhores sat even worse. My mother had been a bloodwhore and it had gotten her killed.

"Rhia said something about me being careful around Lannan," I said.

Leo bit into his toast, and chewed thoughtfully. After a moment, he swallowed and said, "I don't like talking about them. They employ me and I have to be careful in dividing my loyalties. But she's right. Lannan Altos prefers his bloodwhores with dark long hair, muscled, and . . . to be blunt . . . hot. You have the look he'd go after."

Hot? Me? I blinked. I never thought of myself in that category. But it would sound like a come-on if I protested. "Wonderful. Just what I need. Some creaking, ancient lecher after me. One with fangs, no less. "He's going to get a surprise if he tries anything. I don't swing that way."

"You're in for a surprise. Lannan is a golden boy. If I swung his way, it would be hard to resist but I'm straight and under Geoffrey's protection, so he can't touch me. Hey, you have anything to wear to this formal shindig?"

I stared at him. "Dude, I just got in from LaLa land, I've lived on the road since I was six—more or less. Do you *think* I have anything appropriate?" I didn't have time to think about shopping, not with everything going on. But Leo wouldn't let it drop.

"Then let's get going. You were the one invited, you have to look good. I've got a tux they bought me just for these occasions. And I know Rhiannon has some pretty dresses that will work. Finish breakfast. We're going shopping."

Staring at him like he'd just grown another head, I finished my eggs and toast, and silently followed him out to the car.

"I hope you realize I'm not about to spend all of my money on some shiny ball gown," I mumbled.

Leo shook his head. "Don't sweat it. I'll expense the cost. Geoffrey will approve." And just like that, the vampires were buying me a fancy new dress.

❧

After she got home from work and spent a few minutes with Leo, Rhiannon joined me in my room. We had three hours before we had to be at the party and both she and Leo were insistent that I had to dress the part.

"What does one wear to a vampire soiree?" I held up the little black dress I'd bought. It was short, sophisticated, and could pull off cocktails or dancing without a problem. Speaking of cocktails, the thought of what might be on the beverage menu made me a little queasy.

"That's nice—what is it? Silk?"

I nodded. "Leo wouldn't let me buy anything cheap."

"It's got a sweetheart neckline. Hmm," she said, a thoughtful look on her face. "Whatever you do, don't bring attention to your neck. No flashy necklaces or chokers. Not a good place to accentuate."

She smoothed the velvet skirt and top she was wearing. "How do I look? Okay?"

"Okay? That green sets off your hair and turns you into a torch. You're gorgeous. You look Old World beautiful." I paused. "Hey, Leo warned me about Lannan. I'll be cautious. I'm nobody's bloodwhore. *Ever.*"

"I know this is hard." She paused. "How much do you hate them, Cicely? And is it just for what they did to your mother?"

I glanced up at her, trying to figure out how to explain. "I don't. Not really. Krystal was a grown woman and she made her own choices, as stupid as they were. The truth is I don't hate vampires. I just don't *trust* them. No matter how many safeguards you put into place, they're predators and they can lose control. And when a vamp loses control, you're toast."

"Is that how you feel about Grieve now?"

I winced. "I love him . . . but can I ever trust him? I don't know. He's in the court of the enemy. They rip people to shreds. They feed on life energy as well as blood. When you think about it, the Indigo Court is far worse than the Vein Lords. Vampires you can reason with to an extent, and they're willing to make deals. I don't think the Indigo Court Fae are quite so civilized."

I held up the braided red leather belt I'd bought. "What do you think about this belt? I still don't know what shoes to wear."

"The belt's great. Wear these," she said, hunting through my mostly empty closet and holding up a pair of patent leather ankle boots with padlocks. "Cute. Very fetish. They'll go over well."

"I love boots." I slid them on, zipping up the sides and fastening the padlocks. Testing the stilettos cautiously, I hung the key around my neck, then stood to buckle the belt around my waist. "How do I look?"

Rhiannon gasped. "Gorgeous! You look so hot! You need makeup though." She paused, then added, "I never thought I'd be looking forward to a vampire's party. Hell, I never thought I'd ever be attending a vampire's party. Leo leaves me out of his job affairs and that's pretty much the way I want it. But if they can help me save my mother, I'll go." She paused, her words soft. "Life's changed for good. There's no going back, is there?"

I shook my head. "No, there's no going back."

"Do you think Myst is going to kill Heather?"

The question was so plaintive, so unexpected, that it drained the energy out of me and I slumped on her bed next to her.

Shrugging, I shook my head. "I don't know, Rhia. I don't know what's going to happen. But take a little time off from work. Tomorrow, let's go hunting in the ravine. Didn't you say Kaylin was going to be coming over today?"

"He called. Had to make it tomorrow. He'll be over in the morning. You really think we can go into Geoffrey's mansion, into a nest of vampires, and manage to walk out alive?"

I nodded, faking confidence. "We have to stop Myst. We have to find Peyton and Heather. When we come home, we'll go through Marta's charms and look for something to help protect us."

"What if they're feeding off her? Off Peyton? What if they're . . . using them?" The brilliant amber of her eyes grew watery.

"Then . . . we pray they can hold out till we find a way to save them. Your mother is strong—she possesses a lot of power. Peyton's no wimp. Try to keep hope. Sometimes, hope is all we have."

With a sigh, she nodded and gathered up her purse. We put on our finishing touches—makeup, jewelry, and headed downstairs to where Leo waited with a limo— sent from Regina herself.

One thing for sure: Life certainly wasn't boring. And another: Walking into a nest full of party-hearty vampires scared the hell out of me. Especially when I didn't know what they wanted.

# Chapter 10

The limo smoothly glided through the empty streets of New Forest, navigating the ice with ease.

I thought about what lay ahead. Geoffrey would be there. It was his house and as Regent of the Vampire Nation, North American branch, he had dominion over the entire continent when it came to the vampires. Geoffrey was one of the most powerful vampires alive . . . or undead, to be technically correct. But even *he* couldn't touch Regina. She walked among the sacred elite—an extension of the Crimson Queen to whom all of the Vein Lords paid homage. All but the rogues, that is.

While waiting for Rhiannon to come home, I'd flipped through more of *A History of the Vampire Nation*, and ran across a few references to Geoffrey, Regina, and Lannan. From what I could tell, they were all ancient and powerful.

Geoffrey was estimated to be nearly two thousand years old. From what was known, his origins were based somewhere in the Xiongnu period in what eventually became Mongolia. It's thought he'd been a lord during the time period, though he apparently hadn't given out any real details on his early life. And it was rumored that he'd sired Myst—although there wasn't much written about his life during that period.

Regina and Lannan, on the other hand, were far older, with their roots going back to Sumer. Regina had been a priestess of Inanna, so the rumors went, though they couldn't be verified except by her and it didn't appear she'd been chatting up the historian.

What was known was that it didn't pay to say *no* to any one of them. That alone sealed any doubt I had about accepting their offer, whatever it might be. I didn't like the thought of dealing with Geoffrey's crew, but I didn't want their fangs draining me dry, either. As far as betraying Grieve to them, I'd have to figure out a way to save him while getting rid of Myst.

I'd glanced over some of the punishments and inducements the vampires had used on the living through the years and decided that my conscience had needed a good reality check.

Leo and Rhiannon looked like a matched set—it was obvious they were together. I wondered what Geoffrey thought about Leo's involvement with my cousin. If he even bothered to think about it. Perhaps it was beneath his notice.

Ulean had opted to stay home—or wherever it was she stayed when she wasn't following me on the astral. The vamps didn't like astral or Elemental beings hanging out and Ulean had felt it would be safer all the way around.

*I'll be listening from a distance. I'll come if you need me.*

As we pulled into the driveway of the large estate, I wasn't surprised to see a plethora of BMWs, Porsches, Jaguars, and other high-end cars.

The lights of the mansion were sparkling and even from out on the lawn we could tell that the party was rolling. The manor spread across the lot—it must have been a good two acres—a vision in white with gold trim. Three stories high, and probably a basement, it reminded me of a Grecian temple plucked out of ancient Athens and dropped into the middle of New Forest. Columns supported a wide covered deck, and huge granite urns containing rosebushes were spaced evenly around the perimeter of the porch. Music drifted out, I caught snippets of Lenny Kravitz and Gary Numan and Seether, along with voices riding the wind, whispers of conversation in languages far older than any I'd ever heard.

As we headed up the stairs, I glanced back at the others. "Stick together. Don't let them separate us. We don't know what we're getting into and we can't afford to get embroiled in any skirmishes."

Leo nodded. "Remember not to meet a vampire's gaze. It's considered a challenge, and against an older, powerful vampire, we wouldn't last a minute."

Before I could reach for the doorbell, the double doors swung open and a tall, beautifully sculpted man stood before us. He was wearing a butler's uniform and his eyes were the black of night. *Vampire.* He bowed, swinging low.

"Hi, Regina asked me to come—" I started to say but he cut me off.

"You are Mistress Cicely Waters. And with you, your companions Master Leo Bryne, and Mistress Rhiannon Roland." The vampire nodded at each of us in turn. "You are expected. Please follow me."

He stood back and I stared at the door, feeling like I was about to walk right into the giant monster's gaping maw. Once the doors shut behind us, we'd be at the mercy of vampires and nobody knew where we were. I glanced

at the others. Leo nodded. Sucking up the fear, I stepped
across the threshold.

�֎

The foyer twinkled. A chandelier hung from the ceiling,
with a hundred crystals dangling from the incandescent
candlestick lights, and the hallway glittered as if bathed
in diamonds from the refracted light.

"How beautiful," Rhiannon whispered.

Looking to the left, a short hallway forked to the right
directly before ending in a set of double doors, their ivory
surfaces covered in golden scrollwork. Directly in front
of us, a master staircase led up several flights, splitting in
a T at the central landings.

To our right, the hallway forked in a left turn, but the
double doors were open and music filtered out from the
room.

Huge potted plants decorated the foyer, miniature trees
in porcelain urns that must have easily weighed a hundred
pounds without the weight of the soil or plant. Tables lined
the walls—long consoles in marble and wrought brass
and bronze. Paintings lined the walls and as I approached
the nearest I saw the name *Monet* and the brush strokes
and realized that it was authentic. Whoever owned this
estate had money. *Good* money.

The room was lit with chandeliers and a rotating disco
ball, but somehow none of the glitz looked tacky, just
sparkly and brilliant. There were odd scents in the air—
perfumes that I'd never smelled but that made me think
of lush gardens and opium dens.

And then, there were the vampires. I had fleeting
glimpses of actual humans in the crowd, but the vampires
were easy to pick out. Pupilless eyes might be freaky on
Little Orphan Annie, but the vamps made them work. It
would be so easy to fall into the blackness, to lose yourself in that shining void.

They seemed to be dancing in slow motion, strobed by the flashing of the rotating light, caught in freeze-frame to the rhythm of the music. The room was filled with Armani and Vera Wang and Calvin Klein and Yves Saint Laurent's Rive Gauche, and I began to realize these were power players. Old money scented the room, oily and thick and rooted in deals long dust.

"Are there any poor vamps?" Rhiannon whispered, and several of the nearest dancers turned their heads our way. One gave us a long, languorous smile. "Oh shit, they heard me," she added.

I nodded back at the smiling vamp and murmured under my breath, "Yeah, watch your mouth."

"I'm so glad you could make it."

One moment we were standing alone, the next—a woman stood by my side. She held out her hand and I cautiously accepted. Her skin was cool but not clammy, and silken. Golden blonde, with her hair gathered into an elegant chignon, she was no taller than Rhiannon but she wore her power like a cloak.

"I'm Regina Altos, Emissary to the Crimson Queen." She lingered a moment on my hand, rubbing my palm with one finger, before inclining her head at the others. "I'm so glad you and your friends could attend our little soiree."

Leo and Rhiannon murmured politely while I frantically tried to think of what to say next. This wasn't my usual social situation. I scrambled but was drawing a blank. Should I just act like I belonged here? Should I ask her what she wanted? Was it rude to take charge of the conversation with someone who was older than the pyramids? Luckily, Regina put an end to my dilemma.

"Come. We will return to enjoy the party, but for now—a meeting. Your friends are invited to sit in; no doubt you would tell them what we say anyway." She motioned for us to follow her and we wove through the crowd toward the end of the room where I could see yet another door.

On the way, I bumped up against a vamp and he looked down at me, hunger and delight filling his face. Catching my breath, I narrowed my shoulders and hurried past, trying to squeeze through without attracting any more attention than necessary.

Regina led us into a study—which was bigger than our living room at home—and there, behind the desk, sat a man, vaguely Chinese, but he obviously had some other bloodline going on in there, too. He looked to be around thirty, but by his eyes, I knew he was far older than that. He was dressed in a pair of leather pants, a ruffled lavender shirt, and a leather vest. His long, sharp nails were painted with gold and his hair hung down to his waist, free and smoothly onyx. In a word: Stunning.

He stood as we entered the room and motioned for us to take a seat in a conversation area. We sat in a line on the Victorian sofa, and waited.

"Look, they gather together like a litter of kittens," he said, smiling at us. He glanced up at Regina, who let out a throaty laugh.

"Leo, my trusty day runner, it's good of you to come with your new friend and your lovely courtesan." The man took a seat in a wing chair opposite me, and Regina sat in the matching chair to his side.

"Thank you for the invitation, Lord Geoffrey." Leo bowed, formally, then took his place beside Rhiannon. I stared at him. His manner had totally shifted. He was in Geoffrey's pocket for tonight. Once again, I wondered about the safety of having someone so aligned with the vamps living in our house, but thinking about the alternative—being without his added protection—made me just as nervous.

I cleared my throat. "I'm sorry, but we haven't been introduced." I stood and gave him a very short bow.

Instinct told me to reserve shaking hands for people who weren't likely to look at my wrist like a feeding station.

He grinned, then, and glanced at Regina. "You're right. She's got spunk. I smell fear hiding there, too, but she covers it well."

Feeling even more put out, I let out a short huff and that produced yet another response. He leaned forward, his eyes narrowing.

"Spunk can be a delightful quality. Impatience is annoying. Don't push your luck, girl." As a long, predatory smile spread across his face, I felt about two inches tall and just as vulnerable. I eased back into my seat.

"Very good, we understand one another," he added. "As to introductions, yes, you're right. You wouldn't remember me, although I first met you when you were a toddler. And I've never had the pleasure of meeting your cousin. I'm Lord Geoffrey, Regent for the Northwest Division of the Vampire Nation."

Regina folded her hands on her lap. "Cicely, we have a proposal for you. And you must give us an answer tonight. Our proposal is simple: Our Queen requires that you come work for us. And as I said, I make *certain* that the Crimson Queen gets what she wants."

I stared at Regina, with absolutely no idea what to say. If I just stood up and walked out, I'd be toast by morning. And yet, beneath her laughter, I could hear something. I strained to catch the nuance.

*Fear . . . fear came wafting in on the wind, fear of what I represented.*

Very slowly, I stood. "What is it you want me to do?"

"Cicely—" Rhiannon's voice held a warning, but I shook my head.

"Do you really think I have a choice? I have to at least listen to what she says." *Or I'll never make it out of this house alive, treaty or no treaty.*

"Smart woman." Reining in her sensuality, Regina was suddenly all business and her all-business side was just as scary. The look on her face told me she wouldn't stop till she had what she wanted. "Allow me to summon my brother. He's late and he should be here before we go on with this." She picked up a telephone and a few minutes later, the door opened.

The most beautiful man in the world entered the room. Lannan Altos was wearing a crimson brocade smoking jacket over a pair of indigo wash jeans, and his hair fell in a mass of curls to mid-back, the color of spun gold. His face could easily have rivaled Apollo's and the resemblance between him and Regina was clear. They sparkled like the sun together, with eyes black as deep space.

He tilted his head and smiled, fangs lowering. I felt myself falling, falling deep, falling wide, falling like I'd fallen into Grieve's embrace but this was different, there was no sense of connection other than the slender thread of unspoken communication that was passing between us.

*Do you wonder what it's like . . . do you want to know? I'll teach you. All you have to do is give me control and I'll give you reason to hunger for me.*

I felt myself moving toward him, toward that beautiful, rich voice that echoed in my thoughts. I wanted to go, to find out what he was promising.

Leo grabbed my arm even as a tiny voice inside shrieked, *Don't look in his eyes . . . don't listen too deeply to his voice . . . don't let him smell your fear . . .*

Regina laughed. "I see you respond to my brother's charms. Most women do. Lannan, this is Cicely Waters. Cicely—my brother. Now, onto our proposition: We know of your connection to the Fae named Grieve. He's a member of the Indigo Court."

I struggled to keep my voice neutral, but inside, I jumped. The vamps held no love for the Indigo Court, so I wasn't surprised they were aware of Grieve's presence.

What did surprise me was that they knew about Grieve and me. But I couldn't let them think they'd thrown me for a loop.

"And . . . ?"

"All we want is for you to continue what you're doing. Keep an eye on him. Infiltrate his world, and apprise us of all you see and hear. Before you say no, consider this: We know you understand the nature of the Indigo Court . . . the history of what they are, and how they got that way. There will be no playing off sides here. You will be *our* agent." Her eyes, like steel marbles, glistened in the dim light.

"Why me?"

"The Queen has her reasons. If you choose to work for us, you will receive a handsome monetary recompense and other . . . shall we say, *perks*? And you will be under our protection. But if you refuse to volunteer your help . . . we'll be forced to think of other ways in which to ensure your *cooperation*." Her voice dropped and I gazed into her face again. The primal fierceness in her gaze sent me reeling back into my chair.

"So, I either cooperate or . . ."

"Or we'll find less generous methods of engaging your services." Regina leaned down and planted a kiss on my forehead, her lipstick forming a burning pout on my skin. I wanted to wipe it off but she might consider that an insult.

"Can I think it over tonight and give you an answer tomorrow?" Stall for time, any time. I hadn't expected to be offered a job, and one that came with such steep ramifications.

"No. We have to know your answer now. Will you help us?"

I stared at her, feeling trapped. Either I helped, or they'd punish me. And perhaps my friends. "Why do you want me to do this? I have the right to know."

Lannan spoke, laughing gently through his words. "Let's take her to see Crawl. He might convince her." He looked too eager, and I wanted to scrunch away, out of sight, unnoticed.

Regina gave him a hard glance. "Crawl? Are you joking?"

"No. Take her to Crawl. He's hard to resist."

Geoffrey shifted, looking uncomfortable, but he held his tongue and a look passed between him and Leo. Leo hung his head, even though Rhiannon was not-so-gently poking his arm.

"Perhaps you are right." Regina motioned to me. "But I'll be the one to take her. Between you and the Blood Oracle, there'd be nothing left of the girl to help us." She slid her arm around my shoulder and led me over to a bookshelf.

"Wait—where are you taking her?" Rhiannon called behind me.

"Patience, firecracker," Lannan said behind me. "You and Leo stay here. Have a drink with me. My sister will keep your cousin safe. As long as she behaves herself."

❉

Regina pressed a book on the bookshelf—I didn't notice which one, and it slid open, silently, to reveal a dark passage. I followed her in, knowing that I had no choice. I'd left choice behind when I walked through the front door.

"I would not do this," she said once it closed, "but my brother makes a point. This will perhaps convince you more than what we have to say."

"What's the Blood Oracle?" Better forewarned than be taken by surprise.

"Better to ask *who*." She blinked. "The Blood Oracle is the seer of the Crimson Court. He's held his office for two thousand years. His name is Crawl, but never address him directly. You must ask all questions through me. He will no longer speak to mortals, be they magic-born or human."

We passed into a dark room. A table sat in the center, illuminated by a single bulb from the ceiling, and on the octagonal-shaped table rested a crystal, hovering above a clear crimson slab of glass that softly glowed. The feel of magic hung heavy in the room and crawled up my arms like scuttling needles, prickling my nerves. This was heavy magic, old magic. Dark and ominous. The rest of the room was cloaked in inky shadows and I had the feeling that to step outside of the dim illumination would be to put my life in danger.

I started to ask what it was, then stopped. Regina was staring intently at the crystal, her fingers hovering above it, and I didn't want to interrupt her train of thought because I could feel how deep she was sliding. I folded my arms, suddenly cold and dizzy. The magic churned like waves cresting over a boat, and the room started to spin. Regina reached out and grabbed me by the wrist, and the next thing I knew, everything had gone black in a massive rush of wind.

# Chapter 11

The scent of a thousand years raced by, turning back the calendar month by dusty month. Smog and dust and the smoke from a million fires gusted past. Voices—cries lost in the depths of time, whispers from old ghosts wandering past, and the howling of wolves rocked the wind.

My wolf let out a whimper, waking as he stretched to learn what was going on. I tried to comfort him—for I knew it was Grieve feeling my fear, sensing my tailspin, but he snarled as I brushed my hand over my stomach.

A cacophony of sound assaulted my ears and I tried to pull away from Regina, to cover my ears, but then all fell silent.

We stood in a softly lit room. The chamber was huge, with a table in the center identical to the one back at the mansion, crystal and all. The same hum of energy rang through the gem and I tried to memorize exactly what it looked like so I could figure out what it was later.

The chamber we were in stretched farther than I could see, and the ceiling was a good thirty feet high.

The walls were covered with a crimson paper, and the light came from some hidden source. Benches lined the walls, and the floor was covered with magical symbols. Heavy magic rolled like mist around my ankles, making my skin twitch. Whatever had been done here had upset the balance and created a force greater than just about anything I'd ever felt.

Regina touched my shoulder. "Come. Stay on the walkway."

She began to move toward what appeared to be the back of the chamber and I followed, wondering where the hell we were going. We walked along a narrow path of Tuscan gold, bounded by thick black lines on either side. There were no symbols on the tiles and, as we made our way up the walk, I began to realize that if I stepped off the path I'd land on one of the sigils. The runes were active and aware—there was no telling just what sort of spell I'd set off.

As we came to the end of the chamber, a dais rose a good five feet off the floor and Regina lithely glided up and on it. She stopped, turning back to me, and leaned over, extending her hand. I reached up to grasp her fingers and, with barely a murmur, she yanked me up and onto the dais. Blinking at her strength, I waited for her to make the next move.

The curtains covering the back of the dais parted.

"What the fuck . . ." I caught myself before I said anything I'd regret.

Regina gave me a sharp look and I nodded, understanding her meaning. *Shut the fuck up and do what I tell you.*

There, sitting in front of us, sat a bent and twisted creature. Maybe he'd been human. *Once.* It was hard to tell. He sat on a cushion raised a good five feet above the dais, hunched over, his skin blackened from what looked like old, leathery burns—charred and long dried. His hair had devolved into ratted clumps, dreadlocks of the worst kind, and his eyes were glassy, unfettered by eyelids, which seemed to have been burnt away. He wore nothing but a crimson loincloth, and his ribs protruded so strongly that he looked like a stick figure or a praying mantis.

In front of him, a fountain of blood bubbled merrily, ringed by perpetual flames that neither wavered nor changed in intensity. They burned brightly, and the blood in the center smelled warm and sticky and fresh.

Regina stepped up to a pillow on the floor next to the fountain and knelt, her head down. "Great Father of the Sight, I come seeking your wisdom. Crawl, Blood Oracle of the Crimson Court, I seek your vision."

He let out a laughter that sounded like the wind whistling through dried corn husks and I smelled decay and dust and the scent of the tomb. "Regina, Crawl's favorite. The Blood Oracle recognizes you. Stand and ask, lovely bloody daughter, and offer payment for the Oracle's services."

She rose, her skirt brushing the ground. She was wearing a crimson leather bustier and a long black chiffon skirt. Now, she brushed back the skirt where it slit up one side to the thigh and pulled out a golden dagger. She turned toward me and motioned me forward.

"Wait—you aren't going to open my vein with that." I'd keep quiet as long as I thought I was relatively safe but this whole scenario wasn't quite what I'd expected, and things were looking worse the deeper into the night we went.

"You will make a small donation for his service. And you will do so without complaint. Do you understand?" She leaned close and her lips brushed my lips, soft and silken and utterly inviting. I sucked in a deep breath and her tongue slid inside my mouth for just a moment—just long enough to wake my hunger. I tried to pull away but found myself firmly wrapped in her arms.

"Do as I say," she whispered in my ear. "If you resist,

he will come off that throne of his and eat you down to the bones. Crawl is older than almost every vampire alive and you'd do best to appease him with a measly quarter cup of your blood. I'm trying to save your life here."

Her voice cut through the sudden haze of lust that her kiss had sparked off and, shaking, I nodded. She backed away and held up the dagger. "Give me your hand, child."

I held out my hand, trembling, praying to whatever god might be listening that she wasn't going to turn on me and slice me to ribbons for a feeding frenzy. She poised the blade above my palm and with one quick motion sliced through the pad near my thumb. The blade was ultra-sharp and a thin weal of blood rose up.

Crawl leaned forward, his eyes gleaming as he watched the blood seep out of my flesh. Convinced I'd been insane to allow her to bring me here, I tried to control my fear. Regina dragged me to the fountain and waved her hand over two of the flames, which died down immediately. She held my hand over the bubbling blood so my own dribbled into it. After about a quarter cup had been spilt, she gently pulled me back and leaned down, licking my hand clean. As it began to heal remarkably fast, a shudder ran through her and for yet another moment I worried about her self-control, but she let out a long breath and stood again.

The flames around the fountain rose once more and she turned to Crawl. "The payment has been made. Now tell me what I need to know."

Crawl scuttled forward, reminding me of a spider or a long-jointed crab, and leered at me. "She is the one. Tell her that you are correct. She will bring about the war and start the road to our reclamation. You've done well, lovely daughter."

I wanted to pull back, to turn tail and run because Crawl was giving me the creeps big-time and it seemed only a matter of time before he lunged for me and I'd be dead as a bug on the windshield. *Splat*.

Regina let out a soft laugh. "I thought so." She turned to me. "Long ago, Crawl advised the Vein Lords to form a tight net on every continent, to watch over the Indigo Court and keep track of where they were spreading. There is a war coming, Cicely." Her tone told me to ask no questions about it, but her words were icy and so confident that I believed her.

I glanced up at the Blood Oracle, who was leaning off the dais, like a long stick bug. He thrust his face through the flames surrounding the fountain and screamed as he lapped up the bubbling blood.

Regina gave me a soft smile, bowed low before Crawl who took no further notice of us, and led me back to the walkway. I was afraid he might come after us and kept glancing over my shoulder, but a few feet away from the dais, she said, "Have no fear. He is trapped there, unable to leave."

"Who is he?" I softly asked.

Still speaking softly, she said, "Crawl, descended from the blood of ancient warrior kings, is one of the most dangerous vampires walking the earth today, second only to the Queen. She made him. He's her pet. Not only do his second sight and psychic abilities defy categorization, but his entire focus is on preserving the Vampire Nation from harm, no matter what the cost, through his abilities to see into the future. He has no mercy, no fear, no love."

"Is he mad?"

"I suppose, in a way, seeing that he's so old no one knows when he was turned. But as for crazy, no—crazy like a fox, perhaps, but he knows what he does. He has full comprehension. He simply has outgrown any shred of humanity that he's ever had. If he was human to begin with."

"I know you may not want to tell me, but this war . . .

it's with the Indigo Court, right? You say I'm a catalyst. Is that why you asked me here tonight?"

I was trying to sort out things. Crawl's words had sent more than shivers through me. There was a ring of truth about them that echoed in my gut.

"Cicely, I will be honest with you. We need you. And regardless of what you think, you need us. The Indigo Court is dangerous. Myst knows you are to bring about her downfall—she will not let you live. You know how they began."

"Yes, Geoffrey sired Myst. He did, didn't he? He's the Geoffrey who led the raid on the Unseelie Court."

Regina let out a soft huff. "Yes. Geoffrey was younger then, and had not developed the patience and foresight he now wields. The Vampire Nation simply seeks to be prepared to rectify a mistake we made so many years ago. So, we need you . . . and we are prepared to help you in return. If you do not agree, we will make your life a living hell. If you join forces with us, we'll do everything in our power to protect you and your friends. No more now, till we return to the others."

I decided to dare one last question, brought about by what Crawl had said to her. "Can I ask . . . are you Crawl's daughter? Did he sire you?"

She glanced down at me and her smile faded. "Lannan and I carry the power of the Blood Oracle within our veins. It has been a long and heavy life for my brother and me since Crawl first came to our land and took us."

And then, she motioned for me to step up to the crystal with her, and within a few moments, we were back in the hidden room.

✢

As we entered Geoffrey's office, Regina motioned for me to sit down next to Leo and Rhiannon. Shaken and wanting nothing more than to go home, I acquiesced.

"We need your answer, Cicely. Will you accept our contract and hire your services out to us? Or will we be forced to take more drastic means?"

"You realize that you've left me with no choice," I said, already knowing what I was going to do. They were convinced they needed me. They'd as good as said that I was going to help them whether it was voluntary or not. I might as well get what I could out of it.

I cleared my throat. "Assent under threat of punishment isn't exactly conducive to good will. But before we get into semantics, yes, I will help you. On one condition. The Indigo Court has captured my aunt and our friend Peyton. If there's any way you can help us rescue them, then I willingly accept your offer."

"The offer is to you, only, but your friends are tacitly included by association," Geoffrey said. "I'm pleased that you've decided to make things easier. We will do what we can to help you rescue your loved ones. I was appalled to hear Myst's forces would dare to capture Heather, or to kill Marta. Speaking of the offer, Emissary, your brother stepped out to get the contract and the first month's payment."

Regina smiled at him. "Lannan will help on occasion. He's not always a stubborn mule." Turning to me, she added, "We believe in paying in advance for services." She beamed and I truly believed she was proud of what she was saying. "We don't want you to feel used in any way."

I bit my tongue. Pointing out again that I didn't have much of a choice, that they'd use me with or without my permission, didn't seem like the wisest move to make. After meeting Crawl, I *really* didn't want to get on their bad side or they might send me back to him to let him convince me to cooperate.

Rhiannon slowly held up her hand.

Regina laughed. "You have a question?"

"Yes," she said, softly. "We have some information on the Indigo Court, but there's so much we still don't know about them. They kidnapped my mother. Do you know what they want with her?"

Geoffrey stood, pacing behind his chair. After a moment, he let out a hollow sigh that had no breath behind it. "We have our suspicions. The members of the Vampire Nation generally don't pretend to be fond of most mortals. We—true vampires—abide by the Treaty of Supernatural Conduct because it allows us to live alongside your kind without being hunted except by those bearing grudges. But we *do* abide by the treaty—except for the rogues— and we honor our promises. The Indigo Court . . ." He paused and glanced at Regina.

"The Vampiric Fae are chaotic, far more chaotic than we are," she said, after a moment. "You may think us arrogant, but trust me, the world of the Indigo Court is far more dangerous than ours. They honor no treaty, no promises, and consider themselves above every rule except their own. They feed on blood and they feed on magic."

"Where we strive to find some compromise to walk among the living, they seek to make the living their slaves," Geoffrey said. "They hate us. We are their makers and they will never forgive us for being first to walk among the living dead. So they seek those with strength to ever add to their court, in order to eventually destroy us."

While I knew the feeling was mutual, I decided to keep my mouth shut.

"We have a long history—" Regina paused as the door opened and Lannan Altos walked in. "Brother—you're back."

After an exaggerated bow in our direction, he handed a manila envelope to her. She kissed him deeply, tongue and all. I blinked. They'd apparently taken their brother-sister relationship to a whole new level.

"You're lovers? But you're related!" Leo blinked as the words burst out of his lips.

They looked at him, and Regina laughed. "Oh, truly, even the magic-born can seem so *human* at times. Yes, we are lovers, and yes, we are brother and sister. We are also best of friends and mated to rule over our family line."

Leo gulped out an "Oh."

"Any more questions?" she asked.

I decided to chance it. "Yes, actually. On that subject . . . if you are brother and sister, and mated, then why isn't Lannan an emissary, too?"

As she shook the papers out of the envelope and handed them to me, she shrugged. "The Crimson Queen doesn't care for my brother."

I quickly glanced at Lannan, hoping her answer hadn't brought up baggage he might be happy to take out on us, but he just let out a low laugh.

"True, very true. Regina is the mistress of courtly attendance. I do not suffer sycophants and toadies, and you must be diplomatic in order to do what my sister does. I am far from diplomatic."

Geoffrey let out a snort. "Lannan, you are the epitome of politeness when you choose to be and the biggest ass in the world when you choose to be. To work for the Queen," he added, "one must put aside one's ego and submit one's will directly to our beloved liege. And that, you will never do. You want to be cock of the walk, my friend."

Lannan shrugged and cracked a smile. "Can you blame me? I bow to no man, though I answer to the Queen when I must. I answer only to myself at all other times. And," he turned to Regina, "to my love." He reached out and brushed her fingertips with his and an audible spark broke the silence.

At that moment, they both swiveled their heads to look at me and I suddenly felt like fresh meat on the hoof. I quickly buried my nose in the contracts. They were clearly written, though I noticed one loophole that stipulated if I should fail to report to them daily, the Crimson Court had the right to "administer remedy." I also noticed they were offering me twenty-five hundred dollars a month to report to them on whatever I found out. Not bad money, for a job that didn't require eight-to-five or asking, "Do you want fries with that?"

"I'm not sure what this means, but it could mean, oh, so many things." I pointed to the clause. "What kind of remedies are you talking about?" Actually, I had some idea, thanks to skimming through *A History of the Vampire Nation.* "The wording on this has to change somehow."

Regina glanced at it, then looked at Geoffrey. "Actually, nothing *has* to change, but perhaps we can amend it. There must be some guarantee she will not default or neglect her duties."

Lannan leaned his elbows on the back of Regina's chair. "Word it so that for every day she misses sending her report—which can be via e-mail if she likes—she must spend an hour with me, and I, alone, will be allowed to punish her during that time."

A chill went down my back. "What *kind* of punishment?"

He stared at me. "Whatever punishment I choose."

"No blood," Rhiannon said. "You will not take blood from her. And you can't maim her."

Regina gave Lannan a long look and a veiled smile crossed her face. "Lannan would never maim such a lovely young woman."

"Wait." I caught my breath, feeling the world hedge in around me just a little bit more. The only way to avoid accepting their deal would be to leave town, but even then, they'd hunt me down. As she reached for the papers, I pulled them away from her.

"The part about helping us with my aunt—it's not in

the contract. I ask again: Can you help us rescue my aunt and our friend Peyton? If I'm going to sign something that puts my life in danger, I have to make more than a couple grand a month for it."

Regina and Lannan looked at each other, then at Geoffrey. I had the distinct feeling they were conferring without us hearing a word.

After a moment, Lannan looked directly at me. I struggled to keep my composure and realized that if I looked away, they'd say no.

"You seek to up the ante, then you'll up the service to blood."

I started to protest but Lannan held up his hand.

"Once per month, I drink from you," he said. "I won't force you to drink from me, and I promise to avoid enthralling you, at least on a permanent basis. I won't make you my bloodwhore, although I think I'd fancy that. *Yes*, I would. But you *will* remember who your master is. You may be of the magic-born, but you are still but a step away from human and we have not been anything near to human for thousands of years."

Shit. If Grieve smelled Lannan's scent on me, he'd freak. "Won't that tip off Grieve that I'm hanging out with you?" Anything, anything to stave off being a living juice box.

"That remains your problem to deal with as you see fit." Lannan shrugged. He waited, tapping his foot lightly on the floor.

Watching my future narrow bleakly, I shrugged. What choice did I have at this point? And if it helped save Heather and Peyton . . .

"I'll do it," I said grimly. "Just make sure you don't take enough to leave me weak, nor turn me into a blood-whore. If you'll honor bind yourself to that, we have a deal."

"You know, we don't *have* to offer you any of this,"

Geoffrey said. "But we do so out of our respect for your aunt, and for Marta, who we firmly believe was killed by the Indigo Court. That's another possibility . . ."

"What?"

"Perhaps we should have you check in to her death. The police certainly won't. And Anadey has her hands full. You might be able to confirm what we know. Truly, it remains easier to attract flies to honey instead of vinegar."

"And I'm your honey," I whispered, as Lannan took the contracts out of the room to be changed.

Regina smiled and walked over to me. I was still standing, so preoccupied in thought that I didn't even think to curtsey. She stepped so close that I could feel the crackle of energy sparkling around her.

"My brother enjoys his toys. He may play with you all he likes, and I grant you permission to enjoy it—he's a *very good* playmate. But remember: You are never, ever to believe that you can lure him away from me. We are a mated pair. You will not interfere or attempt to play one of us off the other. On the other hand, if you choose to play with both of us . . . I won't object in the least."

And then, she leaned forward and gave me a long kiss on the lips, and her taste and smell were so intoxicating that I didn't even flinch.

# Chapter 12

With Regina's words echoing through my head, I stumbled back. She winked at me but the effect creeped me out—with her haunting obsidian eyes.

"Trust me, I have no intention of coming between the two of you, and I don't have any designs on your brother," I said, my knees buckling. Fucking hell, I'd agreed to give it up to her brother once a month, and I wasn't talking sex. Even *that* would have been better than bloodletting, I thought. Then again, remembering his reputation, maybe not.

"Good. Then as soon as you sign the contracts, you'll be free to leave. You're welcome to stay and join the party, if you think you can stomach it." Her voice was cool and I couldn't help it: I locked her gaze.

A challenge. She was issuing me a challenge. Seeing if I had the guts to deal with their world. I turned to Leo and Rhiannon, forcing myself to steady my voice. "You can go home, but I'll stay for a while."

I didn't dare show fear, even if they could smell it on

me. Vampires were predators, they'd respect me if I held my ground. Well, as much as they'd respect anyone who wasn't part of their world.

"We'll stay with you," Leo said, crossing his arms.

"Healer, it may require a stronger stomach than you have." Regina sauntered over to him and placed one stiletto nail of hers under his chin. "Are you sure you're up to it?"

"He'll manage," Geoffrey said. "He's my day runner. To turn tail would tell me he's the wrong mortal for the job. Isn't that right, Leo?" He gave Leo a look that could only have one answer.

"Of course, Lord Geoffrey." Leo smiled, but I could sense the tension behind his words.

Regina let out a low chuckle. "I promise you safety. With Cicely working for us, and this young lion working for Geoffrey, we will do what we can to ensure you remain untargeted by any member of the Vampire Nation who lives in this area." She paused, then added with a silken smile, "Unless, of course, you issue an invitation."

At that, Lannan reentered the room and Regina was back to business. She held out the contracts to me and I glanced over them again, making sure they hadn't changed anything else without me noticing. But everything looked on the up and up, although I lingered over the promise to give Lannan my blood once a month in return for their help with Heather.

"Pen?" I said.

"Here, consider this the first of many gifts," Lannan said, his fingers lingering on mine as I accepted the Mont Blanc he offered me.

I stared at the pen. Probably worth a good grand, and here he was handing it over to me like it was a stick pen. Slowly, I pulled off the cap. A fountain pen. The contracts were on the coffee table and the dotted line loomed like a demarcation line.

Unsigned, I still owned myself. Signed, and they owned a piece of me. But if I didn't agree . . . too many chances for all of us to get hurt. Too many opportunities for the vampires to prove just how tough they were. And I had no doubt they could back up their threats.

I slowly signed my name and put the pen down.

"Now, just a little more of your blood, please—a single drop, at the end of your name." Regina reached for my hand. She lowered her mouth to my thumb and opened the very end of the wound again, using one fang to pierce the skin. A delicious shiver raced through me and I felt myself rise on wings. Then, she pulled away, and I squeezed one drop onto the paper, at the end of my name.

Lannan held out his hand. I slowly placed mine in his palm and he lifted it to his lips where he slowly licked along my wound with his tongue. Heat rose through my body. I wanted to squirm, to slide into his arms, to feel his lips cover my neck, my breasts, my stomach.

My wolf growled then, deep and angry, and I jerked my eyes open. Lannan smiled, seductive and cunning and wicked all rolled into one.

"Oh yes," he whispered. "This is going to be an interesting partnership."

I gasped, the wind knocked out of me as he leaned down and kissed my cheek, leaving me reeling. Falling back onto the sofa, I desperately tried to control the flood of hunger racing through my body. How could he do that? How could a simple sentence make me want to spread my legs for him? Terrified, realizing how far I'd sold myself into their servitude, I began to shake.

Leo, sitting next to me, placed one hand on my leg and whatever he was doing—whatever energy he was running—began to draw the fear out of me. After a moment, I began to breathe normally again.

Regina handed the contracts to Geoffrey. "Here, we

will need a copy for the Court, and one for Cicely. Please have your staff take care of the matter."

He nodded. "By your will, Emissary."

"And now," Regina said, "let's go have ourselves a party."

Lannan wrapped his arm around his sister's waist. As they led us out of the room, I glanced at Geoffrey. He gave me a long, silent look, and then—in the barest of movements—smiled, but the curve of his lips was sad.

An alarm went off inside, and suddenly, I realized what I'd overlooked in the contract. Oh shit! But it was too late to ask for a change.

There'd been no stipulated end date. I was bound to them for as long as they wanted. I'd just indentured myself to the vampires for the rest of my life, if they wanted it that way.

*

Regina and Lannan led us through the main room, to another set of double doors. She glanced back at us. "Are you sure you're game?"

I swallowed. Now, more than ever, I had to show them I could handle myself. "Yeah, as long as your promise stands."

"It stands," she said, her eyes glimmering. I noticed her fangs were down. She opened the doors and led us into another hallway. We followed the three of them down the corridor until we reached a third set of double doors to the right. They stopped.

Lannan looked us over. "Before we enter, know that you will be safe if you follow some simple rules. No sudden movements. Stick together, unless you prefer to join the fun. You are not to attempt to stop anything you see here—everyone here has agreed to the rules of the game."

That left a lot of room, I thought, considering the

vampires' abilities to charm and seduce. Chances were, there were quite a few people around New Forest—or any town, for that matter—who found themselves at vamp parties without really meaning to show up there. Of course, there were the bloodwhores and the fang-girls and the wannabes, but they came with the territory, and from what I'd seen, the vamps enjoyed toying with those who had reservations more than the willing.

I swallowed, wondering just what was going on behind those massive closed doors. "We understand."

"Then enter our world, Cicely, along with your friends, and perhaps you'll wish to do more than just observe," he said, his voice lingering over my name. I shivered and he let out a soft laugh as he cast open the doors.

✦

As the doors opened, we found ourselves facing two guards. One was tall, the other shorter, but both were stocky. The shorter man had dark hair that curled to his shoulders and he looked vaguely Mediterranean. The taller was blonde, with a beard, and he had a Thor's Hammer tattooed in the middle of his forehead. I couldn't take my eyes away from the tattoo as he caught my gaze.

They eyed us up and down, but said nothing as we peeked inside. The room was huge—easily the entire size of our downstairs at home. At first glance, I thought of a snake pit, softly lit in shades of red. The walls, the upholstery, the tiles on the floor were all in shades of coiled red and bronze, gold and black. No windows shed light into the room, and at first all I could see was a sea of bodies writhing, twisting together in one massive mating ball.

Beside me, Rhiannon gasped, but said nothing. Leo seemed unaffected, but he was used to dealing with vampires and had probably witnessed their raves before. I sucked in a long breath, then exhaled slowly, buying time to adjust to what I was seeing. And then, as Lannan gestured for us to enter, I stepped over the threshold, into a world of sex and blood and passion.

The music shifted from the hard-hitting technowave of the outer party. Here it was sinuous, enticing us to join the dance. A long, single note rose and fell, leading into a drumbeat, a cadence, the heartbeats of the humans filling the room. And everywhere, under the music, the wind carried cries of passion and pain to my ears.

Trying to make sense of the living kaleidoscope, I focused on one area at a time. Over there—a long divan. Three women sprawled languorously across it, their gowns filmy and translucent. Two men—vampires— were taking turns with them; one licking at their necks, the other between their legs.

My stomach knotted as I realized the vamps were drinking blood from both areas and I jerked my eyes away, praying they were drinking from the artery in the thigh rather than anything more painful. But the women were sighing, and one let out a moan that set off a responsive chord within me. I sucked in another breath, reaching to steady myself before I realized I'd taken hold of Geoffrey's arm instead of my cousin's. He gave me a sly smile, but just patted my hand before removing it from his sleeve.

Another pile of bodies on the floor—again, a mixture of vampires and humans, an orgy of movement, limbs entwining, fangs flashing, necks trickling blood, heads thrown back in ecstasy. A moan here, a soft sigh there, and one woman looked up at me suddenly, her chin stained red, fangs down, with eyes so black I felt myself falling into the abyss.

She smiled, winked, motioned. Dazed, I took a step forward, but Leo stopped me. I jerked my gaze away. I heard her hiss but she returned to her bloodwhore—a man in his twenties with taut abs and the face of a Grecian god. Another woman—human this time—slowly licked his rising erection.

Shakily, I turned to Rhiannon, whose gaze was glued to the scene. She was biting her lip and I suddenly realized that maybe it wasn't such a good idea to have someone who'd repressed her fire for so many years—which intermingled with sexuality—around a vampire sex club right now. But there was no walking away. Not with Regina, Lannan, and Geoffrey flanking our sides.

Speaking of Lannan, I realized he was leaning over my shoulder, his lips precariously near my ear. "See anything you like?"

I forced myself to get a grip. "It's all very interesting. So this is where you perform your . . ."

"This is our equivalent of a costume dinner party," he said, laughing low. "You might come across a reference to feeding frenzies . . . as you can see, we aren't sharks, ripping our victims to pieces. We prefer to give pleasure where we take it."

"Somehow, I doubt all vampires hold to that creed. Are you sure you're not part of the Indigo Court?" I was joking, trying to divert the subject from Lannan giving pleasure to anyone, but apparently, my joke fell flat.

Before I could get out another word, Lannan had hold of me and in a blur, we were next to the wall and he slammed me against it. Tightly, he held me by the neck with one hand, pinning me to the wall with his body. Leaning close, his fangs glistened in the dim light.

"Don't ever suggest such a thing again, Ms. Waters, or—protection or not—you will be punished. And *I will be the one* to administer the punishment. And trust me, I look forward to that day. Oh yes, I do." A mixture of pleasure and anger filled his face.

I gulped in a breath of air, knowing now was not the time to try to squirm out of his grasp. That might lead his mind in all the wrong directions and with so much sex and feeding going on in the room, trying to escape was *so* not the thing to do.

"You belong to us now," he added, those brilliant white fangs of his just inches away. "Do not forget—you signed with your blood. Are you so eager for my attention that you willingly break the rules?" The touch of his skin against mine was cold fire. There was no warmth, just unrelenting chill that seeped through his fingers to spread through my body.

"Please, I'm sorry—I didn't mean to offend you. I was just making a bad joke," I stammered. We weren't playing a game anymore, I'd signed away my life and now any mistake I made meant they could collect bits and pieces of me any time they wanted. "I didn't realize how bad of a joke it was."

Leo and Rhiannon struggled in the background. Geoffrey and Regina restrained them, watching, their expressions neutral.

Lannan reached up with his other hand and stroked my cheek, drawing his fingernail down the skin, leaving one red weal. His strength was overwhelming. No wonder people were so afraid of vampires. And yet—if the Indigo Court had the vampires' strength plus their own powers, the other side of the army we were facing was even more terrifying.

I swallowed my pride—a hard, hard thing to do—and lowered my eyes. "I'm sorry. Please, forgive me." Those words cost me hard.

Lannan pressed against me, harder than he needed to, but then, after a moment, he slowly let go and stepped away.

"You've been given your warning. Next time you're so disrespectful, expect punishment. And when the time comes for your first blood donation, I'll enjoy taking it, and I'll make you come so hard that you'll scream my name, even if I can't put you in thrall. You have much to learn, Cicely, and humility is at the top of the list. And I am a *master* of teaching humility."

He turned away abruptly and motioned to one of the vampires who was standing near. She was dressed in a tight corset and long, narrow skirt. Her hair was done up in a bun and she looked flawless. Why the hell did most vampires look good? Even the aged ones, the bald ones, the scarred ones, looked delicious. Well, except Crawl. Crawl had been hideous.

"I need a bloodwhore. Female. Bring me one." Lannan's voice was hoarse and he kept his eyes averted from me.

I slipped away, over to Rhiannon's side, where she and the others flanked me protectively. Regina gave me a severe look, shaking her head slowly. Geoffrey blinked, but said nothing.

The vamp who'd sprung to answer Lannan's request returned, tugging a brunette behind her. The girl was wearing white, which so far had managed to avoid being spattered with blood. I had the feeling that was about to change.

I didn't want to watch, but Regina grabbed me, pushing me forward. She put her hands on my shoulders as she leaned down to whisper in my ear.

"You'd do well to watch, because this is what you will face if you screw up again. And if my brother is in one of his moods, it will be both exquisite and painful. Not enough to enchant you, but enough so you'll *never* forget his touch." She purred, laughing richly. "Or . . . perhaps you'll like it and choose to offer yourself into his stable."

"I wouldn't count on it, Emissary," I said politely, wanting to laugh in her face. But I'd seen just what reaction my sense of humor could spark off and didn't want to repeat my mistake with Lannan, who, at that moment turned to face me, his smile taunting.

He reached over the woman's shoulder and slowly stroked her breast under the white lace gown she was wearing. She moaned, her head slowly dropping back to rest against his chest. Lannan leaned down and, gaze still fastened on me, sunk his fangs deep into her creamy white neck while caressing her breasts. She gasped, her eyes widening as he pierced her skin, driving into her with a fury. Then a sudden glow crossed her face and she began to rub her hips against his groin.

I didn't want to watch. I didn't want to see what he was doing to her, how he was affecting her, but Regina held me fast, and her fingers tightened on my shoulders.

"Watch her—she enjoys his touch. She wants him. My brother's the best lover I've ever had. You really should try him. Maybe when he takes blood from you, you'll change your mind." Regina leaned against me, her breasts pressed to my back. It was freaky to feel no pulse, no heartbeat, no rise and fall of her breath.

Lannan reached down and I heard the sound of a zipper, and then, hiking the woman's gown, he slid into her from behind, thrusting in rhythm to the music, sucking at her neck, the blood trickling down from his chin, which was stained a deep red. The crimson rivulets channeled down the girl's chest in thin, moist lines between her breasts, and the bodice of her gown began to absorb the drops as they spread in the pattern of a tainted rose. She let out a groan, and wanton bliss spread across her face.

I shivered, unable to look away. I had no idea what the others were thinking but I was terrified. What if Lannan had this effect on me when it came time? What if I willingly let him fuck me because the drinking felt so good? I wasn't my mother—I wasn't a bloodwhore and I'd be damned if I'd let him make me one.

Regina's hands on my shoulders were burning cold— fire and ice right through my dress—and images of her trailing her fingers down to caress my breasts flashed through my mind. I caught my breath and she purred in my ear.

"You would fit in with us, Cicely. Give it some thought.

We could use a witch of your powers here in our world. And the turning isn't terribly painful. I would most happily be your sire, if you wished."

Shivering, I said nothing. What could I say? Everything out of my mouth seemed to be a mistake tonight, and I didn't want to make another.

Lannan stepped up the pace, driving into the brunette from behind. He focused on me, keeping me in thrall. I could see his tongue dipping to lap up her blood, his fangs sinking a little deeper, widening the punctures, a flowered bruise spreading across her skin. His thrusts and her cries were driving me crazy and I gasped, realizing that I wanted nothing more than to push her aside, to impale myself on him, *to take her place*.

At that moment, I hated him. But . . . *oh, how I wanted him*.

And then, with a final grunt, he pulled away from her and tossed her aside. She fell to the ground, dazed. His face was a bloody mess, his fangs needle-sharp and dripping, his cock slick and he was hideous again. I shuddered, revolted. He laughed then, quietly tucking himself back in his pants and zipping up. Regina pushed me forward to meet him as he slowly sauntered my way. I wanted to run but he wasn't finished with me. The predator lurked strong behind those icy black eyes of his.

He grabbed me around the waist and I could feel him still rigid, pressing against my thigh. He slid one hand down to caress the curve of my back, and the dress I was wearing seemed entirely inadequate. I might as well be naked.

"You want to fuck? All you have to do is ask. *Beg me*. Or . . . just make another mistake." And then, he leaned down and rubbed his face against mine, smearing the girl's blood across my cheeks as he fastened his lips against mine. The salty, metallic tang filled my mouth as he kissed me deep. And then, without another word, he let go. I stumbled, and when I steadied myself and looked up, Lannan had disappeared into the crowd. The pulse of the music throbbed in my head as the party continued.

My wolf growled, deep and angry and jealous. Somehow, Grieve knew that I had responded to someone other than him.

❧

Twenty minutes later, we were outside, standing by Favonis. Leo and Rhiannon stared bitterly back at the house, and I knew they felt they'd failed me.

Truthfully, *I* didn't even know what to say. I felt dirtier than I ever had and yet . . . and yet . . . a knot in my lower stomach begged for release. The feel of Lannan's hands on my skin kept resounding through my body.

"Cicely . . . are you all right?" Rhiannon's voice filtered through my head. I turned to her. "I shouldn't have let you do it—I should be the one. Heather's *my* mother. I'm sorry. I'm so sorry."

"You wouldn't be able to cope with the vampires. And both you and I know that. If Lannan handled you the way he handled me, you'd be dead by now, imploding in some fiery explosion. I've learned how to build my defenses. You're just learning." With a sigh, I unlocked the doors.

Shaking my head, I climbed behind the wheel. "It was my choice. Don't worry. We'll have money coming in, we'll have gifts, and we'll have their help in rescuing Aunt Heather—and if they can—Elise and Peyton. It's worth a few bloody kisses for just that."

Forcing a smile to my lips, not wanting to tell them about my visit to Crawl yet, I screeched out of the driveway. The roar of the car set me even more on edge, and I floored the gas, speeding the whole way home. And nobody said a word to stop me.

As soon as we entered the house, after we did a quick search, I hit the shower, scrubbing myself until I was raw, trying to rid myself of the sleazy feel of his fingers on my skin. But the bloody taste was still there, even after brushing my teeth, even after I ate half a tin of Altoids in the bathroom.

I slowly padded back to my room and opened the door. As I entered, the first thing I noticed was the window was open. And the second was that Grieve was sitting on my bed, frowning, his eyes narrow and dark.

# Chapter 13

The shock of seeing Grieve made me drop my towel. I stood there, stark naked, staring at him, unable to formulate a single word.

"Aren't you going to say hello, Cicely?" His voice tested me out, his words sliding over me like smooth balm on a stinging wound.

I stood there, closing my eyes as Ulean swept up behind me. I could feel her there, embracing me in her cooling breeze.

*You have had such a horrible night. You need to relax.*

Grieve circled me, his eyes on my wolf tattoo. "I felt you tonight. I felt you respond, I felt you quicken. *Who touched you?* I smell the scent of graveyard dust and tattered shrouds in your aura. What have you been doing?"

I slowly turned, matching his movements as he revolved around me. My pulse was beating in my throat. As much as I wanted to, I couldn't tell him what had happened. Rhiannon, Leo—their lives depended on my discretion. But what could I say instead? How could I deflect his questions?

"We were hanging out in a cemetery, looking for graveyard dust for spells. The energy's strong there." I didn't blink, didn't flinch.

"Then why are you so aroused? Why did your wolf warn me that someone was touching you?" He reached out, slowly traced the outline of my tattoo with one finger. His touch made my body sing.

"I don't know." I thought of telling him that a stranger had put the make on me, but then thought better of it. Grieve would go looking for someone to blame and find an innocent man. "Maybe it had something to do with the energy there."

"Perhaps," Grieve said, placing his hand flat against the wolf's head. "Tell me about when you got this tattoo. There are so many things I can't remember since Myst came to power."

Had the turning affected his ability to remember? It didn't seem possible and yet—Grieve was so like and yet unlike himself that I wondered. Swallowing the lump that had formed in my throat, I said, "When I was fifteen, I dreamed of a wolf tracking me through the city streets. He was protecting me, watching over me. I didn't realize it was your spirit form. At the time, Krystal was hanging out with a tattoo artist named Dane, who was in love with her. He was one of the few boyfriends she had who was relatively sane. He paid for our room and board for about three months."

"Did he ever try anything with you?" Grieve asked gruffly.

I shook my head. "Dane was one of the few who didn't. He was a good guy. One night, we were hanging out, getting stoned. Krystal was out hooking for a few extra bucks. Dane was staring at me and when I asked why, he said he could see a wolf sitting next to me—a beautiful silver wolf with green eyes that came to life as he described it."

"It was me," Grieve whispered softly, drawing his hand across his eyes. "I remember. I did what I could in astral form to watch over you."

"I know that now, but at the time, Dane's vision just sounded so beautiful and I got to thinking about the protector in my dream. I asked him if he'd ink the wolf onto me and he agreed. I know it sounds stupid, letting somebody stoned tattoo you, but I knew—*absolutely knew*—that he wouldn't fuck up, and that I had to have this tattoo. And he'd done the rest of my tats over the previous few months, so I knew he was good at his job. We spent the night getting high on Acapulco gold and he worked on the wolf's head and the roses and skulls for five hours."

I closed my eyes, remembering. Around eight, he'd put in a Gary Numan CD—*Outland*—and played it on a loop, over and over. The only sounds through the hours that passed were those of the Electronica Wizard of Oz, the hum of the tattoo gun, and our quiet pull on the joints that he'd lined up on the table.

I'd watched as the vision from my dreams came to life in brilliant color, first the wolf with his emerald eyes glowing, then the trail of roses and violet skulls that swept across my midsection, from thigh to side. It had hurt, but the pot helped me transcend the pain and lose myself in the experience.

Then, a little after one in the morning, Dane stood back and whispered, "My God, look at yourself. You're beautiful."

And I'd looked down, and found the wolf that had followed me in dream after dream come to life on my skin. And I knew that he would always be with me, would always be watching over me.

"The next morning, Krystal threw Dane out and smacked me across the face. She was convinced I'd fucked him. I finally got her to believe that he'd just tattooed me, but it was too late. That night, Dane was at work in his shop and some motherfucker came in with a gun and blew his brains out, took all his cash, and vanished into the night. Nobody ever caught him. The cops didn't look very hard. Like so many of the people we met on the road, Dane was outside of the mainstream and the police considered him expendable. *Just another tattoo artist biker dude.*"

I fell silent, thinking of the tall blond man who'd painstakingly inked my body. I had fantasies that he would take us in, marry Krystal, give us a settled life. His death sent me into a deep depression, but Krystal had just blown it off, angry that her meal ticket had disappeared.

After that night, I'd guarded the wolf from public view, not wanting to share him with others. He felt like he was alive and sometimes I could hear him growling at me, warning me, calling me. Eventually, I figured out it was Grieve—whether his spirit or memory, I didn't know. The men I'd slept with over the years hadn't liked the tattoo much, but I didn't give a damn. The wolf was part of me and I loved it like a good friend.

"And so here we are. You and I. Together again." Grieve gently traced his fingers over the tattoo and I felt like I was diving off a cliff into a midnight pool, dark and sparkling, so deep that I would never touch bottom. I let out a choked gasp. *Please, no more. I couldn't handle much more.*

Aching to calm the raging hunger within, I slowly lowered my hand to rest on top of his.

"Cicely . . ." His voice was breaking.

"Don't stop. I need you more than I can bear," I said, closing my eyes against the approaching storm. Indigo Court or not, I had to feel him touch me, enter me, make me whole. "I can't tell you what happened, but I can't stand this tension any longer."

Grieve moved in, his hand slowly trailing across my stomach to rest on my hip. He tipped my chin up and my eyes fluttered open. Those luminous stars studding their sea of onyx held me firm.

"Are you sure? Are you sure this is what you want?" He looked almost sad, but I could smell his arousal on the breeze, intoxicating and wild. He smelled nothing like Lannan had. Vampiric or not, Grieve was *alive*, and he was wild and passionate. Regardless of what anybody else thought, I knew he didn't want to hurt me, he wanted to *love* me.

"Yes, please." My words were muffled as he gathered me in his arms and pressed his lips against mine. I closed my eyes, sinking into the kiss. His lips were warm and vibrant, demanding and yet giving. He ran one hand up my cheek to brush my slick, wet hair back away from my face.

"No other man will ever touch you again—not if I can be there to stop him," he whispered, pressing his forehead against mine. He began to kiss me—his lips fluttering over my eyes, my cheeks, my lips, down to my neck. I could feel his teeth against my skin, but he hesitated and drew back.

"Not yet," he murmured, almost more to himself than to me. And then his mouth trailed kisses down my chest, teased my breasts as he slowly tugged on one nipple with his teeth, cautious not to pierce through the skin.

I was so wired all I could think was, *Please, please fuck me*. But Grieve wasn't about to move that fast.

He walked me backward to the bed, and in a blur, his clothes were on the floor. He was lean and strong, his olive skin moist and glimmering. His hair hung over his shoulders like spun silver. *And he wants me*.

As I gazed down his body, taking in his nakedness, I suddenly noticed something—something I'd never seen because I'd never seen Grieve in the light without clothes before. Even the first time, when I was seventeen, I hadn't noticed the mark in the dusk of the summer's evening.

On his upper right thigh, he had a tattoo of my face, of me as an adult, not as a child. A circle of silver roses and purple skulls surrounded my face. The same roses and skulls scattered through the vine near my wolf tattoo.

"That's me! How long have you had that?" I asked, breathless, reaching out to touch my face inked onto his skin.

"You aren't the only one linked in this relationship," he said, gazing down at my finger as he smiled. "Since long before you were born. I didn't let you see it last time. You had to make decisions on your own, without me influencing you. I told you, Cicely, I've been waiting for you. And someday I'll tell you more, when you are able to remember."

My wolf whimpered, a pleading cry, and I pressed against him.

"Make me forget the day. Make me forget everything except your touch." I wanted out of my head, out of my thoughts, out of the bloody sleaze I'd been forced to witness at Regina's party.

Grieve pulled me into his arms again, sliding one leg between my knees and I opened to his touch. As we went tumbling onto the bed, all I could hear was the rushing of winds, the soft hooting of owls, the howling of wolves, and my own heart racing. His hands slid over my body, down the length of my legs, and I let out a sharp cry as his fingers gently rubbed me into a frenzy of my own.

Every time he kissed me, white-hot fire—sizzling to a burn—raced through my body. I let out a cry, then another but he refused to stop and kept circling with one finger, driving me crazy with desire.

*This is what you've been waiting for,* Ulean whispered, and a wind, desert hot and sultry, bathed me in fire. *This is why no other man seems to attract you. Dangerous or not, you were bound, you and Grieve, long before you were born into this lifetime.*

Shaken, spinning, unsure of where my body left off and where Grieve's touch began, the night became a blur of touch and motion and movement. His lips on my lips, on my body, licking, kissing, nibbling, grazing me with those sharp teeth that hurt so good. His hands were a vortex of motion and my own mirrored his hunger.

I reached out to touch him, then—suddenly needing to lead. I pushed him back on the bed and slid down his body, my tongue tasting the sweet musk of his sweat. I trailed down the center of his stomach, over his abs, down toward the fulcrum of his delicious V, down to meet his rising passion, to take him in my mouth, to taste the fiery autumn night that clung to his energy, his very flesh.

"Cicely." His whisper was rough, his voice harsh, but behind my name was a plea for me not to stop, not to push him away.

I licked him full, licked him long in one stroke, my tongue tickling over the long pulse of his cock, circling the head and teasing him hard and harder still. And then, suddenly I was on the bottom, and he was over me, head between my thighs, and the sting of his teeth made me cry out in a choked voice.

"Let me in." He rose above me, hips aiming, and I shifted to meet him as he slowly forged his way into my body, into my heart. The slow rhythm of his movements lulled me into a flower-shrouded haze. The scent of spicy carnations wafted over me and I caught the brief glimpse of a dark grove, where our bodies lay entwined on the ground beneath a mossy tree thick with leaves. Only we were not ourselves—but two others—and yet, *they were us.*

And then, we were back in my bedroom and he was driving harder as the intensity heightened. I tried to remember what he was, who he was, but all I could think of was—*he was the right one*. He was the one I was meant to be with, we were bound. I had no idea how or why, but here we were.

He lowered his lips to my neck and sliced the skin. Our bodies entwined as he lapped at my blood and a brilliant indigo mist began to swirl around us. He sucked harder and I whimpered as he tasted my most hidden secret self, my very essence. After a moment, he moaned, then pulled his face away. I was afraid to look at him, suddenly flashing back to Lannan's bloodstained mouth and chin after he'd fucked the girl.

But Grieve's face was clean, with just a single drop of blood on the corner of his lip, and the look in his eyes was one of life and desire and exquisite joy, and I forgot myself as he began to pump harder. My wolf growled, brazen and feral, and I slid into Grieve's flame. All thought dropped away as the spark became a blaze, and the blaze crowned into a raging fire and there was nothing left but Grieve and me, and our passion.

✣

After, long after, I was lying in his arms, dozing. He tapped me on the shoulder and kissed my forehead.

"What is it?" I gazed up at him, realizing that while, yes, I was enthralled because of the venom in his teeth, there was also some energy far deeper beneath the surface working between us.

"I have to go. I don't want *them* to ask where I've been." And by *them*, I knew he meant the Indigo Court.

"Good idea." Sliding out from between the sheets, I slipped on my bathrobe. "Do you . . . I . . . I'm not sure what to say." Should I ask him when he'd be back? Keep it casual? Everything inside me screamed this *couldn't* be casual and that if he wanted it that way, I was already a goner.

He pressed his finger to my lips. "Hush for now. We

are meant to be, Cicely. Let it go at that for now. There are many problems to work through, considering who holds my chains, but we will find a way. I promise you that. You are mine. Never forget that."

*And considering who now holds my chains, there are more problems than you think.* I thought it, but kept my mouth shut, foreseeing so many land mines ahead of us.

He leaned down and kissed me again. "One other thing. I will tell you something even though it puts me in danger."

"What is it?"

"Heather's alive. And so is your friend Peyton."

I stared at him and his glamour fell away, leaving him looking vulnerable and weary. Could he be telling the truth? Was he toying with me? Hesitating, I touched my hand to my throat. "Alive? You're sure? Where are they?"

"I'm certain, yes. I don't dare try to help you rescue them, but I will tell you that they're deep within the forest, past the ravine, being held captive in the Marburry Barrow. I don't know how long they'll remain alive, but right now, they're there and relatively unharmed." His eyes narrowed and he leaned toward me. "Myst is holding them captive."

"Where is the Barrow? How far into the wood?"

"You can't just walk up to it. You have to find the portal, otherwise it will just look like a large mound of dirt and grass. But if you want to go there, follow the path to the stand of red huckleberries. You'll see a Faerie ring of toadstools on the left." He traced a diagram on the bed for me.

"Faerie ring? Aren't those dangerous?"

"Yes. Step carefully—don't enter the ring because it's a snare. Then, continue for about an hour. Turn right after you walk between the Twin Oaks—you can't miss them, they're the only oaks in the area—and you'll find the

Marburry Barrow. The oaks are portals, though—and they will thrust you into my world and if there are Indigo Fae around, you'll die. I guarantee it."

"We have to try. We can't just leave them out there."

Grieve paused, then added, "Cicely, there are creatures in the wood—dangerous beasts that the Indigo Court breed and train. And then, there are the Shadow Hunters. They . . . *we* . . . bring a new definition to fear."

"I think I met one of their beasts already. A tillynok."

"Tillynoks used to be safe enough, but everything in the wood's been tainted by Myst's energy." He stared at his nails. "I can't help you any more than I have. At least . . . not now, not yet."

He looked at me then, without any façade, and I caught a glimpse of the old Grieve, the Grieve I remembered from so many years ago. The Grieve who had stared at me so sorrowfully when he was preparing me for life on the road with Krystal.

I moved closer to him, wanting to comfort him. As I placed my hand on his arm, he looked up—almost too quickly—his new side warring with the old—and covered my fingers with his. The wolf's head on my stomach let out a low whimper, and I moved in, pressing my hands on his shoulders.

And then—in a blur of movement—he raced to the window and was gone like a leaf caught up in the wind. The curtains around the open window swirled and I ran over to stare out into the night. There, loping toward the forest, ran a wolf. I raised one hand, then watched as an owl rose from the trees—the great horned bird I'd seen before. Spiraling, it glided on the wind, following the wolf back into the wood.

I slowly returned to bed.

*What now?* I had to tell the others. We had to go rescue Heather and Peyton. And Rhiannon and Leo deserved to know that Grieve and I were actually lovers. They wouldn't be happy, but I couldn't keep it a secret. I slipped on my robe and crept out into the hallway, tapping lightly on Rhiannon's door.

She answered, looking sleepy but still awake.

"Leo went to work, but not back to the party. Come in," she said. Closing the door behind me, she bundled me over to her bed and I crawled under the comforter with her. We snuggled like we had when we were children, and as she softly touched my cheek, I realized she already knew.

"So then. Grieve." Her words were measured, but her eyes filled with understanding.

"You can tell?"

"Yes. I heard you both—talking low. And I can see it in your face. You love him, don't you? Terribly so?"

"Yes, Grieve. He came to me tonight. Please, understand. I *needed* him. Grieve has a tattoo of my face on his thigh. Just like I have my wolf. He got it before he met me."

"I . . . I think there's nothing that can keep you two apart. Whatever binds you together is stronger than the Indigo Court or the vampires." She smiled. "Was it good?"

I laughed then. "Yes, oh yes. Grieve is . . . he's what I need. He's who I'm meant to be with. I know you can't help but be suspicious, but Grieve isn't like the others. He fights against his vampiric nature. He isn't truly part of the Indigo Court. He's trying to help us. And he told me where to find Heather and Peyton."

"Alive? Where? Can we get to them now?"

I told her what Grieve had told me. "I think we can trust him."

She sobered. "It sounds like we're going to need more help. We don't dare go through the wood at night. It's far too dangerous."

"We have Marta's stash of goodies to go through. First

light, we'll see what we can fashion for protection. And you said Kaylin will be over tomorrow? Will he help us?"

"Maybe," Rhia said, her smile flickering in the gentle light from the candle that was burning on her nightstand. Rosemary and lavender, it was enchanted for protection, for peace of mind. I inhaled deeply and held my breath, letting the fragrance work its magic on my thoughts.

"When are you and Leo getting married?" I asked after a few minutes.

"I don't know," she said softly. "I adore him. He's good to me and we get along, and I think I want to marry him. But I don't know if we have what you and Grieve seem to have. Maybe every great love story is different."

"I never thought I'd find him again, to be honest. And now . . . it's harder than it ever promised to be." I propped my back against the headboard and pulled the comforter up over us. "What makes you think you don't have the same level of passion that Grieve and I share?"

"I'm so afraid of losing control—because of the fire. I'm afraid of hurting people. Of hurting . . . Leo. I always hold a part of myself back."

I wrapped my arm around her shoulders and gave a tight squeeze. "You have to learn to control the flames, Rhia. You can't let your fear overpower you forever. It will backfire and then where will you be? Where will we all be?"

And then, because we were both exhausted and didn't want to talk about vampires or blood or anything outside the walls of the room, we blew out the candle and slid back under the covers. Holding hands like we had when we were young, we fell asleep to the soft sound of the air cleaner.

# Chapter 14

We were up before dawn. Leo was still asleep, but Rhiannon woke him up because he was likely to recognize some of the charms I might not. Being on the road and working primarily with the energy of the wind put me at some disadvantage. I didn't do things the way a lot of witches did them, and most of my spells were invocations as opposed to actually working with spell components.

We dug through the boxes and bags, looking for anything that might help. I held up an orange ball the size of a walnut. "This is practically trying to jump out of my hand. You guys know what it is?"

Rhiannon took it, sniffed it, and her eyes widened. "Yeah, it's a firespark charm. Can turn even the most moderate of flames into a raging inferno. I don't think I should touch this."

"Ridiculous. You need to get over your fear of the fire. Just because you're carrying something doesn't mean you're going to set it off," Leo said, glancing up at her. Bart rubbed around his legs; the Maine Coon was dragging around a fuzzy mouse and seemed intent on cajoling Leo into playing with it. "And shouldn't someone be making breakfast? I'm starved."

"Make it yourself," Rhiannon said, staring at him with a hurt look. "I'm not your maid or your mother."

Leo leaned back, squatting on his heels. He rubbed his forehead and let out a long sigh. "I'm sorry. I didn't mean to snap at you. It's just . . . things feel like they're spiraling out of control and we have to get a handle on anything that might help us. Like your power over flame. Maybe Anadey can help you?"

I jerked my head up. "He's got a point. She's a shamanic witch and she works with all four elements. If anybody we know can help, it might just be her."

"Fine. I'll talk to her today." Rhiannon frowned. "Do we tell her what Grieve said about Peyton?"

"Not till we confirm it. We want to make certain she's safe before we get Anadey's hopes up."

I ran my fingers through my hair, staring at the massive pile of odds and ends with disgust. "I don't know why Marta left all this to me. I usually just work with energy, not with the actual components. She could have left this to her daughter, or to Peyton—they would be able to put it to better use than me."

"Nope, she had her reasons. Marta never did anything without thinking it through." Leo held up a handful of necklaces. "Bingo—protection charms. Don't know how effective they are, but they feel charged. There are five of them."

"We each get one, then. And a spare." I draped one of the Algiz runes over my head and immediately felt the soft keen of magic shroud my shoulders. "Whoa . . . this *is* comforting. Okay, let's go eat and then—"

The doorbell rang. Leo went to answer and a moment later returned, followed by a guy who looked around thirty. He was Chinese, thin but muscled, and was dressed in a pair of ripped jeans and a black leather jacket over a gray muscle shirt. Combat boots completed the outfit. He carried a heavy backpack, which he dropped in the corner after carefully scanning the room.

"Kaylin Chen, meet Cicely Waters."

Kaylin looked at me. "We've been waiting for you, Cicely—the wind told me you were coming, and to keep an eye out for you."

*What the . . . ?* "You can speak to the wind?" I'd never met anybody else with my abilities before. But he shook his head.

"No, but ghosts can speak through the wind, and I can speak to ghosts." And then his eyes lit up with a golden light, and I noticed that, standing behind Kaylin Chen, stood two translucent figures. Neither one seemed to realize that I could see them.

Kaylin blinked. "What are you looking at?" Then, he relaxed. "You can see them." He spoke so softly that Leo and Rhiannon didn't hear him.

"Yeah, but I don't think the spirits know I can."

"Probably not. They're attuned to me on a level I can't explain, and very few ever know they're with me. Even gifted psychics usually don't tune in to them." He turned to Leo. They clasped arms. "Good to see you, bro. It's been a long time."

"You, too, dude. You been staying out of trouble?"

"As much as I can," Kaylin said. He saluted Rhiannon, who waved.

"You want breakfast?" She flashed him a wide smile and her eyes sparkled.

Kaylin nodded. "Not about to say no."

"Come on, Cicely. Let's cook while we fill him in on what's going on."

I stared at her for a moment. She'd just about bit off Leo's head for asking her to cook breakfast; now she was volunteering the both of us. I glanced back at Kaylin and he winked at me. A glint in his eyes twinkled and I felt a sudden desire to make him happy.

"Dude, you have some sort of charm going on?"

He shrugged. "Only my natural demeanor."

"Right. Come on, Rhia. Let's get breakfast under way."

Kaylin followed the rest of us into the kitchen. His gaze fluttered back to me as he turned one of the chairs around and swung one leg over the seat, coming to rest his elbows on the back of it.

"So, Cicely, you're Rhiannon's cousin?"

"Here, you're on toast duty." I thrust the bread into his hands. "And yes, I'm Rhia's cousin." While Rhiannon whipped eggs for omelets, I dug through the fridge for a ham I'd seen earlier and began cubing the meat to go in the eggs.

"Then you're in off the pipelines," he said, pulling his chair over to the counter where he began to toast the bread. I handed him the butter and as the slices came popping out of the toaster, he spread them thickly and covered the stack with a tea towel to keep the toast warm.

I gave him a questioning look, but it was Rhiannon who answered. "Pipelines—that's what Kaylin calls the freeways."

*Curious*, I thought, but didn't ask why. Instead, I examined the two spirits who stood by his back. As I let myself drift, listening to the wind, I realized that they were a man and a woman, both dressed in long white robes that sparkled with golden embroidery. They seemed oblivious to me, standing at attention, focused solely on Kaylin, almost as if they were guarding him. And then, I knew who they were.

"They're your parents."

Kaylin shifted, barely, but enough to tell me I'd nailed it. He set down the loaf and gazed at me. "How can you tell?"

"It makes sense. The way they're standing reminds me of the cops—or security guards."

Rhiannon scrambled the eggs and ham, sprinkling in a handful of grated cheese, then divided them onto four plates. She glanced up from her work, frowning at the both of us. "What are you two talking about?"

"Cicely can see something neither of you can." He shrugged. "My family has my back. Literally. My parents' spirits travel with me, watch out for me, tell me who to avoid. They don't know everything, but it gives me an edge and I'm trying to get them to help me look for my best friend's killer."

"Then you think the Indigo Court staged his car wreck?" I asked.

"The Indigo Court? I'm not familiar with the name." He finished up the toast and brought it over to the table. "But I know something's taken control of the town and whatever it is, it was responsible for my bro's death. Derek was one of a kind . . . he didn't make simple mistakes like driving when he was too tired."

"You willing to go up against his murderers?" Leo asked.

Kaylin gave us a long look. "I've been looking for a way to fight whatever this force is for months now. I'm already on the front lines."

I bit my lip, trying to decide just how I felt about him. But Leo and Rhia trusted him and they'd know better than I would. "You willing to take a little trip out into the ravine with us today? We're looking for Heather, and for Peyton Moon Runner."

"Haven't got anything else to do. Sure." He dug into breakfast with such gusto that I wondered how long it had been since he'd eaten. But he didn't look poor. In fact, his clothing looked remarkably well made and expensive. Kaylin was an odd duck and I wanted to know more.

"Before this goes any further, how do you feel about

telling me who and what you are? It's only fair." I'd had enough of making deals unseen. My pact with the vampires was weighing heavy on my mind and I wasn't about to fall in unaware with someone else who might try to pull one over on me.

"She's safe," Leo said. "We both vouch for her. By blood, bro."

Kaylin eyed me closely, then shrugged. "All right. I trust you to that." He pushed back his chair and wiped his mouth on his napkin. "I'm a dreamwalker, Cicely. When I was in the womb, my mother was initiated into an ancient shamanic tradition. There was a demon hanging out nearby and it took the chance to enter my soul. It's not *in me*—not as *possessing* me. But the experience changed my very DNA. It opened me up on a psychic level. When the demon entered me, it died, but its essence blended into my own soul during the ritual and now we are one. I am both Kaylin, and what's left of the night-veil."

"Night-veil?" Oh wonderful. Now we were dealing with demons. Although it was hard to imagine any demon worse than the Vampiric Fae.

"They're the creatures that you catch a glimpse of in the shadows—they hide in dusty attics, creep into old basements, and live in rotting barns. Only during the cover of night do they emerge, and they're connected to the Bat Tribe."

I had a lot to learn. So much of this had gone under my radar, living all those years on the road.

"I feel so stupid compared to all of you. So unprepared. Half this stuff . . . I knew it existed because, hell, I'm magic-born. But my life was so far removed from most magic except the spells I could summon. My existence with Krystal was like a bad seventies road movie. I learned what I could, but there are times I think I'm going to be a detriment because of my ignorance."

"You'll be fine. There's more to you than meets the

eye. Just remember: When in doubt, ask." Kaylin gave me a gentle smile and I suddenly felt safe with him. His eyes promised that he'd do his best to help us, and that was good enough for me. He was on our side, and right now that's what we needed.

And so, like that, we had our fourth. We spent the rest of breakfast filling him in on the Indigo Court, and what was waiting for us in the wood.

❧

"I don't like this," Leo said as he carried our plates to the sink. Kaylin was washing the dishes, while Rhiannon and I cleaned the counters. "We're going to get ourselves killed."

"That's probably going to happen anyway, if we don't do something about the Shadow Hunters. But we know Heather and Peyton are out there and we have to at least give it a try. If the four of us go together, we might be able to hold off the tillynoks and whatever else might be out there."

Kaylin stared at me for a moment, then wiped his mouth on a napkin. "Leo's right. We're probably going to get ourselves hurt, but I'm in."

I folded the tea towel and hung it over the refrigerator handle. "Since it's still fairly early, we might luck out and Myst's people will be asleep."

*Some of them will be, but be careful, Cicely. Not all beasts thrive in the dark and the shadow.* Ulean's voice rang clear in my head, and so did her concern.

At five minutes to nine we were standing in front of the path leading into the ravine. The sky was an odd silver color and the scent of snow-covered cedar hung thick in the air. Everywhere, the glint of light on snow sparkled like diamonds, glistening on the ferns and bushes.

Kaylin had his pack, Leo was dressed in khakis and a sweater that matched the surrounding foliage. *Camo,*

I thought. Rhiannon was carrying a lighter and the firebombs that Leo and I made her bring.

I'd opted for the tough chick look: black jeans, black
turtleneck, and my leather jacket. We all wore boots in
which we could move through the snow and slush. For my
weapons of choice, I'd slid my switchblade into a sheath
attached to my wrist, and had stuck my athame in my
boot sheath. Both blades were highly illegal to carry, but
they did the trick.

"Okay, let's head out." Taking a deep breath, I plunged
into the ravine. The path was level for the first twenty
minutes of walking, then slowly began to descend. When
Rhiannon and I'd been children, we'd usually stayed on
this side of the ravine, in the wood near the house. But
today, we had quite a hike in front of us.

The mat of needles and leaves beneath the snow
scrunched as I led the way into the thick copse. Throughout the woods, the call of crows echoed from tree to tree,
and one lone bird sang to announce the coming storms.
I listened to the breeze that had picked up, but Ulean
warned me from playing in the slipstream too much.

*A storm's on the way, with heavy snowfall behind it.
This is an unusual winter and Myst might be behind it.*

Great. Storms were crazy enough on their own. I tried
to stay out of their way because if they could sense you
had tuned in on them, they'd take aim at you like a lightning rod. And those of us who worked with the wind or
weather tuned in to them like a compass needle seeking
north.

I sent a mental hug to Ulean, surprised to feel one in
return. It occurred to me that, now that I was settling
down—and especially if I were to start up some sort of
magical business—I'd need to begin regular meditation
again. I'd taught myself how to meditate over the years
and it kept me sane during my exile with Krystal. Now I

could start to truly dive into my work with Ulean and see just how far we could take our partnership.

*I'd like that.* A smile broke through her words.

*I'd like that, too.*

I turned to the others. "Let's get a move on, rough weather coming in."

As I scrambled to the edge of the ravine, I noted the overgrown state of the path leading down and through it. When I was little, it had been carefully tended, but now it was a tangle of briars and other dangers, all hiding under a blanket of white.

"Watch it, there's stinging nettle along this path and it will be hard to see now. Everything's so overgrown and wild, and the snow over the slick ground won't make this any easier."

" 'Lay on, Macduff! Just don't lead us to ruin.' " Leo was joking but I could sense the tension in his voice.

"Let's hope it doesn't come to that," I said.

The path was slippery, the overgrown foliage slick from the winter's touch. The patches that were clear of plants had frozen, and were slick with black ice. Down below, mist rose from the bottom of the ravine. And the temperature was hovering around thirty-three degrees. Good thing we'd all worn heavy clothing.

I edged my way down, slipping and sliding, occasionally having to lean back toward the slope to balance myself with my hand. At a shout from Rhiannon, I glanced back. She'd landed on her butt in a patch of brambles.

"You okay?"

She nodded as Leo helped her up. "Yeah, a few thorns but nothing major." Shaking off the clinging stickers, she cautiously passed over the slippery spot and I went back to deciphering the best way down.

Ravines in western Washington are usually steep, covered in thorny brambles and stinging nettle and ferns, and they're moist. Fungi grow thick in them, and there's the ever-present sense that the very ground is alive. Add a layer of snow, and freezing temperatures, and you have the perfect recipe for an accident.

The scents of ozone mingling with the cedar and fir created a sharp blend that went straight to my head. Scents affected me more than they did others, probably because of my affinity for the air.

The mist wafted up the side of the slope and I stopped, staring at the coiling, vaporous serpents. If there was anything hidden within the fog, we couldn't see it. Chances are whatever might be cloaked couldn't see us either, but Rhiannon and Leo weren't skilled at quiet navigation. Kaylin appeared to be, and I knew how to soften my footsteps, but with the other two in tow it would be obvious we were coming.

I held up my hand and motioned for them to shut up.

They quieted down, pausing as I listened. At first, the sound of snow falling from the branches to the ground below and the calling of crows overshadowed everything else, but as I tuned in and asked Ulean to separate the sounds for me, the layers began to pull apart. To the left—a small animal running through the overgrowth. Overhead, the trees creaked in the wind, branches rubbing against each other.

As I lowered myself even deeper into the slipstream of sound, I could hear the slow hiss of the mist as it rolled along the ground, alive and looking to cover and obscure. And behind the mist, spirits whispered on their passage through the ravine. Ghostly lips played out laughter and tears, sudden cries, then—just as suddenly silent.

*Still lower, I had to go lower.*

And finally, below the mist, below the ghosts and the susurration of breeze, more whispering. But this time the noise was on a different frequency—not Elemental, but belonging to . . . the Fae. And that meant, *the Shadow*

*Hunters.* But I heard no footfalls to warn me they were near, no vocalized thoughts to indicate they might be waiting below. No, this was different—as though I were listening through earphones to something distant and far away.

I let out a slow breath and turned back to the others. "We're being watched, but I don't sense any immediate danger. I think we're safe enough." I kept my voice as low as I could but no matter what I did, I knew the slipstream would catch it up for the waiting ears and eyes that hid behind the mist.

Turning back to the path, I began to make my way down into the first layer of mist that rose about a third of the way up the sides of the ravine. The fog swirled around me, cloaking everything outside of a couple yards in my path. While I could see my feet through the white swirls, we'd be walking blind here. I waited for the others to catch up.

"Don't fall behind. I'll go slow. We need to keep within sight of one another."

"Will this help?" Kaylin passed me a thin rope. "We can each keep hold of it."

"Sounds good to me. Don't let it catch on anything." I wrapped the end of the rope around my arm and once again headed into the mist. The chill echoed in my lungs, and reflexively I coughed, then whirled at a sudden stir in the wild rosebush next to me.

"Crap!" I stumbled back as a creature leapt out and landed near my feet. Squat, with bloated eyes, it was about three feet high, and had nasty-looking teeth in an oversized mouth. And it latched on to my leg.

I tried to shake it off, but it had a good hold and—oh shit, it was about to bite down. I had no doubt that those teeth would be able to rip right through my jeans and take a good chunk out of me.

"Get it off me!"

Kaylin rushed forward and landed a kick to its mid-section. The creature let go but hissed at him and gathered itself for a leap. Before I could think, instinct took over and I flicked my switchblade open, stabbing the tip square on the creature's back. As I pulled away for another blow, it jumped out of reach, reminding me of a toad, then ran off.

Panting, I faced Kaylin. "What the fuck was that?"

"Goblin dog. Goblins live in the forest with the Fae you know. They're actually part of the whole Fae world, but both Seelie and Unseelie avoid them. Goblin dogs are . . . well, they're intelligent to a degree. They're a cross between goblins and other . . . creatures. Goblins that didn't quite develop normally. They're used as slaves and frontline grunts in wars. In other words: anytime somebody has to do the dirty work and stands a good chance of being offed."

"Oh, how delightful. I've never heard of them. Hell, I barely know anything about the world of the Fae." I paused. "How do you know so much?"

He gave me a long look. "The shamanic tradition my mother was initiated into, the magic that changed my DNA, is steeped in the magic of the Court of Dreams. The inhabitants of the Court aren't fully corporeal and they work on the astral plane. They're well aware of the Fae and I've learned much in the hundred years I've been alive."

I'd never heard of the Court of Dreams but just the mention of it washed over me like a bucket of cold water. Something about the name . . .

"Wait . . . hundred years? You're a hundred years old?"

"One hundred and one, yes." He said it so matter-of-factly that I decided to let that issue drop right there. We could discuss his age and how he managed to get there without looking a day over thirty later on, when we weren't fighting goblin dogs.

"Okay. So, is this also what gives you your ability to see ghosts?"

"Yeah, and my other . . . abilities." Kaylin nodded to the bottom of the ravine. "We'd better get a move on or that thing might come back. And frankly, I don't know if we're armed enough to actually kill it. You landed a nasty blow with your blade and barely slit the skin."

The reality of what he was saying washed over me. We'd barely hurt the creature. What would we do if we were facing something more dangerous? No two ways about it: We had to shape up because chances were good that we wouldn't make it through the next few months without another fight. Kaylin was experienced. And I knew enough to teach street fighting. We'd muddle through.

"Keep your eyes open. If something happens, don't run off into the mist alone. Kaylin and I have the most experience fighting, so Leo, you stick with me. Kaylin, you help Rhia."

Rhiannon moved to Kaylin's side. Leo pulled up front with me.

"We ready? Let's push toward the bottom of the ravine."

I showed Leo how I was inching my way down, stepping sideways on the steep and frozen hill. Then, I'd test my footing before putting full weight on my leg. He followed suit. Every few feet I called, "Check," and Kaylin echoed it back to me. After another ten minutes, I could hear the sound of tinkling water. The stream sounded muffled, and I guessed it was partially frozen over.

"We're almost at the bottom." The fog was so thick at our level that it caught in my lungs, making me wheeze. But sure enough, in another moment we were standing beside the channel through which a rolling stream flowed. Or did, under a thin layer of ice.

"Now what?" Rhiannon asked.

"Now, we cross the stream and head up the other side." This was taking longer than I thought it would. I hadn't counted on the mist, or on being attacked, or on just how rough our footing would be. We still had at least another hour—maybe two—of walking, according to the directions Grieve had given me.

"We need to pick up the pace."

"Here's a stepping-stone bridge," Kaylin said, pointing to a series of smooth, flat stones that had been placed across the stream. They were wet and iced over, but they were an inch or so above the water and if we balanced carefully, we might not end up calf-deep in the stream. I lightly crossed to the other side and the others followed suit.

"Now, up the hill and on to the Marburry Barrow," I said.

But even as the words left my mouth, a noise to our left alerted us and we turned. There, hiding behind a tree, stood Chatter, looking petrified. And Grieve was nowhere in sight.

# Chapter 15

"Chatter? Chatter? I see you!" As I headed toward the tree, he looked about ready to run. I held out my finger, shaking it at him. "Don't you dare!"

Rhiannon glanced at the tree and a huge smile washed across her face. "Chatter! Please, don't go!"

He slowly stepped from behind the tree, eyeing the four of us nervously. After a moment of scuffing the ground, he bowed to Rhiannon. "Miss Rhiannon, it's good to see you again. And dear Ciccly . , ,"

"What are you doing here, Chatter? Were you watching us?" I took a step toward him. He didn't worry me nearly as much as Grieve. Grieve was a member of the Indigo Court. Chatter still seemed like . . . Chatter.

He blushed and shook his head. "I can see why you would think so. No, Miss Cicely. I'm not worthy enough to be used as a spy." By the tone in his voice and the lowering of his head, I could tell whatever self-esteem he used to possess had been beaten out of him. I prayed Grieve hadn't been on the other end of the stick.

"Chatter . . . my friend. What are you doing here?" I held out my hand and he slowly took it. As I pulled him close and gave him a hug, he relaxed just enough to tell me that he was as afraid as we were.

He winced, then shrugged his head to one side. "Just . . . trying to stay out of the way of the Queen and her Court. Grieve's not around today to protect me."

That figured. I had the feeling that life at the Indigo Court hadn't gone easy on Chatter. In fact, it occurred to me we might actually have a better *in* to the Court through him than through Grieve. Of course, if Myst found out . . .

"I bet life isn't very easy now that the Queen of Rivers and Rushes is gone. I'm so sorry. I liked Lainule." I held his gaze, wanting to take away some of the pain I saw behind those limpid brown eyes.

"No," he whispered, a light flashing in his eyes. "Life's been harsh the past few years. I miss the Queen. She was fair and just."

"Will you tell us what happened?" Rhiannon asked. She placed a light hand on his shoulder. He gazed at her, a slow sadness filling his eyes.

*He likes her,* Ulean whispered.

I nodded, slowly. I could see it in his face. Chatter shivered under her touch as she stroked his arm lightly. I glanced at Leo, who was not looking pleased.

"We need to know what's going on. My mother's disappeared, and a friend. We don't know if they're alive or dead."

Relieved she didn't spill Grieve's secret and let on that he'd already told us they were alive, I relaxed for a moment.

Chatter closed his eyes. "I'm so sorry. I'm so sorry about *all* of this. I wish you hadn't come back, Cicely— not to face this mess. And Miss Rhiannon . . . your mother and your friend . . . I wish I could help."

His eyes misted over and he hung his head. "We fought them. So much death. So much blood. We fought and fought. Grieve led a band of us deep into the Barrow and we tried to sneak the women and children out through the portal to the other side. But they caught up with us. There was so much blood and screaming, and little children torn to bits." He wiped his eyes with one hand, but the catch in his voice was like a rusty hinge and I knew he'd been broken.

"Oh, Chatter." Rhiannon slid her arms around his shoulders and he leaned into her embrace. "I wouldn't bring up the memories but we need your help. We need all the help we can get. Will you tell us what happened to Grieve?"

He blinked. "We were caught. They were going to feed on me but Grieve begged them to spare me. They drank him down to the gate of death and then made him drink. Then he just . . . he recovered—so fast. And when he stood again, he looked so strange. His eyes changed. *Grieve* changed. He looked like a wild child and I was afraid he'd finish me off himself, but he just said, *Let me keep him. He's lazy and useless but he amuses me.* My friend would never have said that before the change."

"And they agreed?" I quietly shifted my weight. My feet were going a little numb in the cold but I didn't want to break the mood.

"Yes. So I stay with Grieve most of the time. The others hate me, but Grieve . . . he tries to be himself. I can tell he doesn't like what he's become. He would never treat you so oddly, Cicely, if this hadn't happened to him. There's a constant battle going on inside. I can see it in his eyes. He's always at war with himself."

Chatter crouched on the ground, ignoring the snow. He rested against the tree trunk. "I get tired, so I come out here and breathe the illusion of freedom."

"Do you want to come home with us? We can help

you. You could leave town, get away." I had no idea how we'd manage it but the offer slipped out before I could stop myself.

But Chatter shook his head. "Thanks, Miss Cicely. You and Miss Rhiannon, you're good friends, even though I only really knew you when you were children. But I'm afraid I wouldn't get far. You'd be in trouble and I'd end up dead. And besides . . ."

"Besides what?" What more could there be than to get away and not look back? But Chatter's answer silenced the cynic in me.

"I help keep Grieve sane. Without me he'd give way, fully turn into one of *them*. And I can't do that to him. He was my best friend at one time. Shadow Hunter or not, Grieve's still my blood-oath brother."

I wanted to do something . . . *anything* . . . to help. But there was nothing we could do if he refused.

"I understand. Chatter, will you at least promise not to mention you saw us or talked to us?"

He inclined his head. "I won't give you away. I promise you that." He slowly rose and dusted his hands on his pants. "I'd better go now, before they miss me. I don't want them to come looking for me and find you." Turning, he added, "But be careful. These woods are laden with creatures that could rip you apart. If I were you, I'd go home. Seriously, the woodland is tainted. I don't know if it can ever recover."

I bit my lip, wanting to take him by the hand, drag him home, and send him off on a bus somewhere, but I stepped back. If we interfered too much, we'd only get him in trouble. Or dead.

"Go then, before they sense us. But Chatter . . . if you do see my aunt—Rhiannon's mother—or our friend Peyton . . . if you think of something that can help, then please, let us know."

Chatter nodded. Then, turning to go, he stopped. "The

owl's been looking for you, by the way, Cicely. He asks for you, every day. I'd help, but I'm just . . . don't count on me." He shook his head. "I'm useless. But soon, you must find the owl. If the Shadow Hunters find it, they'll kill it. They hate owls. And—don't trust spiders. The spiders of the wood watch and listen. They're Myst's pets."

He ran then, so fast I could barely track him. In mere moments, he was gone.

❧

We made our way up the other side of the ravine in silence. I could tell the others were itching to discuss the meeting with Chatter, but this wasn't the time nor place for that.

Once we were at the top of the ravine, the going was quicker and we moved silently through the path, our sounds muffled by the snowfall. The clouds had moved in and now a light flurry had started, softening our footsteps even more. Although still overgrown, the trail wasn't as bad as it had been back in the ravine. Someone had to be keeping it under control, and my guess was the Indigo Court. The light fell through the trees in an odd, slanted way, and the silver-tinged sky lent an air of foreboding to the disturbing ambience that filtered through the woodland.

I kept my eyes open for the stand of red huckleberries. I knew them by sight, even without the berries in blossom. Blue huckleberries grew more frequently over the Cascades, in eastern Washington. I was beginning to wonder if Grieve's instructions were right when, within a few minutes, I saw a thick patch of them ahead—there must have been twenty or thirty bushes in one grouping.

"Start looking for the Faerie ring. Don't step inside of it—we need to go around it. Grieve was clear on that. *Don't step inside the ring of toadstools*."

I glanced around. Toadstools were another commonality in the forest—their growth spurred on by the dampness and the thick decay that littered the forest floor. Moss grew heavy in these woods, and ferns, and all plants misty and magical. That they'd be up during the snow was odd, but then again, this was a magical wood and the Fae could work wonders with the flora.

We slowly passed through the stand of huckleberries and I was beginning to wonder yet again if we'd made a wrong turn when Leo said, "I found it."

Off to our left, about ten yards past the shrubs, a wide ring covered the path. A good twelve feet in diameter, the ring was comprised of toadstools that were rust and brown, with white spots that dappled their skin. Some had blossomed out—their tops flat and fully open, ready to spore. Still others retained bulbous heads, tightly closed to stem. Their aroma was heady and bitter: pungent earth, tangy like fermented dirt. The snow within the ring was pristine, untouched by even animal prints, and the trail to the side was clearly visible.

Rhiannon backed away. "There's something wrong with that circle."

Leo knelt beside it, careful not to place his hand inside. He reached down, touching the ground beside the ring. "The magic here is deep—strong. Earth magic, but not friendly to us. I can feel it pulsing through the ground, touching the trees and plants all around here."

I reached out, trying to listen, but my power lay with the wind and there was little I could latch on to. "Kaylin, what do you think?"

Kaylin motioned for us to move back from it. "Rhiannon is right—this Faerie ring is a trap. Don't step inside, don't even put a single finger inside of it. I don't know exactly what would happen, but it's waiting for its next victim."

"Grieve said to skirt the outside of it. From here, we walk for another hour until we come to what he called the Twin Oaks. There we'll turn right after stepping between them, and we'll be at the Marburry Barrow." I glanced at the sky, wondering how long we'd been out here so far. It was cold and getting colder, but I wasn't willing to turn around and go home yet. "Anybody have any idea of what time it is?"

Kaylin flipped open his cell phone. "Reception here, not so good, but the clock says we're going on ten thirty. It took us an hour to cross the ravine and talk to Chatter. So if we keep a good pace, we should reach the Barrow at a little before noon."

"Let's get moving then. I'm chilled through. Walking helps."

I sucked in a deep breath and headed around the mushroom ring, bypassing the danger by keeping to its edge. The tingle of magic followed me, reaching out to jar my senses but otherwise left me alone. One step over the line, though, and we'd be in big trouble.

Traveling was easier at this point, although we had to keep a clear lookout for hidden rocks and roots beneath the snow cover. Twice I stopped, holding my hand for the others to wait as I tuned into the wind, listening to noises coming along the slipstream.

Once, I caught the distinct impression of a shriek that vibrated down my spine, a bolt of fear hidden in the one, lone cry. I kept quiet, not wanting to alarm the others. Not ten minutes later, another noise set my alarms ringing, but what I thought might be another goblin dog turned out to be a rabbit loping by. It stopped for a moment, nose twitching as it stood on its hind legs to look at us, before it turned to dart back into the undergrowth.

"Oh dear! Oh dear! I shall be too late . . ." I whispered under my breath. But since the rabbit carried neither a pocket watch, nor wore a waistcoat, I decided this wasn't our rabbit hole. Too bad Myst wasn't as innocuous as the White Queen.

Sure enough, at about twenty minutes to noon, the

forest began to open out into a clearing and up ahead we could see a pair of oak trees, towering huge. The path led right between them, and beyond, the route blurred to the eye.

"A portal . . ." Kaylin said.

"What?" I turned to him as he joined me at the trailhead.

"The oaks—they make up the sides of the portal. From here, I can't see anything but a barren mound, but want to make a bet we walk through there and bingo, we'll be facing the Marburry Barrow?"

I nodded, slowly. That would account for the indistinct blur around the edges. "You're right, I think. Grieve said they were a portal, that we had to pass through the oaks to find the Barrow. But now I'm wondering whether there might be members of the Indigo Court prowling the outskirts? We know they can go out in the daylight, so what's to prevent them from being there? Maybe I didn't think this thing through enough before suggesting we come out here."

Rhiannon pressed close to my side. "My mother's in there, and Peyton. They need me. I have to try."

Leo frowned. "I brought a few things from Marta's ritual gear that might help us." He set down his pack and began to fish through it, bringing up a handful of what looked like vertebrae. "Snake bones," he said. "I've studied enough to know that these can be used to create a cloud of poison—"

I looked at him. "Poison? I thought you were a healer."

"Heather taught me from the beginning: A witch who cannot hex, cannot heal. The balance of light and shadow—there's a place for the dark, Cicely. You know that from the life you led." He shrugged. "We have to be willing to do whatever it takes, considering who we're facing and what's at stake."

Blinking, I realized just how far down the road we'd come in just a matter of a few days. Danger was no longer a concept. We were staring it in the face. And the world needed both life and death, but in balance. The Vampiric Fae were upsetting that balance.

"Yeah, I get it. You think that the gas would work on the Indigo Court?"

"We don't know, so save it as a last resort," Kaylin said. "I know one way to slip in there and see what's going on."

"And what's that?" I asked, glancing at him.

"I'm a dreamwalker. I'll go in on the astral."

Rhiannon shook her head. "No—it's too dangerous. You could be hurt."

"There's always that chance, but if the odds are with me, they won't notice me before I can get away. The key is, you guys have to be ready to run. You'll have to run fast and hard because they're stronger than we are. But if I can get in there without them knowing, I might be able to pinpoint how to actually enter the Barrow." He handed me his backpack. "Keep this for me, please. It has some important items in it . . . just in case."

"You aren't serious about this—" I began to say, then stopped. Of course he was serious. None of us would be here if we weren't. I'd been ready to stomp right in there and that would have been far more likely to get me caught than if Kaylin slipped in on the astral. "What do you need in order to go in?"

He glanced around. "We need to find a place to hide. I'm going to have to lie down to prepare for this."

*Ask if you can go with him,* Ulean prompted.

I blinked. Say what? I was no dreamwalker and while Kaylin had a century of experience, could he really take another person with him?

*Just ask him. I can go with you.*

Score one for scaring me shitless. But Ulean could see

farther than I could and she apparently knew something I didn't. I tapped Kaylin on the arm. "Listen, do you know how to take somebody with you? Can you do that?"

He jerked around, giving me a hard look. "Why do you ask?"

I shrugged. "Ulean told me to ask if I could go with you."

When Kaylin spoke again, his voice was cold. "I won't risk your life, Cicely. There's no guarantee that they won't have some sort of anti-magic field that will negate the spell. What happens then?"

"Tell me exactly what it is that you do. Then let me make the decision." I sucked in a deep breath.

Rhiannon shook her head. "Bad idea. Don't let her talk you into it." She scuffed her feet. Neither she nor Leo looked happy at my request.

Kaylin let out a long sigh. "When I dreamwalk, I go into a deep trance—and yes, I can drag someone along with me. At some point—it's hard to explain how it happens—I see a door. When I go through it, my body turns to shadow. To the stuff dreams are made of. I can move around in shadow-form and so can whoever I have taken with me. I can spy on people, but I can't take action. I can't get in a fight, for example."

I thought about it for a moment. "Is there a time limit?"

He nodded, slowly. "Of sorts. If I stay out on the astral too long, I run the risk of not being able to come back. I could be trapped as a shadow entity."

"And how long is too long?"

"I don't know," he said. "I've never been out longer than an hour. I believe it depends on the power of the dream-walker, whether someone else is in tow . . . a number of varying factors. And there's another little matter: There are creatures out there, and not all of them are nice."

Oh, this was just getting better and better. Ulean had really set me up. "So we go walking into the shadow and

we might not come back. And there could be nasty crit-
ters. Can we fight them while we're there? You said we
couldn't fight from the astral."

"We can't—not anything on the *physical* plane. But
yes, we can defend ourselves against anything that's out
on the Dreamtime. That is, if we're stronger than they are.
Chances of that aren't very good." He gave me a quasi-
grin. "You still want to come with?"

"Maybe . . ." Only I didn't. But Ulean thought it was
a good idea and she'd never steered me wrong yet. "You
mentioned something about if the spell is negated . . .
what happens then?"

"Then we run like hell. If we can. If the spell's
disrupted—whether by accident or design—we appear
in body wherever we're at. In other words, if we're hiding out near the ceiling over a group of hungry Shadow
Hunters and someone negates the spell, our bodies will
resolidify and we'll fall right into the middle of the
group. And probably land *very, very* hard. This isn't
easy. Dreamwalking is dangerous." He lowered himself
to a nearby windfall and leaned his elbows on his knees,
whistling softly.

I glanced at the Twin Oaks. If we went through in body
and there were Vampiric Fae on the other side, we were
doomed. We'd never get away from them. And nothing
Grieve—or anybody—could do, would save our butts.

"Okay, I'm in! Let's do this!" I sucked in a deep breath.
"Rhiannon, Leo, you guys need to hide—and I mean hide
but good. Whatever happens, *don't* come after us. If we
don't come back—"

"Don't say that!" Rhiannon bit her lip, on the verge
of tears.

"If we don't come back," I said again, with emphasis,
"then get your butts out of this wood, tell the vamps what
happened to me, and don't look back. Get out of town
before nightfall."

Leo slid his arm around Rhiannon's shoulders. "Please rethink this. We can't afford to lose either of you."

"With a little luck and some common sense, you won't have to," Kaylin said. "But Cicely's right. This is our best chance to find out what's going on in there. We won't stay long, just get the lay of the land so we know what we're facing, and then come back. We won't take any unnecessary risks, will we?" He looked at me, pointedly.

I shrugged. "I wasn't planning on it, no. I'm not a lunatic. But Ulean thinks I should go with you, and she's usually spot-on. I've come to trust her over the years—she's saved my butt more than once."

"Then let's do it," Kaylin said. "Get ready to walk into the shadows. It's a cold, dark journey, and there's nothing quite like it in the world."

# Chapter 16

"You'll have to lie in my arms," Kaylin said. When I stared at him, a faint grin on my face, he shook his head, his dark hair swinging around his shoulders. "No, it's nothing like that. I need to be holding you in order to help you shift over with me."

"I kind of thought that's what you meant." I decided not to make him blush any more than he was. If we weren't in the situation we were in, it might be *fun* to make him blush but I reined in that thought for later.

Kaylin lay down on the ground, on his back. He held his arm out and I snuggled against him. It was an odd feeling, cuddling up against a strange man. But somehow, he felt comfortable and safe and I actually relaxed as he rolled over to face me and wrap his other arm around my shoulders, too.

"Don't be frightened," he said, his breath warm and minty against my face. "First, you'll feel a shimmering inside your body—I can't explain it, but like . . . like . . . when you see the lines fluttering on the TV—bad reception. Then you'll feel like you're starting to float. Keep calm. I'll have hold of you; I won't let anything happen."

I sucked in a deep breath and nodded, closing my eyes. I wasn't sure I was ready to see my body turn to vapor. Or shadow. Or anything resembling a nonsolid gas. I could deal with the concept, but to actually witness it might be more than I was up for.

"Keep breathing," Kaylin said. "Don't hold your breath. When we're dreamwalking we don't need to breathe so try not to panic if you notice you're not." He paused. "I still don't think this is such a great idea but here we go. Ready?"

I nodded, forcing myself to inhale-exhale as though I had just laid down to take a nap. Kaylin began to chant, something low and deep and almost out of the range of my hearing. Within seconds, he went from being a geeky cute goth guy to radiating a power that felt far, far older than me. I fought to keep my eyes closed, wanting to look at him.

And then, my body started to melt.

It began at someplace in my third chakra—just above my solar plexus. A wave of water ran through me, emanating from that one spot, undulating through muscle and bone, blood and vein, like concentric ripples on a pond. My body was melting like liquid silver, like the Wicked Witch of the West, like the second Terminator dissembling.

*Keep calm, focus on the feeling of Kaylin's arms around you.*

But Kaylin's arms were melting, too, mingling with the quivering pool that was my body. We were separate and yet linked, blending and yet two distinct beings. And then, the rippling spread out to my hands and feet, fingers and toes, and my flesh swelled and fell away as I felt myself diffuse and spread out. That was all it took for panic to set in.

*What's happening? I'm breaking up!*

*Calm yourself.* Kaylin's whispering thoughts found their way into mine. *As long as I brought you across, I can communicate with you. You're fine. This is just the process of becoming shadow. Only another minute or two and we'll be fully on the astral.*

A gentle breeze blew over my melting form. *And I am here.*

Instead of hearing Ulean's voice on the wind, it rang through my . . . head? Mind, I suppose. Instinct taking over, I tried to breathe but there was no breath, no air to comfort me. Reeling, I turned head over heels, lost in the pull of the astral current that rose up to surround us.

*I can't breathe!*

*You don't need to. Don't think about it. Focus on my voice. Focus on your senses—can you see anything?*

See anything? I didn't have eyes—wait. There was a light. Maybe just the sensation of light, but somehow I was aware of it. And then, I felt something shift and realized I'd just blinked. I glanced down and saw myself in silhouette, a shadow against the astral world in which we were standing. It was me, but in smoke and vapor, without distinct features. I held up my hands in wonder.

"I look like . . . wow . . . I'm not sure what." A cutout of a paper doll? My shadow, run off by its lonesome?

"You look fine—you're exactly as you should be."

Kaylin's words were more distinct. I wasn't hearing them—not with my ears—but they felt less intermingled with my own thoughts now. I looked around and there in the shadows next to me, I saw Kaylin—or rather, Kaylin's shadow.

A thought struck me. If I could see *him*, maybe that meant . . . I slowly turned to my right. There, in a cloud of mist and sparkles—faint cerulean with diamond dust sparkling in the midst—swirled Ulean. She was not female per se, but a vague bipedal form caught in the middle of an ever-spinning vortex.

*My gods, you're beautiful!* I couldn't stop staring at her.

*Thank you, my friend. I'm so happy you can finally see me.*

"We'd better get going," Kaylin said, and I realized he'd missed my exchange with the Elemental. So even here, he couldn't hear her. But . . .

"Can you see Ulean?" I motioned toward the mist and vapor that was my wind Elemental.

He stared for a moment, then slowly inclined his head. "Faintly, but there's static. Perhaps it's because I'm not attuned to the wind."

*He's not bonded with me. Only you can see me clearly here. And only you—or those I choose to—can hear me.*

"Got it." I figured the answer worked for both of them. "What now?"

Kaylin pointed ahead. I followed his gesture and there saw a pair of what looked like beacons, lit up brighter than the Space Needle on New Year's. As I gazed at them, the shapes began to sink through and I realized what they were.

"The Twin Oaks!"

"Yes. If they were just ordinary trees, you wouldn't be seeing them nearly so well. They'd be lit up, yes, as with the auras of all living things, but not like this. Look around. Really try to focus because so much out here depends on learning to open your mind in order to see more than one dimension at once."

Once again I tried to breathe and panicked briefly as no air flowed into or out of my lungs. I caught myself and let my fear settle.

"What am I looking for?"

"Think of Rhiannon and Leo. Then look for them."

I brought Rhiannon's face to mind. Her smile, her red braid, the sparkle in her eyes . . . then I thought of Leo and—

"Whoa . . . there they are!"

Not two yards from where we stood, I could see them, vague and indistinct but their auras shone like the neon of a bar sign. Leo's was green, steady and brilliant. But Rhiannon's aura crackled, her energy looking tight—as if she had clamped restraints on it. Flaring like sunspots, it tried to break free time and again and was yanked back to meld again into her body. The tension was palpable, as if she were wrestling with a nest of writhing snakes.

"Shit . . . she's going to explode someday and it's not going to be long. Look at that—she's got so much repressed energy that it will eat her alive if she doesn't do something soon."

Kaylin nodded. "We have to take her in hand, help her overcome her fear of the fire. She could burn up with that much repressed force."

*Spontaneous combustion.* The thought ran through my head with alarming clarity and I could so easily see her setting herself up for it. Surely she could feel the power shifting, though? Or had she blocked any natural connection out of fear she'd misuse it again? One way or another, we had to help her find balance.

"How are you doing? Think you're ready to go check on the Barrow, or do you need another moment to adjust?" Kaylin—or the inky black shape that passed for him— leaned against a splotch that I finally realized was a boulder back in the physical plane.

I gauged my comfort level. I still felt misty and oddly at loose ends, but I had gotten over my fear of not breathing, and the shapes on the astral were becoming clearer and more defined to my new eyes.

"I think I'm ready. What do we do? And how will

we know if they see us?" I tested out my footing on the ground. Dreamwalking felt kind of what I always imagined bouncing around on the surface of the moon might feel like.

"If we fall into a field that negates the magic, we'll know all too well. The question is: Will they have any seers capable of ferreting out astral entities? Essentially, psychic spies? That's our biggest worry, providing the magic holds. Just keep your eyes and ears open. Focus on the person you want to hear and tune in that way."

He motioned to me and we headed toward the Twin Oaks. A nervousness settled in my solar plexus. It was odd not to feel my body. Was this what it felt like to be an Elemental? Never solid, but instead made of shadow-stuff?

We neared the oaks and the energy between them crackled, lightning bolts in miniature flaring between the trunks. The trees were ancient, with swirling rings in their aura. They were old past counting and their roots ran deep into the world, their veins glowing beneath the surface. They burrowed down—foot after foot the sparkling anchors delved through the soil. They had been alive and growing long before my ancestors set foot on this land.

The energy flowing between the trunks set up a grid of sparkling lines through which we had to pass. I sucked in my breath and wondered if the portal would knock us off the astral, or if it was simply a gateway.

Kaylin paused. "Let me go first. If something happens, then you run like hell and ask your Elemental to escort you to the nearest dreamwalker to see if they will take you back over to the physical side."

"Won't this just wear off?" I blinked. "I thought there was a time limit on the spell?"

"Theoretically. In practice, I don't know." He shrugged. "Here goes nothing. I'll cross over, then return for you if everything's okay." Before I could say a word, he passed through the portal—and in the glare of smoke and mirrors was gone from sight.

⚜

I waited, watching the portal. If I'd been able to breathe, I would have been holding my breath but barring that, I counted seconds. Of course, on the astral—as in the realm of Fae—time ran differently. We could be out here for days and only minutes would pass in the physical world, or vice versa. Still no sign of Kaylin. Where the fuck was he, and what was I going to do if he didn't come back?

I was about ready to follow him—he didn't really think I was going to run off and leave him there if something happened, did he?—when there was a shimmer between the oaks and he reappeared, motioning to me.

I hurried over to his side, Ulean following me in her cloud of starstuff.

"Is it safe?"

Kaylin nodded. "For now, at least. But we were right to worry. There's a group of the Indigo Court Fae near the mound. I don't think they can see us. Let's get our butts over there before that changes."

He grabbed my hand and the smoke of his hand mingled together with mine to form an odd merging of our bodies. It was as if we were conjoined twins, bound by our fingers.

"Hold on to me when we go through the portal. It's a little freaky."

Without any further warning, he dragged me between the Twin Oaks, and I went flying along behind him as he leapt through. The crackle of energy rattled me, disrupting my entire system.

"Crap! Is this what it feels like to be a live wire?" The words jolted out of my mouth as we exited the other side.

"Hush," Kaylin whispered. "We can't be seen, except as a fleeting shadow here or there, but if they have anybody who has clairaudience, or who can hear the wind like you can, they might be able to pick up on us."

I squinted, trying to focus on the physical. The astral was superimposed over the swath of trees, but if I kept my attention on the forest, it became clearer, more distinct.

We emerged into what looked to be a large, circular glade. The forest was lit up like a pack of matches, the energy racing through the trees, flaring with deadly brilliance. Everything was swathed in a sparkle of silver, in tones of deep indigo. The trees were barren, their branches weaving a latticework of silver webs across the sky.

*Rhiannon's vision! This had to be the home base of the Indigo Court. Or at least their headquarters in our area.*

*You're right.* Ulean was drifting along behind us and I was relieved to see that she'd made it through the barrier okay. I hung back, letting Kaylin lead.

The Marburry Barrow was huge—the entire New Forest Conservatory campus could have fit inside—and it looked like an overgrown bump in the ground. A number of figures wandered around the outskirts and from here, I could see a shimmer against the lower edge. No doubt an opening.

The Barrow looked as though it had been built on a circular platform raised some fifteen feet above the ground. Steps along one side led up to the top of the mound itself, and at least two figures were lounging on the snow atop the dome.

I scanned the figures. All had a particular tint to their auras, and I began to understand why they were called the Indigo Court. The energy swirled, indigo and deep purple and black and silver—the colors of night and of shadow. Incredibly beautiful, their energy was magnetic and seductive and I longed to edge closer to the group, to bask in their presence.

Kaylin hissed. Startled, I slipped out of my reverie and looked at him with a grateful nod. I raised my hands to assure him that I was okay.

We watched for a few minutes as I tried to memorize the spot of shimmer that I was sure was a doorway. If we were able to sneak back on the physical, we'd know where to go without having to scout around for the entrance.

And then, it happened. The shimmering door parted for a moment and a contingent of the Indigo Court came out with two figures between them. Two figures who weren't of the Vampiric Fae. Both whose auras read as being of the magic-born, one weaker than the other in power.

*Your aunt and your friend.* Ulean was right behind me.

"Heather! Peyton!" I jerked away from Kaylin, heading for Heather.

"No! Cicely, come back!" Kaylin was on my heels, reaching for my arm. He managed to catch me before I'd gone more than a few yards, but then Heather swiveled in our direction and I caught her little cry on the wind.

At that moment, one of the Indigo Court turned toward us and shouted something, waving in our direction.

Shit! We'd been spotted.

"Run, run as fast as you can, we have to get out of here and off the astral!" Kaylin spun around, dragging me behind him on a breakneck race for the portal.

"But we haven't rescued them—"

"They'll kill us if they catch us!" He yanked me between the oaks and the jolt stilled the protest lodged on my tongue. We headed toward Rhiannon and Leo.

"We don't have time to come off the astral easy," Kaylin said. "This may hurt so get ready!"

He threw his arms around me and there was a numbing

flash as we tumbled, bodies solidifying, the smoke of our shadows dissipating. It was like flying, then being yanked out of the sky by an anchor of flesh.

I blinked hard as I tripped and went sprawling in front of Leo, who hurried to help me up. Kaylin, right behind me, was motioning toward the path.

"We have to get out of here. They spotted us!"

"Oh shit." Leo grabbed up our packs and tossed them to us while Rhiannon headed toward the path.

But it was too late. There was a noise from behind us, from between the Twin Oaks, and three men jumped from the portal. They had pale skin and a cerulean cast to their countenance. *Vampiric Fae. Shadow Hunters.*

I started to run, but in my heart I knew they were faster than we were. They'd catch us and they'd feed on us and that would be the end of everything.

"No!" Rhiannon's voice echoed through the air. She stopped, turning.

"What are you doing? Run!" I reached for her but she waved me off.

"I won't let them hurt us . . . I won't let them take us like they took my mother!" Her eyes flared dangerously and sunbursts writhed around her, struggling to free themselves as she pulled out one of the firebombs.

The men slowed, staring at her warily, but still heading in our direction. They glanced at the rest of us and I could tell they were trying to figure out just what the hell we were up to.

"Don't come any closer. I'm warning you!" Rhiannon's voice was close to breaking. And then, tears running down her face, she raised her arms. "I told you to *stop . . .*"

The next few seconds were a blur. She tossed the firespark in the air, held out her hands, and screamed one word—I couldn't catch what—and a wall of flame came writhing out of her palms. Green and gold and red, a beautiful, deadly burst of fire aimed in their direction, exploding the bomb into a shock wave of flame.

The men shouted and turned to run as the jets licked at their clothing, catching their gossamer tunics alight. The bushes around the portal began to smoke as sparks flew off, sizzling against the snow.

"Rhiannon, pull it back! Pull it back!" I raced over to her side, not sure how to help her restrain the fire that had so long been repressed. She was screaming now, as the flames licked out of her hands, and her eyes had gone wide like a deer caught in the headlights.

"Move!" The voice came from the huckleberry bush to the right, and Chatter emerged. "I'll help her."

He pressed one hand against her arm and she gave him a dazed look. As he began to whisper to her, the flames lessened, and within a few seconds, she sucked them back into herself.

"Now, run—you've bought yourself time, but you've got to get out of here." He bit his lip, looking at all of us. "I can help—I can take one of you. I can run a lot faster than any of you."

"Take Rhiannon. Now!" I shoved her into his arms and she complied, still dazed. He turned and, in a blur, they were gone. "Kaylin, you get out of here on the astral."

"What about you two? I can take one of you—"

"I'll take her." Grieve emerged from the bushes, near where Chatter had been. "You take Leo and I'll bring Cicely."

I stared at him, open-mouthed. "How'd you find us?"

"I followed Chatter—did you really think I'd leave him alone with that crew from the Barrow around? Now shut up and get over here. We have to move before they come back through the portal." He opened his arms and, without another thought, I walked into his embrace, and then we were off in a blur of motion, with my Grieve holding me tight.

# Chapter 17

Grieve swept me up in his arms, and pressed me against his chest as we made a beeline through the wood, faster than I could have ever imagined. While neither vampire nor Fae walked the astral, they could run like the wind—a blur of speed and movement.

I leaned against him, breathing in the intoxicating scent of autumn dreams and bonfires and old ink and pungent earth. The cadence of his heartbeat was different than my own, but he was still alive and breathing. The Vampiric Fae of the Indigo Court scared me speechless, but Grieve hadn't started out as one of them—and I still didn't believe he had been totally won over by his new nature. He wouldn't be helping us if he had been.

We flew through the trees; they went past us in a blur of snow on boughs and gnarled branches and the steady fall of flakes softly drifting down from the clouds. Wind whistled through my hair, streaking it back as we ran. A bevy of whispers whistled past, a flurry of voices buffeting my ears as we raced through the forest. I tried to catch what they were saying but the cacophony was too loud, and finally, I gave up trying.

And then, we were at the ravine, and down and up the other side, and into the yard. Grieve didn't stop, though, not until we reached the porch and I suddenly found myself standing in front of the screen door. Rhiannon was on the other side, waiting, and she opened the door and yanked me in. Grieve followed.

"Have Kaylin and Leo made it back yet?" I asked, a little breathless from the trip.

Rhiannon shook her head. "Not yet." Her face was flushed, and she blew a strand of hair back from her eyes as she nodded to the living room. "Chatter's in there, Grieve."

"Give us a minute, would you?" I put my hand on Grieve's arm. "I need to talk to you."

He followed me into the kitchen. A fervorish light in his eyes broke through the sullen expression lingering in his face. He glanced over his shoulder and then turned back to me. "What is it?"

"Grieve." I took a step toward him. "Thank you. Thank you for saving me. Thank you for letting Chatter help us."

"I had to. I can't let her hurt you, and yet I can't break free of her spell." Grieve gazed into my eyes. "Cicely, I'm so torn between duty and my heart. You make me break every instinct my body pushes me toward." His voice cracked.

And then I was in his arms, seeking his lips. "I love you, Grieve. I always have. I can't help it. You're my enemy but I need you. We need each other."

"How can you be so sure?" he whispered roughly. He wasn't smiling, but the faint curve of his lip was more than I could bear. "How can you know we aren't making a mistake that could cost you your life?"

"I don't care. I know you're dangerous—to both your-self and to me. But we are linked . . . and I don't think there's anything we can do to stop it." I threw my arms around his neck and pulled him to me.

His hands slid over my back, over my ass, leaving a trail of sparks wherever he touched. I sought his lips.

One hand fisting my hair, he darted his tongue between my lips as he fastened his mouth on mine. His touch was silk and fire as the kiss raged through my body, soaking into every pore, every inch of my skin. I moaned softly as he slid one knee between my legs and pressed me back against the counter.

I closed my legs around his, feeling the muscles under his jeans, feeling the power wrapped up in his taut, lean body. He held me fast, his lips moving from my mouth to my cheek, then to my neck where he raked his tongue over my skin, setting off a new series of explosions. His teeth grazed the soft skin there, and I felt a thin trickle of blood run free as he nipped lightly. When his saliva hit the raw skin, a growing warmth sucked me under, spreading through my system like a dark drug. And yet, I had no sense of being a bloodwhore, of being *used*.

Breathing heavy, I pressed against his chest as his hands slid under my shirt to cup my breasts. He rubbed his fingers over my bra as he lapped the thin trail of blood dripping from my neck. The soft slide of his tongue against my skin both irritated and aroused me— there was a sandpaper quality to it, a slight grating and I couldn't get my mind off what it was like to feel that tongue elsewhere.

My wolf growled, low and with pleasure.

Grieve reached for my buckle and I let out a whimper. "Not here, not in plain sight, please."

He quit tugging on the belt. "I forget. The Fae aren't

modest about sex. But Cicely—I want you. I want you now."

Reason hammered against the fog. There was a group of Indigo Fae out to kill us, and here we were, standing in the middle of the kitchen, making out.

"Stop—please, just for now. I need to make sure Kaylin and Leo make it home safely." I pushed against his chest. Damn it, I didn't *want* to stop, not even though I knew he was tasting my blood. I wanted to strip him right here, pull him down on the floor, and fuck his brains out.

He struggled for a moment to hold me, but then lifted his head, his platinum hair falling forward to graze my face, and let go, trembling as I stepped back. A drop of my blood remained on his lips, and his eyes were glowing.

"You taste so good. I want you—all of you, again and again."

His teeth showed, needle-sharp and brilliant white, but I had lost my fear. Whether it was shock from the close call, or just the feeling that *we* were inevitable, I had to trust that he was on our side—as much as he could be.

I shivered, suddenly cold. "I . . . oh, Grieve, I don't know what the fuck I'm getting myself into but I love you."

Before he could respond, I pulled down my shirt, turned, and darted into the living room. Rhiannon was sitting beside Chatter on the sofa and they looked up at me in unison, Chatter with a worried expression on his face, Rhiannon—questioning.

"Have Kaylin and Leo gotten—" Before I could finish, there was a noise at the door and I stiffened. A second later, Leo and Kaylin burst in, slamming the door behind them. Kaylin looked utterly exhausted.

"We lost them, I think. But they know where we live. We have to ward the house and the land. There's no other way to keep them out."

"We'd better start warding the land. I think we have a book about protection spells in that pile over there." I rifled through the stack until I found a grimoire dedicated to purification and protection spells.

"I think I saw something in here when I was leafing through . . . here it is. A spell for warding an estate. We'll need of lot of quartz crystals—they don't have to be large but they have to be spiked on at least one end. We'll need garlic . . . crap . . . *a lot of garlic*, and sulfur, and blood. Our blood."

At that moment, Grieve joined us, slipping his arm around my waist. I leaned back against him and he pressed his lips to my head.

"Cicely, do you realize your neck's bleeding?" Leo pointed to my shirt and I glanced in the bronze-framed mirror on the wall. A trail of red droplets slowly dripped from my neck down my right shoulder to stain my shirt.

Kaylin stared at me. Hard. But he didn't say a word. Leo looked pissed. They both gave Grieve a cold once-over but said nothing more.

"I'll just go clean up," I said, suddenly feeling uncomfortable.

"I'll come with you," Grieve said.

I knew that one step inside my bedroom would be all it would take. I shook my head and pressed my hand against his chest. "Please, wait here. We've got to ward this place before your newfound family sends out a hunting party after us."

"They're more likely to attack the house at night, with all of you here sleeping," Grieve said. "While you change, Chatter and I'll have a little talk about just how we're going to handle this when we have to go back to the Barrow. With a little luck, the Shadow Hunters won't know we helped you escape."

I turned to Kaylin. "Tell Leo and Rhiannon what we

saw. Tell them *who* we saw." And then, I hit the stairs before anybody could say a word.

⚜

By the time I rinsed off my neck and changed my T-shirt for a cami, I felt relatively back to normal. Dreamwalking with Kaylin, and then Grieve's passion had thrown me into a tailspin. I wasn't sure just what the hell to expect next—I just knew that there was no walking away from Grieve, not now.

As I headed down the stairs, I heard a shriek. *Rhiannon!* I leapt over the last five stairs, landing in a crouch, and raced into the living room.

"What's going on? What happened?" I glanced around the room, expecting to see something horrible, yet all I saw was Leo holding her against his chest. But the smell of smoke alerted me.

"Look over there." Leo nodded to one of the chairs.

The upholstery was soaked through, an upturned pan on the floor next to it. A large burn mark scorched the seat. Kaylin gave me a sideways shake of the head and gave a slight nod at my cousin. Oh shit, she'd caught the chair on fire.

"Rhiannon? Did you do that?" I sat down on the other side of her and took her hands in mine.

She nodded. "Yeah, I did. I was arguing with Leo about Chatter and . . . the chair caught on fire. I told you that once I unleashed it, I wouldn't be able to control it."

It was then that I realized Grieve and Chatter were nowhere to be seen. "Where are the two of them, anyway?"

"Out on the porch, talking." She sniffled. "You're right. I have to learn how to master this. Now that the fire's loose, there's no way I can stuff it back down. I get angry and it wells up inside." Gazing at her hands, she turned them palm up in mine.

"I can kill, Cicely. If I don't learn how to deal with this, I can kill without even blinking an eye. I've done it before, I can do it again. Long ago, Marta said they should burn out my powers before I ever fucked up again. Maybe she was right."

"Don't ever say that!" I dropped her hands and grabbed her shoulders, shaking her gently. "You will learn to control this and you will master the flames that are burning inside of you."

She studied my face, searching. "Do you really believe that?"

"Yes. Yes, I believe it." I looked over at Leo, and his jealous face confirmed my suspicions on just what had caused the argument. "We'll ask Chatter to help you. He taught you when you were a child, he can do so again."

"No—" Leo started to say but I stopped him with a single glance.

"Don't *even* go there. *You* can't help her. And Kaylin and I don't work with flame so *we* can't. Chatter's our best bet at this point."

*And just because you're jealous, dude, doesn't mean you can stop her from getting the help she needs,* I thought.

"What about the idea of asking Anadey?" Leo's lips were thin and white and little lines flared around the edges of his eyes. Oh yeah, he had it bad and he was aware enough to recognize that Chatter had eyes for my cousin.

I looked at Rhiannon. "It's up to you—either we ask Chatter, or we go to Anadey's this evening and ask her for help. Whichever you choose is fine by me, but we have to get you help and it has to be soon."

She debated, glancing at Leo, then at the front door. After a moment she whispered, "I guess we'd better ask Anadey first. If she can't help me, then maybe Chatter will."

Leo visibly relaxed. "Good choice," he muttered, but I gave him another look and he shut up. The last thing we needed were testosterone wars running rampant around here.

At that moment, Grieve and Chatter returned.

"We'd best be gone and back to the Barrow," Grieve said. "They'll be expecting us."

"What if they know you two were the ones who helped us get away?" I held his gaze, not wanting him to go, wanting to go upstairs and do unspeakable things with every inch of him.

"Don't worry—they won't. I promise you. But you need to guard this house or get yourselves away from here before nightfall." He lifted my chin, reaching down to kiss me lightly. I ignored Leo's and Kaylin's bristling, and draped my arms around his shoulders, letting him lift me to my feet as the kiss intensified.

Heady. He tasted like summer wine and incense and wild mushrooms and cinnamon, and I let out a faint groan. Grieve sucked in a deep breath and leaned his head back, his teeth glistening and sharp, ready for the strike.

"Grieve—" Chatter's timid voice broke through the sex haze I was drifting in and I gently tapped Grieve on the shoulder.

He held me fast for another minute, staring into my eyes, a triumphant smirk on his face, then he let go and—without a word—turned to leave. Chatter mumbled a hasty farewell, and before we could blink, they were gone from the house and I closed the door behind them.

❈

I turned back to the others.

"Don't say it. Don't say a word. Grieve and I . . . We are whatever it is we're becoming, and like it or not, he and I are linked."

"You *want* it to be that way," Leo said, a slight accusatory tone in his voice. "Don't trust him, Cicely. He's one of *them*."

"No! Yes . . . but not fully . . ." Frustrated, I kicked at the burnt chair. "I can't explain this. Grieve and I have some sort of bond that formed long before he was turned by the Indigo Court. Why else would I have the wolf guardian tattoo and why else would he have a tattoo of me on his thigh? I trust him . . . as far as I can."

"Fine," Leo said abruptly. "You trust him, okay. But what are you going to do about balancing your work for Regina and the Crimson Court, and your feelings for Grieve?"

"It's not like I forgot about the vampires. Trust me, dude. I'm as confused as you are and whatever I do has to straddle both worlds. And I have to decide whether to tell Grieve about it."

"You're going to feed Grieve the information that you're spying on him and his people? How stupid can you be?" Leo jumped up. "I don't care if you fuck him. But are you forgetting the little matter that Grieve's new family kidnapped your aunt and my sister and our friend Peyton? Did you forget *all of them*?" His face contorted and then he punched the air and took off toward the stairs.

"Leo—" I started, but Rhiannon stopped me.

"No, let him go. He's just angry and worked up. I'll try to calm him down. I understand both sides, unfortunately." She turned and raced after him.

Helplessly, I turned to Kaylin. "Is he right? Am I just not seeing things clearly?"

He sidled over to me. "Little girl, you aren't seeing anything but the sheets."

I bristled at the "little girl" but he just snorted.

"Remember, I'm one hundred and one years old. I can call you 'little girl' or 'little child' or 'wayward brat' if I want to, as long as you're younger than me."

"You really think so, do you?"

"I've got seventy-five years on you, Cicely—never forget that, even though I look your age. Rhiannon's right. And you're right. You and Grieve do have a connection. But I also believe that he has you under his power. Probably a venom in his fangs. The Fae of the Indigo Court are extremely seductive, and they inherited the vampire's ability to seduce along with their own natural charms, which pretty much makes them rocket scientists when it comes to sex."

Without thinking, I reached up to touch the grazed skin on my neck. Was Kaylin right? Was Grieve playing a game with me? The memory of his touch, his tongue on my neck swept me under again and I let out a soft moan as I pressed the skin where he'd bitten me.

"Hell, woman, you're lucky I have any honor," Kaylin whispered.

My eyes fluttered open. He was staring at me intently, and I could tell he was aroused right through those tight jeans of his. Blushing, I lowered my hand. "I'm sorry . . . I don't know . . ."

"You *reek* of desire. I can smell you from here. And the look on your face—you're begging to be fucked." He shook his head when I started to protest. "Save it. I'm not standing on ceremony because if I was any other man—a man with a weaker will—we'd be on the floor right now and I'd be screwing your brains out. You'd better go take a cold shower and think long and hard about the situation."

Stunned, angry, I made my way up to my room, where I stripped off my clothes, then hit the shower. I scrubbed the slightly sore wound on my neck—and every other part of my body—with a vanilla body wash, thinking about what Kaylin had said. As I stood under the pounding water for a good half hour, my thoughts began to clear.

*Fuck. Could Kaylin be right?*

After a while, I stepped out of the shower and dried off, feeling self-conscious. Maybe Grieve was on our side—I wanted to believe it. But could we risk Heather's and Peyton's lives if my feelings for Grieve were due to a powerful aphrodisiac in my system?

Slowly pulling on a clean cami and pair of jeans, I

let out a long breath. Truth was, my heart wouldn't let me walk away. And neither would the vampires. They wanted information and I was apparently their conduit. I was caught between two enemies, a pawn for one and in love with the other.

I headed down the stairs, a dozen questions racing through my mind.

Leo and Rhiannon were back in the living room with Kaylin, and they all looked at me as I entered the room. I gave them a wary look.

"I'm sorry. I . . ."

"Kaylin explained what might be going on," Rhiannon said. She was holding *The Rise of the Indigo Court* in her hands. "I skimmed through. Listen to this:"

*Like true vampires, the Vampiric Fae developed a venom in their bite. But the venom is specifically focused. The mutation happened when the first Unseelie were turned. The Fae's sexual powers were infused into the toxin and the controlling focus became of a sexual nature rather than the ability to create general suggestions. In other words, a member of the Indigo Court can sexually enslave someone through their bite. With the true vampires, the suggestion can be of any sort—from something as simple as handing over money to killing oneself. The primary difference, besides the sexual component, is that the venom of true vampires will wear off after a while unless a mutual blood bond is created. But the Indigo Court Fae venom is cumulative and at some point the victim will be hopelessly enslaved, unable to break free. The number of bites this takes is unknown.*

She glanced up at me. "How many times has he bitten you?"

My stomach churned. My feelings couldn't *all* be the

result of a drug, could they? There was a link between us—
we'd proven that.

I shrugged. "Just once . . . twice maybe?"

"You can't let him keep biting you," Leo said.

"At least, not until we find out just whose side he's on,"
Rhiannon added softly. I jerked my attention to her and
she gave me a soft smile. She understood.

*She understands better than any of them,* Ulean's
voice whispered low behind me. *Truth be, there is a danger with Grieve, but not in the manner that they think.*

I wanted to protest, but decided to just roll with it. "I'll
be careful. I won't say anything to him about working
with Regina without talking to all of you." I let out a long
breath, about to head into the kitchen for a bite to eat
when the doorbell rang. "You expecting anybody?"

They shook their heads. I slowly crossed to the door,
but then it occurred to me that the Indigo Court wouldn't
just come knocking. They'd forcibly abducted Heather,
they wouldn't politely ring the bell.

I opened the door but there was no one there. Curious,
I opened the screen door and peeked out, and then I saw
it. On the porch—a huge basket filled to the brim with
what looked like expensive treats.

Reaching out, I poked it with my foot. Nothing moved
or exploded. Finally, I picked it up and carried it into the
living room. The sucker was heavy and I set it down on
the coffee table.

"Apparently, somebody likes us," I said. "Christmas is
still a couple weeks away but it looks like we got a present early."

"Who's it from?" Rhiannon leaned forward.

"I don't know. Let me see if there's a card. Meanwhile,
is there anything to eat? I'm starving." I cautiously opened
the cellophane holding everything inside. I wasn't used to
presents. Krystal's idea of a birthday or Yule gift had been
along the lines of a Happy Meal or a quarter-ounce of pot.

"I'll start dinner," Leo said. "Let me know what it is—and yell if you need me. Rhiannon, why don't you call Anadey?" He headed into the kitchen.

The cellophane wrap was held together by a large burgundy ribbon and bow. I unfastened them and laid them to the side, then peeled the wrap away. As I began to lift out boxes of expensive chocolates and cookies, and imported cheeses and candy—all still tightly wrapped in their original wrappings—I finally saw a card in a crimson envelope. I quietly opened the seal, which was formed of a gold wax with flakes of crimson.

*You know who it's from.* Ulean was behind me, I could feel the gentle breeze of her breath blowing on my ear. An entirely different sensation than when Grieve did it.

*Oh, I know.*

I knew who had sent the basket before I even touched the card, which sported a beautiful bouquet of red roses on the front. As I flipped it open, sloping writing— curved, elegant calligraphy—shone out in red.

*From the Crimson Court to Ms. Cicely Waters & Friends.*

————

*Just a token to celebrate our partnership. Here's wishing for a long and happy connection. Your first blood tithe is due the night after next—please meet Lannan Altos in his office at the New Forest Conservatory on Sunday evening. He will have your first month's salary in advance at that time.*

————

*Best, Regina Altos*
*Emissary to the Crimson Court.*

Fuck. I looked up from the note. I'd hoped for a month or so to adapt to the idea but their message was clear. They owned me, blood, stock, and barrel.

And it was time to pay the piper.

# Chapter 18

I tried to underplay the note. No use getting Rhiannon upset. Meanwhile, we needed to go talk to Anadey and tell her what we'd found out about Peyton and ask if she could help Rhiannon. We called and she agreed to meet us the next morning at her house. We spent the rest of the evening strengthening the wards around the house and playing Scrabble.

The next morning, while Leo and Kaylin volunteered to stay home and try to pull together some sort of protection for the land itself, Rhiannon and I jumped into Favonis and headed for Anadey's apartment.

She was hunched over the table when we quietly entered at her *Come in*, teacup in hand, looking ten years older than when I'd met her the first day. She gazed up at us, her eyes still red from crying. "Any news?"

It was clear she was afraid to ask, but had to.

"Some. We found their hideout, thanks to Grieve. But we had to get out of there before we were caught. Heather and Peyton were both there, alive." And I prayed they still were, after our bumbling efforts. What if Myst had killed them to punish us for our intrusion? It seemed like something she might do.

We told Anadey about our trip, swearing her to silence when we described Kaylin's abilities.

She pushed back her teacup and let out a long sigh. "Okay, so I need to quit moping and do something to help save my daughter. If you have the courage to take on the Indigo Court, I have to find my own will. I'm not sure what use I can be, though. My magic's a lot more subtle than my mother's was. I work with all the elements, but I tend to do so on a more . . . molecular level. It's hard to describe. I don't cast spells so much as rearrange events."

"I wish you could time hop and rearrange Heather and Peyton being captured." I sighed. Time jumping was rare and usually only allowed one to view events, not to interfere in them.

"If I could, do you think I wouldn't have already tried?" Anadey shook her head. "There are more powers in the universe than we can hope to ever understand. And some I hope we never fully know about."

"Anadey, I have a favor to ask." Rhiannon leaned across the table. "I need help. I need your help. The fire's been unleashed from where I hid it all these years. I'm having troubles controlling it now."

Anadey blinked. "Marta told me about you—about the car incident. I wondered how long it would be before you'd open up to the energies again. You can't ever suppress something like this for good. Mother thought you had managed to eradicate it, but I knew better. That's one place we differed."

She stood up and motioned for us to follow her into the kitchen, where she rinsed out her cup and offered us peppermint cookies. "These are Peyton's favorites. I guess I thought . . . maybe if I made a batch they would act like some charm to call her home."

Accepting one of the cookies, I debated whether to ask a question that had been running through my mind. Finally, I decided that it couldn't hurt. "You didn't get along too well with Marta, did you?" I asked.

Anadey let out a stiff laugh. "My mother and I never saw eye to eye, which is one reason she never gave me entrance to her precious Society. The Thirteen Moons Society—at least this branch—was dead before it began, and what remains is a shadow of what they could have had if they'd quit being such asses. Your mother never fully belonged," she added to Rhiannon.

"What do you mean?"

"Heather tried Marta's patience, she was willing to step outside the box. Marta kept a tight rein on the leadership in fear that Heather would take over at some point, before she was ready. I know she was hoping Cicely would come home and take over, but she had no clue just what you had become, my dear."

It hurt to hear her point out my weaknesses. "I never had anybody to teach me how to practice my magic the right way," I said, my words clipped to keep the pain from my voice.

Anadey shook her head. "Oh heavens, do you think I'm criticizing you? Not at all. You have no concept how far you've come by working solitary, teaching yourself through experience. You're far stronger than you believe. For one thing, you didn't have anybody to teach you the *right way* to do things, so you never believed you were doing them *wrong*."

While I thought over what she had said, Rhiannon quietly took over, rinsing our cookie saucers. After a moment, she dried her hands on a tea towel and turned back to Anadey.

"So, can you help me? *Will* you help me?"

Anadey let out a long sigh and nodded. "Yes, but you have to agree to several conditions. You must put yourself in my hands. You must listen to me. I won't teach you the standard practices toward harnessing your powers, but I will help you find the best way for *you*. Every witch is different, every spell caster and sorcerer needs to learn their own path if they are to truly coexist with the energies they have locked inside them. Whatever you might call yourself, you're of the magic-born, and you're a daughter of the fire. Will you take direction from me, even when you're afraid?"

Rhiannon gazed into Anadey's face, the fearful look that was in her eyes beginning to slide away. "I will."

"Then we begin work tomorrow—Sunday, so be here at sunrise and prepare to stay all day. We'll fast-track you. And, both of you, if there's anything I can do to help bring my daughter home, you will let me know? Because somehow, for some reason, Cicely, I think you are at the heart of this and both Heather's and Peyton's safety rests on your shoulders."

Wearing such a heavy cloak of responsibility weighed me down. As I left the apartment, I glanced back to see Anadey waving through the window. At least Rhiannon would get the help she needed to rope in her powers, to use them instead of letting them use her.

❖

By the time we got home, Leo and Kaylin had warded the land as best as they could. It felt better—stronger, like we had a cushion separating us from the forest. I decided to spend the afternoon combing the pages of *A History of the Vampire Nation*, while Rhiannon flipped through the *The Rise of the Indigo Court*.

We needed to familiarize ourselves with both bloody worlds as much as possible. Most of the texts seemed Biblical, in that there were long lists of names—who begat whom and who sired whom—and brief encounters by people who had lived and died centuries ago.

The afternoon slid by and as evening arrived, Kaylin and Leo made a beeline for the local fried chicken joint and returned with a couple of buckets of chicken and biscuits. As they came through the door, I looked up.

"You made sure that they don't have any cross contamination with fish there, right?"

Rhiannon nodded. "Not a problem. Not a fin or scale in the joint. Just chicken." She sat the food on the table and gathered some napkins and plates for us. "What are you doing?"

"Reading till my eyes have crossed. And I finally found something that I think we need to know. Listen." I reached for a drumstick with one hand as I held the book open with the other.

*The Najeeling Prophecy (see Chapter 7: Examining the Book of the Undead) speaks of a member of the Indigo Court who will rise to power, hand-in-hand with his traitorous love. Together, they will bring about the necessary events that will set in motion the final war in which the Vampire Nation will go to war with the Indigo Court. The outcome of the war is not known; the investigator who translated the Book of the Undead died in a freak accident before he could finish his translation, and the actual Book of the Undead disappeared.*

"I think this is talking about Grieve and me." I tapped the book with my other hand as I took a bite of the drumstick. Though the word "traitorous" made me uneasy.

"How can you be sure, though?"

"Crap. I knew I forgot something." With all the commotion, I realized I still hadn't told them about my meeting with Crawl. Quickly, I sketched out my visit to the Blood Oracle. "I was going to tell you earlier, but with Grieve . . . and the visit to the Marburry Barrow, it got lost in the scuffle."

"You went to see the Blood Oracle and you didn't think it was important to tell us? Christ, Cicely, you can't just shut us out of stuff like that. We're all in this together, you know." Leo looked huffy and I was beginning to see that he *really* didn't like feeling left out of things. Either that or he was feeling touchy because until I'd returned, the vampires were his territory.

"I meant to tell you, and I just did. So much is happening, it's hard to keep everything sorted out. But yes, Crawl seems to think I'm 'the one' and I have a feeling that this connects to what he was talking about." I shrugged. "Like it or not, the vampires think I'm their special-needs girl. Frankly, I'd rather be anonymous to them. *This* is why they want me to spy on the Indigo Court—they think that by doing so I'll start this big war between the two and they expect to come out victorious."

"Meanwhile, members of the Indigo Court are kidnapping the magic-born to create their own army of vampiric magic using slaves to fight in the war. Think of the chaos if they manage to harness a group of witches as powerful as Marta and Heather—the havoc they could wreak." Leo rubbed the bridge of his nose and I knew he was thinking about his sister.

"They'd be almost invincible." I stopped as Ulean touched my shoulder.

*Something is happening outside. You need to attend to it. Be cautious. They're approaching.*

"Trouble, guys. Ulean just warned me." I put down the book and the food, and cautiously peeked out the front door, Rhiannon on my heels. There was something—I could feel it—on the periphery of the land.

"Wait," I whispered.

She paused, glancing over my shoulder. "Something out there?"

I nodded. Turning, I scanned the yard, not sure what to look for. *Ulean, can you hear me?*

*Yes . . . over at the boundary. Leo and Kaylin did their work well, they cannot approach.*

*What's out there? I can hear it . . . feel it.*

Ulean whisked past me, leaving me with the dizzying scent of lavender and lemon, calming and yet invigorating. It washed away some of the gloom from my aura and I inhaled deeply, letting out a slow breath while I waited. After a moment, she returned.

*You come to a crossroads . . . be careful, Cicely. Please, don't rush into action. Listen carefully. Words carry deception even if they come from someone you love.*

A shiver raced down my spine. What the hell was going on? I slowly descended the steps, Rhiannon behind me. Leo and Kaylin followed.

As we crossed the yard toward the ravine, I felt like we were standing on the edge of a precipice, over a crashing ocean full of sharp, jagged rocks. And one of those rocks was rising to meet us.

Out of the ravine, trailed by a cloud of mist that swirled in their wake, walked five figures. The mist was quicksilver, sparkling indigo, and gray, coiling like serpents in the chill night. The forest fell silent, at least to the ear, but I caught sounds on the wind: the spinning of webs, the shuffle of spiders, the rustle of twisted creatures who had no names.

I stepped over the hose, and when it hissed and became a snake, I forced myself to avoid looking down. Rhiannon gave a little gasp from behind me but I kept walking, my shoes squeaking lightly on the snow. My gaze was fastened on the figures, silhouettes in the night, but their auras were shining with brilliant swirls of cerulean and silver.

*The Indigo Court.*

We approached one another, across the lawn, but they

stopped fifteen yards from the edge of the forest, waiting. As I gauged their distance, I realized they'd stopped right at the line where the men had warded the property. They'd done a good job: The enemy could not pass.

I kept walking and Rhiannon caught up to me, pacing by my side. Kaylin and Leo had our backs and we came to a halt a few yards away from the shrouded figures. I held up my hand and waited. Let them be the first to speak.

One member of their party stepped forward. A woman, from what I could see through the mists that surrounded them like a tangle of living, writhing webs. She stepped forward, dressed in long robes, and then I saw the tumbling red locks that cascaded down her shoulders.

*Heather. Heather, it was Heather, oh great gods, my aunt, and she was a vampire.*

Heather's face was pale as cream, pale as the silver moon, and her lips were rosebud red. Her eyes sparkled black, with the stars of the Indigo Court shining in them.

"Heather!" Rhiannon's cry shattered the night. "No! No!" She screamed then, the fractured pain of her voice spiraling higher and higher. "No, tell me it's not true . . . tell me you aren't one of them!"

Heather turned to her, and a faint look of pity washed over her face, and then was gone. "I'm still your mother—"

"You're *not* my mother! You're a demon creature—filthy vampire!"

And then, Rhiannon raised her hands and her palms crackled with flame. She thrust them forward, the fire racing off of her hands toward Heather, who leapt nimbly to the side. The flames engulfed a small juniper plant, but the snow-covered foliage sizzled and the fire went out.

"You'd best get her out of here." Heather turned to me. "*Now.*"

Too numb to even blink, I turned sharply and motioned

to Leo, who jumped forward to grab Rhiannon by the shoulders. He wrestled her back to the house.

"Heather." I took one step forward, looking to see if Peyton was with the others. I couldn't see any sign of her, though. "It's true then. You're one of *them*."

"Technically, I belong to Myst. She made me an offer I couldn't refuse." A vague look of discomfort crossed her face. "Cicely, they've asked me to speak to you tonight."

I glanced at her companions. Two women, two men— obviously born into the Court. Their skin bore the same cerulean cast that we'd seen in those at the Marburry Barrow. And Heather . . . she was a vampire now, with magical powers. Their slave.

"Why did you let them turn you?" I couldn't help the words, they flew out of my mouth like a swarm of moths toward a light. "What could they possibly offer you to make you give in to them?"

A soft smile spread across her face. "Sometimes, we are given choices. And sometimes, the choice we make is not one we would choose for ourselves, but one we make for others."

Listening to her words, trying to read the wind behind them, I could sense her hidden meanings. She had been backed into this choice.

*The lesser of two evils.* Ulean was by my side. *She chose Peyton's life over her own.*

I closed my eyes for a moment, trying to sort through the illusions. Kaylin, standing beside me, rested his hand on my shoulder and I drew on his strength, welcoming the flow of energy that shored me up.

"Why are you here? What do you want?"

Heather bowed her head. "We bring you a warning."

She stepped aside, and one of the men stepped forward. He looked similar to my Grieve, and yet he was so unlike my love that it frightened me. Grieve struggled against his nature, but this man—here I saw only alien aloofness, a cold ruthless spark that raced from his eyes to his mouth.

"You are being given fair warning by Myst, the ruler of this wood. We know you seek to interfere with our affairs. Be warned that should you continue, we will turn Peyton. For now she is safe, but defy us and we'll destroy every friend and family member you have, and then yourselves. We let you live because your aunt agreed to join our Court if we gave you protection. But that protection ends if you attempt to intervene in the coming war."

I stared at him, and bone-weary, snorted. "What about Peyton?"

"She is alive. For now. Her freedom at this time is not up for discussion."

"Oh yes, it is. Hell, you've already destroyed our families. We're the only ones left. Tell your Queen that you've done your job. Mission accomplished. We've been warned."

"And your response, milady?" For all of his churlishness, he bowed politely.

I glanced at Kaylin, who gave me a single nod.

"Tell Myst to mind her webs and spiders. And tell her that we'll repay her for the *kindness* she's shown my aunt, and Leo's sister. And if Peyton comes to harm, we'll burn down the wood—tear it apart limb by bough by leaf. You go back and you tell Myst that the Indigo Court might rule the forest, but once you step on our land, *I'm Queen here*. And I walk with the Vein Lords at my back, so don't think it will be so easy to destroy us."

The ambassador stared at me for a moment, then nodded. "As you wish, Cicely Waters, but we are not finished yet. I advise you: Don't count on your allies so much that you leave yourself unarmed. Our enemies may still run this town, but we are a force you *should not cross*."

With one last look at Heather, who stared at me

steadfast, unblinking, I turned, striding back to the house. Kaylin fell in behind me. We didn't dare show fear, didn't dare look back. By the time we got to the house, the group of Shadow Hunters had retreated back into the night.

# Chapter 19

Leo and Rhiannon were on the sofa; he was trying to calm her and she was waxing between fury and hysteria. I held her hands, tight, trying to talk her down from the emotional roller coaster she was riding. After a little while and two minor fires—one on a footstool and the other on Heather's jacket that was still hanging by the door—between Leo and me, we managed to soothe her back into a coherent state. I put in a call to Anadey to tell her what had happened and relay Rhiannon's reaction.

"She needs to be with me tonight. I can make her sleep without her dreams playing havoc on the subconscious. Bring her over to Marta's house and I'll take care of her tonight."

"Hold on." I punched the mute button and told the others what she'd said.

"But will they be protected there?" Leo glanced at Rhiannon. "I don't have anything pressing tonight. Maybe I should go with her."

I didn't like the thought of staying at the Veil House alone and was about to say so when Kaylin spoke up.

"If you do, I'll stay here and help guard Cicely."

Part of me bristled at the thought that I needed guarding, but the reality was: If the vampires and Vampiric Fae were going to war, and they both believed I was a catalyst to start that war, I could use a few good men on my side.

"Fine. I'm sorry, Rhia, but I just don't trust your subconscious not to let loose on the place. Anadey wanted you over there at sunrise, anyway. You can get a jump on your training that way."

Rhiannon nodded, pale and looking worn out. "I'm sorry to be such a bother. But you're right. I don't know if I can be trusted in my sleep. Not with what's happened. Are you sure you'll be okay here with Kaylin?"

I glanced at the dreamwalker. His aura was flaring and I could see the energy spiraling off of him. He was on high alert and his parents were standing behind him. "Yeah. We should be fine. Leo, take her over to Anadey's now, before it gets any darker. Don't stop to pack, you'll only be gone for a night."

Without another word, Leo ushered her out to his car and they pulled out of the driveway. As I watched them go, I had the uneasy feeling the night was just beginning.

*⁜*

*The owl is waiting in the woods.*

Ulean brushed against me. I glanced up from the table. Kaylin and I had finished dinner, and we were now sorting out spell components from Marta's stash. I still had bag after bag to go through, but at least I knew now that I was sitting on a treasure trove. Between Leo, Rhiannon, and I, we should be able to come up with a number of spells and charms to help protect the town of New Forest. The question was: Would we live that long?

*Cicely . . . the owl is waiting for you. I know it's dark, but you need to answer its summons. It will fly in from Myst's wood to meet you.*

*What . . . ? The owl?* Blinking, I put down the packet of tiny gems I was sorting through. None were terribly valuable; mostly a lot of semiprecious gem chips and cabochons.

"I'll be back. I won't go far and definitely not outside the perimeter of the land, but there's something I need to check on." I pushed out of my chair before Kaylin could stop me and grabbed my jacket. Before I headed outside, I ran upstairs and snatched up my owl feather, firmly tucking it inside my pocket, and then for good measure, I stuck my stiletto in the boot sheath I always wore on my boots, then headed outside.

I jogged down the cobblestone path, through the gardens at the back of the house. I wasn't sure what I was looking for but I'd know it when I saw it. As I gazed across the lawn to the ravine, I heard a faint *hoot*. Shit, the owl was there.

*Who are you, and what do you want with me?*

*I'm waiting. I'm waiting for you. Don't tarry too long.* The feel of the thought was masculine, though I couldn't be sure. Another wind Elemental?

*No, not another Elemental. I don't know who this one is.* Ulean's words drifted over me, cool and calm. No sense of danger.

And then I remembered what Chatter had said. *The owl's been looking for you, by the way . . . He asks for you, every day. I'd help, but I'm just . . . don't count on me. I'm useless. But soon, you must find the owl. If the Shadow Hunters find it, they'll kill it. They hate owls.*

If the Indigo Court hated the owls, then I'd probably like them.

Pulled, not knowing why but only knowing I must follow, I made my way over to an oak, tall and barren against the winter sky, and jumped, catching hold of a lower limb. I swung myself up into the branches, and began to climb, following the whisper of current that led me on. I wasn't afraid of heights—I'd been running across building tops since I was twelve.

And then, I caught sight of it: a pendant, hanging from one of the branches. It was a milky white moonstone, set in silver on a black ribbon. The owl tattoos banding my arms set up a fuss and I jerked. I was used to my wolf talking to me, but the owls had never spoken—they'd always been silent before.

Slowly, I reached for the pendant. It resonated in my hand, setting up a keening, and the owl feather in my pocket began to vibrate so loud that I yanked it out, staring at the quivering plume. As I watched, it began to smoke, then burst into flames and with a shout I dropped it, watching as the fire quickly snuffed out on its way to the ground.

*What the hell is going on, Ulean?*

*I cannot tell you. This is a journey you must travel, without aid of my vision. But I am here if you need me.*

The pendant began to glow brightly as I held it to my chest. There was no aura of menace about it, no threat. Nervous, yet feeling for all the world that this was the right thing to do, I slid the ribbon over my head and, hesitating just an instant, let the gem come to rest against my breasts.

As it hung against my body, a cool breeze began to emanate from the gem. I clasped it in my hand, closing my eyes, trying to focus on the energy. The gem throbbed in my hand and I heard a faint noise, like the rustle of wings.

I slid deep into the pulsating beat that now echoed throughout my body. A faint music rose on the wind, the echo of an acoustic guitar, the driving rhythm of the drum . . . it crawled through me, resonated around me, flooded me from the inside out like paint rippling down a wall.

*I'll meet you in the forest. In the half light between daylight and dusk, we will meet. But first, you must spread your wings and fly, child.*

That wasn't Ulean.

In a daze, I climbed higher, listening to the strange voice crooning to me on the wind. Ulean began to howl, shrieking in some tongue I could not recognize, a cry of joy and feral pleasure, and her mania buoyed me up.

Higher I climbed, until I reached a branch a good forty feet off the ground. I edged out on it, shaking the snow off to the ground as I stared at the darkening sky and began to shed my clothing. I dropped my jacket and shirt, watching them plummet to the ground, then without thinking, shimmied out of my jeans and panties, and they, too, fell away to the bottom of the tree.

Shivering, I crouched naked on the branch, holding on to nearby limbs for balance. The clouds parted then, a thin sliver to show the brilliant moon shining through. Below, the mist was rising, rolling along the ground, seeping up the trunk like a blanket of soothing smoke.

Under the cloak of cloud and stars, I gazed up at the heavens, unable to think, unable to put words to my thoughts. The necklace beat a staccato tattoo on my soul, the music swirled around me, notes flooding the wind, and the call was too strong. I couldn't ignore it, couldn't shake it off. Inhaling a sharp breath, not knowing just what I was doing or why, I let go of the branch and went into free fall, heading toward the ground.

⚜

As I whistled through the air, something began to shift, and my body twisted inside out. A blink of an eye, and I was gliding silently on the currents, wingtips wide, zebra stripes of black and white. I opened my beak and let out a call, and the screech echoed through my body, raspy and shrill and enough to scare the hell out of every rat and mouse that might be hiding in the yard.

Then it hit me—I was aloft—in flight—gliding through the yard toward the woodland. But the ravine and the forest glowed with a light I'd never seen before, and I veered to my right, avoiding the tree line. There was something in there, something nasty that set traps for owls like me, and I wanted no part of it.

I sailed effortlessly, turning on a wing to glide back toward the house, seeing everything from a vastly different perspective but still retaining my sense of self. In fact, I felt far clearer than I ever had. The necklace still dangled around my throat and I knew that if I wasn't wearing it, I'd shift back into my human form again.

Sweeping over the house, I spiraled, circling around, then coming to land on the bough of the oak. There, near me, the great horned owl perched on the limb, talons gripping the bark. His eyes were whirling as he watched me. I could swear that I saw a tenderness in them, a welcoming home, and I let out another shriek and he answered.

He leapt off the tree, gliding low through the mist, and I followed. We flew in tandem, turning, twisting, spiraling aloft through the fog bank, then swept up again and across the face of the moon, as the true meaning of freedom flooded through my body. Nothing else mattered. Nothing else could mar the expansiveness of the world.

For sheer joy, I did a barrel roll and headed toward the ground, pulling up just in time. The horned owl followed me and we danced our dance. At one point, I saw Kaylin standing on the porch, my clothes in his arms, as he watched us cartwheeling on the wind.

*Ulean, are you here with me? I'm flying!*

*You are, my child. You are coming home to your true nature.*

*What do you mean?*

*There is time enough for that. We will talk later. For now, explore your new freedom, child of the wind.* And she laughed and her currents carried us forward as she rode the slipstream with us.

We passed through a host of spirits gliding through the yard and they dove to all sides, looking terrified as we shattered their composure.

*Can they see us?*

The other owl answered. *Yes, ghosts and owls are closely aligned. We are the creatures of dark magic. We ride in the wake of the Bean Sidhe. We bring tidings from the dead. Ghosts and spirits are part of our heritage.*

*Who are you? What is this? How am I doing this?*

*You, like your lover, are part Cambyra Fae. You are not just of the magic-born by birth, but half your heritage lies within the demonic Fae. Your father was one of the Uwilahsidhe, the owl people.*

Part Fae. *I was part Fae?* My mind tried to process the concept but I kept coming back to one thought. *You knew my father? What was he like? What is his name? Is he still alive?*

*Yes, I knew your father, and your mother, too. And yes, he still lives. His name is Wrath.*

*I want to meet him—is that possible?*

But the owl fell silent as we twisted another loop around the house and he came lightly to rest in the oak again. He let out a piercing call that sliced through the night and I answered.

*Not now. Not here. But he knows of you, girl. He knows of you.*

And then he leapt and dove, and we were off once

more, winging through the dark as he taught me to spread my wings and fly.

❧

Early toward morning, the owl landed on the eaves next to my room. I landed next to him, exhausted, desperately needing to rest. We'd flown through the night, turning, dipping, but ever-always avoiding Myst's forest.

*Time for you to return to your other form.*

I blinked. *My other form.* There had been points through the night when I'd forgotten I had another form.

*How do I do that? I can't get the pendant off.*

*Just focus on letting go. But do so inside or you'll topple off the roof.* Ulean's voice was clear, distinct from the owl's.

As I pondered how to get inside so I could try to change back, Kaylin showed up in my room and eased the window open. He gently reached out and I hopped on his arm, and then he lifted me inside and set me on the ground.

I waddled around, my talons uncomfortable on the hardwood floor, as I tried to figure out how to shift back.

*Just let go of the form . . .*

Ulean's comforting voice filtered through the slip-stream again and I hooted softly, grateful she could read me even though I'd shifted form.

*Just let go of the form . . .*

I calmed my thoughts, reached down deep. Consciously, I let the owl form dissolve, picturing myself as . . . me . . . *Blink.* A few seconds later, I toppled over on the floor, naked except for the necklace.

❧

I'll give Kaylin this much: Instead of staring at me, he immediately covered me with a blanket from the bottom of the bed. I slowly sat up, rubbing my head, which hurt like a son of a bitch. The necklace throbbed gently against my chest.

"Before we even start to discuss this, please go downstairs and get me a cup of tea." I slipped out of the blanket and into the thick terry robe that Rhiannon had loaned me. This time, Kaylin watched.

"Dude, eyes back in head." I stared at him and he let out a soft laugh.

"Sorry, but you aren't exactly hiding it."

"I just changed into an owl and flew around the yard for an hour or two or three. Why should I be thinking modesty after that? I mean, come on, it was . . ." I softened my voice, the sarcasm drifting away. "It was the most incredible thing that's ever happened to me."

He relented. "Sorry, but as old as I am, I'm still young compared to others like me. And you're . . . you have a magnetism about you that's hard to ignore. Cicely, what happened out there?"

"Tea first."

While I climbed into bed, shivering because now I felt cold all the way through, Kaylin dashed downstairs and returned ten minutes later with a tea tray holding a pot, two cups, and some toast and jam.

As we drank our tea and ate our toast, I told him everything. Told him about always feeling a connection to the owl, about getting the tattoos even though I didn't know why I had to, about the owl feather that I'd found on my pillow one morning, never questioning why it had come into my life, just accepting.

"The owl in the wood, he said I'm part Cambyra Fae, like Grieve. Can this be possible?" I stared at my hands, looking at them in a different way than I ever had before. I'd always known I was one of the magic-born, but having someone tell me I was part Fae was like finding out that I'd never really known who I was. I'd never known myself. Not fully.

"Possible? Yes. Likely? It seems so. What else could explain what happened? I suppose it could be an elaborate trap, but it doesn't feel like it to me." He made sure I was comfortable, then headed downstairs after securing my window and making sure the protection charms were strong over it.

As I stared out at the growing dawn, I tried to comb every inch of what had happened, but the beauty of the experience kept flooding in and pushing logic and thought to the side. Within half an hour, I found myself dozing off, and in my dreams, I soared with the great horned owl, still gliding the night sky.

# Chapter 20

The next morning, I was so stiff I could barely climb out of bed. At least, my arms were stiff. My shoulder muscles throbbed with a deep, pounding ache that I'd never quite felt before. I flashed back to the night before, wondering if it had been the transformation—if somehow my wings had been virginal and needed to stretch and carry me to build their strength.

Rhiannon was waiting downstairs, along with Leo and Kaylin. They all looked up at me and I realized Kaylin had spilled the beans. Eh, well, it kept me from having to explain again.

"So how was your night?" I asked, sliding into my chair as Leo set a plate of bacon and eggs in front of me. I glanced up to find them all just staring at me, silent. "What? Okay, so I turned into an owl, went gallivanting around the yard, and boom, here I am, hungry and sore as hell. What more can I say?"

"So Kaylin told us. What do you think it means?"

I stared at my plate. "What it means," I said softy, "is

that I'm not who I've always thought I was, for one thing. Otherwise . . . How can I possibly know everything this signifies? I don't even understand. It's going to take me a long time to sort this out, to assess what impact it's going to have. I always knew I was of the magic-born, but, Rhiannon . . . if my father is Cambyra Fae . . . does that mean yours might be, too? We were born on the same day. Neither of us ever met our fathers. And now, we can't even ask Heather."

Rhiannon paled. "I didn't even think of that. But wouldn't I know?"

"I didn't." My childhood had been a freak show of abnormality, so I'd always attributed feeling out of place to the environment I'd grown up in, rather than blood. After all, I wasn't fully human—I was a born witch—and had never felt "the odd one out" due to my magic.

"Should we tell Anadey about this? She might be able to shine some light on our heritage." The look in her eyes told me she was hopeful of finding out more about her past, too. Heather wasn't likely to tell her anything, now. Heather was lost to us.

I considered the idea. Anadey was the closest thing to an advisor we had. She was Marta's daughter, though not to the core, and she'd known our mothers before we were born. For a brief moment, I wondered if we could trust her, but tossed that worry out the window. We were long past the trust/don't trust stage. We'd passed it the moment we told her about Grieve and the Indigo Court.

"Yeah. I think so. It's Sunday, nobody here works today, do they?"

"About that . . ." Leo shifted uncomfortably. "I woke up to an e-mail that one of my tasks today is to chauffer you in for your first blood offering. Lannan wants to see you at seven tonight."

"Crap, I'd almost forgotten about that. I guess I wanted to forget."

Leo winced. "I feel trapped in the middle. I have the option to leave my contract without retaliation. I'm thinking of giving up my job as a day runner. Especially now that you're working for the vampires, Cicely. I have a feeling you're going to have it harder than any of us, and I don't want to be put in a position to make it worse. I'm afraid that might happen."

I glanced up at him. I hadn't thought about that before. What if they ordered Leo to do something to me—or with me—that neither of us wanted? He'd have no choice but to obey if he was still contracted by them.

*Don't let him.* Ulean's voice was urgent, prodding. *You'll need him there. I promise you that.*

That took care of that.

"Ulean just told me to tell you: Keep the job for now. I won't say that I trust them, but they aren't stupid. I doubt if they'll put our friendship in jeopardy, considering they believe I'm the key to their upcoming war."

"No, they aren't stupid. I suppose you're right," he said.

"So tell me, what happened at Anadey's? Did she start your training?" I wanted to forget about vampires and Vampiric Fae for the moment and concentrate on the living.

Rhiannon smiled, her face lighting up. "Yes, and it's not as difficult as I feared it would be. I already know quite a bit—I've learned a lot over the years from helping Heather with her spells and wortcunning. I have a lot of practice to do, but Anadey taught me one valuable lesson last night—how to pull back the fire when it starts getting out of control. It was far easier than I thought."

She looked so proud of herself that I jumped up and gave her a hug. At least we had solved one of our problems.

"What do we do today?"

"I thought about going out to find Peyton again, but we

barely escaped the first time. I think we should spend the day working on protective charms."

"Are you going to talk to Grieve?" Kaylin gave me a long look.

I bit my lip. "How can I? I'm giving blood to Lannan tonight. Grieve would sense something's up and he'd try to stop me. I need to file a report with Lannan, but I can do that via e-mail. I'll have to tell them about Heather, of course. But I think first I want to take a walk. I won't go in the wood, but I want to find the owl again. See if I can get some answers. Why don't the rest of you start on the charms? I'll be in to help in a little while."

I finished my breakfast and, grabbing my jacket, headed out to the backyard. The oak towered over me and I gazed up through the branches, amazed I'd been able to climb so high the night before. I slowly began to make my way up the lower limbs, cautiously watching my step, and was about halfway up when I heard a quiet susur-ration, a whispered *Hello*. Looking around for the owl, I realized there was no one—be it humanoid or winged creature—around.

*Who are you?*

*You're using me for a perch.*

The tree? But then, Ulean had brought me messages off the slipstream from plants before. The land was far more alive and vibrant than most people thought her. I leaned my head against the gnarled bark and sank into the energy of the ancient wood. Old, well past old, far older than I was.

*I saw the coming of the new people to this land.*

Well over six hundred years old, then. As I snuggled against the tree, letting the trunk shield me from the wind and the chill, I began to doze, sliding easily away from my conscious mind.

*Where is the owl?*

*He will be back. He and I are friends. He guards against the forest creatures, the Shadow Hunters.*

*Who is he?*

*The Guardian of the Forest. He was driven out of the ravine along with the Queen of Rivers and Rushes. She is not dead. She is biding her time.*

*I wish I could talk to her—so much is going on.*

*You may get your wish, young Cambyra. You may get your wish.*

*It's true then—what happened last night? I was an owl . . . I flew.* And a stream of images from the night before blanketed my mind, taking me back, sinking me deep into the freedom the skies had showered upon me. I murmured gently, almost asleep in the cradle of the tree, feeling protected and cared for.

*You must wake up, owlet. You have miles to go before you sleep . . .*

*"The woods are lovely, dark and deep, But I have promises to keep, And miles to go before I sleep . . ." A poem. You can't read, how did you know the words?*

*So many things pass through the slipstream. Did you truly believe I would not hear them as they cross my path? I am sorry, owlet, that you must journey to the bloody fanged ones . . . but truly, they are less dangerous than what waits in the woodland. Sometimes, the monsters are terribly beautiful, and the heroes loathsome. Go now, rest. Your friend will return for your next lesson in flight. Rest assured. He keeps watch over you.*

And then, my eyes fluttered and I woke to full consciousness, freezing again as I realized it was time to get down, out of the tree.

Ulean rode my shoulder. *The tree, he is old and wise, but not so old as me. But you can trust him. Trees are like that—once they choose a side, they seldom switch.*

As I joined the others in making protection charms,

I sorted through the herbs and crystals carefully, but my thoughts were a million miles away, soaring in the dark sky.

❦

At seven on the dot, I was standing outside of Lannan's office in Vecktor Hall, at the New Forest Conservatory. Leo stood beside me, the limo we'd arrived in waiting in the street in front of the building. Nervous, wondering how this was going to work, I raised my hand and hesitantly knocked.

"Enter." The word echoed through the hall as the door slid silently open. I glanced inside to see Lannan sitting behind his desk.

Altos's office was as oddly contradictory as was he. The furniture was old, heavy, dark, and handcrafted, but electronics filled the shelves, and just like at Marta's, there was a minimalist feel to the décor once you moved beyond the basic furnishings. But the atmosphere reminded me of peaches left on the vine just a little too long.

The suite was done in burgundy and black, with a large divan against one wall. A tapestry hung on the wall and, as I looked closer, I realized it was a picture of a woman being fucked by a large wolf, while a man stood by, masturbating. I shuddered, averting my eyes. A second wall was covered with books, and a desk, ornate and hand-carved from ebony, sat near the books. A door led into another room.

I glanced around for anybody else, but we were alone. Leo stood outside. Lannan glanced at him briefly and waved him off.

"Come back in an hour. We should be done then."

Leo looked like he wanted to do anything but leave me there, but he walked away, his eyes flashing fury. I sucked in a deep breath, stepped over the threshold, and waited for Lannan to speak.

"I see you chose to dress for comfort." *A statement.* "Next time, wear something sexy." *A demand.*

Great. He wanted the full show. He was a master gamesman, that much I could already tell. But I'd play along. I knew how to pick and choose my battles.

"Yes, sir." My voice sounded like a mouse's squeak in a giant auditorium. I forced myself to stand still in front of his desk. Make him initiate the first move.

Lannan looked up at me, his dark eyes glittering. If there had been some spark of light in them, some semblance of humanity, I might have been able to keep it together. But those abysmal orbs sucked me in and I found myself starting to shake. He was a *vampire*, a Vein Lord, and he was going to be drinking from my body tonight.

He slid from behind the desk and silently crossed the room. "What brings you to this fear? The thought of offering me blood?" His voice was soft, so soft I could barely catch it, and he leaned in, nuzzling my neck. "You are a lovely thing, and your scent fills the room. You know vampires have a sense of smell, even though we don't need to breathe?"

As he lingered by my shoulder, my heart skidded to the side. I already had come to loathe the man, yet his very proximity was like an aphrodisiac and even though my mind and heart resisted, my body was responding to whatever pheromones he was putting out.

"Oh, Cicely, not all payment has to hurt. Mine usually does, but keep in mind that I can—and shall—make it a pleasure for you. Blood offerings aren't always torture." He lifted my chin with his hands. "Don't worry, in less than ninety minutes, you'll be safe at home, with your friends."

But the look on his face told me I'd never be the same.

✦

Lannan let go and walked over to a small stereo system in an entertainment center and flipped on the music. Sinuous strains wove out, coiling around me, followed by a throbbing beat. He poured a glass of wine and handed it to me. I stared into the liquid, wondering if it was safe.

"I have no need to drug you. I could mesmerize you and take anything I wanted . . . if I *chose* to."

I froze, the drink halfway to my lips. *Ice,* I thought. *The ice maiden. Stay still, remain in stasis, freeze-frame, do not respond. Let him do what he will and then walk away like it never happened.*

"You understand that I drink from you as my right according to contract. You offer yourself to me." His voice was soft. Too soft.

I said nothing.

"Say it. Tell me that you have chosen this. I want to hear it from your lips, from your curving, sensuous, ever so life-quickening lips."

Again, silence. I stared at the stereo, willing myself to dissolve into the music. Become the chords, become the melody . . . float away on the breeze with the notes as they passed. Ephemeral.

"Cicely. I command you." And his voice was so strong I couldn't disobey.

I turned to stare at him. "I give my blood to you, I've chosen to do this. I signed the contract. Now do what you will."

His dark eyes flared and he let out a small grunt as he began to circle me. I stood at attention, unresponsive, not turning to follow. I managed to keep it together till he stopped in back of me and leaned in close. Then the panic started.

"I can make this ecstasy, or incredibly painful. Which do you think I should choose?" he whispered.

"That is up to you, sir." Struggling to keep my voice even, I began to breathe in shallow bursts. I'd rather have it hurt, to remind me of what he was.

"You must have some idea of what runs through my mind." He pressed his lips against my ear, as his hand began sliding down my right arm, his fingers icy cold against my skin. "What do you think I want to do to you? Tell me."

Damn him. It was another order. Command filled his voice and I couldn't disobey. Even though he'd promised not to enthrall me, that didn't mean he couldn't play head games and mind tricks.

I opened my mouth, unwilling to speak but unable to stop. "You want to fuck me. You want to drink me."

"Elaborate," he whispered, lifting my hair to the side and pressing his fangs against my neck. He didn't break the skin, but I could feel them there, poised, just waiting. "How would I fuck you, Cicely? What would I do to you? Tell me, in detail."

I wanted to cry but my eyes were dry. I wanted to run but my feet were frozen to the ground. My lips opened and I heard myself speaking even though I tried to bite back the words. "You'd slide your hands under my shirt and rip it off. Then, you'd unhook my bra and cup my breasts." As he licked my neck, a whimper escaped from my throat.

"You'd like that, wouldn't you? You'd like for me to undress you? What would I find if I slid my fingers down deep in your pussy? Are you wet, Cicely? Don't lie to me, because I can check, and if you lie, the punishment will be far more severe."

Shivering as his hand slid around, flat against my belly and up under my shirt, my heart wanted to run, to push him away. But my body wanted to drag him down and let him do what he would. Lannan had a drug—one he didn't need to inject or shove down my throat. Pure pheromone, pure aphrodisiac. No wonder bloodwhores flocked to the vamps.

"Yes," I whispered. "I'm wet."

"Where are you wet? Tell me." Again the soft coaxing as he pressed against my back. I could feel him, rigid and hard and furious.

Stumbling over the words, I blurted out, "My pussy. I'm so wet I can't stand it."

Lannan laughed then, raw and coarse. "Good—very good. You want me?" When I didn't answer, his voice thundered through the room. "Answer me, woman. Do you want me to fuck you?"

A cry ripped out of my throat. "Yes . . . No . . . I hate you."

With another laugh, the soft, sensual Lannan was back. He slowly peeled my shirt over my head and tossed it on the floor. Then he unhooked my bra and that, too, went on the floor. My breasts bounced lightly as they fell free of the satin and he let out a low groan and reached out, touching just the nipples. I bit my lip, trying not to show my feelings as the points hardened beneath his touch. I wanted relief so desperately, I thought I was going to cry, but I didn't want him to triumph—didn't want Lannan to win.

"Good girl." His voice was low, but still carrying the command. "Now we can get down to business. I want you to beg me to drink from you. Beg me, Cicely. On your knees, with your lips on my feet. Beg me. *Now*."

I fell to my knees, unable to disobey. My forehead brushed his pants legs as I pressed my lips against his polished leather boots. "Please . . . please, drink from me, Lannan."

He lightly tipped my chin up with the toe of one boot.

"I can't hear you—a little louder, please. And more heart-felt."

My face flushed, burning. If he wanted to humiliate me, he was doing a damned good job. I wanted to stake him right there.

"Lannan, please drink from me. *Please!*" I forced all the sarcasm into my voice that I could, but I still sounded desperate and he let out a sharp laugh.

"Better. Only you forgot *My lord and master*. But I'll let that slip this time." He stepped back, yanking me up and into his arms. "Oh girl, if I weren't using incredible restraint, I'd be in you, reaming you so hard you'd never, ever forget me."

I let out another whimper. *No, please, don't let him go through with it.* I knew he was going to browbeat me, but please, oh please, don't let him lose control. My body was responding to him as my heart sank and a tear finally squeezed out and slowly wound down my cheek.

Lannan grabbed me by the shoulders and forced me to stare into his unblinking, ebony eyes. They glistened like dark jewels. The look on his face was cold again, the soft sensuality gone in the blink of an eye.

Numb, trying to ignore the rumbling desire that echoed through my body, I shivered as he whirled me around, pressing me face-first against the back of the divan. His hand reached around to squeeze my nipple so hard I let out a shriek. Squeezing my eyes closed, I held my breath and waited.

The music shifted. Nine Inch Nails blared through the room, the driving beat catching me up. Lannan's laughter grew louder, his icy hands groping me as he leaned close to my neck. No warm breath to tell me he was there, but just a chilling presence.

And then he plunged toward me, his lips licking my neck, as he grunted and pierced the skin. The pain was exquisite, sending me soaring so that I lost track of my anger, lost track of my fury and rode the wave so high that I came right there, screaming as his tongue rasped against me, coaxing the blood to the surface, one crimson drop at a time.

As my blood entered his mouth, *communion*, a connection forged between us. It coiled like a serpent and I fought it off, fought the hunger to give in and beg him to take me under, to turn me, to make me one of his own.

"No—you're not supposed to enthrall me," I whispered.

*Stop, please, stop. Don't stop. Don't leave me hanging. Don't leave me unfinished, untouched. Tear me to pieces and rebuild me, make me new, make me strong, make me scream, make me love you.*

Closing my eyes, I desperately searched for something to block my rising desire. I thought of Grieve, of Heather, of my cousin . . . of everything except for the soft sound of Lannan's insistent lapping, but I couldn't hold on to the thoughts and I slid ever deeper into the crimson shadowed lust that filtered through my senses.

"I'm not enthralling you. This is only your first donation. It will feel better each time." And then he pressed against my neck again, drinking deep, and a euphoria washed over me that superseded every dark and overripe dream of ecstasy I'd ever experienced.

*Except for one.*

The memory of soaring as an owl over the darkened house rose up and I caught hold. I held on to it—pouring myself into the feel of the wind under my wings, of the sights and scents and sounds. The memory became a beacon, a lifeline and tether to which I held tight as Lannan's passion buffeted me. That moment—gliding into the night—was the most sublime experience I'd ever undergone. Pure, feral, primal, clean . . .

Even as Lannan's tongue against my neck drove me

toward orgasm, even as I lost my control and threw myself into the dance, my mind held tight to the single image of myself-as-owl. A burning ember began to grow in the pit of my stomach, and I knew that someday, in the future when we were free from the Indigo Court, I'd return to Lannan and stake him through the heart to repay him for the depths he'd brought me to.

Then, lust hit me full force and I came again, shrieking in pain as much as pleasure as he pulled away, my blood dripping down his chin, a crazed, triumphant smile spreading wide across his face. But the part of myself I needed to save, the part of myself that could never be beaten or stripped of dignity, soared, riding the winds, winging high and wide and free.

# Chapter 21

I said nothing as he handed me a bandage for my neck, which was still oozing. My knees weak, I stumbled. Lannan caught me up and—with a gentleness that belied his nature—he carried me over to the sofa and sat me down, exiting into the other room for a moment and returning with a glass of milk and a couple of chocolate chip cookies.

Staring at the food, awash in the contradictions that had rampaged through my evening, I could only look up at him, puzzled. "What . . . why . . . ?"

"You need food. I drank deep from you, but some sugar and a night of rest will restore you. Eat and drink, now, and put on your shirt. The wound is covered and shouldn't leak onto your clothing."

He returned to his desk as if nothing had happened.

I shook my head. "How can you be so nonchalant? How can you act as though you didn't just ravage me? You made me come, you made me scream your name, damn it. And you act like it was nothing."

Lannan raised his head, his golden hair falling forward as a perplexed look crossed his face. "Do you want it to mean something?" he asked softly.

"No—yes . . . I . . ." I stared at the cookies in my hand. "You drink from me—you steal my blood and act like nothing happened, like it's just a stop at the water cooler. Do you know how violated I feel? How angry I am at you right now?"

Perhaps it wasn't the wisest thing to yell at a vampire, but I felt hot and overtired and my mind had slid into a fog bank. Thickly, I bit into the cookies and sipped the milk, hoping to clear my head.

Lannan frowned, then slowly stood and crossed back over to me. He took the glass and food from me and put them on the coffee table, then helped me slip back into my bra, fastening it from behind, and then guided my shirt back over my head. Afterward, he sat beside me and took my hands in his, gazing at me so long I began to get nervous.

"Cicely, you truly are a gem. Most of the magic-born have an arrogance to match even the Vein Lords. But you . . . there's something different about you." He brushed my hair back from my face. "You're my type, you know—long dark hair, brilliant eyes, curvy and solid. Listen to me, Cicely. My kind—vampires—we're at the top of the food chain. We are no longer human. You—be you magic-born or human—are our prey. I drink from you because I can, because I want to. Your feelings really play no part in the matter either way."

Once again furious, I pulled my hands away. "If I'm just a juice box on legs, then let me go home since I've served my purpose tonight. Don't bother trying to explain yourself, because you can't. You can't ever hope to make me sympathize with you."

"Girl," he said, pulling me close so that I could smell my blood still on his lips, "listen to me. If the Indigo

Court rises up, then you'll sympathize with us so fast and so hard that you'll beg me to turn you. They would eat you alive, like piranha going after a deer that stumbled in the water. They wouldn't care about your cries or your feelings or your pain—they'd eat you to the bone with your heart still beating. Don't be so quick to turn up your nose at me."

I sat very still, trying not to anger him again. He looked about two steps away from backhanding me across the room. But he let me go then, and flipped open a cell phone.

"She's ready to go home. Wait for her out front. Don't come in."

I stared at him as he snapped the phone shut. "Leo will be waiting for you in the limo. I advise you don't tarry long. The night is dangerous, and there are monsters abroad far more fearsome than I."

Shaking, I stood and polished off the cookies and swigged down the milk, then gathered my purse and headed out the door without another word. As I slowly descended the stairs of Vecktor Hall, I heard a rustling in the bushes nearby and something whispered my name on the wind.

*Cicely . . . Cicely, I need to talk to you.*

It wasn't Ulean—she'd chosen to stay home since vampires didn't care for Elementals much.

*Who are you? What do you want?*

*You must come speak to me. I'm staying by Dovetail Lake. Please, come tonight.* The voice was female but I felt no hostility, no deceit, in it.

*I don't know—it's been a rough night . . .*

*Please, stop on the way home. I must speak to you about Grieve.*

*Grieve? What about Grieve?*

But the voice drifted away, with simply a *Meet me by the boat moorings. I'll be waiting for you.*

I headed for the limo, pulling out my cell phone. Rhiannon answered. "Don't ask me how things went, please. Not now. I need you to do something for me. I want you to go stand in my room and say out loud, 'Ulean, Cicely needs you to meet her at Dovetail Lake right away.' Will you do that?"

"Of course, but what's going on?"

"I don't know, but somebody wants to meet me there and I swear, I've heard the voice before—it came in on the slipstream, and it seems like . . . something I heard when I was very young."

"Should I come, too?"

"No," I said, thinking it over. "You and Kaylin stay and keep a watch on the house. I won't be long, and Leo will be with me." As I hung up and crawled in the limo, it occurred to me that life had gotten terribly complicated, terribly fast. My old life had seemed a nightmare, but I wasn't sure this new one was any better. *Except that I have Grieve and my cousin*, my mind peeped up.

I smiled. *True*, I whispered back to myself. *I have Grieve and my cousin, and both are worth fighting for.*

❧

Leo didn't have anything to do after driving me home, so after an argument about it, he acceded to my demand to stop at the lake. I slipped out of the limo, warning him to stay inside. "You have to be able to get away in case it's a trap. If worse comes to worst, I can try to turn into an owl again and escape."

"I don't like it," he argued, but in the end, I won and he stayed. I played the *I just got bitten by a vampire so do what I want* card on him.

Dovetail Lake was a small lake or a large pond, depending on how you looked at it, an ellipse of dark water hidden away down a lonely road. Surrounded by a thicket of alder and fir, of cedar and weeping willow, the lake was a local hangout for weekend warriors looking for a quiet fishing spot. It wasn't suitable for swimming—the lake was deeper than it was wide, and gave way suddenly once you got past the edge. The last time I'd been back home, two local boys had drowned trying to snorkel in it.

I quietly edged down to the boat mooring and waited by a stand of frozen rushes and cattails that were ragged and weather-beaten. The water was restless and dark, frothing around the pilings as the wind ruffled its surface. I leaned against one of the railings—cautiously, they didn't look all that sturdy—and thought I heard something in the bushes around the side of the lake.

As I turned, a shape appeared from behind one of the scrub alders crowding next to the shore. She was shining, gloriously beautiful and wreathed in silver fire. I caught my breath and slowly stepped off the dock, back onto the icy ground, and made my way over to her.

"Lainule." I stared at the Fae Queen who stood before me, cloaked in the ragged robes of summer. The look on her face sang of sadness and loss, of pain and the weariness war can bring. A stirring inside rang a bell of recognition, and I knelt before her, realizing that if I was Cambyra Fae, then I was of her people, too. I looked up at her gentle touch on my head.

"Stand, Cicely. I'm grateful to see you. I'm glad you got my summons to bring you home." Her voice danced over the words, lightly, playing a musical scale with each syllable. She was as beautiful as Myst, as terrifying as Myst, and yet Lainule didn't strike my heart with the same sense of dread.

"Lady. You were the one who called me back?"

"I . . . yes, and my guardians. The owl summoned you home, Grieve summoned you home, and I . . . I summoned you home. We need you, Cicely."

"But what can I do?" I looked at her, helpless. "I can't fight Myst—she'll tear me to pieces."

"No, you cannot fight her directly, but there are ways to hurt her, to knuckle her down. She's defiled the Courts, defiled the Seelie, the Unseelie. She's destroyed the Court of Rushes and Rivers and she is an abomination against the very code that makes up the essence of our people. Your people, too, as you now know. It's time to bring her into the open, to wage war, to stop her."

Lainule stroked my chin, smiling, and her smile was feral and fearsome but it called me close to her. I stepped into her embrace and she murmured soft words in my ear, stroking my hair, kissing me gently on the forehead.

"I didn't want to let you leave when you were so young, but it was necessary. You needed to become your own person, away from New Forest, away from our people, before you could return to join us. You needed to embrace both sides of your heritage, and learn how to stand strong on your own feet. Your mother was sacrificed, so we might have you."

I looked up at her then—she was tall, oh so very tall and radiant—and her smile blinded me. "My mother . . ."

"Your mother was chosen to be your mother by me and by your father."

"What about Rhiannon? Is she like me?"

"That is for her to find out, but her path lies along a slightly different road. The fire is thick within her."

"Can I meet my father—" I'd always wondered who he was, always wondered why he'd left my mother after getting her pregnant with me.

"In time." She gently pushed me back, looking me over. "Pretty, girl. You have grown up lovely."

"What can I do? How can I help fight Myst? How can I free Peyton before they kill her?" I searched her face, praying she would care enough to help me.

"Peyton? What will happen, will happen. Peyton's fate is not in my hands, but in yours. For now, go home and wait. Grieve will come to you and you are not to speak of this meeting. But you two belong together. He's not the enemy—not in the long scheme of things." Lainule turned to go, then stopped and looked over her shoulder.

"Welcome home, Cicely—both to New Forest, and to your newfound family. You may work for the vampires, but you are mine at the heart of all things, at least this time around. And you will obey me over any other, or I will most assuredly sacrifice you in this game of chess that Myst and I are playing."

And then, she vanished into the brush and I watched her light disappear as she blurred and was gone from sight.

❧

"I don't know what to think. First, we have the war between the vampires and the Vampiric Fae, and now, another battle—this one between Lainule and Myst. And I'm caught in the center of the vortex. The Indigo Court is my enemy twice over and I don't even know what we're fighting about other than to keep them from destroying everything they touch."

Leo, Rhiannon, and Kaylin sat in the living room with me. I looked up, confused and in pain. Lannan's bite ached on my neck, and my forehead felt hot. I was embarrassed about my reaction to him but my body kept prodding me, reminding me that while I'd orgasmed several times, my body still longed for actual touch and connection with someone to whom I could give my whole self—body *and* mind.

"At least we know the Queen of Rivers and Rushes is alive. And if she's on our side—so much the better." Rhiannon glanced at the clock. "Anadey wants me over there at dawn again—she's got me on a training schedule so that I meet with her before work every day for the next few weeks. While that won't be enough time for me to learn how to use the fire properly, she said by the end of this week I should be able to control it without a problem—to pull it back and prevent the accidental breakthroughs."

"If only your mother had trained you during your childhood. This wouldn't have happened." Leo frowned. "Heather seems so levelheaded . . . seemed . . ." His voice drifted off and he blushed. "I'm sorry, I shouldn't bring her up right now."

Rhiannon shrugged, her eyes sparkling with tears. "I have to accept what's happened. And Marta would have kicked Heather out of the Society. By the way, I heard through the grapevine today that all remaining members of the Society besides Tyne, Marta's grandson, have skipped town. Vanished." Rhiannon shrugged. "They're smart. I'm half tempted to do so myself, now that Heather's lost to me."

"We can't. We can't let the town fall to Myst—she'll just spread her horrors to the next town, and the next. And besides, we have to rescue Peyton."

Kaylin patted me on the shoulder. "We'll think of something. I created a few offensive charms today, and I've also rigged more than one Molotov cocktail. If we have to, we'll burn our way in and take her by force. We can do a lot of damage with fire to the Indigo Court."

Suddenly feeling wiped, I slumped back in my chair. "Sounds good to me. We should just burn the whole damned forest down. Make sure my owl pal is out of there and light the match. Okay, I'm going to bed. Rhia, I'll call you at work tomorrow to see what's going down. Leo—don't you tell the vampires about my little to the docks tonight."

He shrugged. "As long as they don't ask . . ."

"*No*—do you understand? You just keep quiet about it altogether. I have no desire to see them start up another feud. Not on my account."

I pushed myself out of bed and headed for the stairs, turning to shake my head. "And life just goes on as normal. People are shopping, going to work, as if nothing is happening—but we've got dead and missing everywhere. You'd think somebody would say something."

Kaylin stood and stretched. "Oh, the townsfolk know something's up, but they don't want to be next. Old superstition: Talk about something, you bring it too close. And not always a superstition. Good night, Cicely. Sleep well."

I trudged up the stairs. As I entered my room and stripped off my clothes, a sound at my window startled me and I turned. Grieve was waiting outside. I pushed up the sash and nodded him in, too weary to do anything else.

"How can you get past the wards when your charming family can't?" I stared at him for a long moment. "And when the fuck were you going to tell me what they'd done to Heather?"

Grieve hung his head. "It only happened yesterday. I had no idea they'd send her to you before I could get here to warn you."

"Fuck you, too." I turned to him. "And you—what's your part in this? To convince me to leave well enough alone? To turn me and make me one of Myst's slaves like Heather? Apparently your adoptive kin seems to think a war's brewing. According to them, I'm not supposed to interfere."

Grieve started to move closer; he suddenly froze. "Who have you been with? You've been . . . Were you fucking somebody? Somebody . . . *dead*?" He was suddenly beside me, holding me by the shoulders. "Have you been with a *vampire*?"

I tore away from him, too angry to be afraid. "No—I didn't let a vampire *fuck* me, but I let one *drink* from me. It's in my contract. Your spies seem to know everything about me, so you might as well, too."

"What do you mean?" He looked stricken and let go of me. "I'm sorry, I shouldn't have shaken you like that."

"You damned well better apologize. Here's the deal: I've been forced into working for the Crimson Court. *Because I know you.* As a side bonus, they were going to help us get Heather back, which is more than I can say you offered. To gain their assistance, I had to agree to a monthly blood donation. But now, my sacrifice is useless—at least as far as Heather's concerned."

"Cicely . . ." He lifted his head, wincing. "I'm so sorry . . ."

I waved away his words, no longer caring if I hurt his feelings. He could have stopped them, somehow saved Heather if he'd really wanted to. I truly believed it, despite what Lainule had said.

"Sorry doesn't mend fences or bring people back from the living dead. No, your people have turned her, and there's no chance to save her. She's gone to us—her life and everything she stood for wiped out in the blink of an eye. We've lost her and the best we can hope for is a bloody staking and putting her soul to rest. But maybe I'll luck out. Maybe my contract isn't all in vain. Peyton is still out there and we're going to rescue her, come hell or high water."

"So, you really are working for the Crimson Court?"

As he stared at me incredulously, I snorted. "Did you not hear what I said? And so what? *You* are aligned with the *Indigo Court.* Thrust and parry, my love. Thrust and parry. We're both pledged into the arms of hell, now."

He gave me a sideways glance. "Who was it? Who drank from you?"

I realized that—Fae or not—he was playing the testosterone card. I'd had enough of tiptoeing around.

"Fine. You want to know? I'll tell you. Lannan Altos, a professor at the conservatory. And yeah, he drank my blood, he made me beg him, and he made me come so hard I about lost consciousness when his fangs hit my neck. He thoroughly enjoyed himself and even though I tried to block him out, I came over and over again."

"I don't want to know this—"

"*You asked!* Once a month, I owe him a cup of my lifeblood, or however much he seems to want. Maybe I should just forfeit my life over to them for good now and get it over with. You should know what it's like to work for unyielding despots."

I expected him to walk out the door, to jump out the window and be gone. But Grieve just dropped to the bed.

"I never thought you'd go to that length to get them back," he whispered.

"Just what *did* you think? That we'd let your newfound family tear them to shreds without putting up a fight? Bleed them out, rip them to pieces? Rhiannon and I are cousins. Heather's my aunt—or was. Now she's Dead Woman Walking and guess what? It's tearing us apart. Do you know what happened when Heather came here? Rhiannon tried to fry her own mother."

At his startled look, I moved in closer.

"Yeah, that's right. I said she tried to fry her—tried to burn Heather to ashes. Her mother's a vampire, a slave to a sadistic queen. Heather's magic is a weapon of the Court now. So Rhiannon tried to kill her."

Grieve dropped his head to his hands and his shoulders started to shake. I stared at him, shocked into silence. He was crying, and they weren't crocodile tears. I knelt beside him, tipped his chin up, looked him square in the face.

"I was coming to tell you tonight about Heather. I was so afraid you'd tell me to leave, that you would never want to see me again."

The tears streaked his face, winding in rivulets down

his cheeks. He was so alien, and yet so familiar to me. I knew him, knew him from the inside out. I was wondering when to tell him about discovering the truth about myself when I flashed . . .

❧

We were sitting together on the top of a hill, and he was holding my hand. Only he wasn't Grieve, and I wasn't Cicely, but we were there, together, staring at a bloody pile of bodies that surrounded us.

"My love, we're doomed. You know that, don't you?"

And I—and yet it was not me—nodded. "They'll be here any minute. This time, they'll never let us go. What are we going to do?"

He held up a bottle. "We can escape to the future with this. We drink this together and we'll be bound to return, to find one another again in a different time. And with the grace of the gods, we won't be torn apart by our families, by our cultures."

He stroked my long hair back, shaking his head. "I love you more than life itself," he whispered. "They're going to kill us, you know that. They're going to torture us, tear us to shreds."

I nodded. They were coming for our heads, and there was no place left to run. I took the bottle, recognizing the potion within. We'd die, yes, but it would set in motion a future for us to return, to find each other again, to finish what we'd started in this life.

"We've left a trail of carnage, that's for sure. Your people can't stand my shadows," I said.

"And your people can't stand my light. *My sweet Cherish*. Please—don't let them part us. Who knows if we'll find each other in the Land of the Silver Falls? This will bind us to the Wheel and we will return, together."

I popped the top on the bottle. "Remember me, Shy. Remember me, and come find me. If I choose to return to this world, then I must have your promise that you'll look for me."

He placed his hand over mine as I held the bottle to my lips. "I promise to you, Cherish, by my blood and my heart, I will search for you with my dying breath."

I tipped the bottle. Drank half the potion and handed it to him. He downed the rest, and we curled up, holding one another, listening to the distant shouts of those hunting us. They'd find us, all right, but we'd be out of their touch. We'd be off into the future.

And we'd find each other again, one way or another.

✳

Shaking, I sat back and stared at him. "We were together . . . before. I thought we might have been."

"Cicely . . ." Grieve gathered me into his arms, the tears flowing freely now. "I told you that I've been waiting for you. And now you've remembered, and we can truly be together again. I love you. I've loved you for lifetimes. And now, here we are and I won't let you slip away this time."

Together, yes, but once more, on opposite sides. Working for bitter enemies, pledged to ruthless factions out for each other's blood. But all of it washed away as he sought my lips, kissing me deep. He washed away the feel of Lannan's hands on me. Grieve slid his lips against mine, against my throat, licking at the marks that Lannan had left, leaving his own scent, his own claim. I tugged at his shirt and within seconds, he was as naked as I was.

I wanted him, needed him to cleanse me of the memory of Lannan's touch. I ran my tongue down his stomach, down his thigh, around him as he grew thick and hungry. Grieve moaned and pulled me up to face him. He slid me onto his lap and I knelt, straddling him. He tucked one arm around my waist, the other under my butt, holding me, keeping me balanced, and as we rocked, rhythmically, I lost myself in the reflection of his eyes. And as we rode the dark wave, I forgot about vampires and wars and humiliation, and remembered what love was.

# Chapter 22

After, Grieve took me in his arms and the swirl of stars in the black globes of his eyes made me dizzy. "I know you flew last night. I know you found out what you are. I couldn't tell you—I had to let you find out on your own."

Feeling slightly feverish, I leaned my head against his shoulder. "I wouldn't have believed you if you did. What do we do now, Grieve? Myst controls you and I work for her enemies. And now, she's got Heather—a very powerful witch—and who knows how many others of the magic-born that she's turned?" Lainule's warning hung heavy in my heart and though I wanted to tell him—wanted to assure him she was okay, I kept my mouth shut.

"I'll help you get Peyton back. I'll think of something . . . there has to be a way." He slid back into his clothing.

"How? We have to act fast—if they try to turn her, her half-breed blood may just very well kill her for good."

Grieve frowned, thinking. "We'll create a diversion so that I—or Chatter—can sneak her out. There has to be something to capture Myst's attention enough to rally most of her guards."

"Burn the forest. We start a fire. That should rout enough of them." I pulled on my nightgown and bathrobe. All I wanted to do was sleep—sleep off the sex, the bloodletting . . . sleep off everything.

"You can't burn the forest! You can't even think of doing something so horrible. The Golden Wood is our home, our land." The look on Grieve's face took me aback.

I shook my head. "I'll do whatever it takes, and nobody else has to like it. Besides, the snow won't let it burn, not more than enough to get her notice."

"Wait—give me tonight. I'll figure out something. Please, don't do something so rash." He sounded so plaintive that I relented.

"All right, but if you haven't got a plan by tomorrow, I'm taking a match out there and torching it. Understand? I'll do whatever I have to in order to save any of their victims who happen to remain alive in the Barrow."

Grieve nodded, then kissed me once more and slid out the window, vanishing into the night. Exhausted, I locked it, replaced the protection charm, and crawled into bed. The wolf on my stomach was rumbling, satisfied, and yet . . . there was something there . . . something odd . . .

Ignoring the slightly queasy feeling I had, I turned out the light and was asleep before my head hit the pillow.

❧

The next morning, Rhiannon was gone to Anadey's by the time I got up. Kaylin had apparently decided to take up residence because he was still there, and making breakfast at that. Leo had crashed out on the sofa in the living room. I frowned. It was time we got some order into the house.

"Yo, Kaylin, you going to live here or what? If so, let's

get you set up with a room. And why didn't Leo go to bed last night? He and Rhiannon are sharing her bedroom."

Kaylin flipped the pancakes, then handed me a double-shot latte with a sprinkling of cinnamon. "Yeah, I think I'll stick around for a while. I have a place to live but you need me. As for Leo, he kept saying he could hear things outside. We'd go check every hour or so, but never saw a thing. I guess he couldn't sleep."

"Well, Grieve showed up last night in my room. He's promised to figure out a way to get Peyton out alive." I sipped the steaming liquid, grateful for the faint buzz of caffeine that was already rampaging through my system. I'd heard that it took forty-five minutes for the drug to hit the bloodstream. I didn't believe it. "Damn, dude, this is strong."

"All the better to wake you up. So how's your neck this morning?"

I reached up to finger the area where Lannan had dug into me. The edges felt hot, raw. "Will you take a look? I've been queasy ever since I left his office. And not just because of what happened—it's something else."

As Kaylin gently brushed aside my hair to examine my neck, I winced. My stomach was getting worse. Just then, my wolf rose up, whimpering. A ribbon of fire raced through me, so dry that I felt like I was kindling held to a match. I clutched my stomach. My wolf was sick. Grieve was sick.

"Help me, Kaylin . . . I don't feel so good." I tried to stand up but my knees buckled and Kaylin caught me. Through the fog that was encompassing my mind, I heard him yell for Leo to wake, and then the next thing I knew, he was carrying me upstairs. I let out a little moan as he jostled me, turning at the landing. The sound of footsteps behind us penetrated the haze.

"What's wrong with her?" Leo's voice echoed through the blackness. I realized my eyes were shut and attempted to force them open.

"I don't know. She complained about being hot—not feeling good. Look at the wound on her neck. What the fuck?"

Leo sucked in a hiss and I managed to open my eyes just a crack. "Water. I'm burning up."

Kaylin brushed his hand across my forehead. "She's hot, but not terribly so. Get her some water. Hurry."

My eyes closed again as Leo's face disappeared and I reached out, seeking comfort from the one who knew me best.

*Ulean, are you here? Help me, please.*

*I am here, girl. You will be all right. You're not the one who's sick.*

*What do you mean? I feel like I'm dying.*

*I know, girl. I know, but trust me, you aren't. Ride it through, the wave will pass, and I'll do my best to pull you out of it enough for Leo to help you.*

*What wave? What are you talking about? Why does my stomach hurt so bad if I'm not sick?*

*Because, girl . . . Grieve is sick. Terribly sick. You have to ride it out, climb out of the communion in order to help him.*

And then, Leo's hands were behind me, lifting me up so I could drink. The water was cool as it ran down my throat, ice on a burn, and I let out a single cry as my stomach cramped again.

*No! Please, no! Out . . . let me out . . . now . . .*

The slipstream eased just enough. I saw a chance to break out of the communion and leapt for the opening. There was a ripping sound, a horrible whining as if my wolf had been mangled and then—in the soft blink of an eye—I landed safe inside myself, the connection severed. My stomach ached from the spasms, but the pain began to diminish. The fog was lifting.

With Kaylin's and Leo's help, I slowly sat up, trembling. "What the fuck was that? Something's happened to

Grieve! I know it." I tried to get up, to make it to the door but they stopped me and forced me back onto the bed.

"I need to examine you, Cicely." Leo held up a small kit. "I brought my healer's case when I got your water. You can't get out of bed until we know what happened."

"I *know* what happened." I tried to shake him off. "Grieve is sick and my wolf felt it. I tuned in to him. Let me up."

"Sit still and allow Leo to do what he needs to," Kaylin said, holding me fast. He was stronger than he looked. "Just what are you planning to do? Race out there into the wood to find him? Run right into Myst's arms?"

Kaylin caught my gaze and I froze. He was right. What the hell could I do? Get myself caught? Out Grieve as a traitor? Resigned, I let Leo check me over. He listened to my heart, then took my temperature, and finally, using a cotton swab, he rubbed gently across the puncture wounds on my neck. I stared at the oozing liquid on the cotton.

"Crap, am I bleeding?"

"More . . . puslike. Either Lannan didn't brush his fangs before he bit into you or . . . Hello, what's this?" Leo held out the swab and murmured a few words I couldn't hear, then watched. The tip of the swab where the droplets were had turned bright pink—fuchsia to be exact.

"What's that mean?" I stared at it. Barring lipstick or flowers, anything that color couldn't be good.

"Poison. You were poisoned . . . but not with anything like arsenic. This is . . . a bacteria? Virus maybe? You were infected with something when Lannan bit you, Cicely." Leo looked at me, his meaning clear in his eyes.

"And when Grieve licked the wounds last night, he got some of whatever this is in his system. And he's terribly sick. But why is he sick and I'm not? We both have Cambyra blood in us, so it can't be against the Fae."

Kaylin shook his head. "Maybe it's not meant to hurt the Fae. But I still bet you anything Lannan's fangs were coated with whatever this is."

"If not the Fae then . . . oh . . ."

And I saw. The Indigo Court. The Vampiric Fae.

"Do you think . . . could the vampires have made their first attack against Myst? And could I be their weapon?" I pushed myself out of bed, striding to the dresser, where I leaned toward the mirror. I knew it—knew it in my gut. The vampires had used me as their own personal Typhoid Mary. "I wonder if this thing can spread? And if so . . ."

"If so, then the Indigo Court may be in for some casualties. Or at least a nasty bout of stomach flu."

"Grieve's sick. I can't do a damned thing to help him right now. What if he dies? What if they used me to kill him?" I whirled around. "I need to speak to Lannan. *Now!*"

"You can't," Leo said. "Lannan's asleep for the day. You won't be able to talk to him until tonight."

"Then I'm heading out to Dovetail Lake. Lainule may know something about this and by gods, she's going to tell me." Frantic, terrified I'd lost Grieve a second time, I raced down the stairs, Kaylin and Leo on my heels.

"Are you sure you want to do that?" Leo grabbed me by the wrist and spun me around. "I think you should just wait . . . wait until I can talk to the vampires tonight."

*He knows something,* Ulean whispered.

I stared at him. There was a flicker in his eyes. Ulean was right—his eyes read guilt all the way through. "What do you know about this? Tell me. Now! Before I bitch-slap you across the room. *And trust me, I could do it.*"

Leo backed away. "I can't tell you."

"You'd better tell me. I learned to fight in the streets, boy, and you're smart enough to know you'd better not piss me off." I started for him, fists clenched.

Leo jumped back another step and held up his hands.

"Okay! Okay . . . stop. Don't hurt yourself. Or me." He paused, then shook his head. "Sit down and I'll tell you what I know. But if Geoffrey finds out, I might as well impale myself on a pitchfork."

I crossed my arms, waiting. "This better be good."

"Good? Not likely. But the truth." His eyes flickered and he let out a long sigh. "I heard Geoffrey and Lannan talking—neither one knows I eavesdropped and if they find out, I'm toast. They were discussing the best way to get in a first attack on the Indigo Court. Someone—not Crawl, but someone of his stature in the Vampire Nation, has apparently figured out a virus that affects the Vampiric Fae. It spreads through close contact, like kissing, hugging, shaking hands."

"Or sex and feeding on blood."

"Right. And it causes a massive breakdown of the ability of the Vampiric Fae to handle daylight. The vampires are trying to even the playing field, I think. If the Indigo Court can only come out at night, then they're on par with the vampires and won't have the advantage of being able to wreak havoc while the vamps have to sleep."

"Holy crap. Then Grieve's reacting the way he is—"

"Because it's daylight. I think . . . I think the virus or whatever it is worked. And when he went back to the Court, he began spreading it. And those who catch it, will spread it further. The vampires are hoping to create a pandemic."

I gently rubbed my hand across my wolf, wanting to find Grieve, to tell him to get out of the light, to get inside and stay in the dark.

"I'd like to kill Lannan," I said softly. "I want to be the one to stake him. He knew that Grieve would respond to my fear and anger. I *know* he knew it. I don't know how they assembled their information, but they know all about me and I'll bet you anything they know I'm part Cambyra Fae."

"Cicely—this may not be a bad thing." Leo took my hands and I glared at him. He let go, but wouldn't shut up. "We're fighting the Indigo Court. No, not Grieve, but everybody else there. Put your emotions aside, at least as far as he goes, and look at this logically. We can use this to help us get Peyton back. By tomorrow, the Court's going to be in shambles and we can use that turmoil and chaos as a cloak."

Bleakly, I stared up at Kaylin, who nodded but said nothing. Leo was right. As much as I hated Lannan, I had to admit the plan was ingenious. And by the very nature of what was happening, the prophecy was coming true—the vampires were causing Grieve, via me, to become an unwitting traitor and carry the virus back to the rest of the Indigo Court.

Which made me wonder, which had come first—the plan? Or the prophecy? Or had some vampire-cum-scientist somewhere engineered this infection, and then the higher-ups—maybe Crawl or the Queen herself—had the foresight to take an ancient prophecy and make it happen?

No matter what, Grieve and I truly now were the traitorous lovers of the Najeeling Prophecy. Because I knew, in my heart, from my link with Grieve, that he was suffering horribly right now. And others of the Court would soon be suffering, too. And there was nothing I could—or should—do about it. To run in there to save Grieve would be tantamount to helping the Indigo Court, and I couldn't do that. Not even for love.

I lifted my head slowly, staring at Kaylin and Leo. "Get ready," I said in a hoarse whisper. "We're going to have a talk with Lainule. We need her help, and I owe her my allegiance, it seems."

After calling Rhiannon and telling her to wait for us at Anadey's, we headed for Dovetail Lake. I revved up Favonis, wondering why I'd ever bothered to come home. The world was bleak, and I couldn't seem to find one bright spot to hold on to . . . not even though the sun was shining in the impossibly cold and bright and harshly snow-blanketed world.

❧

By the time we got to the lake, I was more than depressed: I was furious. And fury would carry me a lot further than moping. I hopped out of the car the minute I turned off the ignition and went stomping toward the rushes, kicking up the snow. Kaylin and Leo followed, at a distance.

"Lainule! I know you're here!" I stopped, and forced my thoughts into the slipstream. *I know you can hear me, you know who I am and you'd better come out or I'll broadcast it far and wide that you're still around here.*

*Don't toy with her, don't threaten her, girl. You know that's not safe.*

*I don't care, Ulean. We're being played like pawns between three rival forces and I'll be damned if I give away all of my power. We're going to at least get one thing out of this and that's Peyton, back alive and safe.*

The susurration of the winter breeze turned into an icy blast as the reeds parted. Lainule, flanked by two men who reminded me of Grieve and Chatter in the old days, stepped out from between the parted bushes.

"You dare to summon me with such language and threats?" Her voice was low but the power behind it sent me reeling back. I stumbled into Kaylin's arms and he steadied me.

Lainule might be beautiful in the night, but during the day she was blinding. Radiant, even under summer's torn and shredded cloak, her eyes were the blue of morning sky and her hair the color of spun platinum woven with auburn strands. She looked at Kaylin, then at Leo, then back at me.

"What do you want, Cicely? It had better be good for

such an entrance into my world." The Queen of Rivers and Rushes brushed back the stand of cattails and rushes and nodded for us to enter.

I hesitated for a second, then marched through. Kaylin and Leo followed more slowly. As we passed through the parted bushes, the winter fell away and we were standing by the lake during summer—the trees were in full leaf, the sun gleaming warm and golden overhead. The ice and snow were gone and the water rippled gently as a light breeze drifted past.

"We're . . . Where are we?" The sudden shift had taken the wind out of my sails and I smiled as the sunlight warmed me through. It felt so good compared to the harshness of winter that I just wanted to find a soft spot on the grass to lie down and sleep and dream.

"You asked to speak to me. I will not stand around the parking lot of Dovetail Lake for all the world to see. So I brought you into my domain. What there is of it, for now." She let out a long sigh and her eyes looked red from weeping.

I frowned. "What's wrong?"

"I am tired, child. Weary and heart sore. But such is the way when you belong to the world of the immortals. Come, sit and rest. You have the time here. Tell me what's so urgent that you would come seeking me out."

Her guards escorted her back to a makeshift throne— an old cedar stump that had been hastily carved into a royal bench, complete with footstool and armrests. As she ascended to take her place I had a sudden glimpse of what she'd been forced to leave behind. Beyond her possessions and her forest, she'd been stripped of her roots. Lainule was the Queen of Rivers and Rushes, the sovereign of the land in New Forest, and now she was hiding out in a temporary encampment, trying to stay one step ahead of Myst.

I let out a long breath. "Did you conspire with the

vampire Lannan Altos to infect me, so that I might contaminate the Indigo Court by passing a virus to Grieve?"

She gazed at me, her eyes steady and clear. "Not just a virus, Cicely. *Plague.* And yes, I know Altos and his bloodthirsty companions. This is not the time to retain old grudges. We have a common enemy. It behooves us to work together in order to eradicate Myst and her vermin. When you seek to exterminate a threat, you don't use sugar water instead of poison."

I nearly swallowed my tongue. "Poison? But Grieve—you used your own Prince to carry the toxin back to Myst's camp."

"Sacrifices must be made. And since he isn't born of the Indigo Court, there's a chance he will survive. I will do what I have to do, take the risks I have to take. And you . . . while I said before you are mine, I have no problem sharing you with the vampires in order to accomplish our goals."

*Sharing me?* A sudden thought struck me and I stared at her, wondering if I could be right. *No . . . but yet . . .*

"Are you behind the Crimson Court insisting I come work for them?"

Lainule smiled, and her smile was both fierce and bright. "Oh, Cicely. One thing you will learn, as you come to know your father's people more and more—we do not flinch in the face of danger. We do whatever is necessary."

I shivered. I'd never considered the Fae to be pacifists, but I had not realized they could be so ruthless.

*We . . .* I had to include myself in that. I was half-Fae.

Lainule leaned forward and tipped my chin up, looking into my eyes. "Never make the mistake of envisioning your people as gentle creatures, playing silver pipes and darting around the flowers. We are warriors and lovers: We are the chosen of the Mother to guard her wild sanctuaries and to rule the realms of Maeve and Danu, of Aine and Mielikki. Of Pan and Herne and Cernunnos and Tapio. Do you understand?"

I nodded, my stomach leaping from one knot to another. Lainule seemed taller, stronger, more powerful than I'd first thought, and she could squash me between her fingertips if she wanted to. I had no doubt that, if my death would strike down Myst, she'd see to it that I was sacrificed.

"We help keep the balance in check, and when one—such as Myst—seeks to upset that balance, we go to war in any way that we can. Winning is paramount. And I'll use every resource available to strike back at the Mistress of Mayhem for invading my domain and slaughtering my people. Whether it includes you and Grieve—I'll do whatever is necessary. I have always done what is necessary."

I wanted to protest, but something in her words—a finality that rang a chord of déjà vu—stopped me. There were no more words. I couldn't defend Myst and her people, even if *those people* included Grieve. As much as I loved him, I couldn't put his safety before stopping the Indigo Court.

"Can you help us save Peyton? We were thinking that this might be the time to strike. If this . . . poison . . . works like you say it does—they'll be off guard and not paying much attention to her." I stared at the ground. "If you can't, then I warn you—I'm going in on my own to rescue her. I have to. My loyalties are to my friends and family first. Now that they've turned Heather, my first order of business is to save my friend, even if it costs me my life."

Lainule rested a hand on my shoulder. "I cannot send my people with you, but I will give you this . . . take it, use it in good conscience. Do not lose it." She handed me a delicate lacquered fan made from oak. "It will help you to control the wind. And when you change into owl form, it will travel with you."

I blinked, taking the fan. It hummed with magic, strong and brilliant and magnetic. With a soft hush, I opened it wide and felt the wind stir.

"One wave of the fan, and you call a strong gust. Two waves, and you call a potent wind. Three . . . and you can walk on the wind. But it has limitations: It may only be used by you, and only when your wind Elemental is near. Ulean has kept me abreast of all your comings and goings over the years and she is linked to this fan."

"Ulean? You've used her to spy on me?" Feeling a sharp sting of betrayal, I jerked my head up. Ulean had never, ever told me she was in touch with the Queen of Rivers and Rushes.

Lainule touched her finger to my lips. "Shush, child. The Elemental had no choice. She is bonded to you, but she was originally mine. I gave her to you to protect you."

"*You* . . . gave her to me? I knew you'd asked Grieve to show us the bonding ritual but I didn't know . . . I didn't know Ulean was yours." And then I looked up at the Queen and saw something in her eyes that I couldn't quite read. "Why are you helping me? Other than the fact that I'm half-Fae? Why choose my mother to bear a Cambyra's child?"

Lainule motioned toward the portal leading out of her realm. "It's time for you to go," she said, ignoring my question. "Use the fan to help you in recovering your friend. Kill as many of the Indigo Court as you can. And if you can . . . rescue Grieve and perhaps we can figure out some way to break the connection between him and Myst's Court. Also . . . Chatter—he was always one of my favorites even though he was born outside of a noble match."

I dropped into a curtsey—the best I could, considering I was in jeans and a leather jacket. "Thank you. I'll do my best. And if we can somehow save Grieve from himself . . ."

"I know. You love him. You've always been on opposite sides, child, as far back as time goes. Perhaps this time, the two of you can get it right."

"Then you know—"

"It's time to leave. Stay longer in my domain and the years will fly by outside. For now, you leave but a moment after you entered."

As we turned to go, she called out, "Kaylin—the Court of Dreams is but a step away from my own domain. Watch closely. Your demon is about to awake."

Kaylin jerked around, but Lainule's guards thrust us back through the portal and we were standing in the middle of the snow again, thick flakes now pouring from the sky. I glanced at my watch. We'd been gone all of five minutes.

"Come on. Let's gather Rhiannon from Anadey's, and then . . . then let's go hunting. We're about to become soldiers in this three-sided war, although I'm not sure just whose side we're on."

Kaylin remained silent, looking pensive, but Leo snorted. "I think we make up the fourth side, Cicely. Haven't you figured out yet that we've got our own little army right here? Let's get a move on, because if the Indigo Court is really being hit in the gut with whatever poison or virus that was sent back through you, now's the time to dive in and see what damage we can do."

We headed back to Favonis. To war. To battle. To rescue Peyton. And hopefully . . . to survive.

# Chapter 23

When we showed up, Anadey and Rhiannon were just finishing a few energy-control exercises. We waited until they were done, then went over what had happened with Lainule and Grieve, and what we were planning.

"I'm so glad Lainule is alive, but that she's dealing with the vampires is unsettling. The Fae and the vampires tend to distrust and dislike one another. She must be in desperate straits if she's turning to them for help."

"Her people were massacred. She's holding court just off a parking lot by the lake. I think that qualifies as desperate," I said.

Anadey motioned for us to wait. "Let me see if I have anything that might help you. I'd go with you but I'm older and stiffer and I'd slow you down and that's the last thing you need going into this."

I nodded. While I had my doubts she'd slow us down that much, now was not the time to find out. "Tell you what you can do to help: If we succeed, we're going to need the house to be so protected that even a fly can't get through the shields. While we're out hunting for Peyton, can you do something to shore up our warding? Because what we're about to undertake is tantamount to waging war on the Indigo Court. I guarantee, they'll be out for revenge."

*Especially if we manage to steal away Grieve and Chatter,* I thought.

"I can do that." Anadey examined the fan Lainule had given me. She shivered as she touched it. "This is heavy, old magic, Cicely. Not the kind you just hand out on a whim. Keep this safe and don't lose it."

*She speaks the truth. You have been gifted generously from the Queen of Rivers and Rushes. Don't underestimate what that means.* Ulean blew through my hair and I could sense a tingling in her words, which always indicated she knew more than she was saying.

*What do you know about all of this? I had no idea you belonged to Lainule before Grieve bonded the two of us together.*

*That is for the Queen to tell you. Not my place. But I will be with you today, and I will help you learn to use your fan to greatest advantage.*

Anadey poked around in her stash and came up with several items. One, a small bottle filled with a red liquid, she handed to Rhiannon. "You know how to pull your flame back in, so now you should be able to use this. The potion will magnify your fire, but I have only one dose so drink it at the moment of your last resort."

To Leo and Kaylin, she offered small jars, also filled with liquid. "Iron water. It won't bother those with half-blood of the Fae, but I guarantee this will burn and scar its way through a full-blood, even of the Indigo Court."

Turning back to me, she let out a long sigh. "You are one of the Owl People, and you can harness the wind with your fan . . . I'm not sure what I can give you that's stronger than what you already have. But I have one thing . . .

it belonged to my mother and I found it in her personal ritual gear."

She held out a silver torque. It was wound silver, and the ends came together in the front in the shape of two flowers. "Those are belladonna flowers—deadly night-shade. Somehow, it seems to fit you. Marta never wore it, but she kept saying that one day it would find a home."

I took it, and it radiated magic in my fingers, though a subtle, slow, deep energy that ran in the currents of the ley lines and the high mountains of the earth. The tat-too on my left breast suddenly tingled and I looked at the wound silver torque. *Belladonna flowers* . . . deadly nightshade like the ones in my tattoo. There was a con-nection, though I didn't know what.

Glancing up, I met her eyes. Anadey gave me a weary smile, one that said she knew just what we were facing and was holding out as much hope as she could.

"We'll do everything we can to bring Peyton home," I said. "But say a few prayers for us, because we'll need it."

"I will . . . I'll start weaving my spells of protection the minute you leave here." She motioned for us to fol-low her into a spare bedroom. There, in the center of the room, was a loom. "I weave my magic into threads and cords. I'll work on one for your land—a long thin cord to be buried deep around the perimeter. I don't know how long it will take me to get it done, but I'll start it now."

She took her place at the loom and, as we silently filed out of the room, she said without turning her head, "Bring my baby home. If you can. You're the only hope she has."

✳

"Dress in black and white. We've got snow and dark trees out there," I said, sorting out what we could take with us. We were facing at least a two-hour march through the woods to the Barrow, if last time was any indication.

We gathered in the living room, gearing up for our search-and-rescue mission. Dressed in the thickest jeans I had and a black turtleneck, I slid on a pair of wide-heeled Doc Martin boots, and then fastened the wrist brace on my right arm that held my switchblade like a pro.

I slipped the torque around my neck and felt a deep humming race from the tattoo on my breast to spread throughout the rest of my body. Whatever the torque did was connected with my Fae heritage, I'd decided.

The stiletto athame went in my boot sheath, and I buckled on a thigh strap and slid another pair of knives—double-bladed and balanced for throwing—into the holders. Blades were the one weapon I'd learned how to use while living on the streets with my mother. Uncle Brody used to tell me: *A good blade is better than a good husband; you can rely on it more.*

The others had changed into denim and leather, too. Even Rhiannon. She, Kaylin, and I made sure our hair was braided back, hard to grab. Rhia brought out her makeup and we used the white eyeliner pencil and the mascara to smudge camouflage stripes across our faces.

Kaylin held up a pair of daggers, whirling them around like the master he was, then slid them neatly into the matching sheaths hanging from his belt. He added a set of polished black nunchakus and several small shurikens.

Not to be outdone, Leo held up a short staff, lithely twirling it around, reminding me of a modern, more handsome Friar Tuck. Even Rhiannon had a weapon, though when I saw what she was carrying, I took a step away from her. She had fixed up a couple of Molotov cocktails and was stowing them in a green grocery bag.

*Joy, oh joyous flamefest.*

*At least she's claiming her power,* Ulean whispered in my ear.

*Yes, she is at that.*

"So, let's go over this one more time. Our goals in

this order: Get in there and get out alive. Rescue Peyton. Bring Grieve and Chatter out. If possible, kill Myst. That's a long shot but I thought I'd throw that in there, just for good measure." My wolf hadn't spoken all day and I was worried that Grieve might be too sick for us to find him, but a quiet voice inside whispered he was probably sleeping, since the light hurt him now.

"We ready?" I looked at them, waiting.

"As we'll ever be." Rhiannon nodded grimly. "And if you should see Heather . . ." Her voice trailed off, then she cleared her throat. "If you should see Heather, stake her if you can." She held up four wooden stakes, then handed one to each of us.

I caught her gaze. "Are you sure?"

She didn't even flinch. "I'm sure."

"Okay, then . . . let's do this."

And we were off, out the door, into the storm that had finally broken.

❧

Two hours of travel meant that we'd reach the Marburry Barrow around three in the afternoon. Still daylight enough to take advantage of the plague Lainule had unleashed on the Indigo Court. As we silently crossed the yard toward the ravine, the wind snapped at our heels and the snow swirled in a mad dance around our faces. The hike into the ravine would be harder this time; the storm was barely getting started.

*We don't have storms or snow like this often.*

Ulean whistled past. *Myst rules the winter. She is of the Unseelie and still carries the cold weather magic in her veins, Vampiric Fae or not. She brings it with her and I'm afraid winter for this town will be hard and long this year, as long as she is rising in power.*

*Were you with Lainule for a long time?*

*Yes.* Ulean's answer was faint, as if she were looking

over her shoulder as she spoke to me. *Lainule and I go back a long, long, long way.*

*Back to when Grieve and I were together before?*

A very short *yes*, and she fell silent and I got the distinct feeling she had no interest in pursuing that thread of conversation.

The path was covered over and, while still visible through the trees, was difficult to navigate. The rocks and branches littering the trail were covered and it would be entirely too easy to twist an ankle or trip and fall here. I focused on leading the way, cautiously testing my footing every time I came to a suspicious lump under the blanket of white.

The forest was silent, the silence of sick rooms and hospitals, of muffled cotton, of a world lost in the frozen white. We picked our way along the trail as the snow fell thick and heavy. Wet, it would pack in and freeze tonight and I thought about what Ulean had said. Myst had the power of winter at her fingertips, and she'd nestled in for a long night's journey in New Forest. If her people now could only come out to play at night, and with the true vampires walking the night, it crossed my mind that maybe we should change our sleep schedules so we weren't so vulnerable during the darkness.

Thirty minutes in—we were going slower because of the weather—and we came to the ravine. I wanted to take a different route down—they might be watching us—but we didn't have the time to check out how safe the descent would be off path. Taking a deep breath, I plunged down, one step at a time, using a deadfall branch to test the way. With the bracken and vine hidden beneath the snowpack, it was doubly dangerous.

I thought I was avoiding all the traps, but without warning, caught my toe underneath a blackberry sucker and went sprawling face-first to roll about ten feet down the ravine before managing to slam into a tree.

"Are you okay?" Kaylin scrambled down the hill, kneeling beside me.

"Fuck." Wincing, I pushed myself to a sitting position. "That smarted. The snow kept me from getting too torn up by the brambles." As he pulled me to my feet, I checked to make sure nothing was broken and dusted off my jeans.

"Warning—incoming!" Leo's voice ripped through the air.

I jerked around, looking back up the hill to see one of the Indigo Fae slipping out from behind a tree. The look on the man's face was tortured, and his eyes—mad. He lunged for Rhiannon, grabbing her around the waist from behind and forcing her head to the side. He bared his teeth and dove for her neck. She screamed as Leo grabbed for the Fae. The man swung wide, backhanding Leo into the snow as if he were a dust speck. *Fuck, he's strong!*

I scrambled up the ravine, but Kaylin was ahead of me. He had whipped out his daggers and with silent, deadly accuracy, sent both spiraling through the air to plunge into the side of Rhiannon's attacker.

The Shadow Hunter let go of Rhia and whirled around, crazed and bleeding. He let out a low hiss and lurched to the left, the daggers still embedded in his side. As he swung around, moving twice as fast as Kaylin was, even *with* blood gushing out of his side, he held up one hand and Kaylin dropped to his knees, a dazed look on his face. Damn it, he was using magic.

The bleeding man turned his face to me, his mouth open in a hideous stretch, his fangs glistening next to the razor-sharp teeth. He began to morph, his body twisting as he changed form into a hideous, twisted doglike creature. The next moment, he leapt, lunging for Kaylin's throat.

Without a second thought, I swept the fan twice at him, whispering, "Gale force." And a huge gust of wind hurtled toward the creature, knocking him over and knocking me on my butt in the backlash.

Leo grabbed his walking staff and cracked the creature over the skull while Rhiannon thrust out her hands and whispered something.

A short burst of flame seared the monstrosity's skin and he screamed, disrupting his shift. Within seconds, he was back to normal—or at least, I supposed it was normal; maybe it wasn't—and groaning as he rolled on the ground, trying to douse the flames.

Kaylin, shaken out of his trance, leapt up and, using two of his shurikens, threw them to land directly in the throat of the Indigo Court Fae. With one last shudder, the Shadow Hunter lay still.

I crept up beside him, staring down at the unblinking man. He was handsome, strangely compelling even in death, with rigid cheekbones and glassy eyes, in which the stars had gone out.

"Christ, that took work," Kaylin said, retrieving his daggers. He wiped them in the snow, then dried them on the bottom of his shirt. "And he was hurting. Did you see his expression?"

"He looked crazed—and yes, in pain." I stared at him. I'd never killed anybody before. Or helped kill anybody before. It was an odd sensation. I searched for guilt, but felt none. He'd been out to kill us and he wouldn't have hesitated to tear us apart. "I wonder if his shapeshifting . . . is that how they feed?" I was thinking about Grieve. Did he shift into that form now, too?

"Yes." Rhiannon slipped up beside me to stare down at the man. "But don't worry," she whispered. "Grieve wasn't born to the Indigo Court. I'm sure that he doesn't do that."

She was probably lying to spare my feelings, but I was grateful for the illusion right now. A glance at her showed she was holding steady. Anadey had already worked wonders with her and I looked forward to seeing her after a few months of steady practice. My cousin was going to be one hell of a force.

"You think he was in pain because he's out in the day, even though we're under a cloud cover? If he's infected with whatever plague Lainule and Lannan cooked up . . ." Leo knelt beside the Shadow Hunter and began searching his pockets. At my quizzical look, he shrugged. "Why not see if he might have something we can use?"

And just like that we became looters as well as killers.

He held up an odd-looking blade made of obsidian. The blade looked so sharp that I was almost afraid to touch it, but when I took it in my hand the energy seeped right through me, chilling me through. I almost jerked away but that would have been a dangerous mistake and I caught myself. The energy was sinking deep, curling around my nerves, sucking me into a numbness that felt oddly familiar.

"Help . . . me . . ." The words became molasses in my mouth and I rolled my head back, sinking to my knees.

Kaylin reached over and lifted the blade off my palm. "Your eyes . . . they were shifting, changing to—I'm not sure what. But I saw something there."

The fog began to lift. I shook my head. "Don't let me hold that again, it scares me." And it did. It made me think of sinking in quicksand, of being sucked down into the tar pits, of being consumed alive. "But we need to know what it is. Is there a way to transport it safely?"

He nodded, hoisting off his backpack. Retrieving a small box from the pack, he slipped the blade inside, then wrapped a rubber band around the box and replaced it in the pack.

"It should be fine for now. But yeah, I think we'd better find out just what the fuck's up." Reaching out, he rubbed his hand up my arm and I shivered. Kaylin did things for me, definitely, and if I hadn't been with Grieve, I'd be so right there. "You okay?"

"Yeah, but we'd better keep our eyes open. If one of the Shadow Hunters is still out and about, you can bet more are. And they aren't very happy right now, which tells us that Lainule's plan seems to have worked, at least to some extent."

We resumed our trek down the side of the ravine. I was more cautious in my footing and, muffled by the thick cover of falling snow, we silently descended to the bottom. The stream had totally frozen over, though I didn't trust the layer of ice to hold us, so we cautiously navigated the stepping stones again.

On the other side, we started back up the hill.

"Look," Rhiannon whispered. I followed her gaze.

Stretching between two of the firs was a giant spiderweb, the strands shimmering with frozen droplets to create a sculpture in ice and silk, a monument to Arachne, a tribute to perseverance. It was huge, at least twelve feet from top to bottom, and the guylines were anchored a good fifteen feet between trees. A shiver ran up my back as I watched, waiting.

Slowly, out from behind the tree, scuttled the sculptor, the creator. The spider's body was easily the size of a salad plate, the jointed legs spreading out to easily two feet in diameter. The golden orb weaver was milky white, with shimmering gold markings on its body, and it scurried into the center of the web. Another joined it, and a third, and they waited, watching us.

"Motherfucking son of a bitch . . ." The sight took my breath away. I wasn't fond of spiders, but these gave me the creeps in a way most others never had. A wave of malevolence rolled off of them, toward us.

*They are deadly in their bite—they are not your typical orb weaver. Be cautious, for these are Myst's pets.*

*Snow weavers.* Ulean blew in next to me on a chill gust, filled with snowflakes and ice.

I nodded, slowly, unable to tear my gaze away from the sight. They were beautiful and horrible, sparkling with energy that beckoned me to come forward.

*Cicely, they are mesmerizing you. Please, say something and break their hold. Speak, child. Speak.*

A sudden gasp and I realized it was me—I'd been holding my breath and my body had taken matters into its own hands. I shook out of the trance and hurriedly turned to the others.

"Don't look at them too long—they have some sort of control and they will lure you in and kill you. Or bind you for Myst. They're magical, and they belong to her." I reached out and shook Rhiannon, then Kaylin and Leo, making sure they weren't caught, like I'd just about been.

"Then she knows we're here? Are they her eyes and ears?"

"The owls and spiders hate each other," I whispered, looking back at the spiders to make sure they were still in their webs. And in truth, when I looked at them, I wanted to strike down the web. They gave me the feeling of overripe fruit, or cloying sweets covered with translucent flies.

"And you are Uwilahsidhe . . . of the owls." Kaylin stared at the spiders. "Should we try to kill them? Is it too late?"

"I think the question is, can we kill them?" I looked at him, and we read each other's eyes. He slowly shook his head. I gave him an affirmative nod. "No. We leave them. I have a nasty feeling that we'd be playing Russian roulette."

*You are right, they are far stronger than you can believe. But they will stay in their webs. Fire will not hurt*

*them, so your cousin should put away her flame. Just*
*watch where you walk. There are others in the forest.*

I whirled around to see Rhiannon bringing out one
of the Molotov cocktails. "Stop." I motioned for her to
put the bottle away. "Ulean just told me that fire won't
hurt them—their magic is too strong. But they stay in
their webs. Just be cautious as we continue, not to stum-
ble into a stray web because there are, apparently, more
of them."

And so we continued on our way to the Barrow, but
now Myst surely knew we were coming. And we'd killed
one of her people. I knew that the Mistress of Mayhem
would be waiting with open arms and ready teeth.

# Chapter 24

We came to the circle of mushrooms and cautiously skirted it, taking extra care since the path was now obliterated by snow. A few footprints here and there showed someone had been through here recently. As we turned to head toward the Twin Oaks, I heard a noise from off to the side. Before I could raise my fan in readiness, Chatter stepped out of the trees.

"Chatter!"

He rushed over to us. "Something has happened—Grieve is sick. Indigo Fae all over are ill. The light is making them sick and they can't come out, but even staying in the dark doesn't help too much."

Rhiannon reached out and gently slid her hand down his arm, which seemed to calm him down. "It was unwitting. Cicely was—"

"Rhia—stop." I couldn't tell Chatter what had happened, nor Grieve. Lainule would have my head if I spilled secrets. "Chatter, how is Grieve? I thought he might be sick, my wolf tattoo has been upset all morning." A twist here, a little lie there, it added up but my life was no longer mine and I'd do what I had to in order to protect my family and friends.

Chatter looked at Rhiannon, confused for a moment, then turned back to me. "He's not in the main Barrow. We seldom stay there and Myst seems not to mind. I can take you to him, but it's still dangerous."

"We'll go with you but Chatter, if I have to I'll kill any of the Indigo Court that threaten us. You must understand that right now." I looked into his eyes, holding his gaze. "I can't have you turning on me if something goes down."

He shook his head. "No, I won't. And if you take out a few of them, I won't stand in the way. The Shadow Hunters live to kill and to hurt." His eyes glazed over for a moment, then he wiped the fog away and led us off the main path. "Follow me. You don't want to go toward the main entrance of the Barrow. It's too dangerous. Myst has guards out in full—they're in pain due to the light, but she doesn't care. That's part of their job. But it makes them worse."

We were breaking through the undergrowth now, heading into thick forest. Navigating it in good weather would be tough, but with the winter holding us hostage, it was harder. The snow was piling up—a good foot now, and I sunk deep with every step, having to slog through the heavy, wet drifts.

Within minutes we could no longer see the path and I wondered if we'd be able to find our way back, but Chatter gave me a shake of the head when I opened my mouth and I fell silent, trusting him. If he said we should be quiet, I'd be quiet. We wound around through cedar and fir, over fallen tree trunks, under heavy arching branches filled with snow that silently showered us in the sparkling, harsh land that the forest had become.

At one point, Chatter held up his hand and we stopped.

A small crossing in front of us loomed, and there, making its way slowly through the clearing to the other side, was a creature forged of ice. It was hard to make out the shape, though it was vaguely bipedal, and it gleamed with streaks of blue and purple frozen within its gleaming crystal shell.

I gasped, but kept silent. Ulean stirred at my shoulder.

*Ice Elemental—very rare around here. Usually they're found on glaciers, or at the Poles. They're dying out, you know, as the glaciers melt. They will be a casualty as the world warms, unless another ice age is sparked off again.*

It was so beautiful that I wanted to creep forward, to run my hand down the creature's sparkling side, but I restrained myself. I glanced at Leo, Kaylin, and Rhiannon, who stood just as rapt as I was.

*It's beautiful . . . does it know we're here?*

*I cannot tell. Ice Elementals are far, far from the world of warm-bloods. They live outside of time, coming to life during the winter and fading during the summer unless they live in the lands of the long nights.*

As it vanished into the undergrowth on the other side, Chatter waited for a moment, then motioned us on. We followed him deeper into the forest. For an hour, we followed the Fae, stopping now and then as he checked the slipstream for any Shadow Hunters.

Finally, up ahead I saw the entrance to a cave leading into the hillside. Chatter pointed to it and we headed toward the dark opening. As he stood back, waiting for me to enter, I sucked in a deep breath and paused.

*Is it safe, Ulean?*

*No place in this woodland is safe, Cicely, but I don't sense danger at fingertip's length.*

I entered, followed by the others. Chatter brought up the rear. He stopped, turned to the entrance, and in a low voice chanted a few words. A sparkling light filtered over the opening, cloaking it, and I realized he'd just made it harder to see from the outside.

The chamber was pitch-black, but after a moment, little Faerie lights began to light the inside and I found myself staring at a cozy living room. Several seats carved from oak were placed around a center pit, over which a rotisserie had been placed. A small stalagmite rose from the ground, a bowl chipped out on the top. Fresh water bubbled into the bowl, continuously cycling.

Chatter let out a long sigh. "We should be safe enough for a little while. I have to check on Grieve." He motioned to the benches. "Sit down, please." With a wave of the hand, he lit the stones beneath the rotisserie on fire and they blazed a merry warmth. "Warm yourselves while I'm gone."

"Let me come with you." I walked over to his side. "I have to see him. Please."

"If you're sure . . ." He cocked his head. "I don't know if it's a good idea."

"Chatter, we're here to take Peyton, Grieve, and you home with us. I'm going to see him, one way or another." I held his eyes and felt myself falling into his gaze. He blinked slowly and I found myself moving toward him, but then shook my head. "Don't try that on me. I'm part Cambyra Fae. I know what you're doing."

"Cicely, how can we go with you—"

"Shut up." I held up my hand. "You don't have a choice in this. Chatter, we're stronger than you think, and we'll do everything necessary to save our friends, ourselves, and this town. I love Grieve. He loves me. Take me to him."

"You may not like what you see." A sullen look washed across his face, but he wiped it away. "All right, follow me. But only you. Grieve would not tolerate more than your company right now."

"Are you sure you want to go alone?" Kaylin asked.

I shrugged. "I don't have a choice. Just keep alert out here."

I followed Chatter to the back, where another opening led to a narrow passage. It led so far back into the mountain that I couldn't see the end of it, but several chambers opened off of either side. Chatter led me to the first one and we slipped through the opening, ducking our heads in order to do so.

The chamber was fitted to be a bedroom. Soft lights lit up the inside, delicate and sparkling, and in the corner was a bed. The bed was carved from rock, piled high with moss and blankets. A dresser to the left looked like it had been plucked out of the Victorian era, and to the right, a divan and table, both from the Art Deco years. But my focus was on the bed, for resting in the center of the blankets, as still as death, was Grieve.

As soon as I entered, he began tossing and turning. My wolf gave a whimper—now that we were within touching distance it would be hard to keep the connection from re-forming. I rushed over to his side but stopped when he sat up, a ferocious look on his face.

"Stay back, I'm having trouble controlling myself. Even around Chatter." His eyes shimmered, the stars in them sparkling, calling me forward even as he warned me back.

"Grieve, what's going on? What's happening?"

I didn't dare tell him that I had caused this—in his condition, who knew what he'd do? Guilt warred with triumph—the thought that we might be able to get a leg up on the Indigo Court through this plague danced in my heart like Tinkerbell dancing on Hook's grave.

"I don't know, but it's hit a number of the Indigo Court." He struggled to sit up. "Now's the time for you to rescue Peyton, if you're ever going to. She'll be easier to get out of here."

I bit my lip. "You can't help me, can you? You're too sick."

He shook his head, drawing his hand over his eyes.

"I'm managing to hold on. But the true Vampiric Fae—the ones born to the Court—are having trouble maintaining. Some are slipping into madness, others into their brutal natures fully. I'm afraid that whatever this is, will make them more dangerous than ever once they adapt to it."

His words hit like ice water. "Adapt? Isn't it . . . nobody's dying from it, then?"

"Not that I know of, but it's created a condition where the daylight is like poison. Unlike the true vampires, we aren't dying from it. Just incapacitates and seems to bring out the inner beast."

I sat down on the chair near his bed, closing my eyes. What had Lainule and Lannan done? Even if they couldn't effectively fight during the day, they were still terribly dangerous and they weren't going to go *poof* into a pile of ashes like the Crimson Court when the sunlight kissed them. The plan had backfired, in a terrible way. Now they'd be less able to reason.

"What's wrong? Cicely?" Grieve pushed himself up on his elbows. "Are you okay?"

I nodded bleakly. "Yeah. I'm okay. But we have to get Peyton and Chatter out of here." With a horrible finality, I realized that taking Grieve home with us wasn't an option. Even my love couldn't blind me to the fact that he was far more dangerous, closer to the edge than before. He could survive here, among his crazed brethren, but Chatter—Chatter couldn't.

Grieve stared at me for a moment, reading my face. "You wanted me to come, too." Wincing, he gripped the side of the bed and let out a low moan. I moved toward him, but he held up his hand.

"No," he said, his voice ragged. "We can be together at night, but until I find out what's happening, I don't dare touch you during the day. You'd intoxicate me too much, I'd want to drink from you too deep and I might hurt you."

"Grieve . . . I love you. I love you," was all I could say, staring at him from across the divide that had suddenly sprung up, a gulf that threatened to sweep us away from each other.

He paused, a dark smile creeping across his face. "I could turn you. You could become one of us, now that you know you're part Cambyra Fae. We could be together and hunt through the night. You'd love the power that it brings. And you'd be with your aunt then."

Horrified, I turned to Chatter, who shook his head, cautioning me not to speak. "Grieve. Grieve? Where is Peyton?" he said, moving a step closer to my fallen lover.

"Peyton? The magic-born Were? Where do you think she is, you dolt? She's in the gaol. Idiot." Grieve's smile grew darker, more feral, and he reached out his hand. "Bring me my lover. I need her. Need to feed . . ."

"No—no. Grieve—come back to yourself. Grieve, can you hear me?" I jumped up. "Don't let this suck you down. Don't let it eat you up. Can you understand? You've been infected by some illness and it's hurting you. Fight it. Please, please fight it."

Grieve snorted, but then a moment of clarity passed across his face. "Cicely . . . get out of here. Please. I don't want you seeing me like this. I don't want you hearing the horrible things I say." He struggled to sit up again. "Listen to me. I love you, Cicely Waters. You're my one love. You've always been my love. Whatever happens, remember that. Chatter, help her to get Peyton out of here while you can. My guess is that the gaol isn't heavily guarded right now. Myst is probably up in arms—and sick herself. And Chatter—don't come back. It's too dangerous for you now."

With another cry, he twisted to the side, bringing his legs up to his chest. My wolf howled as a sharp pain lanced through my stomach and I fell to my knees with a scream. Chatter grabbed me up and tossed me over his shoulder, carrying me out of the room, dragging me toward the main chamber even as I beat on his back, trying to stop him.

"No—I have to help Grieve. Put me down!"

"You can't help him," he said, setting me down once we were out of the room and far enough away that I couldn't just run back in. "There's nothing you can do to help him. He has to work through this himself. Come. I'll help you with Peyton. Grieve's right—she probably won't be guarded too heavily at this point."

He led me back to the main chamber and I followed, unable to think. My wolf was begging me to return to Grieve's side, to give in, to let him do what he would so we could be together. But the torque around my neck began to vibrate, gently humming, soothing me, and a warmth spread through my chest from the Fae girl tattoo, down toward my wolf where it washed over the tattoo in a glow of moonlight, easing the pain. My head cleared enough for me to shake away the thought.

As we reentered the room, the others looked up.

"Come on. Chatter's going to help us find Peyton and get the fuck out of here." I headed toward the door.

"What about Grieve?" Rhiannon asked.

I slipped my gloves back on. "Forget it," I whispered. "We're leaving him here. It's for the best."

Chatter gave them a shake of the head and the look on his face said enough that, without another word, they stood and followed us out into the snow.

❉

We had to climb up the hill next to the cave. Slipping and sliding, we worked our way through the undergrowth, holding on to branch and bough, pulling ourselves up some of the steeper inclines. Boots sliding on ice slicks, teeth gritting as we struggled through the heavy, wet snow, we managed to finally pull ourselves over the top of the slope. I rolled over on my back, staring into the frost-laced sky, letting the flakes kiss my face with their delicate touch.

"Gods, that was hard. I'm in shape, but damn, that was like slogging through mud." I pushed myself up to a sitting position, frozen through, my muscles aching like I'd just run a marathon. At this point, I just wanted to get through the rest of the day alive. Happy wasn't a factor now that I'd seen Grieve.

And carrying the secret that I'd been responsible for his illness—and for potentially making our battle with the Indigo Court worse—didn't help. Guilt ate at me, and even though I hadn't willingly participated in Lainule's plan, the fact was that I'd entered into the contract with the vampires and I'd agreed to obey Lainule.

"Hurry," Chatter said. "We don't have much time before dusk and who knows what the return of shadow will do for Myst and her people? With the way things are, this might have strengthened them."

With that lovely thought lingering in my mind, I let him pull me to my feet and we headed off again, one slogging step at a time. Thanks to the time in the cave, I wasn't as frozen, but the temperature was dropping and the snowflakes were growing smaller and more furious. This was sticking snow, biting snow that would pile up all night.

Kaylin slipped up beside me. "What went on back there with Grieve?" he asked in a low voice. I shook my head, not wanting to talk about it, but he wouldn't let up. "I know something happened. What was it?"

Turning my head to him, I kept my voice low. "He's being overtaken by his darker nature. And he says that this *cure* that Lannan and Lainule thought they found may just make the Indigo Court a lot fiercer and more dangerous to deal with. You should have seen him fighting both the pain and his urge to give in to his vampiric nature. Kaylin, it's all so fucked up."

He slipped an arm around me and helped me along, not saying another word. The look on his face was enough. He may not have approved of Grieve but he wasn't taking any delight in the unfolding events. As we trudged along behind Chatter, I leaned my head on Kaylin's shoulder and he tightened his grasp around my waist.

After another twenty minutes of slow, cold going, Chatter held up his hand. Kaylin let go of me as we all gathered around the Fae. We were on top of a ledge, over-looking another ravine. Down below, I could see three guards standing in front of what looked like the mouth to another cave.

"The gaol," Chatter mouthed.

The guards looked anything but attentive. One was bent over, puking his guts out near a huckleberry bush. Another was moaning and rocking back and forth. The third was managing to stand upright, but he leaned on a nearby tree stump and looked in danger of passing out. Finally, a piece of luck.

I sucked in a deep breath, planning out the approaching battle in my mind. They were weak, but even weakened, they were formidable foes. We'd have to get down there and kill them before they could raise an alarm.

It struck me that the thought of murdering three strangers didn't even make me flinch, and I looked up, shocked and numb. Kaylin met my gaze and gave me a small nod.

*He understands. He's been alive a long time, Cicely, and not all of his life was easy or painless or free of death and blood.* Ulean's touch was gentle on my skin.

*What am I becoming, that I can contemplate killing three people I've never met just because of who they are?*

*You're becoming the person you need to be. You're*

*becoming the person you really are inside: a survivor.
A warrior. A leader. A woman who will do what is necessary to rescue her friends and family. That's what it
means to love, Cicely. That's what your mother could
never teach you because she put herself first, always.
You're growing into the woman who can proudly wear
her wings and fly.*

Ulean brushed around me. I thought of Peyton, and of
Grieve. Of Heather and Elise, Leo's sister. I thought of
Kaylin's best friend, and the nameless others who'd lost
their lives to these creatures. And those who were next
on the list.

Sucking in a deep breath, I checked my blades and
pulled out my fan. The others silently readied their weapons. We were ready. If Myst wanted mayhem, then we
were going to ram a boatload of it down her throat.

Without another thought, I went barreling down the
slope at the three guards, waving my fan twice, driving
the gale on before me.

# Chapter 25

We brought down a minor avalanche with us, the snow cascading behind us in a wave of smoke. There was very little roar, since only a small slope of snow broke off, but as we surfed the frozen white, a lightning bolt split the sky and thunder rocked the air. Snow lightning—crap! We were getting full special effects for this.

I came to rest—on my feet, luckily—in front of the guard who had been doubled over, puking his guts out. He'd jumped back when the snow cascaded down the slope, and his gaze rose to meet mine, his eyes ringed with the same mad haze that I'd seen wash over Grieve's face. Before he could react, I flicked out my stiletto and lashed out, slicing his left arm across the bicep.

He let out a growl and spun around, his foot catching me across the stomach. In a daze of pain, I went flying back into the snow. As I struggled to my feet, I pulled out my fan.

To my left, Rhiannon and Leo had engaged the second guard. Leo planted his staff in the ground and used it to propel himself up and over the guard's head, catching the man's neck between his legs with a scissor kick. The man twisted, trying to free himself, and Leo flipped away from him, landing in a crouch. Unbalanced, the guard went down. As he struggled to regain his footing, Rhiannon held out her hands and a blistering flame shot forth, engulfing the Vampiric Fae.

To my right, Kaylin and the third guard were into it. From appearances, Kaylin was winning. There was blood all over the snow and none of it appeared to be coming from him.

Chatter was skirting the perimeter, looking for anybody, particularly other guards, who might be hiding out.

Ignoring the pain in my side, I quickly turned back to my own attacker and held out the fan. As I waved it twice, whispering, *"Gale force,"* a gust of wind so strong it knocked me back off my feet raced past, directly aimed toward the guard. It hit him square in the chest, sliding him along the snow a good ten feet before slamming him against the face of a boulder. He went limp and I raced up, switchblade ready.

Before he could regain consciousness, I slid my blade along his throat, severing the skin from ear to ear. As blood fountained out, his head fell back, still attached to his neck by a sliver of flesh. With a final gurgle, his body relaxed and I knew he was dead.

*Be cautious how much you use the fan. It has limitations that Lainule didn't remember to tell you about. And . . . repercussions.* Ulean swirled around me, a twisting vortex as she helped lift me to my feet with her currents.

I turned to see how Rhiannon and Leo were doing. Leo was limping, and the guard's knife was bloody. Chatter was on the run toward them, but he was too far away. Kaylin and I converged on the Indigo Court Fae as he swung around and—like the creature we'd met earlier—his mouth began to distend as his body shifted.

"He's turning into one of those doglike creatures!" I couldn't use the fan, the others were too close, so I flipped out my switchblade and tried to jump him.

The Fae met me with an outstretched fist, managing to punch me directly in the shoulder. I clutched my arm with a groan. How the hell could he be so strong? As I struggled to get out of the way of his second blow, Kaylin leapt in with his nunchakus and went to work. Leo circled behind and brought his staff down across the man's head and, with a loud crack, he was down. Except the Fae was just stunned. He was already starting to regain consciousness and when he did, he'd begin his transformation again.

Rhiannon pushed to the front and held out her hands.

"No," I said softly. "Let me do it. Don't bloody your hands, Rhia."

She let out a harsh laugh. "They've been bloody for half my life." And with that, she let out a spray of fire that melted the snow around the Fae and caught him aflame. He shrieked once, then Kaylin threw one of his daggers with deadly accuracy and the Fae lay dead.

We stared at the carnage around us. Leo was limping, but the cut he'd received was superficial and Chatter bound it up with a strip of cloth cut from one of the guard's tunics. My ribs and shoulder felt bruised, but I'd live. Kaylin and Rhiannon were untouched.

We turned to the cave. Peyton was in there, somewhere. The question was . . . were other guards waiting for us? There was only one way to find out. I pushed to the front and stepped over the threshold.

✦

The cavern was actually a tunnel illuminated by a trail of purplish sparkling lights. It led into the mountainside. I glanced around—nobody in sight. Yet. Motioning for the others to follow me, I headed down the passage, trying to be as silent as possible. Ulean was at my shoulder, I could feel her.

"Is this the prison?" I stopped, motioning to Chatter.

He slipped up beside me and nodded. "I've been inside a couple times, when they locked me up as punishment. The tunnel continues, with side passages—some are holding cells, others are guard quarters, I believe. I don't remember which is which."

The tunnel was made of granite, and at first I wondered if it had been an old mining tunnel, but looking closer it seemed too smooth. No miners' picks had chipped away at this passage. No, it looked almost like glass in its even surface. I stopped briefly and slid my fingers across the smooth wall, closing my eyes. A shiver ran up my back. The passage was magical, the energy flaring from within the very structure of the rock.

Sucking in a deep breath, we started down the hall again, Kaylin behind me, then Chatter, then Rhiannon and Leo. As we came to the end, I peeked around the corner. Several of the chambers Chatter had mentioned buttressed the main channel to the right, then another turn at the end. Slowly, cautiously, we moved to the first side entrance and stopped a few feet before it.

*Can you see what's inside?*

*I cannot tell for sure—this place is full of magical traps and wards—but Peyton is not there. That much I know. There is someone in there, however.*

I nodded, then turned back and whispered what Ulean had told me to Kaylin, who passed it back to the others. They looked to me for a decision, though by the look on Leo's face, I could tell he was nursing a faint hope it might be his sister. Torn, I tried to decide what to do. If we tried to sneak past, whoever it was might raise an alarm, or take us from the back. No, we were going to have to face them, whether they were one of the enemy or a prisoner.

*And there's no saying a prisoner won't also be your enemy.*

*Thanks, I needed that.*

I swung in through the door, hoping to catch whoever it was off guard. The person whirled. *Fuck, one of the Indigo Fae.* A woman this time. She was lying on a bed and as she tried to sit up, blinking, pain filled her face.

I didn't wait. I lunged for her and landed on top of her, holding her down as I raised my switchblade high. Biting my lip, I brought the blade down right in her throat. She let out a hiss, and threw me off, sitting up. I went sprawling to the floor, ducking, as Kaylin flipped over me and landed a kick right in her stomach.

She landed back on the bed and reached for her throat, trying to staunch the bleeding, but the activity had just spurred on the flow and now she frantically tried to press her hands against her throat. Kaylin pulled out one of his daggers and within seconds it was over.

I stared at my hands, at the blood spatters that were covering me. *What was I becoming?*

Kaylin must have noticed my expression. He moved to put his arm around me. "We're doing what we have to do. If you want to save Peyton, we have no choice. These creatures—and they are creatures, mind you—would eat you alive and I am not joking. I think I've figured out what the book was talking about when it mentioned *feeding frenzy.* Can you imagine a group of the Vampiric Fae, turning into those creatures, attacking a woman? A child? They'd eat them to the bone, without bothering to administer a killing bite first. *Feeding frenzy.* Think about it."

Chatter sucked in a deep breath. "That's exactly what happens. I've seen it," he said. "Children, women, it matters not to them. They have no conscience, and they love the mayhem. They feed on the fear they cause, as well as the flesh." His mouth pursed, looking like he was going to cry, he shook his head. "They revel in the blood."

I looked up at him, and the image flashed through my mind. I could see it, all too vividly. *Feeding frenzy.* They were the piranha of the Fae world. I thought again of the people who'd disappeared. Of Heather and Peyton and Elise . . . oh gods . . . *Elise.* I turned to Leo, who was white as fresh-fallen snow.

"My sister. If she's not here, and they haven't turned her, then they ate her. Just like that . . . in a flurry of blood and bone."

Rhia pressed against him, taking his hand. "We don't know that," she said softly.

"Yeah, we do. Because if they didn't force her to turn, then that's what happened. I know my sister. She wouldn't voluntarily help them." He rubbed his hand over his eyes, looking sick. "I want them dead."

"We seem to be accomplishing that," I said, wiping my blade on my pants. My mind and hands were forever stained with blood so why not my jeans. "I guess this is what it means to be a warrior."

"That's about the size of it. You do what you have to do, Cicely. And what we have to do now is find Peyton. Chances are we'll be fighting more of them—and we have to take them down before they give a warning." Chatter looked stronger than I'd seen him since the old days. He was standing tall.

"What do you think will happen to Grieve?" I whispered.

He shook his head. "I don't know, but we don't have time to speculate right now. Let's move on."

We crept down the hall to the next chamber, which was empty. Then the third, before the bend in the tunnel. I peeked around the corner, cautiously. There, behind a set of iron bars, was Peyton. She was naked, huddled beneath a ragged blanket, but I could see her eyes. They were normal—she hadn't been turned. She glanced up and saw me, and bolted to a sitting position. I pressed my finger to my lips and she nodded.

"Can anybody pick locks?"

Kaylin pushed to the front. "Let me."

While he worked, Peyton searched her cell, finally setting for tying the threadbare blanket around her, toga style. I realized she didn't have any clothes and that would prove a problem for her on our way back home through the storm.

A moment later, Kaylin sprang the lock and the door opened with a faint squeak. Peyton hurried forward and fell into my arms. I held her close for a moment, whispering to her.

"Are you able to travel?" I didn't bother asking how she was. I figured that was opening a can of worms that was better left for when we were safe.

She nodded. "But they took my clothes and shoes. I have nothing to wear except this blanket." Her arms looked bruised and when I looked closer, so did the side of her face, though she wasn't sporting a black eye.

I turned back to the others. "How are we going to get her home? She can't spend two hours out in the cold wearing a blanket. And nothing the guards were wearing will fit her—she's far taller than most of the Indigo Court Fae."

"I have an idea," Leo said. "Peyton, can you turn into a cougar?"

"I thought she was a werepuma," I said.

"Same thing—cougar, mountain lion, puma . . . they're all different names for the same cat. I know, I've studied that side of my family history," Peyton said. "And yes, I can but not in here. There's some magical barrier that's preventing me from shifting in the cell."

I glanced down the tunnel. What if Elise was here? What if others were here? "Should we . . ."

Leo touched my arm. "Not now. We came to save Peyton, Chatter, and Grieve. We can't take Grieve with us, but we have Peyton and Chatter. If my sister's here," he whispered, "she's on their side. And if not, she's dead. Let's cut our losses and go."

*He's right. You need to leave. The afternoon is wearing away and you must be home before dark because the Indigo Fae will be back to full strength then, and worse. They are changing. Whatever Lannan and Lainule infected them with, it backfired more than you think.*

I nodded, Ulean's urgency spurring me on. Motioning to the others, we headed back the way we'd come. We managed to make it out of the cave, back into the waning afternoon. The snow was still falling and so thick that it was hard to see more than ten yards ahead. The minute we left the cave, Peyton began to shiver. She stepped to the side.

"Peyton, listen to me. If we find ourselves in a fight, take off. Head for the house. Anadey's working on a stronger warding for us and she might have it ready by now. For the moment, we should be safe over the boundaries, but I don't know how long that will last." I had a nasty feeling we weren't out of the frying pan yet. And who knew what lay waiting in the fire.

"I understand. Thank you, all of you . . ." she said, drawing her hand in front of her eyes. Tears sparkled behind her snow-kissed lashes, and then without another word, she shifted quickly, and a gorgeous tawny cougar stood there.

I motioned to the side of the hill, and then stopped, looking around. The bodies of the guards we'd taken down were missing.

"Hell, someone's been here. Get a move on."

"We could take you back. I can take one of you through the shadows and Chatter can run—" Kaylin started, but I shook my head.

"There are three of us, one would be left behind and I won't do that. Hurry up." I struggled through the fresh snow over to the slope and began to make my way up. The others followed suit, Ulean assisting us by gusting at our backs to give us a shove.

We managed to make it to the top and head back through the path, led by Chatter. He stopped, though, a few minutes later. "They might be waiting along the path, and they won't take chances. They'll send more than we can handle. I know another way, but it's dangerous."

Mutely, I glanced at Leo and Rhiannon. They nodded. So did Kaylin. Peyton let out a soft huff. Turning back to Chatter, I let out a long sigh. "Let's go. Lead on."

He silently turned to the right and plunged us through the undergrowth. We were fighting snow a good eighteen inches deep by now, and undergrowth so thick that we had to push our way through. I thought about our footsteps, but with the rate at which the snow was falling and the coming dusk, they'd be covered soon. Especially if we walked in single file.

The afternoon wore on, and by my watch, we had a little over an hour till the sun officially set. The only good thing about sunset was that the vampires would be up and maybe, just maybe, we could hope for some help from them. But then again, they had no clue as to what we were doing. There was no cavalry to rescue us, no gods in the machine.

We silently plunged forward, Peyton huffing gently. She was probably warmer than the rest of us. In her Were form, she'd be used to the cold and snow. Chatter stopped every so often to give us a chance to catch up and make certain we were still altogether. I was beginning to wonder what the danger part was when we came to the edge of the ravine. But there was no easy descent here—the edge was sheer, and boulders covered the slope and bottom of the great ditch.

An alluvial deposit—common in Washington State, from when the great glaciers had moved across the land. In their retreat, they'd left vast swathes of rocks and boulders—a blanket of stone to cover parts of the land. An avalanche here meant a rockslide, a danger itself.

The snow atop the stones only increased the danger of turning an ankle, twisting wrong, getting a foot caught in between rocks. I stared down at the wash of stone, my stomach plunging. It would take us a good two hours to make it to the bottom, and the climb on the other side, once we crossed the frozen stream, would be exhausting.

Chatter stopped, kneeling to examine the snow at the edge. "This won't be easy going. But . . . I can take you down, one by one. I can get you to the bottom, but I'm afraid I won't have the reserves to help you up to the other side."

"But can you do so without hurting yourself? That's one hell of a steep climb." I stared down the slope, uneasy. If we were caught down there, we'd be trapped.

"I don't know, to be honest. But I'm willing to try." He looked up at me, his eyes soft and luminous. "Cicely, Grieve would want me to do everything I could to help you. Please, let me help you."

I nodded, then. But before we could move, Peyton brushed against my hand and let out a soft huff. She padded to the edge and easily slipped over the side. For her, the going was far easier. One less person for Chatter to have to carry. Another thought struck me.

"I can fly down, if you take my clothes so I can change again, after."

"Are you sure?" Rhiannon gave me a long look. "You've only flown the one time."

"I flew all night." And then I heard it—the soft screech from the tree overhead. I glanced up. The great horned owl. He swept down and circled me. "I'm taking that as a sign."

Immediately, I began to strip as fast as I could. I handed my clothes to Chatter. "Take Leo and my clothes down first, then Rhia, then Kaylin. I'll meet you at the bottom."

As soon as I was naked, with the others staring at me like I'd lost my mind, I swung up into the branches of the nearest tree. I kept the fan Lainule had given me, the handle looped around my wrist. I climbed higher, trying not to slip on the snow, my body shivering with each branch. The owl landed on a branch nearby and I clambered over to crouch beside it. My pendant hung around my neck, softly glowing, and the owls on my arms began to tingle. I stared at the owl. It swept out of the tree, and I sucked in a deep breath and dove with it.

The ground hurtled up, but my body shifted faster. I had no clear thought on how it did so, but within seconds, I pulled up, gliding with the great horned owl. We spiraled around one another, and I sensed an odd familiarity. The last time, I'd been so focused on actually flying that I hadn't fully noticed, but now I sensed a kinship with the owl. Was it one of the Uwilahsidhe?

*Come, fly to the other side.*

*But my clothes—I can't wait that long for Chatter to bring them up and we don't dare chance him wearing himself out.*

*Then to the bottom of the gorge. Fly and land softly on the trunk near the cataract.*

I gazed down, saw the trunk he was talking about. The tree had fallen along a series of small falls that were frozen over, on the other side of the stream. I swept down, spiraling, reveling in the feel of my wings on the wind. The horned owl hooted softly as we landed at the bottom. It waited beside me as I waited for Chatter. Within a moment, a blur raced down the hill and stopped on the shore beside me. He appeared, holding Leo around the waist. I turned back to my companion.

*Thank you. Will you watch us on our way through the wood? Can I contact you when I'm in human form?*

*No, you cannot read my thoughts then—we are connected, but only when in owl form. But I will come with you, I will watch over you the best I can. Now change back and get dressed.*

I shifted back, dressing quickly in the freezing air as the snow swirled around us. Chatter headed back up the slope, a blur in the deepening shadows, as Peyton gingerly made her way across the stream. Within a few minutes, we were all at the base of the ravine that would lead us to the Golden Wood and home again. As I stared up the slope, a noise behind us startled me.

Turning, I could see a group of the Vampiric Fae. They were making their way down the alluvial deposit. They were coming for us and both Heather and Myst were with them.

# Chapter 26

"Hell! Move. They're on the way."

We scrambled for the slope of the ravine. Peyton didn't have much problem in her four-footed form, and Chatter was quick, but the rest of us weren't so nimble. I grabbed branch and limb, ignoring the brambles that pierced through my gloves, ignoring the needle-laden boughs that slapped me in the face as I half-crawled, half-climbed my way up the slope. The ravine was steep, but luckily had plenty of rocks and trees to gain leverage on. My breath coming in white puffs, I charged upward, trying not to focus on how close they were.

*They are almost down the slope on the other side. Hurry.*

Shit, they'd traversed the swath of rocks and boulders like they were skipping stones. I pushed ahead. And then, Chatter was at my side, and we were racing in a blur up the mountain. I blinked and found myself standing on the top of the ravine.

"Chatter—you're too tired—"

"Let me do this." He vanished again, a blur down the slope. I took a moment and glanced around. Nobody over here on this side, thank gods. Although I'd really love it if some hero came charging in to save us, but that wasn't going to happen. I pulled out my fan, gearing up for what I knew was coming. At that moment, Chatter appeared again, Rhiannon in tow. Peyton crept over the top, still in puma form. She slunk over to my side.

Kaylin was helping Leo, trying to drag him along faster. Chatter took a deep breath and—looking exhausted—headed down again.

"No—you can't bring them both." I stared in horror at Myst and her crew. They'd reached the bottom and were lithely crossing the frozen stream. This was going wrong. So wrong. Myst wasn't supposed to come with them. I knew in my heart we couldn't stand against her.

I turned to Rhiannon. "Go—get moving back to the house."

"No. I'm staying here with you." She pulled out her bag with the Molotov cocktails in it. "We go down together or not at all."

I took a deep breath. "Let's make a pact then. If they catch us, if they try to turn us, we do whatever it takes to avoid that fate. I'd rather be torn to pieces than work for them."

She nodded. "I know Heather did it to spare Peyton, but I wish she hadn't." She spoke softly, but I could hear the catch in her voice.

Chatter appeared at the top, Leo in his arms, as Kaylin dragged himself over the edge. We were all exhausted, and Chatter looked like he was going to pass out.

"How far are we from the house?" I tried to gauge where we were.

"Ten minutes as the crow flies. Fifteen on foot." He pointed toward a copse of cedar and fir. "There's the path that leads into the ravine, through that stand of trees over there.

I could vaguely see it in the approaching dusk. Nodding, I said, "Let's do what we can to make it hard on them and then run like hell. If we can get over the border to our land, then we should be safe for the night. That is, until Myst finds a way to break the barrier."

I opened the fan and focused on it. *Ulean, what's the worst damage I can do with this?*

*You do not want to know. Each time you use the more powerful energies, the fan will own you a little more.*

*Tough. We need it. I'd rather be possessed by a fan than by Myst. Now, tell me.* I focused on her energy, trying to drive home the urgency.

*You have a point. Very well. Vortex force. But be prepared to run. It will not be safe and you cannot control the power once you've set it loose.*

Taking a deep breath, I said, "I'm going to unleash a tornado. Whatever you have, start it now and move back. This thing is dangerous."

Without a word, Rhiannon lit the bottles with a lighter and tossed them into the ravine. She held out her hands and a stream of flame came searing out to explode the gas-laden bombs, sending a flash flood of fire down the slope. She jumped away, as did the others as I swept the fan twice and whispered, *"Vortex force."*

Ulean slipped up beside me and I felt her joining in, helping warm the air around us so that it collided with the cold. I kept my focus on the currents as they began to whip into a counterclockwise spiral, creaking and moaning as they picked up speed. Another few seconds and there was a roar as the monster came to life.

With the sound of a freight train rattling by, gusts of dark clouds began to spin. The funnel cloud engulfed Rhiannon's fire and swept down the slope, a blanket of swirling flame on a deafening ride. My ears popped from the changing air pressure.

"Run. Now!" I turned and headed through the trees at breakneck speed, following the others who'd already taken off. Ulean howled along beside me, buoying me up and along. I leapt over a fallen tree trunk and hit the path, veering toward the house. We ran like the hounds of hell were after us, not looking back, not knowing whether Myst and her followers were on our heels or if we'd staved them off.

And then, breaking through the tree line, we were across the border, onto our land, and a soft glow lit up the perimeter of the yard. Anadey stood on the porch, watching anxiously as we skidded to a halt. We were home and Peyton was with us.

❧

I turned, gasping for breath, in time to see Myst and Heather come to the edge of our property, followed by a half dozen guards. My heart in my throat, I watched as they traced the border, but did not set foot across it. Whatever Anadey had done, it was holding.

Straightening my shoulders, I faced them—the Mistress of Mayhem and her Court. She gazed at me, steady, her luminous eyes sparkling like stars, her skin the color of sky on a clear, late evening before twilight fully hits. Her gown flowed into the shadows, diaphanous shades of blue and black and gray and silver. *Beautiful,* I thought. She was so incredibly beautiful and terrifying.

Myst cocked her head to the left, then the right, and let out a slow laugh.

"Cicely Waters. You think you have won?"

I shook my head. "If we'd won, you'd be dead."

"Good, then. Don't underestimate me. Child, do you even have a clue as to who you are? As to who you *were*?"

The great horned owl circled overhead, coming to rest in the oak behind me. I cleared my throat and returned Myst's gaze, willing myself not to flinch.

"I am Cicely Waters, born of the magic, born of the Uwilahsidhe. I know who I am. And I know what you are." It was foolish to challenge her, but I wanted her to understand that I understood she was a vicious monster. A crazed Queen out for blood. "I walk with the Crimson Court at my back."

She inclined her head gently and, turning to Heather, lightly traced her hand down my aunt's cheek, softly caressing her. Then, without a second thought, she backhanded Heather so hard that my aunt went sprawling to the ground. Heather lay there, staring up without a protest. I heard Rhiannon stifle a cry, but I didn't turn, didn't show any emotion.

"A thought," Myst said, turning back to me, her gaze narrowing in on me. "If I treat my friends thus, consider how I treat my enemies. Then decide which side you wish to be on. Your precious Grieve is *mine*."

"No!" I jerked, unable to stop myself. "What do you mean?"

"I claim him for my own. *He will be my consort.* And you, my dear . . . Don't you remember who you used to be? Think, think very hard." Her eyes begin to swirl and I felt myself falling deep into her spell.

*A glimpse . . . standing deep in the forest, and Grieve was beside me only he was not Grieve but Shy. And I was there . . . I was Cherish . . . and this time I looked down at my hands. They bore a faint cerulean cast. With wonder I reached up and touched my teeth. Razor-sharp and two small fangs. And I turned to Shy, who smiled at me, loving me, and I knew that I was a traitor to myself, to my race, to my mother.*

"No," I whispered. "I wasn't one of you! I was Cambyra Fae!"

Myst laughed. Deep and rich, her voice echoed through the night. "You *are* Cambyra Fae *now* . . . but oh yes, I can see you remember. Good-bye for now, *child*. We will meet again. Soon. And you will remember how you turned on your family. Grieve isn't the *only* one who's been searching for you through the years. Remember this: I never forget a grudge." And then, she turned and like a shadow in the night, she and her companions were gone.

I turned back to the others, who stared at me, silent and waiting. With a sickening feeling that things had just gotten a whole lot worse, I nodded to the house. "We're safe for now. We need rest."

And we went inside and shut the night and the snow and the demons out.

# Chapter 27

I plugged in an e-mail to Lannan, demanding to see Regina, Geoffrey, and him the next night. There was too much I needed to report for me to type it all out. I also told him in no uncertain terms that Lainule should be present, and that I'd be bringing my friends. We were all in this together now.

Peyton was downstairs, reunited with her mother, and we left them alone for a bit to enjoy their homecoming. We still didn't know what the Indigo Court had done to Peyton, but she'd tell us when she was ready. She seemed okay, and I hoped they'd just roughed her up a little.

Rhiannon and Leo were cooking dinner. Kaylin was working on some magical charm—I didn't know what. A knock at my door sounded and I pushed myself away from the desk and called, "Come in."

Chatter entered the room. He joined me on the bed, crossing one leg over the other. "Thank you, for letting me stay here."

"You're on our side now, like it or not. At least they

won't beat you anymore. Grieve never . . . he didn't . . ." I wasn't sure I wanted to know, but he shook his head.

"Grieve never laid a hand on me. I told you before, he did what he could to fight his nature. Now though, who knows what's going to happen? And with Myst claiming him, how long can he hold out against his Shadow Hunter side?"

I winced. "She can't have him. He's mine. And I'll do everything in my power to stop her. To free him." A sob choked up in my throat and Chatter pulled me into his arms, holding me softly as I wept. After a few minutes, I sat back and rubbed the tears from my eyes. "Crying won't help."

"What did Myst show you that made you so angry?" He gently tipped my chin up, his eyes soft and doelike in the dim light of the candles I'd lit.

I bit my lip. How could I tell him what I suspected? How could I admit that once, I'd been on the other side, as vicious as she was? Grieve and I had switched sides this life, but a gulf a mile wide still divided us. I only knew that I loved him, and I'd do whatever it took to kill Myst and free the Golden Wood. Even if it meant trucking with vampires, aligning myself with Lainule, slicing throats . . . whatever we needed, I'd do it.

*Anything* to keep Myst from winning.

I shook my head. "Never mind that. Leave it for tomorrow. For when it's light again and the Indigo Court hides in pain."

He nodded, standing to go. I watched him silently leave the room.

After I'd logged off my computer, I patted the pendant around my neck. The reassuring pulse of magic beat through my body. Beyond vampires and Fae and Vampiric Fae and magic, there was this—my legacy. My father was Uwilahsidhe, and I had his blood in my veins. And perhaps someday, I would meet him.

I stripped off my clothes and opened the window. A swirl of flakes flew in from the snow-covered night. It was beautiful, a blanket of sparkling white. I stared down, eager to let go of the day's events. My fan hanging around my wrist, I leapt lightly to crouch on the sill. I let out a smile as a fierce, feral pride rose up.

Lannan could suck me dry. The Vampiric Fae could enslave my family. The vampires could start their war. We'd won our battle today: We'd rescued Peyton and Chatter. It was time to celebrate. Small victories were important now.

Tomorrow, I'd have to face the stark reality of what had happened, but tonight—tonight I could escape.

And nothing they could do would change who I was—or what I'd discovered about myself. I stared up at the swirling storm. Winter had moved in with Myst, a vengeful winter out to blanket us all with the chill of the Indigo Court, but we weren't done yet. We had lived and would fight another day.

The owl tattoo on my arm let out a piercing screech as I let go and fell toward the ground. In the blink of an eye, I twisted, shifting, and went gliding up into the night sky, free from everything and everyone.

The great horned owl met me, gliding in from the oak. Silent shadows, we flew over the house, riding on the currents provided by Ulean, who chased by our side, laughing. And her breath gave us a tailwind that propelled us onward as I left war and blood and death behind.

# Play List for *Night Myst*

I write to music a good share of the time and have been sharing my playlists on my website. I finally decided to add them to the backs of the books for my readers who aren't online.

—Yasmine Galenorn

3 Doors Down: "Loser"
Alice in Chains: "Man in the Box"
Beck: "Scarecrow," "Dark Star"
The Bravery: "Believe"
CC Adcock: "Bleed 2 Feed"
Chester Bennington: "System"
Chris Isaak: "Wicked Game"
Cobra Verde: "Play with Fire"
David Bowie: "China Girl"
Dead Can Dance: "Yulunga," "Indus"
Death Cab For Cutie: "I Will Possess Your Heart"
Depeche Mode: "Personal Jesus," "Dream On"

Everlast: "One, Two"

Gabrielle Roth: "The Calling," "Dolphin," "Raven," "Mother Night," "Luna," "Seducing Hades," "Black Mesa," "Stone Circle," "Rest Your Tears Here," "Totem," "Night Whisper," "Zone Unknown," "Avenue A"

Gary Numan: "Innocence Bleeding," "Prophecy," "Crazier," "My Breathing," "Before You Hate It," "Dead Heaven," "The Angel Wars," "Noise Noise," "Stories," "Telekon," "My Brother's Time," "Hunger," "Devious"

Gorillaz: "Clint Eastwood"

Jace Everett: "Bad Things"

Jay Gordon: "Slept So Long"

King Black Acid: "Great Spaces," "Rolling Under"

Ladytron: "Black Cat," "Ghosts," "I'm Not Scared," "Burning Up," "They Gave You a Heart," "Predict the Day," "Versus"

Led Zeppelin: "When the Levee Breaks"

Lenny Kravitz: "Fly Away"

Little Big Town: "Bones"

Live: "TBD"

Low with Tomandandy: "Half Light"

Metallica: "Enter Sandman"

Nine Inch Nails: "I Do Not Want This," "Sin" [long], "Get Down, Make Love"

Nirvana: "Heart-shaped Box," "You Know You're Right"

Oingo Boingo: "Dead Man's Party"

Orgy: "Blue Monday," "Social Enemies"

PJ Harvey: "This is Love"

Puddle of Mudd: "Psycho"

Red Hot Chili Peppers: "Blood Sugar Sex Magik"

Saliva: "Ladies and Gentlemen"

Seether: "Remedy"

Steppenwolf: "Jupiter's Child"

Tangerine Dream: "Dr. Destructo"
Thompson Twins: "The Gap," "All Fall Out"
Toadies: "Possum Kingdom"
Tori Amos: "Little Amsterdam," "Professional
    Widow"
Wayne Static: "Not Meant For Me"
Ween: "Mutilated Lips"
Zero 7: "In the Waiting Line"

Dear Reader:

I hope you enjoyed *Night Myst*, the first book in my new Indigo Court series, and I hope you're looking forward to reading *Night Veil*, the next book in the series, available summer 2011. For those of you new to my books, I wanted to take this chance to welcome you into my worlds. For those of you who've been reading my books for a while, I wanted to thank you for taking a chance on Cicely's adventure. I loved writing *Night Myst*, but I also love writing my other series—The Otherworld series (aka Sisters of the Moon)—and want to assure my longtime readers that, yes, there are more books coming in that series.

And that's why we're including the first chapter of *Harvest Hunting*—book eight of The Otherworld series—in the back of *Night Myst*.

If you're a new reader, you'll get a taste for what my trio of half-Fae, half-human demon-hunting sisters are like. And if you've been reading The Otherworld series for a while, I wanted to give you a sneak peek at the first chapter of *Harvest Hunting*, available in November 2010.

So without taking more of your time, I'd like to present the beginning of *Harvest Hunting*, and I hope it whets your appetite for the next book!

Bright Blessings,
Yasmine Galenorn

My nose quivered. Something smelled wonderful. I followed the scent through the crowded hall until I found myself standing next to the buffet table.

My sister Menolly and I had just stood beside our sister Camille and witnessed her marriage to her third husband. Three—count 'em—three husbands. Simultaneously. Trillian had been decked out as the best goth groom ever, wearing black leather pants that matched the obsidian gleam of his skin, a black mesh tank, and a velvet cloak the color of blood.

Morio and Smoky had worn what they had to their first wedding with Camille: Smoky wore his long white trench with a blue and gold vest, a pale blue button-down shirt, tight white jeans, and his ankle-length silver hair coiling around him like dancing serpents. Morio wore a red and gold kimono, with a dress sword hanging from his side and his dark hair rippling down his back.

And of course my sister looked good enough to eat, her jet hair glistening against her gossamer priestess robes, so sheer I could see her bra and panties through them. Now that she was an official priestess of the Moon Mother, she was expected to don ceremonial garb for most important occasions.

The four of them had gathered before Iris, who again presided, and together they underwent a variant of the Soul Symbiont ritual designed to bring Trillian into their fold. Menolly and I had worn gowns—hers of black with shimmering crystals, mine of gold—and stood as witnesses again.

Now we were into the celebration part of the affair.

I glanced at the calendar on the wall. October twenty-second and we were well on our way to Samhain, the festival of the dead. It had been a month, almost to the day, since we'd unsuccessfully raided Stacia Bonecrusher's safe house.

Thinking about Stacia forced me to face another thought, one I'd been trying to avoid. I glanced across the room at Chase Johnson. The detective was sitting at a table by himself, watching the celebration with a quizzical look on his face. Unable to help myself, I headed in his direction. He watched me approach, his expression carefully sliding into neutral. I took the chair opposite him.

"It's a beautiful wedding." I nervously played with the napkin resting on the table next to me. "Don't you think?"

"Yes, lovely." He blinked, long and slow, and I wondered what he was really thinking. "Camille seemed a little stressed, though. What's up with that?" Even though his tone was normal, I knew there was nothing normal about Chase. Not anymore.

"Our father refused to attend the wedding. Not only does he disapprove of her marrying Trillian, but his official stance is that she's turned her back on her duties for the Otherworld Intelligence Agency by becoming a priestess and agreeing to enter Aeval's court. He refuses to condone her behavior by showing up, and the day she actually pledges under Aeval's rule . . . I'm afraid of what's going to happen."

"Turned her back on her duties? That doesn't seem fair, considering all she's done for the OIA. I know Sephreh's your father, but damn, that's cold." He sipped his champagne, sounding more himself than he had the entire past month.

I glanced at the fading scars on his hands. His body had healed remarkably fast from the deep knife wounds that had laced his skin and punctured several of his organs. But it would take a long, long time for him to heal from the potion that had saved his life. The Nectar of Life had torn his entire world apart and put it back together in a crazy new patchwork. And our relationship appeared to be a major casualty—on rocky ground, at best.

"When she promised to train under Morgaine, and *especially* when she agreed to dedicate herself to Aeval's Dark Court, Father took it as a personal insult. But Camille doesn't have a choice; she's under direct order from the Moon Mother herself."

"Yeah, I got that," he said, fiddling with his glass.

"She did everything for us when our mother died, and without her the family would have been ripped to shreds. Father was extremely cruel to her last time they spoke and I'm pissed off that he didn't show today. Our cousin Shamas has been trying to fill the void, but it's just not the same."

"What did he say?" Chase played with his goblet. "By the way, will alcohol hurt me . . . *now*? I haven't had a drink since before the accident."

"No, you'll be fine. You can still eat and drink anything you want. It's not like you were turned into a vampire." I stared at my hands. As loyal as I was to our father, I couldn't blind myself to the truth. "At his last visit, things went from bad to worse. By the time he left, Camille was on the sofa, curled up in a ball, sobbing. Smoky came in at the point when Sephreh threatened to disinherit her. In turn, Smoky threatened to shift into his dragon self and crisp our father."

"Crap. The fallout from that can't be good."

"Things were at a standstill until Menolly stepped in, told Father to go home and Smoky to chill. But definitely *Not Pretty*. Not at all."

"A mess all the way around, then." Chase morosely picked up his champagne flute and downed the last of the sparkling wine. "And so . . . here we sit." He stared across the table at me. "I don't know what to say, Delilah. I don't even have a clue on how to start."

Part of me wanted to cry. Nothing seemed to be working out the way we hoped it would. I blinked back my tears.

"How about you start by telling me how you're doing? We've only talked three times in the past two weeks." I didn't mention that we'd barely kissed since he'd healed up and returned to duty.

Chase contemplated the question, looking at me through those limpid, soulful eyes. They'd only grown more luminous since he'd drunk the Nectar of Life. His aura had shifted. Some spark, some force I couldn't put my finger on, was changing him.

"How can I answer that when *I* don't even know? What am I supposed to do? Jump up and shout, *Rah Rah*, now I'll outlive everybody I've ever known in my life'?" He slammed the goblet on the table so hard it almost broke.

Stung, I blinked back the tears. "Giving you the Nectar of Life was the only option we had—unless you prefer the thought of dying."

Shifting in his seat, Chase let out a long sigh. "Yeah, I know. I know. And believe me, I am grateful. But damn, this stuff does a number on your head. It's more than the realization that I'm going to live a thousand years. There's something . . . nebulous . . . about it. The nectar ripped open a part of me. Something I'm afraid to face." He slowly reached out and took my hand.

I stared at him for a moment, but he remained silent. Both Camille and Chase had come through the autumn equinox worn and weary, covered with blood. Camille had bathed in the blood of the black unicorn as she sealed a fate with which the Moon Mother challenged her:

sacrificing the horned beast to his phoenix-like destiny
while on the Hunt of her life. And then she'd been thrown
under the wheels of Aeval, and would soon be forced to
descend into the realms once ruled by the ancient Unseelie Queen.

And Chase . . . no less life-shaking. He'd been bathed
in his own blood and was now—by human terms—
practically immortal.

"Whenever you're ready to talk about it—"

"What? You'll play shrink to the mutant?"

"*No. I'll listen.* As your girlfriend." I stared at him, the
virulence of his anger rankling me. "Chase, this isn't fair.
We'd planned on you drinking the nectar anyway—"

"I know that! But you told me that the ritual required
preparation, and now I understand why. I'm *not human*
anymore. I don't know who—or *what*—I am. A thousand
fucking years to look forward to and *I have no idea what
to do with them.*"

Fed up and too tired to deal with his angst as well as
my own, I pushed back my chair. "I guess . . . it's hard
for me to understand what you're going through. I'm
trying—I really am. But until you can figure it out, you
don't seem to need me around."

"Wait! It's just . . . Oh hell, I don't know what to say."
He slumped back in his chair. "I want to say that everything's okay. I feel like I should be thinking, 'Wow, now
my girlfriend and I can be together for centuries.' But
Delilah . . . I have to tell you the truth. I don't know if I'm
ready for that kind of commitment now that the opportu-
nity is actually here."

Tears stung behind my eyes, but I blinked them back.
"It would seem that Sharah is doing a better job taking
care of you than I am."

The elfin medic who worked alongside Chase in the
Faerie–Human Crime Scene Investigations Unit had
been overseeing his care as the potion worked its way

through Chase's system, changing every cell, altering his very DNA.

Chase snorted. "Maybe that's because she's *not* taking care of me. Sharah is offering me advice, but she's not coddling me or treating me like some freak who needs kid-glove handling." A look of pain crossed his face and he dropped his head to his hands and rubbed his forehead. "I'm sorry. I'm sorry, Delilah. I love you, I really do, but right now it seems like I'm no good to either one of us."

My stomach churning, I sat on the edge of my chair again. "Yeah, I know. But Chase—please, don't shut me out."

"I need to be on my own for a bit. To think about things. Besides, Camille needs you more than I do now. Her life's a mess, too. And Henry . . . poor Henry doesn't even have a life anymore. Go enjoy the party. Be there for your sister. She deserves the support. And . . . and if you meet somebody and . . . if you *want* them, I won't ask questions."

I tried to protest but he shook his head. Feeling abruptly shoved out of the nest, I scurried toward the door, biting the tears back. Chase was right about one thing: our friend Henry Jeffries had fared worst of all. He'd been working in Camille's bookshop—the Indigo Crescent—when the demons broke in. They killed him and blew up a good part of the shop in order to warn us off. We still hadn't gotten the smell of smoke out of the walls.

As I neared the door, a voice echoed from behind me. "Delilah, you okay?"

When I turned I saw Vanzir, the lanky dream chaser who was demon bound to my sisters and me. Over the past seven months, we'd slowly been forging a friendship. Menolly and Vanzir hung out a lot. Vanzir and I talked from time to time. Camille kept her distance, but she was growing less leery of him as the weeks wore on.

Vanzir's eyes whirled, a kaleidoscope of colors without any names. His David Bowie goblin-king hair was spiked and platinum, and he looked uncomfortable out of his leather pants and ripped tank. But he made the tux and tails work.

I shrugged and said, "I guess."

"*You guess*, my ass. You sense anything wrong out there? Demons?" Vanzir leaned against the wall in front of me, giving me the once-over.

He didn't have a clue what was bothering me.

"*Men.* Even you demons are clueless." As he stared at me, I shook my head and pushed past him. "I'm going to take a run outside. I need some air."

"What? What did I say?"

As Vanzir let out a snort, I sidled to the door, slipping out while everyone was focused on toasting the happy . . . well, not *couple* . . . the happy marriage. Camille would understand. She'd forgive me for skipping out. Because pretty much only she and Menolly knew what I was going through. What we were *all* going through.

⚜

Rhyne Wood Reception Hall was in one of the larger parks, and the city leased it out for celebrations and parties. Camille had decided to hold the reception here because, unlike her impromptu marriages to Smoky and Morio, this one had been planned, with over a hundred guests. And those numbers took space. Rhyne Wood had a dance floor, a nice big kitchen, and catering staff.

Situated in Fireweed Park, the mansion was a small part of the thousand-acre wilderness buttressing the shore of Puget Sound. I stayed away from the edge of the butte overlooking the inlet—I hated water—but there were plenty of paths and trees and bushes to lose myself in. As soon as I was far enough away from the mansion to comfortably feel out-of-sight, I shifted into my tabby self, my primary Were form. Everybody always thought it hurt, but really—if I went slowly—it didn't. Just a blur and a haze as life shifted perceptions.

Free of clothing—except for a bright blue collar—I took off, racing into the undergrowth, reveling in the scents that flowed like hot chocolate on a cold autumn night. And it *was* cold, but my fur kept me warm and cozy. My worries floated away as I bounded through the rain-sparkling grass, romping in the misty evening, chasing the few moths still braving the rain-sodden evening.

I leapt at one, an Anna's Blue, and caught it in my mouth. With a quick *nom nom*, I swallowed and wrinkled my nose as the feather-light wings tickled my throat. A moment later, a rustling in the grass distracted me and I raced in the direction of a thicket of alder trees surrounded by dense huckleberry bushes.

I knew enough to not get too near the bushes—they had nice, sharp thorns perfect for snagging my tail. But I could smell whatever was hiding there, and the scent set my pulse to racing. I wanted to chase, to stretch my legs and feel the thrill of the hunt. I needed to rip things apart, to act out my aggression. And whatever was in the bushes, I might be able to play cat-and-mouse with.

As I skirted the huckleberry, the rustling grew louder and then out popped another . . . *cat*?

Puzzled, I cocked my head, staring at the creature. *Not cat*. But what the hell was it? Fluffy, bushy tail, cute, dark with a light stripe . . . I knew I'd seen one somewhere, but I couldn't remember where. Wondering if it might be friendly, I took a hesitant step toward it. As its big, bushy tail fluttered in the wind, so pretty and tempting, I promptly forgot my manners and pounced.

The creature swung around, turning its butt toward me, and lifted its tail.

*Oh shit!*

Just as I remembered what it was, it took aim, shook

its ass, and a wide spray came shooting toward me. I yowled and turned tail, but not before getting drenched by the foul-smelling perfume. At least it managed to miss my eyes, but I didn't wait around for the skunk to get in a second shot. I hightailed it back toward the mansion.

As I reached the steps, I slowed. What the hell was I supposed to do? If I ran in there as a cat, I'd stink up the joint. If I ran in as myself, it would be worse because I'd be bigger, hence giving off more of the odor. I paced nervously in front of the steps, wanting the nasty scent gone. *Now.*

Luck was with me. Within minutes Iris and Bruce appeared on the porch with their champagne. Iris glanced around, her nose wrinkling, and I let out a plaintive yowl.

"Oh, good heavens!" Iris shoved her glass in Bruce's hand and came racing down the stairs. I stepped out from the bush I was hiding behind, and she stared at me, eyes wide, a look of horror on her face. "You poor thing. Oh dear, how are we going to get you home?"

Just then, Rozurial slipped outside. He looked at Bruce, holding the two champagne flutes, and then down at Iris and me.

"That's not who I think it is, is it?" He barely muffled his laughter and I hissed at him. "Oh, yeah, babe. You have a little BO problem, know that?"

"What should we do with her?" Bruce asked.

Iris stared at me, cocking her head, and I could see the wheels turning. "Rozurial, you take her home through the Ionyc Sea. I'll head home with Bruce in the car and we'll get her cleaned up."

She leaned down and shook her finger at me. It was tempting, but I had learned not to swat Iris while in cat form. She wasn't above scruffing me and holding me off the floor, even though she was barely four feet tall.

"Listen to me, Delilah, and I know you can understand

me so you'd better do as I say. Don't you dare turn back into yourself until we take care of this. I guarantee it will be far worse with all six-foot-one of you skunked, rather than just yourself as a little pussycat. Got it?"

I stared at her and blinked. If I disobeyed her on this one, she'd have my hide. Slowly, I let out a complacent meow.

"Good. Now, Rozurial, you take her home. And I don't want to hear any fuss about it—*just do it*. Honey, will you let Camille know where we're going?" Iris motioned to Bruce, who hurried back inside.

Roz picked me up and I snuggled against the incubus, rubbing my chin on his chest. I had the feeling I wasn't going to like what Iris had in store for me, and I wanted comfort. Purring loudly, I gave him my best *good kitty* look and he snorted, rubbing my ears.

"Eat it up, beauty. Eat it up. Come, you'll be safe enough, just don't try to jump out of my arms." And in the blink of an eye, we leapt into the Ionyc Sea and crossed a world to travel fifteen miles.

Roz set me down outside, warning me not to enter the house until Iris had tended to me. "I'll be back in a moment to keep an eye on you, though smelling like you do, I doubt anybody's going to be a bother."

He vanished into the studio-cum-shed that he shared with Vanzir and my cousin Shamas. With Camille's three men staying with us, and Bruce shacking up with Iris part of the time, we had built ourselves quite the extended family.

I tried to sniff out if there were any enemies near, but the scent of skunk infiltrated every pore. My eyes hurt, my nose hurt, my throat hurt, and I was getting queasy. It felt like the mother of all hairballs was churning in my stomach. I hunched near the porch, trying to avoid being seen by any would-be heroes of the animal world.

Roz came back after awhile, dressed in a pair of

skintight jeans and a muscle shirt, and he sprawled on the ground near me, on his back, staring up at the stars, his long curly hair spreading on the ground beneath him.

"Look at the sky, fuzzball." He ruffled my head. "Look at all the stars whirling around . . . I've walked among them, you know." His voice dropped and took on a sinuous cadence. Even in cat form, I found it soothing and seductive.

"I've danced through the aurora borealis, skated my way through the Ionyc Lands. When I was searching for Dredge, I followed any and every lead, wherever it led me. I journeyed from the Northlands to the Southern Wastes, from Valhalla to the gates of Hel, looking for that motherfucker. I've seen so much beauty and terror in my life that you'd think nothing would faze me . . . But the stars . . . they're still the ultimate treasure. Pristine, luminous, and always out of reach."

He rolled over onto his stomach and plucked a long blade of grass, tickling my belly as I stretched out beside him. "I know you're worried about Chase. But Delilah, you have to let go, if that's what he needs. The Nectar of Life plays havoc with humans when they aren't prepared. You saved his life, but he lost something he wasn't ready to lose. His mortality—in the human sense—is a huge part of what makes humans . . . well . . . human. When you have such a short time to live, you make the most of it. Now, you need to stand back and let Sharah help him. She knows what to do."

I knew he was speaking the truth, I just didn't want to hear it. But he was right. Camille and Menolly had been telling me that for days, but coming from them, it felt like sisterly meddling instead of advice. I let out a little yowl.

"Yeah, I know you know, and I know you don't like it, but take my advice this time, okay? I understand what it means to have life ripped apart and drastically changed."

And I knew that Roz did understand. He'd lost his

family to Dredge; he'd lost his wife when Zeus and Hera decided to use them both as pawns. He'd been changed from Fae to incubus in the blink of an eye. Chase's life had been turned upside down in that same fraction of a second, though not as harshly as Roz's.

A car pulled into the driveway. Bruce and his driver. And Iris. They jumped out and I saw they'd brought Vanzir home, too. Probably a good thing. He wasn't the most decorous guest, and I had a feeling he'd be happier here than hanging out late at a party where most of the guests avoided him.

Iris ran inside, and in less than ten minutes, she dashed down from the back porch, wearing a rubber apron over what I recognized as a dress she kept for the grungiest chores. She stood over me, hands on her hips.

"Well, I don't know how you got yourself in this fix, but let's take care of you." She leaned over and scooped me up in her arms, her nose twitching. "You reek, girl. What did you say to that skunk?"

I wanted to protest—*It wasn't my fault, I didn't do anything.* But I knew that—even if I protested in cat—Iris would understand and call me on it. Truth was, I'd invaded the skunk's territory and threatened it by pouncing.

Iris carried me against one hip as she went up the back steps and into the enclosed porch, where I saw something so horrible waiting for me that I squirmed, desperately trying to get away: A bath full of what looked like dark, thick water.

She struggled, her thick rubber gloves losing their purchase on me. The minute her grip weakened, I bolted for the door to the kitchen, which was standing open.

"Come back here! Delilah, get your fuzzy butt back here *right now!*"

I galloped toward the stairs, but before I could get there, Vanzir was standing in front of me, a snarky grin on his face. Faster than I could blink, he reached out and snagged me up. I squirmed but he held fast and carried me at arm's length to the porch, where he unceremoniously dumped me in the water. Iris slammed the door so I couldn't get into the house again, but I'd already given up, resigned. I was already wet, I might as well let her give me the bath.

The scent of tomato juice cocktail broke through the smell filtering into my nostrils, and I took a cautious lick of the water.

*Not bad, not bad.*

Iris began to scrub me with the juice, straight, and I hated to admit it, but it felt good. I detested the smell of skunk—it was making me nauseated—and if Iris thought that a bath in V8 would help, then I'd let her bathe me. I even relented enough to let her scrub my tummy. She took off my collar and I felt suddenly naked. After all, that collar contained my clothing. When I changed back, if it wasn't on me, my clothes wouldn't be either.

After about ten minutes Iris motioned to Roz and they moved to the side, leaving Vanzir to hold me in the tub. He had a snarky grin on his face.

"Puddy tat like her bath? Puddy happy?" he crooned.

*Good for you I know you're just teasing*, I thought, *or you'd be dead by now.* Vanzir was our slave, and if we chose, he'd die. Enslaving him had been the only way to keep from killing him when he defected to us in the first place.

I settled for chomping on his thumb. He raised his eyebrows, but that David Bowie–Ziggy Stardust platinum shag barely moved. I wondered how much gel he used to get it to stay in place.

Iris and Roz came back, and she lifted me out of the bath and dipped me in a bucket of warm, clear water to rinse off the tomato juice.

"Uh-oh," she said.

That didn't sound good.

"Oh, Mama." Roz let out a snort. "She's not going to like that at all. I wonder if . . . will it translate over?"

*What? Will what translate over? What the hell was going on?*

"Delilah, honey, I think you'd better shift back now. Vanzir, would you fetch a towel? She's not going to want those clothes, I guarantee you that. What a pity—your beautiful gown. You'll have to replace it."

*My gown!* Oh, no! I hadn't even thought about that, but Iris was right, the skunk had ruined my most elegant evening dress. My *only* evening dress.

She sat me down and I sniffed the air. Hey—what the hell? I still smelled like skunk! Letting out a huff, I shook my head and water flew everywhere. Iris jumped back.

"I know you're not happy, but please—mind your manners. I would prefer to smell as little like skunk as possible. Now, here's the towel. Boys, be nice and quit teasing her."

She took the large beach towel from Vanzir, who was grinning ear-to-ear by now. *Oh, he was going to get his.* Iris held one end while Roz held the other. She stared pointedly at both of them until they averted their eyes. Normally I wouldn't give a damn, but right now I was in a pissy mood, and the Talon-haltija knew it.

I shifted back, slowly, because I was in no mood for any nasty muscle spasms. The slower I shifted, the easier it went. As I stood up, feeling rank, I wrapped the towel around me. Iris's gaze traveled up to my face.

"Oh my stars," she whispered, her eyes wide. "I had *no idea* that was going to happen."

"What? What's going on? If somebody doesn't tell me soon, I'm turning back into a cat and going on a shredding binge."

"Hey, Red," Vanzir said, once again ruffling my hair. Only this time he had to reach up to do it.

*Red?*

"No . . . no . . . You don't mean what I think you mean, do you?" I took off for the bathroom, the smell of skunk with a side of tomato following me.

As I flipped on the light and stared in the mirror, I let out a groan. My beautiful golden hair was now rife with brilliant highlights. I looked like Ronald McDonald, only tiger-striped. The tomato juice had dyed the lighter parts of my hair, and now I was a patchwork of pink, rust, and burnt orange. And none of it looked good.

"Fuck! Fuck, fuck, *fuck me*."

Iris peeked around the corner. "I'm so sorry, Delilah. I had no idea tomato juice would do that. And it didn't take care of the smell, either."

"I reek, and my hair looks like a dye bomb went off in it!"

I dropped to the edge of the tub. I loved my hair. It wasn't fancy, it wasn't anything super special, but it was mine. Now I looked like I was doing a bad Lil' Kim impersonation.

"Well, hop in the shower, maybe you can scrub some of the skunk scent off. Meanwhile, I'll see what I can find out. I've never had to deal with this before—no one I've ever known has been skunked. Not that I remember." She headed out of the bathroom, muttering to herself.

I grimaced, then looked at myself in the mirror again. I'd always loved the combination of my emerald eyes and golden hair, but now I looked like I'd gone punk. Bad. Very bad. Splotches of pink-to-orange dappled the gold, and even where it hadn't, my natural color had become brassy.

"Crap. One more thing to deal with." But right now, I needed to focus on getting the stench off me.

"Here we go," Iris said, coming back with a basin filled with a bottle of hydrogen peroxide, a box of baking soda, and some dish soap. "Fill the bathtub."

Mutely, I did as she ordered, backing off as she poured

a cup of the baking soda into the churning water. Then she added the quart of peroxide and about a quarter cup of dish soap. I stared at the briny bath and gingerly stepped in when she gave me a little shove.

Far from a nice, fresh, minty bubble bath, which I'd willingly take, this felt more like she was scrubbing off the last seven years of skin. By the time we finished washing me and my hair, I was bright pink from the vigorous use of the loofah. As I rinsed off under the shower spray, I could still smell the skunk, but at least it was muted. *A little.*

"Oh, dear," she said, looking up at me.

Wordlessly, I peeked in the mirror. Now, in addition to pink, orange, and brassy blonde, I had platinum patches from the peroxide. "Crap," I said again, shaking my head. "What can we do about my hair?"

Iris bit her lip. I'd never seen her look quite so remorseful. "I'm not sure. I have no idea how hair dye would react on you, given your half-Fae heritage. Let me do some research on spells. Maybe there's something we can do magically."

"Forget about asking Camille to touch my head," I muttered. "I remember perfectly well what happened when she tried to make herself invisible. She was nekkid for a week and couldn't do a thing about it. And didn't even *know* it until somebody told her that her clothes were invisible."

A knock on the door interrupted us. I wrapped the towel around me and Iris answered. It was Vanzir.

"Delilah—it's Luke, from the bar. He wants to talk to you."

Luke? Luke was a werewolf who worked at the Wayfarer Bar & Grill, owned by my sister Menolly. He occasionally came over to dinner, but if he was here instead of on duty, there must be something wrong.

I stared down at my towel-wrapped torso. At

six-foot-one, I was lean, though not gaunt by *any* stretch of the imagination. You couldn't see my bones—they were all covered by a nice layer of muscle.

"He'll have to deal with me being half dressed. I'm not climbing into any of my clothes till I find something that will prevent the skunk smell from spreading to them."

Wandering out into the foyer, I nodded at the tall, lanky werewolf who slouched against one wall. Luke could be mistaken for a cowboy except for the scar that laced its way down his cheek. A faint smile flickered across his lips. The ponytail that hung down his back was tidy, but gave me the impression that his hair was flyaway and tousled by nature.

He touched the hat he wore. "Miss Delilah, how you doing? Ran into a skunk, did you?"

"That obvious?"

"Between your . . . perfume, and the new dye job up top, yeah. I bet Iris used tomato juice to no effect?" A lazy smile took the place of the worried look as he flashed a wink at Iris. She blushed.

I nodded. "Yeah, something like that. And then some quasi-crazy peroxide mix. You don't happen to have a cure, do you?"

"Maybe," he said. "At least for the scent. I'll have to go back to my apartment to get it. Learned to make it years ago when I was still running with the Pack. We found out firsthand that tomato juice did a number on light colored fur. But first, I have need of your services, if you're willing."

"My services?" I started to bristle, suddenly all too aware of my semi-naked state.

"You're a PI, aren't you?" He was doing his best to keep his eyes on my face, though I saw them drop a couple times, then swiftly scan back up to look me in the eye. Kind of cute, actually. He was blushing. And, mingling with the skunk, the tomato juice, and the chemical scent of the peroxide, I could smell his musk, though not so thick as to indicate arousal. But he liked women, that was for sure.

"Oh. Um . . . yeah." I edged into the living room and nodded for him to follow me. "What do you need?"

I motioned for him to sit and he edged onto the sofa while I curled up in the rocking chair, making sure nothing was showing that shouldn't be. But before I could sit down, Iris slipped in and spread a grungy sheet beneath me. Great. I was beginning to feel like Typhoid Mary.

"My sister was coming out to live here. She said that she'd had a vision, she needed to come up here—to live in Seattle for some reason. She left the Pack, which is a big no-no unless you're excommunicated like I was."

"Did she say why?" I was beginning to wonder about lycanthropes—the Were system wasn't the same in all species, and I'd heard rumors that amongst the wolves, rules were very patriarchal. Not conducive to free-thinking females.

"Yeah . . . I'll tell you why in a moment. Anyway, she called when she hit town this afternoon. She was going to check in, then rest a bit and show up at the bar around eight. But she never showed. I called the cops but they don't put out missing person reports on Supes for forty-eight hours, which is bullshit. My sister came all the way from Arizona and I'm worried. I checked with the hotel. They said she checked in today at two, but they haven't heard from her since."

"Any chance she got caught up visiting someone else?" Interested now, I pulled a notebook off the end table next to me and began to jot down notes.

Luke shook his head. "Nope. She didn't know anybody else here, but she was adamant about being summoned to this area. That's the word she used—summoned. I'm especially worried because she's pregnant. A werewolf who is seven months pregnant just doesn't disappear. She should be nesting, creating the lair for the pups . . . or children, so to speak." His voice belied his calm exterior, and I could hear the panic welling just below the surface.

"What's her name, and do you have a picture of her?"

He handed over a faded picture from his wallet. As I took it from his hands, I noticed the calluses that had long embedded themselves into his fingers and palms. This man had seen hard work, harder than he was doing at the bar, and his skin was covered with faded scars.

I took the picture and gazed at the young woman staring back at me. She looked about twenty-five—misleading, of course, given the long-lived nature of the Supe community. She had Luke's eyes. Feral and yet . . . a yearning hidden behind the wariness. Long wheat-colored hair drifted down her shoulders, honey-kissed and vibrant. She was beautiful, luminous, and dangerous.

"Her name is Amber. Amber Johansen. We haven't seen each other in years."

He left something unspoken. Something that told me Luke had a suspicion about what had happened.

"What do you think is going on?" I caught his attention, turning on my glamour, willing him to open up.

He sucked in a deep breath and let it out slowly, locking his gaze on mine without flinching. "I think that rat's ass she calls a husband came after her. She told me over the phone that she was being followed down there, and my guess is he's trying to *convince* her to come back to the pack. His ego—the ego of the Pack—neither takes it well when their women leave. Rice is an abusive motherfucker, and I'm afraid he'll track her down and kill her."

And then, slowly, he crumbled. "Amber's the only family I've got."

"We'll find her," I said, sliding my hand over his. "We'll do everything we can to find her." But inside, I was praying we weren't too late.